Sheila O'Flanagan

If You Were Me

headline
review

First published in Great Britain in 2014
by HEADLINE REVIEW
An imprint of HEADLINE PUBLISHING GROUP

First published in paperback in 2015
by HEADLINE REVIEW
An imprint of HEADLINE PUBLISHING GROUP

6

Cataloguing in Publication Data is available from the British Library

ISBN 978 1 4722 2693 8 (A-format)
ISBN 978 0 7553 7845 6 (B-format)

Typeset in ITC Galliard by Palimpsest Book Production Ltd,
Falkirk, Stirlingshire

Printed and bound in Great Britain by Clays Ltd, St Ives plc

MIX
Paper from
responsible sources
FSC
www.fsc.org
FSC® C104740

Headline's policy is to use papers that are natural,
renewable and recyclable products and made from wood grown
in well-managed forests and other controlled sources. The logging
and manufacturing processes are expected to conform to the
environmental regulations of the country of origin.

HEADLINE PUBLISHING GROUP
An Hachette UK Company
338 Euston Road
London NW1 3BH

www.headline.co.uk
www.hachette.co.uk

Sheila O'Flanagan is the author of many bestselling novels, including *Things We Never Say*, *Better Together*, *All For You*, *Stand By Me* and *The Perfect Man*.

Sheila has always loved telling stories, and after working in banking and finance for a number of years, she decided it was time to fulfil a dream and give writing her own book a go. So she sat down, stuck 'Chapter One' at the top of a page, and got started. Sheila is now the author of more than nineteen bestselling titles. She lives in Dublin with her husband.

Sheila O'Flanagan. So much more than stories.

'Romantic and charming, this is a real must-read' *Closer*

'A big, touching book sure to delight O'Flanagan fans' *Daily Mail*

'A spectacular read' *Heat*

'Another first class "can't put it down" novel from Sheila O'Flanagan' *Woman's Way*

'Her lightness of touch and gentle characterisations have produced another fine read' *Sunday Express*

'A thought-provoking read that will keep you guessing right up until the end' *New!*

'A captivating novel of family ties and romance' *Sun*

In 2013, Typhoon Haiyan devastated the Philippines. In order to raise funds to help the survivors of this disaster, Authors for the Philippines held an auction in which authors, agents and publishers offered items for auction. My offering was an acknowledgement/dedication in my next book.

This is that book and the winning bid was one which helped to push the total raised to over £55,000. The bidder wants to remain anonymous but I am delighted to dedicate this book, as requested:

To Jean, from her three much-loved sons.

Acknowledgements

Writing is a solitary occupation, but getting the book into print requires lots of outside expertise and support. I'm very fortunate to have some amazing people on my side. So my thanks to:

My agent, Carole Blake
My editor, Marion Donaldson
My copyeditor, Jane Selley
The fantastic team at Hachette/Headline
My worldwide publishers and translators

As always, love and thanks to my wonderful family.

Gracias to Colm for everything.

Thanks also to the booksellers and librarians who continue to champion the cause of reading for pleasure.

And thank you beyond measure to my readers who are the loveliest of people, you always bring a smile to my face with your messages. You can contact me through my website, Twitter and Facebook pages. I hope you enjoy Carlotta's story.

Chapter 1

Hora Zero (Zero Hour) – Rodrigo y Gabriela

When I open my eyes and focus on the clock beside the bed, I realise with absolute horror that I should have been awake an hour ago. I blink a few times in sheer disbelief and then check the time on my mobile phone. The clock and the phone are in complete agreement. So now I'm late. Not just a little bit late either, but properly, horribly, maybe-miss-the-damn-train late. And missing the train means missing the plane. Missing the plane means missing Dorothea's party. And missing Dorothea's party . . . I leap off the bed with the agility of an Olympic athlete. Missing the party isn't an option. I need to get out of the hotel room and into a cab as fast as I possibly can if today isn't going to morph from triumph to disaster in the space of a couple of hours.

In a corner of my mind (the tiniest sliver of a corner of my mind, to be exact) I tell myself that I might be overdramatising a little, although I'm not really a dramatic sort of person. In my business life – the life I was living a few hours ago – I'm famed for my ability to be cool and calm under pressure.

In fact, I'm pretty much unflappable in the face of near disaster. But we're talking about professional pressures and corporate disasters. This is entirely different. I may be overreacting to missing a party, but it's my soon-to-be mother-in-law's seventieth birthday party. I'm supposed to be handing over flowers and making a speech about what a wonderful person she is. It's important to me and to my fiancé, Chris, because although we're pretty rock solid as a couple, the dark cloud on our horizon is his mother. She doesn't like me and I . . . well, I don't like her very much either, to be honest. I'm constantly doing my best to change her view that I'm a poor choice of future wife for her only son, but I never quite seem to manage it. If I fail to show at her party it will be a major black mark against me, and all my months of trying to be nice to her will have been in vain.

Nevertheless, as I slide my arms into my silk blouse, I can't help wondering if I've deliberately overslept, if some unknown place in my psyche stopped me from waking up so that I wouldn't make the train in time. I'm a big believer in listening to your subconscious, but I'm not going to listen to it today. I know I didn't oversleep on purpose. Dorothea's party is just as important to me as this morning's breakfast meeting was. Deliberately missing her party would mean I want her to lower her opinion of me, and it's already low enough. Which is annoying because, without trying to blow my own trumpet or anything, most people would think I'm a reasonably good bet as a daughter-in-law. I'm single, solvent and free from emotional baggage. Though God knows, as far as Dorothea Bennett is concerned, even the Virgin Mary wouldn't have met her exacting standards for her only son's future wife.

Why on earth didn't I set my phone alarm? I certainly

didn't expect to fall asleep when I came back to the hotel to relax after the meeting, but I'm the sort of person who plans ahead. I'm practically pathological as far as advance planning is concerned. So surely I should've anticipated the possibility of nodding off when I stretched out on the hotel's king-sized bed with its luxurious duck-feather mattress topper and cool, comfortable pillows. But the thing is, I don't normally sleep during the day. I find it hard enough to sleep at night. Four hours out for the count was totally unforeseeable.

I sweep my cosmetics into my bag, not bothering to check that the caps on the various tubes and pots are properly tightened. Nor do I bother putting my make-up brushes into the funky leopard-skin pouch that my god-daughter, Natasha, bought me last Christmas. I can sort all this out afterwards. Right now, getting out of the hotel is my main priority.

I pick up my hairbrush and run it through my hair, which is short, dark and sticking up in spikes on one side of my head while stuck flat to the other, as though I've been hit by a brick or something equally solid. Spiky is how I usually wear it, but in a slightly less frantic style. I take my sparkly clip from the bedside locker and shove it into the centre of the spikes, where it glitters beneath the single halogen light over the mirror. My green eyes, surrounded by sleep-smudged mascara, glitter too; I think it's with stunned disbelief that I overslept. I feel my chest tighten with stress and I think that at least a heart attack would be a reasonable excuse for missing the party. I take some deep, calming breaths. A heart attack isn't the solution. Really it isn't.

I turn away from the dresser and stuff the balled-up tights

on the floor beside my bed into my case, before slipping into my high-heeled shoes. Putting on the tights will slow me down, and I don't need them – I only wore them for the breakfast meeting earlier because I always wear tights in a business environment. It feels more professional than going bare-legged. Besides, when I can afford the luxury of putting tights on at my leisure, these are a particularly nice pair which do good things to my slightly too thin pins. They're black, with a criss-cross pattern running up the side and a tiny diamanté star at each ankle. Not that it's important what they look like. Not that anything is important right now other than getting to the station in the next half-hour.

I leave the room, throwing one last hurried glance behind me to make sure I haven't left anything behind. But given that I didn't unpack when I arrived yesterday evening, there's nothing for me to leave. I stand in the corridor at the lifts and jab the call button about half a dozen times. I know it doesn't make the lift come any faster but it helps me to rid myself of some of the pent-up anxiety I'm feeling. And some of the anger too. I'm so angry at myself I can feel my teeth grind as I debate whether it might be quicker to lug my case down ten flights of stairs, or exercise a little patience and wait for the lift.

I stifle a sudden yawn. I can't be tired now, I simply can't. I don't remember the last time I slept for four hours on the trot. I know that today is a bit of an exception, what with the jet lag from yesterday plus this morning's early meeting, but all the same . . . I wonder if I'm suddenly turning into someone who needs her full eight hours. The thought horrifies me. What about future breakfast meetings? Will I be the one to arrive at the last minute looking puffy-eyed and bedraggled because I can't haul my ass out of bed? Will I be the one to nod off at an important point in the presentation? I shudder.

Usually when I have a breakfast meeting I'm one of the first to arrive and I ensure I look smart and groomed and totally in control. It doesn't matter that I don't like meeting clients before dawn, or that I'd much prefer to have had my fruit and full-fat yoghurt, possibly followed by a Danish, before dealing with spreadsheets and PowerPoint presentations. I don't eat at business breakfasts because it's impossible to look efficient and impressive when you've got puff pastry flaking down your jacket or a smear of bitter-orange marmalade on your cheek. That's why I passed on the food that was provided by Ecologistics this morning, even though I was ravenously hungry. But I drank a gallon of coffee to make up for it, which is why it's bizarre that I fell asleep at all. Usually, after more than one cup, I have to clamp down on a caffeine rush and its associated jitters. But I guess jet lag trumps caffeine as far as I'm concerned. Even though it's never bothered me before.

Finally the lift arrives. The doors slide open and a sextet of fit, healthy-looking young people dressed in blue tracksuits and with name tags hanging around their necks move to one side to make room for me. There is a sports conference being held at the hotel today and tomorrow. Clearly athletes schedule meetings at far more reasonable hours.

I'm thinking that if I hadn't asked for a late checkout this morning I probably would have been woken by a chambermaid wanting to make up the room. I hadn't been going to bother keeping it at all, but then decided it might be a good idea in case I felt like relaxing for a while after the meeting. My habit of micro-planning has backfired spectacularly.

I suppose Mateo, my colleague, will be amused when he finds out.

'We have turned you into a Spaniard,' he'll say. 'Needing your siesta.'

He hasn't turned me into a Spaniard. Or an Argentinian. Or anyone else who needs a siesta. I haven't changed a bit over the last weeks while I worked on the project that took in both sides of the Atlantic. Not that I've ever seen anyone in the offices of Cadogan Consulting, the international company we work for, taking siestas. Everyone works the same core hours, which are laughably supposed to be nine-to-five. Most of us work a lot more than that. The only people who take siestas in Spain or Argentina are proprietors of small local businesses, like family-owned shops or garages. And, unfortunately, the employees of Ecologistics, the struggling firm who'd hired us to tell them how they could return to profitability and strength.

Ecologistics is based in Seville. Mateo and I had visited the corporate headquarters (a dull, square concrete building on the outskirts of the city) at the start of the contract over six months ago. Then we'd gone to the other Ecologistics offices in Europe, before heading to their base in Argentina for a few days. We'd taken notes, shared our thoughts about their operations and come up with a survival plan. This morning, at the breakfast meeting, I was the one to give them the bad news. That survival would be tough. And messy. And hard. Something they probably knew already. They just needed to hear it from someone else. And that someone was me.

When it comes to standing up in front of our clients and delivering bad news, I'm one of the company's first choices. Dirk Cadogan, the grandson of the founder of Cadogan Consulting and our current CEO, once told me it was because I am a velvet assassin. I looked at him in confusion and he explained that when I walk into a room everyone assumes that because I'm a small, slim woman with snazzy tights and a sparkly clip in my hair, nothing I say is going to be too terrible. And then I wield the axe in my Orla Kiely bag, and they're left shell-shocked.

I told Dirk that he was being appallingly sexist, which made him flinch. Using words like sexist in the workplace is like lighting touchpaper these days. As soon as it's out of your mouth someone immediately starts thinking Labour Court and some kind of discrimination case, but I laughed after I spoke. Because the truth is, it doesn't matter how we'd like things to be; the workplace is full of -isms of some kind or another and the trick is negotiating them without losing your dignity. I work with what I've got. If clients are softened up by the fact that short with sparkly clips is unthreatening, well, that's a good thing. I'm happy to cultivate that image. It doesn't bother me in the slightest. Same as I don't mind when Mateo walks into a room and everyone's eyes are drawn to his one-metre-ninety body, his broad shoulders and the six-pack abs rippling beneath his cotton shirt. Chris hasn't met Mateo, which is possibly a good thing. I don't need my fiancé worrying about my work colleagues, and Mateo, though undeniably attractive, isn't my type. Anyhow, working with him is a temporary arrangement. Normally I'm based in Dublin with occasional stints in London and an annual trip to New York. Cavorting around Spain and

Argentina was an exception. A nice exception, as far as working in completely different environments goes, but more time-consuming and stressful than usual. As well as more exhausting. I'll be glad to get home.

Anyway, I did the velvet assassin thing with Ecologistics earlier and told them where they were going wrong and what they'd need to do to get the company up to speed again. Not surprisingly, the plan called for a certain amount of rationalisation, which is really another way of saying job losses. Even though it was almost inevitable, I hated having to point this out. I don't like being the person who's the cause of someone else losing a job. Every time I have to do it I feel sick. But I also have to accept it. I lay it out as calmly and as professionally as I can because that's what I'm paid to do. And I justify it by saying that in the long run, more jobs will be saved if the company concerned takes our advice. In any plan that means people are let go I always include substantial salary cuts for the senior management who got them into this mess in the first place. It's the least I can do and it makes commercial sense. But you'd be surprised at how many so-called leaders don't want to share the pain. In my velvet-axe-wielding way, however, I attempt to make it an essential component. And to be fair to Antonio Reyes, the CEO of Ecologistics, he was completely accepting of it, and indeed of the plan in total. Antonio's support is good news for me, because it means a further contract for Cadogan and more fees for the firm. I texted the news to Dirk immediately after the meeting, and his reply reminded me that I have a ninety-five per cent record in getting companies on side, which continues to make me one of his top consultants. Getting Antonio on board will mean a decent bonus for me this year, which was why I was feeling very happy when I said goodbye to Mateo as we left the Ecologistics building. He didn't come back to the hotel for an extra hit of celebratory coffee because he was heading directly to Cadiz. He has family there. Dammit, I think, if we'd had coffee together maybe I'd have stayed talking to him and I wouldn't have fallen asleep at all and I wouldn't be panicking now.

The lift stops at every floor between mine and the ground, which isn't doing my stress levels any good at all. When we eventually arrive, I push my way past the sports conference people, pause briefly at reception to tell them I've left the room, clatter out of the hotel and stand on the pavement, looking for a cab. The sky, which was a glorious blue earlier in the morning, is now a lowering grey and it feels like it's going to rain. So much for my junket in the sun, as Chris keeps calling it. These clouds are every bit as dark as they can be in Dublin.

I push random weather thoughts out of my head and clamber into the taxi that has just pulled up outside the door.

'Train station, please,' I say in English. 'As quickly as possible.'

He seems to understand both the destination and my request for speed, and I get the feeling that he's taking it as a personal challenge. He puts his foot to the floor and we squeal away from the kerb as though we're in an action movie. And as we do, the heavens open and the rain starts to fall. I've never seen rain like it. It's as though someone has opened a celestial sluice gate. A torrent of water seems to have simply cascaded from the sky, flooding everything beneath. The cab driver swears softly under his breath. I understand the tone if not the words as he switches his windscreen wipers to fast, although he might as well not bother for all the difference they're making, because this is like driving through a river.

Nevertheless, I'm hoping that the rain will delay the train and allow me an extra few minutes to board. Flooding on the tracks maybe. Sodden points. Though obviously not enough flooding or sodden points to force a complete cancellation of the service. That possibility throws me into a flap again. I can't have the train cancelled. I just need my taxi driver to get me there in the next twenty minutes. And he will. He's giving it everything he's got. He's the Jenson Button of cab drivers. (Actually, glancing at his face in the rear-view mirror, I reckon he's more the Jeremy Clarkson of cab drivers. But never mind. As long as he gets me to the station in time, I don't care who he reminds me of!) I remember Mateo's words yesterday as we glided out of Madrid's Atocha station on our way to Seville.

'Renfe prides itself on punctuality,' he said of the national rail company. 'If the train is more than five minutes late, you get your money back.'

I heartily approved of that when he told me. I still approve of the concept. But I'm hoping that they're going to have to do a big payout for a six-minute delay today. Although if Jeremy Clarkson keeps on at this rate, I'll be there in time to sashay coolly along the platform, laughing at myself for worrying at all.

We swerve around a corner into a narrow road. Although the Hotel Andalucia is on the outskirts of the city and it seems totally unnecessary to go through twisting streets that feel as though they should be only for pedestrians, I'm reckoning that Jeremy is taking a short cut. He negotiates a few hairpin bends with great aplomb, turns on to a main street again, swears once more – loudly this time – and then crashes into the back of a stationary van.

OK, I tell myself as I'm flung forward and my seat belt restrains me, this hasn't happened. I haven't just been involved in a car crash in Seville. But Jeremy is now swearing very loudly and opening the driver's door. Like magic, a crowd has gathered around us, all talking loudly and gesticulating wildly. The crash wasn't actually that bad. It was more of a shunt really, because we'd just come round a bend and Jeremy wasn't going that fast. But the owner of the van is yelling at him and I'm suddenly worried that there's going to be a fight. I don't want to be involved in their fight. I don't want to be involved at all. I don't need to be. Nobody is hurt. I look around anxiously.

Neither driver is taking any notice of me. I open the passenger door and slide out of the rear seat. Random onlookers glance at me curiously, and then someone asks me a question but I've absolutely no idea what they've said and shrug unconcernedly. Which is no mean feat because I am the complete opposite of unconcerned. I'm as concerned as it's possible to be. I'm losing precious seconds standing around in torrential rain while the two drivers compete to see who can shout loudest. And then I hear the sound of sirens and know that the police are coming.

The police means witness statements and all sorts of time-consuming things. I'm a law-abiding citizen and I want to do my best to help, but there's nothing I can add to this. Certainly not in Spanish. And I can't hang around for something that might take forever. So I sidle around to the back of the taxi and pop the boot. I raise the lid slowly and ease my suitcase out. Even though I've been travelling for nearly three weeks, it's not a very big suitcase. It's bigger than the ones budget airlines allow you to bring into the cabin, but otherwise it's pretty neat. I put it on the ground beside me and glance around. The only person looking at me now is a baby with a tiny pink bow in her mop of dark hair, snuggled up in a pushchair. I give her a complicit smile and a wink and then edge myself away from the fracas. By this time I'm utterly drenched and so is my case. But my departure hasn't been spotted. I start to walk more quickly and then, at a set of traffic lights, I cross the road and turn a corner. I have no idea where I am. But I'm still determined to make the train on time.

I don't know which direction I should be walking in. The Santa Justa station is quite big, and I reckon it must be visible from a reasonable distance, but all I can see are rain-darkened buildings and orange trees. Despite the rain, there's a heady scent of orange blossom in the air. In other circumstances I'd quite like to be here, soaked to the skin and inhaling orange blossom. It's not something many of my colleagues would imagine me doing, but it's sort of earthy and lovely and . . . I don't have time for this. I slick back my now soaking hair and look around me. I don't know which way to turn and my ankles are chafing from the high-heeled shoes. Maybe I should've waited to put on the tights after all. I feel like crying. I even gulp. But then I stop myself. I never, ever cry.

A white car with a green taxi light appears through the rain. I almost run out in front of it in my eagerness to stop it. The car glides to a halt and I open the passenger door.

'Train station,' I tell the driver, heaving my case on to the seat beside me. I think he's grateful for that. I'm pretty sure he didn't want to get out and put it in the boot.

I drip all over the back seat as he puts the car into gear. I've lost precious minutes thanks to Jeremy's shunt. I'm still feeling a bit guilty about abandoning him, but I have to make this train. So I push him to the back of my mind and peer out of the window as we make a couple of turns and then finally, thankfully, approach the railway station.

There are loads of cars either parked or waiting outside. My driver pulls up as close as he can to the entrance, and I pay him way more than I should. I've suddenly remembered that I didn't pay Jeremy at all and I feel guilty again, but only for a moment. He didn't get me to my destination, did he? But I'm here now. I heave a sigh of relief and run into the station. Well, I don't run exactly, because my ankles are in agony now from my shoes, but I do a sort of fast hobble, dragging my case behind me.

The train for Madrid is scheduled to depart in three minutes, from a platform at the other end of the station. I take a deep breath and half run, half limp the length of the concourse before flinging myself towards the platform where the sleek white train is standing. I breathe a sigh of relief and offer up a silent prayer to St Jude. I'm not at all a religious person, but it's good to have spiritual help at times of trouble and I'm well known to the patron saint of lost causes, who has got me out of a jam on more than one occasion. I'm thinking that he's come up trumps again when a railway employee, in her neat uniform, stops me. She says something in Spanish and I look blankly at her.

'The train is closed,' she tells me in perfect English.

'No it's not,' I protest. 'It's there.'

'But closed. There is no more access.'

'I must have access.' I realise my voice is shrill and I try to take it down a notch. 'I have to catch that train.'

'I'm sorry.' To be fair, she does sound regretful. 'But the gates close two minutes before the departure of the train. So that it is on time,' she adds helpfully.

It didn't take me a whole minute to run the length of the platform, did it? I'll have to start taking my gym membership more seriously if it did.

'I won't delay it,' I assure her. 'It'll only take me a couple of seconds to board.' I slip off my shoes so that I can run faster and she looks at me in astonishment.

'It's not possible,' she says.

'I'll be really quick,' I tell her. 'I'll just jump into the first carriage and – oh!'

I watch, horrified, as the train begins to glide slowly and majestically out of the station. Without me.

I've missed it.

Dorothea will never forgive me.

Neither will Chris.

This can't be happening.

'I am sorry, Miss . . . Carlotta.' The railway employee reads my name from the e-ticket, deciding to ignore the O'Keeffe part, which seems to cause pronunciation problems outside of English-speaking countries, and looks at me sympathetically. 'Perhaps you can buy a ticket for the next one. It leaves in two hours and twenty minutes.'

I don't know what to say to her. It's as though my brain has disconnected itself from my body. A train leaving in two hours and twenty minutes is of no use to me whatsoever. A train in two hours and twenty minutes won't get me to Madrid in time for my flight. I want to ask about other possibilities and alternatives but I can't speak. Because I still can't believe that my train really has left without me. I'm furious and gutted at the same time. I should never have agreed to come to Seville at all. It hadn't even been part of the original plan. Antonio and the rest of the board were supposed to come to Madrid to meet us. But Antonio's mother had been taken ill earlier in the week and he didn't want to leave the city, so he asked if Mateo and I would make the trip to Seville instead. And I agreed because I thought it was kind of sweet that the chairman of a multinational company, even one in the sort of trouble that Ecologistics was in, would want to stay near his mother instead of putting business first. It occurs to me that men and their mothers have become an irritating complication in my life.

'Would you like to buy a ticket for the next train?' The employee is still trying to be helpful.

'I don't know,' I say eventually, as I look at the now deserted track. 'I need to think.'

'Of course,' she agrees. 'There is a customer lounge in the station for passengers with your class of ticket. You can freshen up there. And my colleague will help you.'

'Thank you.' It's not freshening up I need, it's drying off. And a train. I need a train to Madrid right now! But I follow the direction in which she's pointing and push open the door to the lounge. The receptionist makes a comment about the weather in Spanish and then English, and on hearing of my dilemma is equally sympathetic about the missed train, although she also emphasises the punctuality of the high-speed system. I'm beginning to hate it by now and I'm wishing that I could be in Dublin's Connolly station, where I'd be a hundred per cent certain they wouldn't mind being a minute or two late once they knew how critical the whole situation was. Efficiency has its drawbacks, I think unhappily as I sit down in the lounge and take out my iPad. I click on the train timetable and try to figure out my next move. Which isn't going to be phoning Chris and telling him that I'm stuck in Seville. There has to be some way of making it home in time. And I'm going to find it.

Chapter 2

**Solo Quiero Caminar (I Only Want to Go) –
Paco de Lucía**

Coming up with solutions to impossible problems is what
we're trained to do at Cadogan Consulting, where I am an
executive. Even though we're not one of the biggest consultancy firms in the world, we're certainly one of the most
respected. Being that bit smaller has allowed us to take a
closer interest in our clients – at least that's what Dirk
Cadogan insists. It's not entirely corporate bullshit. We have
a can-do mentality at Cadogan, which in my view is why
we are one of the most successful consulting companies in
the world. We're not allowed to use the word 'impossible'
even if we're looking at an impossible situation. We have to
come up with something, no matter how difficult it might
seem.

Before going any further in my not-allowed-to-be-impossible
quest, I spend five minutes changing from my wet suit into
a pair of jeans and a slightly crumpled top that I've taken
out of my case. I can't think properly when I'm soaked to
the skin. I also change my heels for a pair of flats before

putting my head under the hand-dryer for a couple of minutes to dry out the spikes. Then I head back into the lounge to click my way through bus, train and plane schedules so that I can find a way in which I can be in Dublin in under six hours. And eventually I do find the solution. There's always a solution. Only this isn't one I think will work for me. Because basically the only way of getting from Seville to Dublin in time for Dorothea Bennett's seventieth birthday party is to hire a private jet.

It says a lot about my state of mind that I seriously start looking at the cost of private jet hire. The first thing I learn is that there isn't a schedule of fares like on an airline page. You have to ask for a quote. I hesitate and fill in the information on two different charter sites. They're supposed to come back instantly, but I guess they think I'm taking the piss, because the clock is ticking and after five minutes I still haven't got an instant reply. Finally one of the companies comes back saying that they can't fulfil my request as they need at least twenty-four hours' notice to provide the service. I snort. What's the point in saying that you provide a round-the-clock executive service if you don't do it when people actually want it? Surely to God there are important celebrities fetching up at airports around the globe every day of the week wanting planes right away? What if I was Lady Gaga or Angelina Jolie or someone equally VIP? Would they fob me off with a twenty-four-hours'-notice demand? I don't think so. But I also don't think I have Gaga or Angelina's resources, despite my decent salary plus bonuses at Cadogan. The sites don't quote rates on their home pages for a reason. And the reason is that if the cost is an issue then you can't afford it. I come back to earth and realise that it's utterly ridiculous for me to even think I can charter a plane. It doesn't much matter anyway. The owners of the other site clearly know I'm not a serious contender for one of their latest-technology jets. They haven't even bothered to reply.

I've wasted more than thirty minutes in the lounge and I still haven't come up with a viable solution to my problem. There are no direct flights from Seville to Dublin, and none from Seville to Madrid that will connect with my flight either. Nor can I see any from other Spanish airports that will get me home tonight. I can't afford to hire a private jet and there are no other options. Despite all my promises I am going to miss the party. I take out my phone and scroll to Chris's number. But my finger is trembling as it hovers over it. I'm great at being the velvet assassin when I have to deal with the head of an international company. I can look anyone in the eye and tell him (it's nearly always a him) that my plan is his only hope for survival. I can fend off all sorts of protests and objections and remain totally unmoved. But I feel sick to the stomach at having to tell Chris that I won't make it tonight. Even though I was dreading the party, I don't want to let him down. But it's looking increasingly likely that I will.

I spend another fifteen minutes checking and rechecking the train times and flight connections because I still want to believe there's a solution. I want to make it home. I want to keep my promise. I feel myself tense up again as I flick through screen after screen without finding the magic bullet that will make everything all right. Eventually I admit defeat. Because there really is nothing.

Once I accept that there's no chance of making it back to

Dublin tonight, a certain calmness descends on me. Realistically, it's probably the same kind of calmness that Anne Boleyn felt on the scaffold just before they chopped her head off – a sort of horrified resignation coupled with a disbelief that this is really happening. Nevertheless, I can't quite bring myself to dial Chris's number yet. Calling him would make it all real, and I'm not ready to deal with reality.

I decide that the best thing to do is to actually organise my train to Madrid and my flight for tomorrow so that I can at least show that I've been busy. So I book the flight (which is horrifically expensive because it's so last-minute) and I go to the receptionist at the lounge desk to ask if she can change my train ticket. There's a bit of discussion about this because she's saying I have to buy a new one and I'm trying to simply transfer the one I have. I don't know if I'm getting things right because it's all becoming more and more confusing to me, and eventually I lose my temper a bit and just say 'fine, whatever' like a moody teenager talking to her parents. I realise instantly that I've been rude and start apologising, and the receptionist is kind and forgiving and tells me that travel can be stressful. Although she then goes on to fly the flag again about the high-speed network, saying how much more relaxing it is going to Madrid by train rather than by air. At this point the only thing that will lower my stress levels (which have shot up again during our conversation) is a beam-me-up transporter device, but it's obviously not going to be invented and installed in the next five minutes, so I thank the receptionist and walk out of the lounge, dragging my case behind me while at the same time trying to stuff the new tickets into my bag.

I have another dilemma, which I'd totally forgotten, and

that's somewhere to stay for the night. I suppose the best thing is to try the Hotel Andalucia again, although now that I'm stuck here, it would be nice to stay in the city and do a little sightseeing – if it ever stops raining, that is. In all the work that I've done for Ecologistics, I haven't got to see much of the cities I've had to visit. It's been air terminals, office blocks and chain hotels most of the time. And even though the Andalucia isn't part of a chain, it's very corporate and too far from the old quarter to be able to take in any of the historical sites and buildings. Antonio Reyes asked me, after the meeting, if I would be staying on in Seville to explore. This was the best time of the year for it, he said, in his beautifully accented English. While the orange blossom covers the trees and before the heat becomes unbearable. I told him that I was too busy and he said 'another time perhaps', adding that he would be happy to show me around the next time I returned.

I'll go back to the Andalucia. It's too wet to explore now, and besides, I can't allow myself to enjoy my unexpected night in Seville. I can't allow myself to think, even for a second, that it might be considerably better fun than being at Dorothea's party. Which it would be, of course, if I'd chosen to be here rather than finding myself stranded.

I have to ring Chris. I can't put it off any longer. He'll have finished his clinic by now and will be expecting a text from me to say I'm on the train. He likes getting updates on where I am and what I'm doing, even if he doesn't always reply to them. I'm usually quite happy to send them, because it's nice to know that he cares. But right now it feels controlling. I know it isn't, I know every single thing I'm currently feeling is influenced by my overwhelming guilt about having overslept for the very first time in my entire life, but I wish I didn't have to tell him about my stupidity.

I take the phone from my bag and decide that it's far too noisy on the concourse to make a call, so I walk outside. The ferocious pounding of the rain has eased slightly, but there are rivers of water flowing down the road. It's noisy here too, with taxis disgorging passengers and people milling around dodging each other and the rain, but eventually I find a quiet corner and dial Chris's number.

'Bennett,' he says when the call connects. He always answers his calls with his surname, even when they're from me. It's probably because he never checks to see who's actually calling him before he speaks.

'Hi.' I try to sound cheerful and upbeat.

'I was wondering when you'd ring. How was the meeting?' Even though he's not a businessman himself, Chris likes to hear about what he jokingly calls my fat-cat lifestyle. The fat-cat adjective is based on the fact that I have an expense account and occasionally take clients to the kind of restaurants that cater primarily for men in suits. Chris only wears suits (usually dark but with a vibrant tie) when he's in his consulting rooms, because he knows that his patients are always reassured when they see him looking professional. But he's not a boring businessman. He's an ophthalmologist who specialises in laser surgery. He has to look like he knows what he's doing.

'It went well,' I say.

'How many did you consign to the scrapheap?'

'Thirty over the next two years,' I reply.

'Did you have to?'

'The business will be saved and so will lots of other jobs. And . . .' I'm speaking quickly now, 'you can't be nasty about it because you're forever complaining about too many administrators sitting on their behinds doing nothing, which is what was happening at Ecologistics.'

There's nothing he can say in reply. The ophthalmic clinic went through its own rationalisation programme a year ago when one of the money managers realised that costs were getting out of control. In fairness, only three people were let go, but I was very proud of the fact that I didn't say a word when I heard about it.

'Anyway,' I continue, trying to sound assured and confident but feeling my knees begin to tremble, 'I've run into a bit of a problem.'

'What sort of problem?'

'I . . . um . . . I've missed the train to Madrid.'

'You've what?' I don't blame him for sounding incredulous. My pathological punctuality is one of the things about me he likes the most. It's a counterpoint to his habitual lateness, a habit that many medical consultants seem to think is their right. But time is money in the field of commercial consulting and I'm never, ever late. Except for today.

'I'm sorry.' And here I lie to him, because I don't tell him about sleeping late at all but make a big deal instead of the shunt by my Jeremy Clarkson driver.

'Are you all right?' he asks, a note of concern in his voice. 'Are you hurt?'

'I'm absolutely fine.' I'm relieved to hear his anxiety on my behalf. 'It wasn't that bad. But you know how it is in these situations,' I add, suddenly terrified that I've underplayed my hand and wanting him to stay at least a little bit worried about me. 'Everything was totally chaotic and I was a bit shaken up.'

There's a silence as Chris absorbs this information and finds the eventual flaw.

'But didn't you allow enough time?' he asks. 'I can't believe that a simple tip would delay you so much.' He knows me. He knows I usually factor in time for the unexpected. He knows I hate being late.

'It was hard to get another taxi.' The lies are coming more fluently now. 'And it was chucking down rain, which made things all the more shambolic. Still is,' I add, as I glance at the leaden skies.

'In Seville?' He sounds surprised.

'I guess it does rain here sometimes.'

'So how long until the next train?' asks Chris.

'Um . . . that's the problem. It won't get me to the airport in time.'

'You're kidding me, right?'

I wish I was.

'You can't be telling me you're going to miss my mother's birthday party!'

'I'm checking out options as we speak,' I lie yet again. 'But there's a possibility I won't make it, yes.'

'But . . . but what about your speech and the floral presentation?'

There are times when I think that Chris is a worse micromanager than me. The speech and the floral presentation are the least of my worries right now. Anyone can say a few words and bung a bouquet at the old bat, for heaven's sake! I tell him that perhaps Lisa or Pen could do it if I don't make it.

I'm sure either of Chris's sisters would be happy to stand in for me. They're always perfectly polite when I meet them, but any thoughts I had about being friends with either of them have long vanished. Like Dorothea, they keep any warmth they have well under wraps. They weren't that keen on me having a role in the birthday celebrations in the first place.

'But you insisted you wanted to.'

OK, he's starting to do my head in now. The speech and the flowers aren't the key issue here. What's important is that – in the entirely likely situation that I don't make it to Dublin in time – he points out to his mother how devastated I am at missing the event and how I'm with them in spirit.

'And hopefully I still will.' I'll probably burn in hell for the lies. 'I'm doing my best to sort out an alternative flight.'

'I thought there was only one. You said before that you couldn't get home earlier than this evening because there was only one.'

I usually have to keep reminding Chris about my travel arrangements. It appears that this time he actually listened to me.

'I know. It's such a pain that there aren't any direct flights from here either. But I'm trying to route though Barcelona. Or London. Or something.'

'How likely is that?'

'Tricky,' I concede. 'But if it can be done, I'll do it.' I'm not going to tell him that it can't. Not yet.

'It's a bit of a mess,' says Chris. 'It's also so unlike you.'

I know. That's why I'm in such a flap. That's why I'm telling lies!

'I'm doing everything I can to get there,' I assure him. 'I don't want to be the only one missing. I want to tell your mum what an amazing woman she is and to present her with the flowers. I want her to know how happy I am about marrying into her family.'

'I know you do,' says Chris. 'It's just that we've been planning this for weeks, Carlotta, and it's a blow that it might not turn out right. Pen and Lisa have worked so hard and they want everything to be perfect.'

'And so do I,' I tell him. 'You know how much I want to be part of it. I want to prove to your mum that I'm a worthy addition to your family.'

That's the truth. I was hoping that fawning over her at a family occasion would make my future mother-in-law see that I'm not the daughter-in-law from hell.

'She knows that already,' says Chris.

It's good that he thinks his mother likes me. But I know different.

There are many reasons for my lack of favour with her, and one of them is that I'm not Amanda Geraghty, Chris's ex-fiancée, who completely met with her approval and who I'm pretty sure she secretly hopes will reappear just before the wedding and whisk him out of my arms. Amanda is a teacher at an exclusive private school, which makes her career choice eminently suitable. Her father is something in finance (though not a disgraced banker or anything like that). Her mother is very distantly related to some English earl, which is why my nickname for her is the Countess. I've never met her but I've seen photos in which she looks very aristocratic, with her perfectly coiffed ash-blonde hair, her porcelain skin and her sapphire-blue eyes. Chris has known Amanda since their college days and they were engaged for two years.

According to him, they simply drifted apart. But Dorothea was gutted when they finally called it a day. At least that's what Penelope told me at my first dinner in the Bennett home, a three-storey over-basement house in Rathgar. Pen, who – like her sister – works in the health service (which is another acceptable female career choice as far as Dorothea is concerned), actually lives in the basement, which was converted into a self-contained flat about five years ago; this means she spends a lot of time in the house with her mother. I visualise them sometimes, sitting together at the kitchen table, wondering what on earth it is that Chris sees in me. I like to think that he sees I'm a normal woman. The Bennett girls, with their constant talk about public service, are too good to be true.

George, Dorothea's ex-husband, is a former Chief Justice. I met him briefly just after Chris and I got engaged. He's a bit pompous and self-important, but basically he seems like a decent enough man. Dorothea divorced him because she thought he was too lenient with the criminals who appeared before him during his time on the bench. Well, that's what I like to think. The truth is that George had a bit on the side, and Dorothea found out and gave him his marching orders before he even had a chance to apologise. I'm not sure that he would have, actually. I reckon it was his moment of rebellion. But it cost him dearly, because Dorothea kept the beautiful house and George has ended up living in a small apartment in Donnybrook on his own. Nice area, and probably a nice apartment, but nothing on what he had before. I can't help smiling to myself when I think that Dorothea bested the country's supposedly toughest ever Chief Justice. But that's Dorothea for you. She's far more of a velvet assassin than I'll ever be.

Chris currently divides his time between living with Dorothea and with me at my small home in Harold's Cross.

He also owns an apartment near Belfield which is currently rented out to a couple of lecturers at the nearby university. When we get married, the plan is to live in Harold's Cross before ultimately selling both it and the apartment and buying somewhere together. In the background, too, is the fact that Chris will eventually inherit the Rathgar house. Dorothea wanted us to move in as soon as we got married, but obviously I've already said no to that. I couldn't imagine what it would be like to live with my own parents after I was married, let alone my mother-in-law! Actually, I don't know how Chris manages to live with his mother either. But maybe it's because he's more laid-back than me. And, like I said, it's a big house. (All this talk makes it sound like Chris is a bit of a mammy's boy and under Dorothea's thumb, but that's not the situation at all. He lived in Russia for a couple of years when he decided to specialise in laser eye surgery, and he did a year in the States too. There's no case of arrested development or Oedipus complex or anything, I can assure you.)

Amanda doesn't seem to have been worried about living with Dorothea, though. That had been the plan for them. Every so often I ask about her, but Chris is always dismissive, saying that their engagement was a mistake.

'Your mother didn't think so,' I told him one night. 'She liked Amanda very much.'

'And me not so.' I was merely stating a fact.

'Ah, she just likes to put my girlfriends through the mill,' said Chris.

'She gave the Countess a hard time?' I couldn't keep the scepticism out of my voice and Chris laughed.

'She was always slightly in awe of Amanda,' he admitted.

'But you and I make far more sense than me and her ever did. Besides . . .' he pulled me close to him and nuzzled my cheek, 'you're far, far hotter than she ever was.'

And that was the end of our discussion about Amanda Geraghty. She might have some aristocratic blood in her veins, but when it comes down to it, being good in bed is a much better proposition!

Nevertheless, I'm certain Dorothea wanted me to be an Amanda 2.0 upgrade, and was deeply disappointed when she realised that Carlotta 1.0 was inferior in every respect. When she first heard about my job, she almost visibly recoiled.

'So basically you're the sort of person who goes into a company and charges lots of money for telling them the blindingly obvious,' she said at the excruciatingly awful dinner.

'If it were blindingly obvious they would have done it already,' I replied mildly.

'The dogs on the streets usually know how to solve problems that consultants take forever to do.'

'You have specific experience?' I asked.

'Look at our country!' Her eyes, flinty blue, bored into me. 'This government and the one before it hire far too many people to tell them what they already know. Every time a change to the constitution or some controversial legislation is required, they bring in armies of consultants to tell them for an enormous fee what every person in the country could tell them for nothing.'

'That's not exactly the sort of consulting I do,' I told her.

'It's all the same.' Her voice was obstinate. 'A rubbish waste of money.'

She sat back in her chair, satisfied that she had put me in my place. There's no question that at that moment I was wondering if I was taking on more than I could chew with Dorothea Bennett. And then Chris intervened smoothly, telling his mother that I was very highly regarded and that I had helped to save many struggling companies and that they all seemed to think my services were worth it.

I flashed him a grateful smile, then busied myself with my food. Dorothea had cooked sole on the bone for dinner. I'm not a big fish eater, but this was exquisitely prepared and delicately flavoured. Dorothea is an excellent cook, and she's perfectly aware that home cooking is another of my failings. When I next glanced up, she was sitting ramrod straight in her chair, which made her look tall and imposing. She'd dressed almost entirely in black that night. Perhaps it was some kind of subtle signal of her distress at losing her son to someone as undeserving as me. She looked both grieved and elegant in the dark Chanel suit, teamed with a cream silk blouse. Her blue-rinsed hair was pulled back into a chignon so that the diamonds in her ears were clearly visible. Dorothea always wears a lot of jewellery. In addition to the earrings, she sported a gold necklace and matching bracelet, plus a selection of rings on both hands. I could see that she was a formidable woman in a million different ways and I knew that having her as a mother-in-law would be a trial. Nevertheless, I've worked with many people who were a trial, and I know I can work with Dorothea too, especially as Chris wants so much for us to get along.

Which is why, when plans were made for her seventieth birthday, I insisted on being involved. Chris was initially doubtful, not because he wasn't pleased at my interest, but because, he said, Dorothea's party was primarily a family occasion. I pointed out that I was family too and that this was an opportunity for me to show that to his mother. Chris looked startled, but immediately agreed with me and talked to Pen about it. She decided (although I can't help feeling somewhat reluctantly) that I should be the one to give Dorothea a bouquet after she'd cut her birthday cake. I was delighted to finally have a role in the proceedings, although Chris said he'd have to check with Dorothea that she was comfortable with it too.

'You're telling your mother that there's going to be a surprise bouquet of flowers?' I looked at him in astonishment.

'She doesn't like surprises. She likes to be prepared. Besides, she'd be expecting it anyway, just not expecting you to give it to her.'

I suppose the Bennetts can't help not being a spontaneous, fun-loving family, which makes it all the more surprising that when he's with me, Chris is both. But I told him that of course he should get his mother's approval for me to be the flower-presenter. Then I added that I would say a few words too. I'm quite good at speeches and he knows this. He squeezed my shoulders and kissed me.

'I know you think we're mad,' he said. 'And I admit that we are a bit. But it's easier to go along with Mum's foibles than argue about them.'

Apparently there was a bit of debate about my precise role in the grand celebration (I didn't ask what it was they needed to discuss), but eventually Dorothea conceded and I was officially elected flower-presenter-in-chief. I was also given the green light to say a few well-chosen words. Clearly the Bennetts placed far more importance on handing over the bouquet than I did, but if it kept them all happy, who was I to complain?

When everything was agreed, I composed a short, hypocritical speech to say how wonderful Dorothea was and how she was the linchpin of the family and how lucky I was to have met her only son. In between practising my presentation for Ecologistics, I'd stood in front of the mirror a few times and delivered my speech for Dorothea. Even if I say so myself, it was charming.

And now utterly useless.

'So when will you know about the flights?' asks Chris. 'You must have memorised the schedules at this stage. Surely you've got a good idea of what will work.'

'I'm still running through them,' I tell him. 'I'll . . . call you back.'

'Text me,' he says. 'I have a full list this afternoon, starting in ten minutes.'

'OK.' I feel my shoulders slump. 'I really am sorry,' I tell him again.

'It isn't your fault,' says Chris. 'I'm sure Mum will be very understanding.'

And I know for a fact she won't. I should tell him now that there isn't a chance of me getting there on time, but I can't bring myself to do it. It'll be easier by text.

'I'll get back to you as soon as I can,' I promise.

'And to Pen,' he reminds me. 'So that if you don't make it she can organise someone else to do the flowers.'

We're not co-ordinating an Olympic opening ceremony here, I think to myself. It doesn't really matter who does the deed. I'll be in her black books anyhow.

'Of course,' I say.

'Well, look, I hope to see you this evening. But obviously if you're going to be late, I might not be able to pick you up at the airport as planned, so you'll have to get a cab.'

'I know.'

'I've got to go,' says Chris. 'I can't keep my patients waiting.'

'See you later,' I lie. 'Love you.'

I always end our conversations with 'love you'. His usual response is 'Love you Lots', which he thinks is an amusing way to abbreviate my name. But this time there's a tiny hesitation before he says the words. I don't blame him for being annoyed. If I were him, I'd be annoyed too.

Chapter 3

Romance Anonimo (Anonymous Romance) – Narciso Yepes

I put my phone back into my bag and walk quickly to the taxi rank. I'm wondering if Jeremy Clarkson's Doppelgänger is still caught up in dealing with his accident, and I feel terrible for abandoning him without paying. I'm getting tired of all the guilt I'm carrying around today and I'm relieved when the driver of the cab I get into is a different man entirely.

The rain has stopped by the time we pull up outside the Hotel Andalucia, and with a speed never seen in Ireland, the grey clouds are already beginning to disappear, revealing a washed blue sky. The air is significantly warmer and I can make out the scent of the orange blossom again.

I pay the taxi driver and walk up to the reception desk at the hotel. I haven't seen this receptionist before, but I tell her that I stayed with them the previous night and that I need a room again for tonight. She frowns slightly and begins to tap at her computer terminal with her long, pillar-box-red nails.

'I'm so sorry, Miss O'Keeffe.' She pronounces it *Kay-fay*, which sounds slightly exotic. 'But we are fully booked for tonight.'

I look at her in disbelief.

'We have a conference,' she explains apologetically. 'From a sports institute. And there are still guests from the *feria*.'

The trackie-clad athletes. Of course. And there was a huge festival here last week, according to Antonio. But a fully booked hotel? She has to be having me on. This entire day has to be having me on!

'We are booked completely for both tonight and tomorrow night.'

I feel my composure begin to crack and I'm afraid that this time I really will burst into tears. How can everything be going so spectacularly wrong for me? Over the years I've learned how to be organised and punctual and efficient and unflappable. And yet today all of that has come crashing down around me. Today I've been late and chaotic and shambling, and things are still going wrong.

'Let me see if we have rooms in our sister hotel,' says the receptionist. 'It's on the other side of the city and—'

'No.' I shake my head. 'Not yet. I want to think about what to do. Thank you.'

I walk away from the desk and sit down in one of the enormous white armchairs dotted around the foyer. I appreciate now that I made a ridiculous mistake at the Renfe desk in the train station. I changed my ticket to Madrid to tomorrow when I should simply have changed it to a later train today. Which I now realise is the option the employee was trying to offer me. That way I would be in Madrid tonight and it wouldn't matter if every damn hotel was full because I could camp out in the airport if necessary. I can't believe I've been so monumentally stupid.

I breathe deeply through my nose, and exhale softly through my mouth in the way that I learnt in the managing-stress classes that Sive, my best friend, made me go to in college. I need to get myself on top of things again. I need to regain control of my life. Would it be better to go back to the station and try to switch trains yet again? I remember from the schedules that there are plenty more this evening. It's the most sensible option. It's the option I'm going to take. I stand up.

And then I hear him call my name.

Because the accent is Irish, the very first thing I think is that it's Chris, even though I know that's utterly impossible. So if it's not Chris, it must be someone from the Dublin office of Cadogan Consulting. But none of them should be here in Seville. And none of my confident colleagues would say my name in such a hesitant way.

I look up, my expression puzzled. And then I see him. I stare at him for what seems like forever, trying to put the voice with the man. He smiles as I get slowly to my feet.

'Carlotta? Carlotta O'Keeffe? Is it really you?' He walks towards me.

He's tall. Taller than Chris and easily as tall as Mateo. He's leaner than both of them. He doesn't have the defined abs of Mateo, but beneath the faded green T-shirt he's wearing, I can see that he keeps in shape. His hair is dark blond, slightly long and curly. His face is chiselled. His eyes are sapphire blue. I can't decide if he's handsome or beautiful. Beautiful seems like the wrong word for a man who is, despite the curly hair, very masculine, but there is a beauty in the way he holds himself and the way he's moving and I suddenly remember it, although back then he wasn't tall and lean and breathtakingly handsome to go with it. If I'm right, of course.

I remember my mother's words. 'That Luke Evans is a beautiful boy. It's a pity about—' and then she broke off because I walked into the room.

'A pity about what?' I asked, but she shook her head and didn't answer.

I wondered if she meant that it was a pity he was beautiful, because twenty-odd years ago beauty wasn't a desirable attribute for a teenage boy. They wanted to look cool and tough, not sweetly angelic. But Luke didn't seem bothered by his curly locks and perfect features. He rose above it.

His family, mum, dad and four sons, lived at the end of our road. The Evanses were flashier than most of us on Blackwater Terrace. Mr Evans was the first to pave over the small front garden to provide off-street parking for his 4x4 and his wife's Mini Cooper. They were the only two-car family on our street. They also had satellite TV before anyone else. And mobile phones. My mother used to make disapproving noises whenever she talked about Mr and Mrs Evans, so maybe, I remember thinking one time, maybe she thought it was a pity Luke had the parents he had. I assumed it was because of the flashiness. Even if they could have afforded it, my parents weren't the flashy sort. They're still not.

It's definitely him. Here in Seville. Looking at me with an expression of delight and surprise.

'Carlotta. It is you, isn't it?' He's smiling.

'Luke?'

'What in heaven's name are you doing here?' he asks.

I'm lost for words. The last time I saw Luke Evans I was fifteen years old. We'd gone on our first date together. After that, I never saw him again. Until today.

Chapter 4

**Cuentos para la Juventud (Stories for the Young) –
Julian Bream**

We've been looking at each other for what seems like forever
and I still haven't said anything. I've no idea what to say.
I never expected to see him again and certainly not here,
not now. Instead of coming up with words, I'm thinking
of the very first time we met, the day the Evanses moved
into the house in Blackwater Terrace. I was thirteen years
old and reading in my bedroom when I heard the enormous
removal truck pull up outside number 34, followed by two
cars from which the Evans family emerged.

Richard Evans was an imposing man. Tall and broad-
shouldered, he was classically good-looking and radiated
confidence and authority. His wife, Murielle, was slim and
attractive, and wore her blonde hair pulled back into a ponytail. Despite having four children, they looked younger and
more glamorous than any other set of parents on the street.
For a time, all the boys wished that Richard was their dad,
and all the girls longed for a mother as cool as Murielle.

I was too young to be interested in the Evans boys,

although for the older girls a family with four sons was a definite opportunity. Kyle was the eldest and aged about nineteen when they moved in. Luke, at thirteen (just a few months older than me), was the youngest. The two in the middle were Jordan and Wayne. The three older boys were all well-built and muscular like their father, and wore their hair in the tight buzz cuts that were popular at the time. Luke was different. His frame was smaller and softer, his face was longer, and as for his hair – well, those golden curls gave him an almost cherubic appearance. I wondered how he'd escaped the barber's razor.

It was over an hour before the removal van left the street, by which time all of the neighbours had, at one point or another, found a reason to walk past number 34. My mother, who'd gone by just as the last item was being taken out of the van, informed us that they seemed to be a very modern family. She didn't say that as though it were a good thing. My dad grunted and returned to his paper. I didn't care one way or the other, but my sister, Julia, quizzed Mum about them when she returned from her usual Saturday afternoon shopping expedition with her friends, and asked if she thought any of them were a good bet. Julia is four years older than me, and back then she was constantly on the lookout for new boyfriends to add to her tally of broken hearts. She's the beauty in our family, and at seventeen she had her pick of the local lads, flitting from boy to boy like an indecisive butterfly. She went out with Kyle Evans for a while but broke it off long before the family left Blackwater Terrace. Kyle was Julia's rebellion, because my mother hadn't wanted either of us to be involved with the Evans boys, even though I was never sure why.

Anyway, I'd no intention of being involved with them. At thirteen, I was a scrawny, miserable-looking girl with long, stringy hair, a flat chest and no sense of style. As well as which I was short for my age, smaller than all of my friends by quite a distance. My father used to frown when he looked at me and would ask my mother where the hell I'd come from, because he was a tall man and Julia took after him. Even Mum wasn't short. I'd obviously inherited an unknown ancestor's mutant gene and I wished I hadn't. I hated being small. Even though I was officially a teenager, most people still treated me like a child, and when it came to boys – well, they thought I was a kid too.

I met Luke because Mum asked me to go to the shops for an extra bottle of milk in the early evening. (She always asked for bottles of milk even though bottles had been discontinued years earlier. In fact I've never seen milk in a bottle in my life.) I'd been reading a girls' magazine and was happy to stop because it was talking about how to keep your boyfriend happy and obviously I didn't have one to worry about. So I took the money from the jar on the kitchen counter and cut through the laneway at the back of our house to reach the cluster of shops on the main road.

I spent a few minutes reading the headlines in the evening newspapers before going to the till to pay for the milk. Luke Evans was ahead of me. He was buying packets of sweets, crisps, Coke and chocolate.

At the risk of making my parents sound like characters from a Dickens novel, I have to confess that neither crisps, Coke nor chocolate were regularly available in our home. Dad didn't receive an extravagant wage from the factory in Tallaght where he worked, and although Mum had a few part-time house-cleaning jobs in the nearby, more affluent, suburbs of Terenure and Rathgar, we lived on a tight budget. Consequently, rubbish snack foods weren't a big part of our lives and the lack of fizzy drinks, sweets and crisps never really bothered us. Chocolate, of course, was a whole different ball game. The biggest treat in my life now is to sit down and eat a bar of Green & Black's milk chocolate, totally uninterrupted.

So when I saw Luke Evans struggling to fit a final large bar of Cadbury's Fruit & Nut into a plastic bag, I couldn't help giving it an envious glance.

'It's not all for me.' His tone was defensive and I realised that my look might have seemed disapproving rather than envious.

'I didn't think it was. I saw you all move in today. Probably your mum doesn't have time to cook.'

'We're having fish and chips tonight,' he told me. 'This is to keep us going.'

'Fair enough.' I wasn't going to comment on the Evanses' food choices. I'd been the butt of jokes myself in the past, when girls in my class sniggered at the sandwich, apple and water that Mum packed for my lunch, while they tucked into at least one salty or sugary snack. Besides, going on the physique of the boys and their father, it didn't seem to be doing them any harm.

'It was a long day.'

'Did you have to travel far?'

'Dundalk,' he replied.

Dundalk is near the border with Northern Ireland. It takes less than an hour to get there from Dublin these days, but back then the trip took a lot longer because you had to go through a series of small towns, each of which caused time-wasting traffic jams.

'Why did you move here?'

We'd walked out of the shop together.

'Oh, something to do with Dad's work,' replied Luke. 'I don't know. I didn't get a choice.' His tone was bitter.

'This is a nice place to live,' I said.

'Dundalk was near the sea.'

'So's Dublin.'

'It's not the same.'

'Did you leave friends behind?' I asked.

He considered that for a moment. 'None that matter.' He grinned suddenly, which lit up his face. 'Maybe you're right. Maybe this will be the start of a new life for all of us.'

I shot him a glance. I wondered if something terrible had happened in Dundalk that they needed to start a new life.

'Oh, not this way!' I steered Luke away from the main road and towards the laneway. 'This is quicker.'

'Thanks.'

'And I don't know if you've already ordered the fish and chips, but I wouldn't go to the Capri. I know it's the nearest, but Mum says they reuse the oil too much. We go to Manolo's. It's beside the chemist.'

'Thanks,' he said again.

'If you like Chinese food, you should go to the New Mandarin.'

'What's wrong with the old one?' he asked.

'Huh?' And then I got it. 'I suppose there must have been an older one at some time,' I said. 'But it's been called the New Mandarin for as long as I can remember.'

'I suppose it must be good if it's been around forever.'

'We don't get Chinese food much,' I admitted. 'But Mum says it's the best place.'

'Your mum seems to know all the good places to get food.'

'Not that it matters to us,' I told him. 'We don't eat out a lot. Or get takeaways. Mum cooks most of the time.'

'Mine doesn't,' said Luke. 'The only thing she's good at is spaghetti bolognese. Otherwise it's microwave stuff for us.'

I was a bit shocked at this. My mother used the microwave for defrosting food and reheating leftovers. I was astonished at how fearsomely strong the Evanses seemed to be on the sort of diet that would make Mum gasp with horror. Well, Mrs Evans wasn't strong, of course. She was pretty. And Luke was . . . well . . . he was cute. He reminded me of the kind of kid you'd see in a Disney movie. *Home Alone*, maybe. Or something like that.

'This is me.' The laneway emerged almost beside our house.

'That was a lot quicker than going by the road,' said Luke.

'I use it all the time. But not at night,' I added. 'People smoke and drink in it at night and it's not safe.'

'Thanks for the info.' He reached into the bag and took out a Bounty bar. 'Here. Have this.'

'I can't.' All chocolate was exotic in our house but Bounty was the most exotic of the lot.

'Of course you can.' He looked at me as though I was crazy. 'You've given me all sorts of useful local knowledge. It's a thank you.'

'Well . . .'

'My mother would be very annoyed if I didn't say thank you.'

I hesitated and then took the Bounty.

'See you around,' said Luke.

'Yeah, see you.'

Sometimes I look back on my childhood years and I think that I must have been one of the most naive people on the planet. I accepted everything my parents told me. I didn't spend my meagre pocket money on illicit bags of crisps and bars of chocolate. I was compliant and obedient and I never asked any questions. I didn't feel hard done by, though. I enjoyed my childhood. But the best two years of my life were the two years when Luke Evans was in it.

Even though I'm jolted back to the first time we met, I'm feeling the way I did when I realised I wouldn't ever see him again. And yet I was wrong about that, because here he is now, standing in front of me, not cherubic any longer but masculine and handsome.

'What brings you to Seville?' he asks again. 'You look great, by the way.'

The one thing I can be a hundred per cent sure about is that I don't look great. My hair is all over the place thanks to drying it under the hand-dryer at the station, I didn't bother to redo my make-up, and my blouse is a creased mess over my jeans. Which are my faded, loafing-around jeans, not the bum-hugging straight-legged ones that make me look marginally taller and significantly slimmer. If I'd ever imagined meeting Luke Evans again, I would've pictured myself in one of my kick-ass suits, so that he'd know that I'd turned into a confident, competent person. The kind of person that people didn't mess with. That people didn't walk out on. But life never works out like that, does it?

'I'm here for a meeting,' I tell him as I try to smooth my hair. 'Well, I've done the meeting. I should be on my way home.'

'Don't tell me I've run into you for the first time in – how many years? Ten, twelve . . . no, it must be more, and you're leaving already!'

'Closer to eighteen,' I tell him as I mentally calculate it and reel in shock myself at the result.

'My God,' he says. 'It doesn't seem that long at all . . .' His voice trails off.

'What are you doing here?' I ask. 'Do you live here?'

'No, I've come for a wedding. Not mine,' he adds quickly. 'A friend is getting married tomorrow.' He looks at me thoughtfully. 'Would you like to come? You could be my plus one . . . although obviously if you're on your way home . . . Please don't be on your way home, Carlotta. It'd be lovely to talk at least.'

'I'm not going straight away. But I *am* going tomorrow, so I can't help you there. Besides, I'm sure you have your pick of plus ones.' The words are out of my mouth before I can stop them. But it's true. Luke Evans could've had any girl he wanted eighteen years ago. I'm sure they're still flinging themselves at him now.

He laughs. 'If only. I did have a plus one for a while but she found someone else and . . .' He looks urgently at me. 'Have you plans for tonight? Can we go somewhere? Talk. Catch up.'

'I was about to go to the station and catch a train to Madrid,' I tell him.

'You don't have to be there tonight do you?' he asks. 'There are plenty of trains in the morning.'

'I can't stay here,' I say. 'The hotel is full. Have *you* a reservation?' I add, and blush because I realise it could sound like I want to share his room or something. Which obviously I don't!

46

'No,' he says. 'I'm borrowing an apartment in town for the weekend. I was just collecting something here.' His eyes narrow. 'You can stay with me if you like.'

He says it so casually, as though we're friends who see each other and stay with each other all the time. But it's been eighteen years. And we were only kids back then. We never got around to being anything else. Which maybe wasn't entirely his fault. But he still could've called.

'That's really nice of you.' I keep my voice as steady as possible. 'But I can't impose.'

'It's not an imposition,' he tells me. 'There are three bedrooms in the apartment.'

'What about the owner?' I ask. 'I'm sure he . . . she . . . doesn't want stray people staying there.'

'The owner, my friend, is the girl who's getting married.' He grins at me. 'Anita. Her parents live further out of town and she's staying at home tonight because she's getting married from there tomorrow.' He smiles. 'She was a girlfriend years ago.'

And they're still friends. Even though she's getting married to someone else. Which doesn't surprise me in the slightest, because Luke was such an easy person to be friends with. Dammit, even though I thought I'd turn and walk away if I ever saw him again, I'm talking to him now. He has that way about him. He draws you in.

'And she's letting you stay in her apartment?' Despite everything, I'm a little surprised at this.

'We've known each other for ages, and I've had the keys for years,' he says easily. 'She knew that it would be difficult to get anything in Seville right now, what with the *feria* and everything.'

47

Taking Luke up on his offer would save me a lot of hassle, but I can't help feeling that I might be causing myself a lot of grief too. Basically, I'm thinking of staying in an apartment with a man I hardly know. A man I *don't* know, for heaven's sake, because the last time I saw Luke Evans he was a teenager. Who knows what his life's been like since his Blackwater Terrace days? Who knows what sort of person he's become?

'It's in a great location,' he tells me. 'Near the cathedral. Wonderful for sightseeing.'

'I don't have time for sightseeing,' I say.

'Everyone has time for sightseeing in Seville.' He sounds slightly shocked.

'I really don't.' I sigh. 'All I need is somewhere to crash so that I'm up and ready in time to catch the train to Madrid tomorrow.'

'Of course you're welcome to simply stay and crash,' says Luke. 'If that's what you want.'

'It's just . . .'

'We were friends.' His voice softens. 'We're still friends, Carly.'

Nobody but Luke has ever called me Carly. Chris calls me Lots. My family and friends occasionally call me Lottie. Hearing him say it sends a shiver down my spine.

'We haven't seen each other for eighteen years,' I remind him. 'Hardly friends now.'

'That doesn't mean we can't be friends again.' He smiles his wide, open smile. 'And even if we're not, you can still stay in the apartment with me. No strings, no problems.'

I'm torn. I glance at the crowds milling around the reception area and think that it'll be the same all over the city. And that it would be lovely to stay in an apartment in the old part of town. And that perhaps I could do a little bit of sightseeing if the rain has stopped.

'It's a nice offer,' I begin.

'It makes sense,' he says.

'No strings?'

'Absolutely none,' he promises me.

With anyone else I'd still have said no. But this is Luke and he was once my very best friend. And maybe, in the end, it was better that there'd never been anything more between us.

'OK then.' If Chris were to call me and say that he was staying with an old friend who turned out to be female, I know that I'd be annoyed with him. Which is stupid, isn't it? But he doesn't have to know. Besides, I trust Luke. No matter what.

Chapter 5

Calle Abajo (Lower Street) – José de Córdoba

'I'll just get the car,' he says, 'and meet you in front of the hotel, if that's OK.'

'Sure.' I nod, and he strides off to the bank of elevators beside the reception desk. I'm wondering if I have time to nip into the Ladies' and freshen up a bit, because I know I must look a total disaster area. But he's seen me like this now and he might get the wrong idea if I appear on the hotel steps looking like my groomed, corporate self.

Staying with Luke is a sensible thing to do, I decide as I walk out of the lobby and wait outside the building. We were best friends long before he ever asked me out. We promised to be friends no matter what. And people don't change. At least . . . I think of how Luke has changed. How much taller and leaner he's become. How his face has matured. How his hair has darkened. How he's no longer a teenager, he's a grown man. But inside he's the same, isn't he? Just like I am. And that thought makes me suddenly doubtful. Because I'm not actually the same inside as I was at fifteen. How could I possibly be?

There's a continuous stream of cars picking up and dropping off guests, and I glance in admiration as the latest glides to a halt near me. Then Luke gets out and offers to put my bag in the boot.

'This is your car?' I gasp.

I've always wanted to own an Aston Martin ever since I saw the movie *Goldfinger* in which James Bond drives around in the famous one with the changeable number plates. All my male friends believe that an Aston is one of the most beautiful cars in the world. And Luke Evans is driving one. I'm gobsmacked.

'You like it?' He's smiling at me as he takes my case and places it in the open boot.

'How can I not?' I reply.

I look at it in awe, and I realise that other people are looking at it with varying shades of envy too. It's a V12 Vantage, in traditional gunmetal grey, and it appears both powerful and elegant all at once. I'm almost afraid to get inside, but when I do, I inhale the smell of the cream leather and I can't help running my fingers along the walnut dash. I'm in love with it already.

'OK?' Luke gets into the driver's seat. It suddenly clicks with me that it's a right-hand-drive model, but it doesn't appear to bother him that he has to drive on the wrong side of the road. He spins away from the hotel and joins the stream of traffic while I sit back and enjoy the ride.

Luke is a good, confident driver but I feel myself tense as he takes the Aston through streets that are becoming narrower by the minute. Seville wasn't built for Aston Martins. The old quarter wasn't built for any kind of car. The consolation, I think, is that it doesn't matter which side of the road we should be driving on; the streets are too narrow for anything other than heading straight down the centre. I'm hoping they're one-way. But Luke seems to know where he's going.

'I've stayed here a few times,' he tells me as he turns into the narrowest street so far. 'Always convinced I'll get lost, though.'

He stops the car in front of a double gate set into a wall. He gets out and taps a code into a keypad. The gate rises upwards and I see a very steep ramp leading into what must be an underground garage.

'And now for my favourite part.' Luke edges the Aston forward and we crawl down the ramp, which veers sharply to the left at the bottom. I'm blinking in the sudden darkness and wondering how in God's name Luke can see anything. But he's relaxed as he manoeuvres the car carefully around the bend and into a small space between two concrete pillars. Then he cuts the engine and sighs.

'Always scares the shit out of me,' he says. 'Even when I'm not driving one of the world's most brilliant cars.' He opens the door. 'C'mon.'

There's a tiny lift in the corner of the garage, with barely enough room for the two of us plus my case. We're standing shoulder to shoulder and I can feel the warmth of his skin through the thin fabric of my blouse. I ignore the forced intimacy and keep my eyes fixed in front of me.

The lift shudders to a stop on the fourth floor, causing me to sway slightly. Luke puts out his hand to steady me but I tell him I'm fine, not to worry. The doors open slowly and I step out into a dim hallway. As I move to one side, a sensor light comes on in the high ceiling. Luke takes a small bunch of keys from his pocket. He selects one, inserts it into the lock of the plain wooden door opposite and pushes it open.

It's equally dim inside the apartment. Luke walks along a short, narrow corridor; I hear the noise of shutters opening and then suddenly the passageway is filled with light. I move towards Luke and I gasp again, because this apartment is as fabulous as the Aston Martin. The walls are painted off-white, the floor is highly polished parquet and the furniture is either restored antique or fantastically authentic-looking reproductions. The windows are long and narrow and are giving spectacular views of the city.

'Oh wow,' I say as I stand beside Luke and gaze out over the rooftops. 'This is amazing.'

'I know,' says Luke. 'This place has been in Anita's family forever. She had it redone a few years ago. It used to be ultra modern – it still has some great technology – but it's perfect now, isn't it?'

'Absolutely.' I look at the catch on the window that opens out on to a narrow wrought-iron balcony. 'Can I undo this?'

'Sure.'

I open the window and step outside. I've never been afraid of heights but can't help a moment of dizziness as I lean on the iron railing. It's worth it, though. The sky is now a brilliant blue, all traces of the earlier clouds completely gone, and the jumble of buildings beneath shine white and bright. There are oases of green too, palm trees and maybe some more orange trees, I think. I'm lost for words.

'Would you like a coffee?' Clearly Luke has seen this view enough times not to be enthralled.

I turn back inside. 'Coffee would be lovely.'

'Coming up,' he says.

He leaves me in what is obviously the main living room. I've decided that everything in the apartment is genuine antique not fantastic fake, and consequently I'm almost afraid to move in case I knock anything over. There are occasional tables dotted around, on which vases and other ornaments have been artfully placed, and I'm reckoning that they're worth a few bob, if not utterly irreplaceable. I wonder what it would be like to live here, and then I think that Chris would be able to tell me that, because Chris's parental home is a bit of a homage to antiques and art too. Dorothea has her favourite pieces on display, and whenever I visit I'm generally afraid of barging into a stray table and knocking over a priceless statuette, thus cementing my place in the hall of unsuitable potential daughters-in-law forever. I'm always so careful around Dorothea's home that I look as though I have some kind of weird walking ailment – one that makes me scuttle sideways every time I'm near a piece of furniture.

I glance at my watch. I suppose the preparations for the birthday party are now in full swing and that everyone is looking forward to a fantastic evening. I wonder if Chris has told Dorothea yet about my missing the train, and how she feels about it if she knows. I'm hoping she'll feel at least a flicker of sympathy, although I can't help thinking she might be revelling in *Schadenfreude* instead.

I wish more than anything else in the world that I hadn't gone to sleep after the meeting. I think now it was the strain of having to remember so much, and in a language I don't speak, that exhausted me. I know that Mateo was astounded by my ability to make our presentation in a foreign language, and to appear to completely understand every word I said. I could see the awed expression on his face as I addressed the board in my temporarily acquired Spanish. It wasn't as incredible as it might sound, because a lot of my presentation was bilingual – most of the board of Ecologistics is English-speaking – but even if I say so myself I was a total triumph this morning. I wanted to be able to tell Chris about it tonight. I'd already imagined leaning against his shoulder in one of the quiet moments, telling him how brilliant I'd been and how pleased everyone was with me, and having him say that he was proud of me. Dirk had phoned me again just before I'd fallen asleep to say that Antonio Reyes had contacted him personally to say how impressed they were with what Mateo and I had done. Well done, he'd said. You're a gem, Lottie.

Maybe Chris wouldn't have thought so. Maybe he would have been affronted by the idea of me standing up and parroting the Spanish words and phrases I'd only learned the day before. Maybe he'd have considered it a cheap trick. Unethical even. But I never pretended afterwards I could speak fluently. I'd admitted as much, in English, to Antonio. Although I didn't tell him the complete truth. I just said that I could read more than I could speak, which was basically honest.

If I close my eyes, I can see it all again now. The text beside the pictures on each PowerPoint slide. And I can hear the words as Mateo had recorded them and as I'd listened to them. I can fit each sound with each word on the text but the grammar eludes me. Not that it matters anyway. The presentation is over. I don't need to retain anything. I shake my head and the slides dissolve, leaving nothing but a blank screen.

'Coffee,' says Luke and walks back into the room.

* * *

I don't remember exactly when we became friends. I didn't see him for ages after the day they moved in to Blackwater Terrace, and I can't honestly recall the next time we met. But when the school term started we got into the habit of walking there together, leaving our houses within a few seconds of each other and falling into step as we turned on to the main road for the twenty-minute journey. Sometimes we talked about school, sometimes about friends or family or TV programmes we'd seen; sometimes we walked in near silence. It didn't really matter to us. We enjoyed each other's company.

My classmates started sniggering and muttering about me having a boyfriend, and making kissing noises whenever they saw Luke in the distance, but it didn't bother me. I told them that he was a friend who was a boy which was an entirely different thing. (Julia had used that phrase about the latest guy she was going out with and I liked it. So I borrowed it. Just as I occasionally borrowed her favourite jumpers without telling her.) Because they didn't get a rise out of me, the girls stopped their teasing after a few weeks, although I knew they talked behind my back while wondering what the point in having a friend who was a boy, as opposed to a boyfriend, actually was. There was, as far as they were concerned, no benefit to boys who were friends at all. Some of them were peeved at me for apparently taking Luke Evans out of play for girls who were prepared to be more than just friends with him. After all, as my mum had said, he was beautiful.

A few times during our friendship he went out with girls. At first I thought it was the end of walking to school together or helping each other with homework projects. But Luke seemed to take having a friend who was a girl and a girlfriend who was a girlfriend in his stride. And I wasn't the slightest bit jealous of any of the girls he went out with, because to me he was still a friend. With hindsight, I'm sure the girlfriends didn't feel the same way.

Maybe if Luke and I had first met a few years later things would have been different between us from the off. But at thirteen, he was my confidant and I was his. The only physical contact between us was an occasional platonic hug to show support, or sympathy or understanding. It worked for me, though, because it meant that Luke had my back and I had his. It was comforting.

The first time Luke comforted me with a hug was the day that he found me sobbing because I'd aced all my end-of-term exams and I'd been accused of cheating. In answering a history question on the reign of England's Henry VIII, I'd managed to write down, verbatim, my history book's text on the subject. I'd done almost the same in geography, business studies and biology. Mrs Trent, the principal, had called me into her office and told me that she was going to have to talk to my parents.

These days parents are much more likely to side with their children than the teacher. I know this because my next-door neighbour in the terrace of artisan houses where I live is a teacher. She complains that it's hard to enforce discipline when parents are more concerned with their children's rights than their responsibilities, and when most of them are ready to challenge her authority at any given moment.

My parents, by contrast, trusted the teachers implicitly, and when Mum got a phone call to say that Mrs Trent wanted to talk to her about a serious issue, she hotfooted it to the school without talking to me about it first. In fairness to her, when she heard about the wholesale quotations from the books, she looked at me with resignation and then explained it all to Mrs Trent, who regarded me in complete astonishment.

'None of her teachers noticed this,' she said. 'She never answers questions in class.'

'She was ostracised for being a bit of a smarty-pants in primary,' Mum pointed out.

'Why didn't you tell me?' Mrs Trent was looking at me as though I had two heads. 'I didn't believe it was a real phenomenon.'

'Neither did we,' said Mum. 'But with Carlotta, it seems to be.'

'I see,' said Mrs Trent. 'It does present us with a challenge.'

'I know.' I spoke for the first time. 'The challenge of deciding if I'm a genius or a parrot.'

'Let's go for gifted.' Mrs Trent smiled at me. 'And let's assume that you'll use your gift well, Carlotta.'

I do my best. But I'm still never sure if it's good enough.

Luke looked at me from his amazing blue eyes when I recounted this to him, and then he asked, 'Is it true?'

'I'm not gifted or a genius,' I told him. 'What I have is called eidetic memory. People are wrong to call it photographic. It's not like I look at a page and remember everything on it straight away. I have to read it. Sometimes more than once.'

'And then you remember it perfectly?' He was astonished.

'Nearly,' I admitted. 'Close enough.'

'But that *does* make you a genius,' he protested. 'You

should be doing your Leaving exams already. All you have to do is read the books and remember them.'

'There's more to exams than that,' I reminded him, although every year there's a debate about how they're nothing more than rote learning and how students can't think for themselves. 'You have to be able to answer questions, not just quote the book.'

'But if you can remember the whole book off by heart . . .' He was looking at me in wonder. 'That would be pretty amazing.'

'I don't remember every single thing,' I protested. 'I read stuff, I remember it for a few days, I forget it. When it comes to doing exams, though, I can swot up for each one the night before and I remember everything I've read fairly easily.'

'That is sooooo cool,' he said. 'How d'you do it?'

'I don't know,' I told him. 'I know that some people do memory tricks. They memorise long lists and can repeat them back perfectly. I don't do that. I read something, I close my eyes, I see the page again. And I don't know how I do it.'

'Wow,' he said. 'You'll go places with a brain like that.'

'It's not my brain,' I tried to explain. 'It's just my memory.'

But ever after that he used to call me brainbox. He was the only person I never minded using the phrase.

It does sound cool when I talk about it. Most people have the same reaction. That it's genius. But it's nothing of the kind. It's a party trick, that's all. I don't have great insights into the burning questions of the day. I'm not a radical thinker. I'm certainly not a genius. I'm just an ordinary person who can remember stuff for as long as I need to.

That's how I managed the bilingual presentation. Mateo

did up the PowerPoint slides and then he read them out to me while I looked at each one. It's not just my visual memory that's special. I remember sounds too. So I could put the sounds of the words with the written text in front of me and remember it. It's a bit of a con really, and Cadogan doesn't send me all around the world repeating it, but Dirk felt I was the right person to present to Ecologistics. And it paid off, because we got the business.

'Coffee,' says Luke again, and I realise that he's been standing there patiently while I've been remembering.

'Sorry,' I tell him as I take the small cup from him. 'I was daydreaming.'

'I know,' he says. 'I recognise that look on your face.'

'Am I so readable?' I ask.

'You always were to me.' He sits down on one of the antique chairs and tentatively I do the same, willing myself not to spill coffee over the elegant mint-green brocade.

I sip the coffee, unsure of what to say now that we are alone in a room together. Luke says nothing himself, but drinks his coffee in a couple of gulps before putting the cup on the polished table beside his chair.

'I should've shown you to your room and let you unpack before plying you with coffee,' he says. 'I'm still completely stunned at meeting you here.'

'Colour me stunned too,' I say in reply, and we both laugh.

Laughing helps. Suddenly the atmosphere between us, which had been building up to something awkward, has eased again.

'C'mon.' He stands up. 'I'll show you to your bed for the night.'

I drain my coffee and follow him. He pushes open a door

to a darkened room. Once again, when he opens the shutters and the light pours in, I can see that it's tastefully and expensively decorated. The walls are the same off-white as the rest of the apartment. The double bed has an old-fashioned brass frame and is covered by a white sheet with a blue floral pattern, as well as a mountain of pillows enclosed in crisp white pillowcases. The chest of drawers is painted in distressed cream, as is the big wardrobe. Despite the fact that the view from the window is a hotchpotch of rooftops, towered over by a massive cathedral, the room has an open, rustic feel to it.

'Is this Anita's room?' I ask. Much as I need somewhere to stay, the idea of sleeping in the bed of a woman I don't even know makes me feel uncomfortable.

'Nope,' says Luke. 'This is a guest room. I'll be in the other guest room. Anita herself has a far more glamorous bedroom.'

'The apartment must be huge.' I can't imagine how much it must cost to have a three-bedroom apartment in a restored building like this.

'It used to be two separate apartments until her dad bought the second one and knocked them together,' explains Luke. 'There's a shower room and loo through this door here . . .' He shows me. 'So you have everything you need.'

'It's great,' I tell him. 'Thank you so much.'

'I thought perhaps you might like to visit the cathedral later.' He nods towards the window. 'Unless you've been already, of course.'

I shake my head and am about to remind him that I'm not here for sightseeing, but then I remember that I had wanted to see something of the city and that this is my opportunity. Surely it's better to have Luke, who apparently knows the place, alongside me rather than to schlep aimlessly about by myself. So I say that I'd love to see the cathedral and he suggests that we head out in twenty minutes or so when I've had time to freshen up. Catching sight of myself in the full-length mirror beside the chest of drawers, I see how much of a wreck I look. It's a miracle that Luke recognised me at all.

I agree that twenty minutes is all I'll need to get ready, though honestly I'd need about twice that to feel properly presentable.

And I need to take some time to phone Chris.

Chapter 6

Alma Libre (Free Spirit) – Juan Carlos Quintero

My memory is both a blessing and a curse, though obviously it's part of who I am. That's what I said to Chris when, after our first few dates, I told him about it. Because of his medical training, he already knew everything there is to know and he was initially sceptical about how much I could remember. But when he gave me a textbook about eye conditions to read and I was able to recite chunks of it back to him, he couldn't help being impressed. He was so impressed, in fact, that he arranged for a neurologist to do some tests on me to track my brainwaves. I put up with two sessions of sitting in a room with electrodes all over my head and then told Chris that I'd had enough of being a lab rat. But apparently the tests were of some use to the neurologist, so I felt I'd done my bit to advance medical science.

I think Chris is proud of my ability, in a weird sort of way. Having an unusual gift makes me more than just a girl he met at the clinic where he worked. It makes me special.

I was never Chris's patient. I don't know if ophthalmic

surgeons can be struck off for gazing deeply into their patients' eyes and telling them that they love them, but fortunately the situation didn't arise. I met him when I went to the eye clinic with Sive. She was thinking about getting the same laser eye surgery I'd had done a couple of years earlier. Having been blind as a bat before it, I still wake up every day marvelling at the fact that I can see the time on the clock beside my bed without having to peer myopically at it (well, except today of course). Anyway, Sive, who's one of the most practical and competent women I know, was uncharacteristically squeamish about the whole eye thing, and so I offered to go along with her for her consultation.

She had the very last appointment of the day. She works as a liquidator, settling the affairs of businesses that have gone bust, so she's been very much in demand over the last few years. The only time off she takes during working hours is strictly for childcare emergencies. She's my god-daughter Natasha's mother, and like me, she says she's afraid of being found out, of the men she works with realising that she isn't quite good enough. Sive shouldn't need to worry, because she's properly clever, but I think all women, no matter how brilliant they are, always worry. It's frustrating and probably unhealthy but it's the truth.

Anyway, while she was having her consultation my mobile rang. It was Dirk, but the call dropped each time I tried to answer, so I went outside, phoned him back and listened as he told me about a new account the company was getting which, he thought, was prime material for me. Dirk is a good guy but he talks way too much. I was afraid that Sive would be out of her consultation by the time he eventually ended the call, so I hurried up the stairs and into the clinic, colliding with Chris Bennett as I pushed open the door.

There was the usual flurry of apologies, me telling him I was sorry, him saying that no, it was all his fault, and then we both looked properly at each other and – well, I don't know – it was like something popped inside my heart. It wasn't because he was fantastically good-looking, although he could certainly give Ralph Fiennes in his *English Patient* days a run for his money. It wasn't anything he'd said, because all we'd both done was apologise to each other. It was just instant attraction. Obviously I covered it up well, walking past him with a nonchalant air, but it was all I could do not to look over my shoulder as I turned into the waiting area. I told my beating heart to slow down and then I helped myself to coffee from the machine. When I turned back, Chris was standing in the waiting area too.

'My nurse says you were treated here a couple of years ago,' he said.

I nodded.

'Clearly not by me,' he said. 'I don't leave my patients so blind that they walk into complete strangers.'

At first I thought he was serious. He'd kept a straight face as he spoke but then he broke into a broad smile. I smiled too.

'How have you been since your surgery?' he asked.

'Great,' I told him. 'That's why I persuaded my friend to come along.'

I told him about Sive and he nodded and said that she'd probably be looked after by Dr Metcalfe and I said that Dr Metcalfe had done my eyes and he was fantastic and Chris

65

said that indeed he was, although, he added, he would've liked the opportunity to study my eyes in more detail himself. He said that they were lovely eyes. He had a preference, he added, for green eyes. His own were almost navy.

Anyway, that was the start of it. Sive had her surgery and it went great. She's claimed ownership of my relationship with Chris ever since, happy that she brought us together. When I showed her the engagement ring, she shrieked with delight, flung her arms around me and said that she knew that deep down she was a great romantic. And then she insisted we go and have lots of cocktails together to celebrate. Which we did. She's going to be my bridesmaid. I was hers.

I dial my fiancé's number and he answers after the fourth ring.

'Bennett.'

'It's me.'

'I know it's you.'

'Same as I know it's you.'

'Huh?'

'You always say Bennett,' I tell him. 'But my name comes up when I ring. So you know it's me. You don't have to say your surname. You could just say hello.'

There's a pause. 'I'm used to saying my name,' he tells me. 'It's automatic. But you're right. It's odd. You should have pointed it out before. Sorry.'

That's the thing about Chris. He's understanding. And logical. I like logical people.

'I won't be home tonight,' I say. 'It's just not possible.'

'I guessed as much.'

'I'm really sorry.'

'It can't be helped.' He's trying not to be annoyed with me, but I know he is. I don't blame him. If the shoe was on the other foot, if he wasn't going to make it to a party for my mum, I'd be annoyed too.

'So how are the party preparations going?' I ask him.

'Fine, I presume,' he says. 'Pen has it all under control. Lisa's here now too. I told them you probably wouldn't make it, so Lisa will present the flowers and Pen will make the speech. She had one prepared, just in case.'

In case what? Had they already expected me not to show up? Had they thought – hoped – that Chris and I would've split up before Dorothea's birthday? I realise that I'm grinding my teeth again.

I'm sure they'll be just as delighted as Dorothea not to have me there, I think, and then chide myself for being mean-spirited.

'You know I wish I was with you.'

'Yes.' His voice suddenly softens. 'I do. And I have to admit I was a bit pissed off with you when you called earlier. Mainly because you've never been late for anything in your life before. But the traffic accident wasn't your fault, and you can't be expected to factor a lunatic driver into your journey time.'

Now I feel awful. But I allow Spain's answer to Jeremy Clarkson to shoulder the blame.

'I haven't said anything to Mum yet,' he tells me. 'I didn't want to disappoint her in advance.'

It's not going to be a disappointment to her. It's going to be something that'll be held against me forever, the big let-down by the unfavoured fiancée. Though I don't say that out loud.

'But mostly I'm just sorry for us,' he says. 'It's going to be a great night and I wanted you beside me.'

'That's what I wanted too.' My words are heartfelt.

'I'm sure you're fed up with being in soulless hotel rooms showing crappy foreign TV,' remarks Chris.

'Pretty much.' That's true. I am. It's just not happening tonight.

'People who don't travel for work always think it's glamorous,' he adds. 'You and I know different.'

'We sure do.'

'So what are your flight details?' he asks.

'The plane doesn't land until close to midnight tomorrow,' I tell him. 'There wasn't an earlier one.'

'Maybe that's a good idea,' he says. 'It'll give me time to work on my hangover.'

'You're expecting to be hung-over?'

'The girls have ordered lots and lots of champagne. And I know it's not supposed to give you a headache, but it does.'

'Try not to chug back too much.' There's amusement in my voice.

'I'll do my best.' He chuckles. 'I hope you won't be too bored yourself.'

'I'm just going to go for a bit of a wander.' I tell him that the rain has now stopped and he agrees that a walk would be nice. But I still don't tell him about Luke Evans and the beautiful apartment I'll be staying in. I should, I know. But I don't want him to get the wrong end of the stick.

'Phone me at some point during the party,' I say suddenly. 'So that I can be part of it.'

'Lovely idea,' says Chris. 'I will.'

'In that case . . . talk to you later. Love you.'

This time there's no hesitation.

'Love you Lots,' he says.

I end the call and allow myself a sigh of relief. Everything's OK between Chris and me. He understands. He doesn't blame me. He's one in a million.

Then I put away my phone and open my suitcase.

I rummage around until I find a pair of fitted trousers that give me longer legs even in my flat shoes. I also locate a pretty red blouse that brings out the green in my eyes and the dark espresso of my hair. My hair, though . . . I look at it in the mirror and run the brush through it a few times. It's still spiky in the wrong places, but that can only be fixed by washing it and I don't have time to prance around having a shower and washing my hair. Anyway, it doesn't matter how it looks. I'm not . . . well, this isn't a big night out with Luke. It's just sightseeing. I find another sparkly clip and slide it in among the spikes.

When I've finished dressing, and have sprayed myself with my Jo Malone Grapefruit perfume, I walk back into the living room. Luke is stretched out on one of the delicate antique chairs, engrossed in his mobile phone. He looks up as my shadow falls across him.

He doesn't say anything about me looking lovely or more presentable or anything like that. He merely puts the phone into the pocket of his jacket and leads the way out of the apartment.

It's hard to believe that it was raining torrentially a couple of hours ago. The sky is now the colour of bluebells, without even a wisp of cloud. The pavements, save for a few minor puddles, are almost completely dry. The air is warm and the sun is hot. I blink in its brilliance and take my sunglasses out of my handbag.

'This way.' Luke leads me down the narrow street we drove along earlier, cuts through another equally narrow one, and then beckons me into a wide plaza. The cathedral is enormous, totally dominating the plaza and the surrounding area.

'The third largest in the world,' says Luke. 'Apparently.'

'It's amazing.'

'The Giralda – that's the tower – used to be a minaret,' says Luke. 'When the Christians decided they wanted to build a cathedral on the spot, they used it.'

We walk around the building until we arrive at the front entrance, an imposing Gothic archway with a studded door that leads into the cavernous building. I'm not really into churches or cathedrals but this is the city's dominant building and it seems wrong not to visit. Perhaps one of my problems with famous cathedrals is the amount of gold and silver they seem to have on display – here there are all sorts of chalices and other finely wrought objects, and it's not that I don't think they shouldn't be preserved, but I can't help wondering about the wealth they symbolise.

Luke isn't much into it either – it appears his main reason for bringing me to the cathedral is to show me the view of the city from the top of the bell tower. I'm wondering how many steps we're going to have to climb, but it turns out that access to the top is by walking up ramps. This was, Luke says, so that the muezzin could ride horses up for the call to prayer. Fit horses, is what's going through my mind when we're halfway up. There are thirty-seven ramps and it's an exhausting climb. I make a promise to myself to definitely schedule more gym time when I get back to Dublin. But the view from the top is worth the effort. I stand beneath the bells and gaze out over the city, and can't help feeling a little bit glad that I missed the train. Because it would have been sacrilege to stay in Seville and not come here.

There are plenty of other tourists taking photos and gasping in delight at the views, but there's also a sense of awe amongst us that this was ever constructed in the first place.

'They started building the cathedral in 1401,' Luke tells me. 'They were still working on it a hundred and fifty years later. I guess they had a different concept of long-term then.'

I nod. I can't imagine anyone deciding to start work on a building that would take fifteen years now, let alone a hundred and fifty. I think of the men labouring through the summer heat without any of the hoists and cranes and machinery that we have today, and I'm humbled by their efforts. I wonder how many of them fell to their deaths – I'm pretty sure health and safety weren't the predominant aspects to building work back then. I shiver.

'All right?' asks Luke.

I tell him what I'm thinking, and he nods slowly.

'But they were part of something that has endured for centuries,' he says. 'How many of us can say that?'

He has a point. But I'm sure the wives and mothers and daughters of the workers felt differently. I'm assuming that all the workers were men. Women's equality probably wouldn't have been high on the agenda in the fifteenth and sixteenth centuries either.

Luke asks if I'm ready to descend to ground level again,

and I tell him that I'm happy to leave the ghosts of the Gothic builders behind. Coming down is nearly as hard work as going up; it's difficult to keep my balance on the steep ramps and I'm half walking, half running, just like everyone else. Luke is ahead of me, and every so often I have to put a hand on his shoulder to steady myself.

'You'll like the next part more, I think,' he says.

'I will?'

He grins and leads me through the cathedral and out through another door, into the orange garden. It's the neatest garden I've ever seen, serried ranks of orange trees set into a cobbled area. Luke says it was a cloister and a cemetery but all I can think is that it's serene and beautiful, and that the scent of the blossom is heady and enchanting. I could happily sit here for hours, although perhaps the constant stream of other tourists would eventually drive me mad. I can't help feeling we're like ants crawling all over precious buildings and sites, getting in each other's way, and always somehow thinking that it's the other people who aren't properly appreciating what they're seeing.

'Better to experience it than not,' says Luke when I share my thoughts with him.

'I suppose you're right.' I get up from the seat where we've been sitting and wipe my dusty hands on my trousers.

'One of my English friends told me that the oranges from here are made into marmalade and sent to the British royal family every year,' says Luke. 'I don't know if it's true, though.'

'I like Seville marmalade,' I tell him.

The thick-cut version was very popular in our house when I was growing up. Dad loved it and always had two slices of toast loaded with it before going off to work in the mornings. The first time I had some I scrunched up my nose in disgust, but after a while the bittersweet taste grew on me. At the weekends, when I have the time to savour it, I often forgo the fruit, yoghurt and Danish to have toast and Seville marmalade accompanied by freshly ground coffee for breakfast. My mind skitters back to this morning's meeting at Ecologistics. It seems like a lifetime ago.

'Would you like something to drink?' asks Luke as we finally leave the cathedral. 'Another coffee? A cold drink?'

Although the sun is now low in the sky, it's still warm, so we both decide that something cooling is what we need. Luke orders a beer and I opt for sparkling water at a pavement café overlooking the square. I watch the horse-drawn carriages that are lined up outside the cathedral ready to set off on city tours.

'Would you like to do a tour?' asks Luke.

I shake my head.

'So how would you like to spend your night in Seville?' He looks enquiringly at me. 'Anything you've always wanted to do? Go to a flamenco show? The opera?'

'Opera, me?' My eyes widen. 'What do you think I've become over the last eighteen years, Luke Evans? Some kind of culture vulture?'

'You look like you've become someone important,' he says after a moment's consideration. 'Someone who knows what she wants.'

I'm surprised at this. He's seen me in crumpled clothes and with mussed-up hair, hardly the image a woman of importance would like to present. And as for someone who knows what she wants . . . well, that's open to question. Earlier today I wanted to be a woman on a flight to Dublin.

Now, I want to sit in the orange-scented air forever. What we want changes all the time.

I say this to Luke, who smiles slightly.

'I used to think I knew exactly what I wanted,' he says. 'When we lived in Blackwater Terrace. But it didn't turn out like that.'

'Maybe that's a good thing.' I'm careful not to ask why.

'Maybe.' He looks thoughtful. 'I suppose overcoming obstacles is all part of it.'

I want to ask him about the obstacles, but I don't. Before our one and only date, I thought Luke and I shared everything, and I never worried about asking him questions. But it's different now.

'You've obviously found what you want,' he adds. 'And who. I see you're engaged.'

I'd been wondering if he'd noticed. I'd asked myself if I should mention it. But it seems crass, doesn't it, to meet someone you haven't seen in years and inform them you're engaged. As though you're either trying to be triumphant or putting down some kind of marker. I glance at the ring on my finger. It's spectacular. When Chris proposed, he'd already bought it. He didn't quite go down on bended knee, but he put the blue velvet box on the table in front of us, in the intimate city-centre restaurant that is one of our favourites, and pushed it towards me. I opened it without speaking and I know that my eyes widened when I saw the huge solitaire diamond sparkling under the restaurant lights. I put it on straight away – it fitted perfectly – then Chris signalled for the waiter to bring champagne, which arrived amid a muted round of applause from the other diners.

There was a great kerfuffle at work the following Monday

when I turned up wearing the ring. The women clustered around me, oohing and aahing, and although I hardly ever get involved in relationship talk with my colleagues, I spent the rest of the day being congratulated and telling everyone how wonderful Chris was. I felt different, somehow, as an engaged person. As though I'd found my place. Maybe that's what Luke noticed too. Maybe that's why he seems sure I know what I want.

'His name is Chris.' I tell Luke a little bit about him and he says that he sounds like a nice guy and he wishes me lots of happiness in the future.

'When's the wedding?' he asks.

'September.'

'And have you gone all Bridezilla yet?'

I look sceptically at him. 'Me? You've got to be joking.'

'Even the calmest of women go a bit bonkers over their weddings,' he points out. 'Anita did, and she's one of the most sensible people I know. Apparently she'll be arriving at the church in a horse and carriage and they'll be strewing rose petals in front of her as she walks. This is a girl who spent most of her formative years in hacked-off jeans and Doc Marten boots.'

I chuckle. 'No rose petals for me. I've booked the hotel and the music. I've agreed a menu. Invitations will go out soon. Honestly, it's not that much of a deal.'

'Carlotta O'Keeffe!' He looks astonished. 'It *is* a big deal.'

'It's not,' I protest. 'I don't want rose petals or special balloons or . . . or white doves with the rings in their beaks! It's a day with a meal, that's all. Well,' I add, in case he thinks I'm completely unromantic, 'the ceremony is a big

75

deal, of course it is, but everything else is just window-dressing. And you know me, I'm just not into that.'

'You're still the least romantic person in the whole world,' he says. 'Do you guys send each other Valentine cards?'

I know he's remembering our past conversations. How we both agreed that Valentine's Day was nothing but a commercial con.

'Yes,' I admit. 'But we don't go out to dinner that day. We both think it's a desperate waste of money.'

'As practical as ever,' he says.

'Sorry to disappoint you.'

'I'm not disappointed.' His eyes twinkle. 'I'm pleased to know that some people really don't change.'

'You have, though.'

He looks at me curiously.

'You own an Aston Martin.'

And that's why I'm afraid Luke Evans isn't the person I once knew. And why I don't really know if spending a night in the same apartment as him is such a good idea after all.

I'd never known a family to own as much as the Evanses. There were the two cars, for starters. Nobody else in Blackwater Terrace had two cars back then – although now I'm pretty sure that there are at least two for every house. It's impossible to find a parking space on the street, which drives me crazy every time I visit Mum and Dad. But when the Evanses moved in, their two-car status was a major talking point. As was the erection of their satellite dish, which was totally cutting-edge as far as the residents of Blackwater Terrace were concerned. The first time I went inside their house, I was taken aback by the sheer quantity of stuff on display. The house was an Aladdin's cave of new technology. In the days before iPods, each of the brothers had his own Discman. There were three TV sets in the house – an enormous one in the lounge, a portable one in the kitchen and one (Luke told me) in their parents' bedroom. They also had a Nintendo games console and a boxy grey PC.

When my eyes widened at it all and I told Luke that they must be really rich, he snorted and said that it was only stuff.

'But great stuff,' I remarked, and then he said that it would probably all be replaced by other stuff in a few years because technology was changing all the time. I wasn't really into technology – I'm still not an early adopter of anything, though I love my iPad – but I was impressed by everything the Evanses had. Not only by the cars and the gadgets, though, but also by the patina of newness about their possessions. In our house, the furniture, though of a decent quality, was old and shabby; the ornaments and photos on the walls had been there for as long as I could remember, and we were still using the same crockery we had when I was a toddler. (I know this, because Mum used to moan about not having a matching jug after I knocked it over and smashed it when I was learning to walk.)

And then there was Murielle Evans's style. She never left the house without looking stunning in full make-up and jewellery. She always dressed as though she were going to some kind of important function. Her shoes had heels that meant the furthest she could possibly walk was to her car. Mum was dismissive of her. She said that the woman clearly had too much time on her hands because who could possibly afford to spend an hour in the morning putting that look together?

Bottom line, though: the Evanses brought bling to Blackwater Terrace. It never occurred to me to ask why they'd moved there instead of to a much bigger house in the far more salubrious suburbs of Terenure or Templeogue nearby.

But while Richard and Murielle Evans, and Kyle, Jordan and Wayne, seemed to live it large and were happy to be seen with their latest acquisitions, Luke was uncomfortable with it. He wore designer jeans and tops because Murielle bought them for him, but he didn't seem to have new clothes every week like his brothers, and he rarely appeared on the street with his Discman or any other piece of technological equipment.

'I don't like stuff,' he explained to me. 'It starts to take over.'

I didn't know what he meant.

'My dad has to work harder and harder to keep what we have,' said Luke when I asked him to elaborate. 'He's not happy with one of anything. He always wants two. And then he wants a newer version. And to get all this he has to work more. It doesn't make sense.'

'It's good to have nice things,' I said mildly.

'When you need them,' countered Luke. 'Not just because you want them.'

In the capitalist about-to-be-Celtic-Tiger home that Luke lived in, he was the odd one out. A teacher at school once commented that if Luke worked hard he could be as successful as his father. But Luke said that he didn't think people should be judged by what they had. Who they were, he said, was more important. Mr Kelleher was totally taken aback by Luke's response and quickly changed the subject, while Luke busied himself with doodling on the corner of his copybook.

I wasn't exactly sure what Mr Evans did, but it was something to do with insurance. He actually called in to our house one evening to talk to Mum and Dad about it. Knowing how down-at-heel our home appeared compared to the Evanses', I took myself off to my bedroom because I didn't want to be there when he realised that our TV was ten years old and that we didn't have a PC or a games console. Afterwards, Dad said that Luke's father was a really good salesman but that he wasn't going to buy whatever it was that Mr Evans had been selling. I remarked that he clearly made a lot of money doing it, and Dad shrugged dismissively. I suppose Mr Evans's high-powered business talk wasn't the kind of thing that sat well with my dad.

'It's not that,' he said. 'It's that I'm his neighbour, not a potential client. That man considers everyone fair game. He's always blathering on about his company and his products. Never shuts up.'

Perhaps that was what Luke found hard to take. He was a work-to-live, not a live-to-work, sort of person. But somewhere along the line he'd learned to work hard enough to own a very expensive car. I can't help thinking yet again that I've made a mistake by accepting his invitation to stay.

He laughs at me now, and picks up the keys of the Aston which he'd left on the table.

'I don't own it,' he says. 'I'm doing a favour for a friend. I'll be delivering it to him after the wedding.'

'Oh.' I feel a weight slide from my shoulders, only to be replaced by a different one. He's doing me a favour by letting me stay in the apartment, but like the Aston, it doesn't belong to him. My emotions are catapulting all over the place. It's not something I'm used to any more.

'What do you do?' I ask.

'Work at, you mean?'

I nod. That's what the question usually means, isn't it?

'Admin mainly,' he says.

I can feel the tension creeping through my body.

'Lucky you, that it allows you access to fast cars and great apartments,' I remark.

'Yes,' says Luke. 'I've been very lucky. More than I deserve really.'

I'm beginning to perspire a little and I don't know if it's because of the heat or because we're straying into dangerous territory. I'm telling myself that I'm being stupid, that my thoughts and prejudices are being entirely coloured by Blackwater Terrace gossip, but I can't help it.

However, I smile at Luke and relax back into my seat. The past is totally irrelevant now. What matters is today and the fact that he's here and he's helped me out and that we're sitting at a pavement café watching the sun go down.

My phone beeps.

Chris has sent me a photo of himself in his tux. He looks amazing, all dark and saturnine and gorgeously sexy.

I text back, *Missing you like crazy*, and then I add a smiley on the end.

Not being an early-adopter, I've also come late to the whole emoticon thing with text messages, but ever since

Natasha took my phone one day and downloaded an app with a whole range of icons, I've embraced it.

'This way people will know how you feel as well as what you think,' she informed me with all the wisdom of her eight years as she handed it back. 'It's easy to get the wrong end of the stick with a message. So a smiley helps.'

I hugged her. 'Thanks for saving me from a lifetime of misunderstandings.'

'You're welcome.' Natasha went back to what she'd been doing and left me to enjoy my new app.

Which I do. I like adding pictures of smiley faces, or hearts, or suns, or rain, or a million other things to my texts. It makes me seem like a fun person. And that can only be a good thing because, of course, lots of people don't think that about me at all. I suppose I've clamped down on the fun, emotional side of me over the last few years. Not because I can't enjoy myself, but because I need to be focused and clear-thinking in my work. And I guess I'd begun to believe that my work would always be the most important thing in my life. Certainly, until I met Chris, it was more satisfying to me than relationships. Besides, getting emotional doesn't help when you're trying to be a velvet assassin.

I realise that Luke is watching me as I put the phone away.

'Fiancé.' I'm a little self-conscious using the word. 'We were meant to be at a party tonight.'

Luke looks at me enquiringly and I tell him all about Dorothea's birthday. In fact I end up telling him a lot more about Dorothea than I intended. Including how important it had seemed to me to present the bouquet of flowers to her and make a speech about how great she is so that she

81

realises I'm not the career-obsessed harpy she seems to think I am.

'You're being a bit hard on yourself, aren't you?' says Luke. 'You're too nice to be a harpy.'

I grin. 'Thanks for saying so. However, I guess all mothers have an ideal daughter-in-law in mind, and I'm not hers.'

'Because you work for a living. But so does the upmarket teacher.'

'Because I work somewhere that makes a profit for a living,' I correct him. 'Nobody in Dorothea's family ever has.'

'That's not exactly true, is it?' he protests. 'I'm sure her husband was very well paid, and your fiancé . . .' he winks, 'earns a decent crust telling people they need glasses.'

'It's not like that!' I rush to defend Chris. 'He's a brilliant ophthalmic surgeon. People send him cards thanking him for giving them perfect vision after a lifetime of specs. He makes them happy.'

'I'm sure you make people happy too,' says Luke.

'No, I don't.' Once again I'm forced to face the aspect of my job that I like least. 'I make people unemployed. I make them miserable.'

'If you don't like it, do something else,' says Luke reasonably.

'It's not that I don't like the consultancy part,' I admit. 'I like coming up with rescue plans even if there's a certain amount of collateral damage, which I try to minimise. But that makes it so unworthy in comparison to everything the Bennetts do.'

He shrugs. 'That's their problem. I think Chris is very lucky to be marrying you, and she's clearly a fairy-tale wicked mother-in-law.'

I laugh. 'She's not really. Just a bit – chilly. It doesn't matter. It's not her I'm marrying.'

'Did she try to interfere with the wedding plans?' asks Luke. 'Another friend of mine – sorry, Carly, lots of my friends are women – well, when she was getting married, her future mother-in-law was all over everything. Kept wanting to change things. Drove Sabine up the wall.'

'And now?' I ask.

'I haven't seen Sabine in ages,' confesses Luke. 'She used to live in Marbella but she went back to Germany after she got married.'

Marbella was where the Evanses moved after leaving Blackwater Terrace. Luke is giving me an opening to ask, but I hold back.

'Is there anything special you'd like to do now?' He breaks the silence that has grown between us by changing the subject.

'You don't have to look after me,' I tell him. 'I'm sure you have loads of other things to occupy you.'

He frowns. 'I wasn't thinking that I was looking after you,' he says. 'I was thinking that it's great to see you and spend some time with you. But if you want to be left alone, that's perfectly all right.'

'Oh, Luke, sorry, no.' I've hurt his feelings. I didn't mean to. It's just – well, as a counterpoint to the elephantine memory, I'm totally shit with emotions. As my god-daughter already figured out, I've never been great at saying what I feel or understanding how other people feel. I'm not a huggy, kissy, sympathetic sort of person. Which is possibly why I've done well in a job where I basically fire other people for a living. Luke knew that, back in the day. I thought it was why he liked me.

'It's OK,' he says. He doesn't look as offended as he probably should, which is a relief. 'You always did have a habit
of putting your foot firmly in your mouth.'

'Thanks,' I say. 'I just—'

'Don't worry about it.' He doesn't let me finish. 'What I'm
saying is that if there's something special you'd like to do, I'll
be happy to do it with you. If you want to be left alone to
work, or whatever, that's fine too. And if you want to kick
back and enjoy yourself tonight, you can come with me to
meet the gang. We're getting together later in a very traditional
bar. Then heading off for a bit of flamenco dancing. Not by
us,' he adds rapidly when he sees the look on my face. 'There's
a show. Which sounds tacky beyond belief, but it's the
Riverdance of flamenco. It's really good. You'd enjoy it.'

'I don't want to put you out,' I explain.

'How could you possibly do that?' asks Luke. 'It's lovely
to see you again, Carly. Looking after you would never put
me out.'

Chapter 7

Suite Española: Sevilla – Julian Bream

We stroll back to the apartment through streets bustling with people. They seem to be equally divided between Sevillanos and tourists. I wonder how often Luke has been here. I wonder if he's still living in Marbella. And if his family is too. We've talked and talked but we haven't done more than scratch the surface. In the past, we were always deep below it. But that was then and this is now, and despite what I want to believe, both of us have changed beyond measure.

Even though I decided against having a shower and washing my hair earlier, I know that if we're going out, I'll have to. So when we arrive back at the apartment, I tell Luke that's what I'm going to do and he says fine, he'll watch some TV before changing too. I'm suddenly shy in his company and so I scurry off to the beautiful guest room, slip out of my clothes and run the shower.

It's only when I'm lathering myself with soap that I realise I didn't lock the door. It simply didn't occur to me, and yet when I think about it, I'm basically buck naked in a stranger's apartment with a guy I hardly know. At least, that's how other people would see it. But it's like seeing a newspaper headline. It's not the full story. You have to know all the details to put it into context. I remember once a company Cadogan had consulted for decided to close a loss-making division. There was a huge headline about fifty jobs being axed, and a really heartbreaking story about how people would be left destitute at Christmas. But the thing is, they weren't. Half of them were transferred into another division. Some of them took early retirement. And those who did lose their jobs got a generous redundancy package. OK, I know it's not the same as keeping your job, but the truth is that the division had been struggling for months, and if it hadn't been closed then, everyone would have ended up being out of a job, without the package they ultimately got. I tried to explain that to Dorothea when she tackled me about it, but she wouldn't listen. She said I was nothing more than a spin doctor. But these days everyone likes to spin a story to suit their own agenda. Even the news is political.

So how will I spin this to Chris? I wonder as I pat myself dry with the towel. I don't answer my own question because I already know. I'll spin it by not saying a bloody word!

Luke is wearing a different shirt when I walk into the living room, although I think they're the same jeans. The shirt is blue-checked and it matches his eyes. I wonder if I've over-done it myself, because well turned out though Luke is, he's not dressed up and I . . . well, I decided to change into my favourite dress, a black and white patterned Donna Karan jersey gathered under the bust. I've worn it loads of times over the past few weeks because I know it suits me. I'm wearing my favourite red jewellery – a Swarovski necklace and matching bracelet, which are glittery and fun and go with another of my sparkly hairclips, also ruby red. I've picked red shoes too, and now I'm thinking that there's too much red and too much glitter and sparkle, and it looks like I've made more of an effort than I have. Especially as wearing the shoes is a bit of a gamble because my ankles are still a bit raw from my earlier heels.

Luke stands up and asks if I'm ready to go.

'Sure.' Am I annoyed that he hasn't commented on the fact that I'm wearing a dress? And fashionable shoes? He's never seen me looking glamorous before. I thought he'd say something. I shake my head. What the hell is wrong with me? I don't care how he thinks I look. It doesn't matter. After tonight, I'll probably never see him again. He has his life doing whatever he does, and I have mine, which is structured and ordered and exactly how I like it.

'Can you walk in those shoes?' he asks as I make my way down the stairs.

'They're high,' I concede. 'But very comfortable.'

He gives me a sceptical glance. I grin at him and my bout of bad humour suddenly disappears. Fortunately (because I'm already beginning to regret wearing them) it's only a five-minute walk to the bar where we're meeting up.

'The others won't arrive for a while yet,' said Luke. 'Would you like something to eat?'

I'm starving. My eyes light up and Luke bursts out laughing.

'They do good tapas here,' he says. 'Ideally we should visit a few different bars to try different dishes. But I'm concerned about your feet in those shoes.'

'Don't you worry about my feet,' I tell him. 'Worry about my stomach instead.'

He chuckles and we walk inside. The walls and floor are both covered in white ceramic tiles with a blue mosaic pattern. The seats are wooden benches at tables that accommodate four or six, but right now the bar is half-empty and the only people here are tourists.

Luke says a few words to the barman and then asks if I'd like a glass of sangria.

'You might as well be touristy too,' he adds. 'In the summer, the drink of choice is mojito.'

'I like mojitos, but sangria works fine for me,' I tell him.

'I've ordered a selection of tapas,' he says. 'You're not a fussy eater, are you?'

'As long as whatever it is comes without its head and its tail I'm OK,' I answer.

'Remember the orienteering expedition?'

How could I forget? A gang of us from school went orienteering in the Dublin mountains. Some people do this as a competitive sport, running from checkpoint to checkpoint and trying to cover the course in the fastest possible time, but we were doing it for the fun – Luke, me, Jessica Quillan, Mark Shaw, Belinda Morgan and Peter Carew. Although there were three boys and three girls, none of us was a couple. Mark's dad, who was totally into outdoor activities, drove us to the forest and we set off. We'd all brought small rucksacks with food and drink for the inevitable moment when someone said they were faint with hunger. After about an hour tramping through the forest we decided that time had come and we sat down near a stream. The girls had all made sandwiches. The boys – typically – had brought crisps. Me, Jess and Belinda were berating them for not having chosen healthier options (even as we added crisps to the ham sandwiches for extra flavour and crunch) when Peter Carew, the tallest and strongest of the lads, announced that he would catch us something to eat. He then proceeded to break a branch off a tree and, with a penknife, whittle one end into a point. Once he was satisfied with it, he took off his trainers and his socks, rolled up his jeans and waded into the river. We were laughing at him, certain that he wouldn't even see a fish, far less catch one, but he gave a sudden triumphant cry, thrust the spear through the water and held it up, a wriggling fish impaled on the sharp point.

Jess was promptly sick and Belinda started shrieking. I begged him to return the fish to the water but Peter said that it was practically dead and the least we could do was eat it. He'd make a campfire, he said, and we could cook it.

Luke pointed out that starting a fire in a forest probably wasn't the best of ideas, that we were supposed to be orienteering not camping and that we should probably get a move on in any event. Peter got annoyed with him and the three boys started yelling at each other until Belinda told them that someone would come and we'd probably be in trouble for stopping for food anyway and that we should just get on with it. Which eventually we did. But it took ages before I could erase the vision of the impaled fish from my mind, and that's why I prefer my fish to be filleted and preferably unidentifiable.

There's no need to worry about the tapas. The waiter appears with small plates of skewered chicken in a mushroom sauce, patatas bravas, olives, chorizo, calamari and some soft fresh bread with garlic mayonnaise.

'Tuck in,' says Luke, picking up one of the skewers and sliding the chicken on to his plate.

I do the same, and add some chorizo. The tapas are bursting with flavour and I don't say much at all as I work my way through them. Luke doesn't talk either but the silence isn't awkward, it's companionable. I remember that we were always easy-going with each other, how it never mattered if we weren't talking. Maybe, I think, as he refills my glass with sangria, right now we're easy-going because I'm feeling ever so slightly drunk. Light though it is, the sangria is the first alcohol that's passed my lips in six weeks. I don't touch it when I'm working and I've been with colleagues or clients every single day since we started our tour of the Ecologistics offices. But it doesn't matter tonight because I'm not working, I'm not going to meet anyone I know and . . . My phone rings.

I have to lick my fingers and wipe them in a napkin before I can answer it. When I do, the call has already disconnected. I grimace and hit dial straight away. I give Luke an apologetic look, get up from the table and walk outside. I hate talking on my phone anywhere food is being served, and besides, the bar has filled up a bit more and has become clattery and noisy.

'Hi,' I say when Chris picks up. 'I'm sorry. You went straight to voicemail.'

Another white lie. I'm starting to lose count.

'I was just phoning to say I'm on the way to Mum's. I was wondering if you had a message you'd like to give her.'

A message? For Dorothea? Right now she's the furthest thing from my mind.

'Carlotta?' Chris's voice echoes on the line.

'Only that I hope she has a wonderful evening,' I say eventually. 'And that I'm gutted not to be there.'

'Send your message as a text,' Chris says. 'That way I can read it out.'

'Good idea.' I wish I'd thought of it myself.

'I'll call you when the girls are making the presentation,' he reminds me.

'That's great.'

'How are things in Seville? You're not too fed up, are you?'

'No.' I move to one side as a group of people, talking animatedly, walk past me. The city is coming alive again now that it's getting later. 'But obviously I'd rather be at home with you.'

'Tomorrow,' he says.

'I'll text when I'm boarding. I'm sorry it's so late.' I know I keep apologising to him, but it's because I really and truly am sorry about messing everything up. Even if I'm actually having a lovely time in Seville.

'Can't be helped,' he says. 'You're all right, aren't you?'

'What d'you mean?'

'After the accident. You weren't injured or anything?'

'Not at all,' I assure him. 'I got a fright, nothing more.'

'I think I'll tell Mum you were a little bit hurt,' he says. 'Sounds better that way.'

'OK.' If it gets Dorothea on side I don't care what he tells her. I can always pretend to have a bruised ribcage or a sprained wrist or a twisted ankle.

'Talk later,' says Chris.

We say our usual goodbye, he ends the call and I send him the text with good wishes for her. I add a smiley face and an icon of a birthday cake. Then I walk back into the bar. I realise that the group of people who passed me in the street were Luke's friends, because they're now clustered around our table chatting to him, and he's replying in perfect Spanish. (Well, I'm assuming it's perfect. I'd only be able to understand it if one of them were to say something like 'the results of our ongoing study of the issues facing Ecologistics have led us to the following conclusions').

'Carlotta, you're back.' Luke smiles at me and pulls me into the group, introducing me to people whose names I know I won't remember, because that's not how it works for me. Well, I'll remember the names even though they're unfamiliar, but I won't know which name belongs to which person. It doesn't matter. I don't really need to know. Luke's friends greet me in English and ask if I'm enjoying my stay in Seville and then Luke butts in with some story in Spanish which I realise is the story of me missing the train, because they switch back to English again and tell me that the AVE high-speed trains are super-punctual, which is great if you're on time but not so good if you're a person who gets to things late. Something I've already worked out for myself.

They're nice people, and they all try to include me in the conversation, although every so often they lapse into Spanish and burst out laughing. I try not to think that they're laughing at me. Or that Luke is closer to them than he ever was to me. I'm surprised I even think this, because I haven't thought about Luke Evans for years, so I shouldn't care who his friends are now. But I guess I just feel proprietorial towards him. He lived on Blackwater Terrace and he was my friend before he ever came to Spain and met them.

Because the conversation is bilingual, I'm drifting in and out of what's going on. I think they're talking about Anita now, because I hear her name mentioned once or twice, but when they switch to English again it's to ask me if I've seen the latest Hollywood blockbuster that has just opened. I haven't, so that's a bit of a conversation-killer, and I can see that they're trying to think of things that are inclusive for me. We talk a little bit about my work, which I play down. I discover that Begoña is a lawyer and Carmen is a tax adviser and one of the men, Frederico, is just very rich. There's a bit of laughter about this and they tell me that he comes from a really old Sevillian family which is absolutely loaded. More money even than Anita, chuckles Carmen, and Frederico makes a face at her.

They're all well-off, these Sevillanos. I can see it now. The girls are casually dressed but their clothes aren't chain-store. The men, wearing jeans like Luke, are also wearing expensive watches. I'm wondering how he met all of them, where he fits into the scheme of things. He doesn't own the Aston Martin but he moves in circles where people do own these kinds of cars. How did he get from Blackwater Terrace to here?

I'm pretty sure I already know.

And I wish I didn't.

Chapter 8

Sevillana (Woman of Seville) – flamenco version

One of the men says something to the rest of the group and there's a bout of excited chatter before they begin to gather up their things.

'We're going to the flamenco bar now,' says Luke.

I hesitate. They're all very friendly and are trying to include me in everything, but I'm the outsider here.

'Don't be silly,' says Luke when I murmur this to him. 'You're welcome to come along. They love practising their English on new people.'

I'm not certain about that.

'What else would you be doing?' he asks. 'Sitting alone in Anita's flat?'

'I could be working,' I reply, and he snorts derisively.

'You said you'd done your presentation and it was great, so I can't see what else you have to do. Unless you need some time to think?'

I make a face at him. When I was younger, I liked sitting on my own staring into space. Mum used to call it doing nothing. So did Luke. I always insisted I needed time to think. It's true, I do actually enjoy being alone, emptying my mind. Not tonight, though.

'I'd love to come,' I confess. 'I just don't want to be in the way.'

He makes a dismissive sound and hands me my light jacket which I'd draped over the bench.

We go out into the cooler night air and make our way through the twisting streets again. Five minutes later we arrive at the bar. There's a cover charge to get in and Luke insists on paying for me, even though I tell him that I'm perfectly capable of paying my way.

'You're a guest in my adopted country,' he says. 'Now stop acting the eejit.'

I shrug and follow him inside. I thought it would be bigger, but it's quite intimate and the stage is small. I'm not exactly looking forward to this. Years ago, when I was in college, I did a sun, sand and sea holiday in Torremolinos with Sive. We allowed ourselves to be suckered in by a couple of the excursions, including the traditional flamenco night, which was tacky and horrible. But Seville, as Luke tells me, is the home of flamenco, and we're going to be seeing a proper performance, not just a touristy thing.

Yeah, well. They say that about Temple Bar too, but I defy any Dubliner to think there's anything authentic about the Irish culture on offer in that part of the city.

After about ten minutes, a guy with a guitar comes on stage and begins playing. I like classical guitar and the music is haunting. I'm so engrossed I don't notice that he's been joined by another guitar player, until I realise that he can't possibly be making this music on his own. And then a spot-light is turned on and the first flamenco dancer strides on to the stage. He's wearing the tightest trousers possible and a loose white shirt open to his waist. My mouth twitches. The music is lovely but the dancer is a pastiche.

Until he begins to dance, drumming his feet against the wooden floor, building up into a crescendo of rhythmic sound. And then the woman comes out. She's wearing a skin-tight scarlet dress and has a patterned silk shawl draped around her shoulders. Her hair, midnight-black, is pulled back from her face and secured with a high-backed comb. Her beautiful face is set into an expression of hauteur that Dorothea would kill for. She stands in front of the man and he stamps his feet again. She walks slowly around him, allowing the shawl to slide down her back. The music, which has softened, builds up again, and then, quite suddenly, both dancers erupt into a flurry of steps and movement that conveys desire and passion and frustration and longing, and I realise that I am sitting, breathless, on the edge of my seat.

I've never seen anything like it. It's foreplay through music and motion. He's giving it everything he's got and she's looking at him almost disdainfully, as if to say *I need more and I need better*. She produces a pair of castanets, which she clicks in a sultry, mesmeric rhythm. I am enthralled.

When the dance is finished, I applaud wildly. Luke looks at me with amusement and I give him a defeated smile. I've loved every moment of this.

Both dancers do solo numbers and then another dance together, and it's just as erotic as the first. I can't believe that dancing can be this way. I'm totally blown away by it.

There's a break and everyone chatters about the show and how good the dancers are. One of the group (Begoña, I think) takes some castanets out of her handbag and starts to click them. She's quite good and the other girls in the group clap their hands in time with her.

I suppose learning flamenco here is a bit like learning Irish dancing back home. Though I'm not sure that Mrs Temperly, who taught me when I was in primary school, would approve of the sheer sexuality of what's going on here. We learned the traditional, pre-*Riverdance* reels and jigs, where you had to keep your body ramrod straight and your arms rigid by your sides and there was no room for self-expression at all. You'd think I'd've been good at that, but I was terrible. I'm not the world's most co-ordinated person.

The dancers come back and this time the set is slower and more contemplative. But they finish up with another burst of sound and fury, all flashing eyes and stomping feet, and once again I'm completely caught up in the fire and the passion.

This time, at the break, I go to the Ladies', and afterwards, almost as an afterthought, I check my phone. To my horror I see that I've missed two calls from Chris. I push my way out on to the street and hit dial straight away.

'Where the hell have you been?' he asks as he answers. 'I was worried about you.'

'I'm sorry,' I reply. 'I came out for a while. I've been watching flamenco. I didn't hear it ring.'

'Flamenco?' He sounds astonished, and I'm not surprised. Undoubtedly scarred by my Irish-dancing experience, I'm not usually into dancing of any sort.

'I thought it would be good to do something cultural,' I explain.

'You went out to see a flamenco show when you knew I'd be phoning you from Mum's?'

I can't tell him that, caught up in the passion of the flamenco, I'd completely forgotten about Dorothea.

'I . . . was bored.' It's lame, I know.

'I told you I'd ring because you said you wanted to be part of Mum's party. I thought you could listen in to Pen presenting the flowers and maybe you could say something to everyone, but instead you went out to watch flamenco?'

Oh God. He's really angry with me, and I totally understand it. But he should have filled me in on this plan. Although perhaps it's one I should've thought of myself.

'I really am sorry.' I'll never be able to apologise enough.

'I phoned a second time in case you'd fallen asleep. I know you've had a long day.' Somehow it doesn't sound as though he really believes that.

'Chris, sweetheart . . .' I take a deep breath. 'I didn't miss the call deliberately. I've apologised a gazillion times for missing the train and not being at the party. I can't say it any more.'

'I asked them to wait while I rang you. It held up the entire presentation.'

I didn't think I could mess this day up more than I already have. I was wrong.

'Mum is disappointed,' he adds.

'So am I,' I tell him. 'But there's nothing I can do about it now.'

He's silent for a moment, and then it's as though he's decided he's not going to make an issue of it any more, because he says that he knows I'm sorry but that everything had been so well planned and he, Pen and Lisa had wanted it all to go perfectly and it was just a pity that it hadn't.

'Did your mum like the flowers?' I'd paid for the enormous bouquet.

98

'She loved them,' says Chris.

Ridiculously expensive but worth it. Maybe.

'I want you here,' he says. 'Beside me.'

'I want to be there too.' And I do. All the other stuff –
meeting Luke, meeting his friends, the sensuality of the flamenco
– it's not important. What's important is that I've let Chris
down.

'What possessed you to want to see flamenco?' His tone
is lighter. 'You hate that touristy stuff.'

'I guess I just thought it would be fun.'

'When you get home, we can make our own fun.'

I'm relieved that it's OK between us. I don't want to fight
with Chris. We hardly ever quarrel and I hate it when we
do. Not just because he's usually the one in the right.

'Are you still partying?' I glance at my watch and realise,
to my astonishment, that it's well after midnight. I didn't
feel the night go by so quickly. Then I remember it's an hour
earlier in Dublin.

'Oh, yes. Mum is in her element with so many of her
friends around. She's loving it.'

'Ring me again later,' I tell him. 'When everything's
finished. We can talk dirty to each other.'

'Now that's the best idea you've had all day,' says Chris.

'Look forward to it,' I say. 'I love you.'

'Love you Lots.'

When I put the phone back into my bag, I realise that
Luke is standing in the doorway of the club, watching me.

'How long have you been there?' I ask.

'Not long. I noticed you'd disappeared and I wanted to
check that everything was OK.'

'Everything's fine,' I say. I'm a little embarrassed that

he might have heard me tell Chris I'd talk dirty to him later. There's no real need to be embarrassed, but it was a personal thing between my fiancé and me, not for Luke to hear.

'There's a third act,' says Luke. 'Are you coming back?'

'Would you mind if I skipped it?' Suddenly I've had enough of exotic flamenco dancers and their sensual movements. Besides, I want to be able to hear my phone just in case Chris rings back sooner than I expect.

'No problem,' says Luke. 'C'mon. Let's go.'

'You can stay,' I tell him. 'I'll be fine on my own.'

'Do you remember how to get back to the apartment?'

'I can get a cab,' I say.

He looks at me incredulously. 'For a five-minute walk? Are you nuts? I'll come with you.'

'What about your friends?'

'I told them I might be heading off.'

'Won't they mind?'

'Not in the slightest. They'll be partying till dawn.'

'And then going to a wedding in the morning?' I can't help sounding sceptical.

'The wedding isn't till the evening,' Luke says. 'It's cooler then.'

I nod.

'So come on.'

He links my arm as though it's the most natural thing in the world, and we head back towards the apartment. We walk in silence, but as we approach the cathedral, Luke asks if I'd like a nightcap. He says that he wants to show me a view of the city by night and that there's a rooftop bar he always visits when he's in Seville. I'm a bit doubtful, but

I'm wide awake and I'll easily hear the phone in a rooftop bar. A nightcap would be nice, so I follow him across the plaza and through a glass door. There's a lift directly opposite and he leads me into it. It's as small as the lift in the apartment building, but without the suitcase, we're not squashed together this time. He presses the button for the fourth floor.

When the doors open, I'm completely taken by surprise. I hadn't expected the outdoor bar to be so elegant and chic. There's a lighted swimming pool in the middle of the area, for heaven's sake, and high tables with tall chairs dotted around. There are also cushioned chairs for lounging in. The bar itself is glass and granite and illuminated by LED lighting. Fairy lights are strung in an intricate web around the perimeter, while a Cuban beat throbs from the speakers. The whole thing is very inviting. And it's absolutely buzzing with people despite the lateness of the hour. Luke tells me that the Sevillanos always stay out late and that this is one of the hippest bars around.

I remark that it's not often you'd see a swimming pool in a bar in Dublin. And that it would probably be dive-bombed every night.

'Probably,' agrees Luke as we skirt the water and position ourselves at a high table that has just been vacated. He raises his arm and a stunningly beautiful waitress walks over to us. I can see that the staff, male and female, have been hired for their looks as much as their skills behind the bar, because every single one of them is jaw-droppingly gorgeous. Luke orders two mojitos and I say that I thought that was a summer drink.

'But you probably won't be here in the summer,' he points out. 'So now is a good time.'

I smile and look around me. We're right in the centre of the city and, as in the daytime, the cathedral dominates everything. It's lit up now, and the yellow stone looks warm.

'I can't believe we walked up that tower earlier.' I stare at it. 'It's amazing.'

'Good to get the exercise in before embracing the night-life,' says Luke.

'I'm not embracing it,' I tell him. 'Although maybe I am. I'd planned on an early night tonight.'

'You can't tell me that sitting in your hotel – even if you'd been able to find a hotel – would have been more fun than being out with us.'

'No, I can't,' I concede. 'It was brilliant. I've never seen dancing like it.'

'It's very powerful, isn't it? You can just see them back in the day doing all that come-hither stuff.'

I laugh.

'Well, you can.' Luke is defensive.

'I know. I just didn't expect you to say that.'

'Why?'

'It sounds a bit girlie.'

'Oh don't start that again.' Luke groans and I chuckle.

His brothers used to call him girlie when he was younger because of his curls. I once asked why he didn't get them cut off, and he replied, very seriously, that they made him feel different to the rest of his family. I wanted to know what was wrong with being like his mum or his dad or his brothers, and he said that there was always too much pressure. To be the best. To have the most. To make people respect you. He didn't care, he said, if nobody respected him. In fact he preferred it that way.

I thought it was very odd at the time. Afterwards, maybe not so. But in the end, it didn't matter. Luke left Blackwater Terrace with them. So he was the same after all.

Moving from being Luke's best friend to someone he'd asked on a date happened suddenly. At the beginning of the year he'd started to go out with Helena Murray, a leggy brunette with high cheekbones and rosebud lips, who'd always had a bit of a thing for him but who was popular in her own right as one of the prettiest girls in our year. Luke and I continued to walk to school together because Helena lived a bus ride away. And now I remember that teenage girls definitely don't like their boyfriends having friends who are girls, because Helena said so one morning during break. She nudged me so that I spilled the water I was carrying and then she asked me if I really thought I could hang on to Luke Evans in such a pathetic way. He was her boyfriend, she told me. I was nothing to him. I said that I wasn't hanging on, that we'd been friends for ages and that just because he was seeing her it didn't mean that I would stop being friends with him.

I don't blame Helena for not believing me. Besides, she was right to care. After all, when I saw them together I sometimes wondered what it would be like to have Luke put his arm around me the way he did around her, or kiss me on the lips instead of the bumping of our foreheads that we used to do as a way of expressing affection. Thinking these thoughts made me shiver. Luke and I were happy the way we were. Changing things would mess it up. I knew that friendships with the opposite sex rarely lasted when they changed into relationships. I didn't want to lose Luke's friendship. It meant too much to me. So I kept a lid on any romantic notions I might have about Luke Evans. It was safer that way.

And then he asked me out. To see *Independence Day*, which was showing in a local cinema. We'd never gone to the movies together before. As far as I was concerned it was an activity reserved for people who were properly going out with each other, not just good friends. I'd never heard of a boy and girl going to the movies to watch the film. Nobody did that!

'What about Helena?' I asked.

'I'm not seeing her any more,' replied Luke. 'She's an idiot. Besides, she likes soppy movies about dying people falling in love and stuff like that. She never wants to go to anything worth watching. And I really want to see *Independence Day*.'

I sighed with relief. It was OK. It was still just about being friends because, like Luke, I was a sci-fi fan. Still am, despite my reluctance to embrace new technology. And although I do watch the occasional romcom (every so often I sniff my way through *Love Actually* and *Pretty Woman*), I much prefer movies like *The Terminator*, which Dad rented from the video store when he finally caved and bought a VCR, and which I excitedly watched with him.

'Besides,' Luke said. 'I'd like to go to a movie with you.'

It was his tone rather than his words that made me stare at him.

'When you say go to the movies – d'you actually mean, you know, go to the movies? As in . . . us? Together? Like a couple?' My voice squeaked at the end.

'Everyone thinks we are anyway,' said Luke. 'So we might as well be. I had a row with Helena about it.'

I wasn't sure how to react. Luke never had rows with his girlfriends. He usually got on well with them even after they stopped going out with each other. He just wasn't the sort of person you could stay angry with for any length of time.

'She's very possessive,' added Luke. 'She keeps telling me what I should and shouldn't do. And she doesn't like you.'

There was my proof that official girlfriends didn't like their boyfriends having female pals.

'I told her you were my friend and she told me to choose. So I've chosen.' Suddenly he looked anxious. 'I'm not trying to force you to come out with me if you'd rather not. It's up to you, Carly.'

'I'd love to.' Even though going on a date with Luke could be a potential disaster, I was immensely flattered that he had chosen friendship with me over going out with Helena Murray.

'Cool,' he said. 'I'll call for you tomorrow at six. And afterwards we can go to McDonald's.'

It sounded good to me, although I wasn't sure how a date with Luke would compare with simply going to McDonald's with him as we'd so often done.

'I'll see you then, so,' I said. 'Oh, and best of luck in the debate tomorrow.'

'Thanks.'

Although he was quiet and even shy in private, Luke was on the school debating team. He was pretty good at it. I used to memorise his speeches.

'Bye, Luke.'

There had been a subtle shift between us already. I was

now saying goodbye to my boyfriend. But then he grinned and walked away the same as he always did and I was left wondering if I'd imagined the whole thing after all.

That evening, Julia went out on a date herself. I suddenly realised how much time she took to get ready and how much thought went into choosing the outfit she planned to wear; and I panicked because clothes and make-up weren't my forte. Would I have to dress up? Look different? Be different? Luke liked me the way I was, I knew, but that was when we were just hanging out together. Going on an official date was another matter entirely. Should I buy something new, something he had never seen before, so that he'd appreciate me more? A dress maybe. But if he saw me in a dress, would he laugh at me and ask what I was doing? I thought about asking Julia for advice but I felt too uncomfortable. I didn't want her to know that things between me and Luke had changed. I didn't want her to tease me about it.

After she left, however, I had a bit of a rummage around her wardrobe. My sister always had lots of really fashionable stuff, and although I was too short for her skirts and dresses, I'd occasionally borrowed some of her tops in the past. She never knew about it. I always returned them before she noticed they were missing. A multicoloured silk shirt that I'd never even seen her wear before went well with my favourite jeans and made them look dressed up rather than functional. And I reckoned that if I could also sneak her black boots with a high heel, I'd definitely look like someone on a date. (Back then, I never wore heels. Now, they're an essential part of my wardrobe.)

I couldn't sleep that night. I kept telling myself that I was only going out with Luke, that everything would be fine, but the longer I lay wide awake in bed, the more I fretted that it wouldn't work out and that I'd lose him forever. And then I told myself that if I was scared of losing him, I must feel as though we were supposed to be together. Which felt right to me on one level, but on another . . . I thumped my pillow with my fist and turned it over for the hundredth time.

I didn't realise then that I was setting a sleep pattern that night that I would repeat over and over again. That being awake at three in the morning would be a common occurrence for me.

On Saturday morning, while she was out shopping, I nicked the clothes I wanted from Julia's wardrobe. Then I went to the hairdresser's. I'd never bothered much with the hairdresser before, because I wore my hair long, past my shoulders, and Mum normally trimmed it for me. But as I'd decided to rob Julia's blouse and boots, I reckoned I could spend the money I'd saved by not buying new clothes myself on a professional job that would make my hair look glossy and shiny.

All I wanted was a blow-dry, but the stylist, who'd run her fingers through my hair in a manner that suggested I'd brought a year-old bale of straw into her salon, suggested cutting three inches off the length. I looked at her in shock. My hair might have been a bit dry and straggly, but I liked it long. I could let it fall in front of my face like a curtain and twirl the ends of it whenever I felt stressed, which was quite a lot of the time, because at fifteen everything stressed me. My hair protected me. I wanted it sleeker, not shorter. However, the stylist was very persuasive, insisting that the length wasn't doing my heart-shaped face any favours and promising that I'd look a million times better when she'd finished.

I didn't want to look a million times better for Luke, but I did wonder if I should look a million times better for me. And so I agreed and let her cut my hair and the results were startling.

'You've got the sort of face that would do well with a crop,' she observed as she held the mirror up behind my head to show me how it looked. 'But this is a start.'

I couldn't imagine getting my hair cropped, but she'd been right about losing the three inches. Suddenly I felt older and more sophisticated. I hoped Luke would like it. I hoped he'd like me.

I started getting ready way too early, because I never usually bothered with make-up and so I wasn't entirely sure about how it would work out. It seems impossible now to think of any self-respecting fifteen-year-old who doesn't know her way around blushers, concealers and foundations, but this was a different time, and in any case I was clearly a case of arrested development as far as cosmetics were concerned. I was dabbing my eyes with the eyeshadow Julia had given me the previous Christmas, but which I'd never used, when she walked into my room.

'Hey,' I said indignantly. 'You should knock.'

'But if I knocked, I wouldn't know that it's you who's taken my favourite blouse *and* my good boots.' She looked at me and then whistled. 'And you've got a brand-new hair-style. Which is very nice indeed. Putting that together with the eyeshadow and my clothes, it rather looks as though my little sister has a date.'

'So what if I have?'

'Who's the lucky boy?' she asked.

'None of your business.'

Julia and I weren't especially close. She intimidated me back then because she was so pretty and so popular. Years later she said that I intimidated her because I could remember things. I didn't think it was much of a trade-off really, but I guess the grass is always greener.

'Luke Evans will be disappointed,' she said. And then, because I hadn't been able to keep my face expressionless, her eyes widened. 'You're doing all this *for* Luke Evans? Well, well, well.'

'Shut up.'

'It's about flippin' time,' she said. 'The two of you are perfect for each other.'

I made a face at her. But secretly I was pleased. I liked thinking we were perfect for each other.

'But you're making a mess of that.' She looked at my make-up efforts with a practised eye. 'Here, let me.'

Twenty minutes later, she sat back and regarded her handiwork. 'Off you go, Cinderella,' she said. 'And just this once, I won't say anything about robbing my clothes.'

'Thanks, Julia.' I looked at myself in the mirror and liked what I saw. I hoped Luke would too.

'You're welcome,' she said. 'Have a good time.'

'I plan to.'

She laughed and left me alone in my room. I sat on the bed and looked out of the window. I stayed there until I saw Luke leave his house, so that I was already in our hallway when he rang the doorbell. I answered it with indecent haste, and shouted to my parents that I was going out with Luke. As I stepped outside, I could hear my father yelling at me not to be late.

'Your hair.' Luke was staring at me. 'You've changed your hair.'

'Don't you like it?' I tried not to sound anxious.

'Yes,' he said. 'It suits you. You look completely different.'

'Good different, I hope.'

'It's more . . . yes, good different. I like your top, too.'

'It's my going-to-the-cinema look,' I said.

'You make me feel as though I should have a special look myself.'

'Not at all,' I told him. 'You're grand the way you are.'

He might have said that he hadn't bothered with a special look. But he was wearing a new shirt and I was sure I could smell aftershave on his face.

'I'm really looking forward to this movie,' he said as we waited for the bus. 'Will Smith is great.'

'The trailer looked good,' I agreed.

He smiled at me and I smiled back, and suddenly everything felt OK again.

It felt OK until the moment when the lights went down in the cinema. I wondered if he was going to put his arm around me and start kissing me. Pretty much all of my friends who went to the cinema in a couple didn't see a lot of the movie because they spent the entire time with their lips locked together, which seemed to me to be a desperate waste of a good film. Yet if it happened between us, there was a part of me that was looking forward to kissing Luke. I could even believe it might be worth missing the movie for.

110

In the end, though, he didn't try to kiss me at all. We watched as Will Smith and Jeff Goldblum saved the world by uploading a computer virus into the alien mother ship and we agreed that as an action movie it had ticked all our boxes. We were still talking like friends until Luke took me by the hand as we left the cinema. Neither of us said a word then. He continued holding it until we were in the queue at McDonald's. When he let go, I felt as though part of me had been taken away.

Our conversation over our Big Macs and fries was entirely about the likelihood of Earth ever being invaded by aliens. While we assessed the risk as low, we put a very high probability factor on humankind not being able to defeat any extraterrestrial travellers by using a simple virus. It was a fun conversation. Afterwards we stood hand in hand as we waited for the bus home. This time we were able to talk. Still about the movie. We didn't hold hands during the journey, but when we reached our stop, Luke put his arm around my shoulder before we began walking towards Blackwater Terrace. We approached the laneway that was the short cut from the main road to our houses, and Luke hesitated. I wouldn't have dreamed of walking along it by myself, as it was still a haunt of lads who liked to drink cans of cider, but it was also a place where couples could find a nook for a bit of private kissing. And sometimes more.

I knew that Luke was thinking of cutting through the laneway, and I knew this meant that he wanted to kiss me in a shadowy corner, but we could both hear sounds of slightly drunken laughter and jeering coming from the darkness, and Luke shook his head.

'Not tonight,' he said as he steered me along the main road again. 'I don't want anything to happen to you.' He tightened his grip on my shoulder and I allowed myself to snuggle closer to him. As a first date, I thought, it had been pretty good so far. I'd spent time with someone I already liked, doing things I already enjoyed. And now, safe in his embrace, I felt cherished and cared for. It couldn't get much better.

Well, obviously it could. Because we still hadn't kissed and, realistically, that was what would make the big difference. That was what would move us from just good friends to boyfriend and girlfriend. Even though by now I couldn't wait for it to happen, I was still enjoying the anticipation of the moment. I hoped the actual event would be even better than I was imagining.

We walked past Luke's house and stopped outside mine.

'Well,' he said, turning towards me.

'Well,' I said in return.

'I had a really good time.'

'Me too.'

Our faces were close to each other. I could see into his eyes, darkened by the amber street lights. I felt I could see right through them, into his very being. And I liked what I saw.

'I thought about asking you out before, but I was afraid,' said Luke.

'Why?' I was startled by this admission. There was no need for guys to be afraid of asking girls out. We were always flattered.

'I thought you mightn't want to,' he said. 'And I was afraid it would mess up – well, you're my friend too, Carly. I didn't want to change that.'

I was glad he had the same fears as me. If we were both afraid of the same thing, we were OK. Weren't we?

'We'll always be friends,' I told him. 'No matter what. I promise.'

And then, just as he was about to kiss me, our front door opened.

'There you are!' My dad was standing in the doorway, framed by the light that streamed out of the house.

Both Luke and I moved quickly apart.

'Your mother was wondering where you'd got to,' called Dad.

'I told her I'd be with Luke,' I said.

'She thought you'd be home earlier. She was getting worried. And Mrs Evans called to ask if Luke was here. She was worried too.'

Luke and I exchanged puzzled glances. Murielle wasn't a worrier. And although I was rarely out much past eleven, which a quick glance at my watch told me was the time, I knew that the Evans boys were often out much later.

'Mum did mutter about me being home early tonight,' Luke murmured. 'But I thought she was in one of her moods.'

I shrugged and then called out to Dad that I'd be in in a minute.

Instead of taking the hint, he continued to stand in the doorway. I gave Luke an agonised look and he grinned.

'Tomorrow,' he said. 'I'll call for you tomorrow. We'll go somewhere together.'

I wanted to kiss him now, to hold on to him, but I couldn't with Dad watching us.

'Don't worry,' said Luke. 'We'll be fine.'

And I trusted him because I always trusted Luke. So I nodded.

Then he gave me the quickest of pecks on the cheek before turning away and walking home.

I never saw him again.

Until today.

Chapter 9

Bailando al Fuego (Dancing towards Fire) – José de Córdoba

To my astonishment, I've nearly finished the mojito, which has to be the nicest one I've ever drunk. Cold and minty with a gentle kick and a hint of sweetness. Luke is watching me, a thoughtful expression on his face.

'Thirsty?' he asks.

'I guess.'

My phone rings and startles both of us. I look apologetically at Luke, then turn away from him.

'Hi,' says Chris.

'Party over?' I'm surprised. It's less than an hour since we talked, and I thought they'd keep going a lot longer than that.

'No,' says Chris. 'But I'm alone in my room now.'

It takes a second for the penny to drop. And then I remember the promise to talk dirty. Chris has a bit of a phone sex fetish, I guess. He loves it, and I . . . Well, even though sometimes I get a bit embarrassed about it, it can be fun. Nevertheless, I can't talk dirty in a public bar, with Luke

Evans sitting opposite me. Let alone do anything that makes me feel in the slightest bit sexy.

'What are you wearing?' he asks.

'A dress,' I mumble.

'Is that music playing in the background?'

'Yes.'

'Nice,' he says. 'You can take it off to the music.'

I don't know what to say. My back is to Luke now, and I'm staring straight at the bell tower of the cathedral.

'Tell me what you're doing,' says Chris.

'Um . . . I'm lowering the zip,' I whisper.

'What?'

'The zip.' I'm hoping that Luke is listening to the Cuban music and not me. 'I've . . . The zip is down.'

'Good,' says Chris. 'Now what are you doing?'

'I'm stepping out of the dress.' I've slid off the chair and moved a little further away from Luke. Now I'm closer to a young couple. But they're speaking to each other in a language I don't recognise, and I'm hoping that they don't understand me either.

'And what are you wearing underneath?'

Oh God.

'My black lace,' I say quietly, although actually I'm wearing Spanx, because even though the Donna Karan is reasonably forgiving, I didn't want to bulge. But Chris bought me the black lace and I always bring it with me.

'You look great in black,' says Chris. 'I love sliding the knickers down your legs and putting my lips to . . .'

I cough a couple of times.

'Are you all right?' The seductive tone has gone and he sounds concerned.

116

'Sure, fine, fine.'

'And putting my lips close to yours,' he continues.

I'm flaming with embarrassment here. I let him do all the talking, only adding an occasional breathy 'yes' from time to time and hoping that he's enjoying his own performance enough not to notice that my participation is minimal.

'Long, lovely strokes,' he says, and I reach out for the remains of my mojito, which I throw back in a single swallow. Unfortunately, I misjudge putting the glass back on the table, and it misses completely. I yelp and jump out of the way as it falls to the ground and shatters.

'What the hell was that?' demands Chris.

'I . . . um . . . I was stretching out and I've knocked over a glass.'

'Oh.'

'I was sort of carried away,' I tell him.

There's a silence. I clutch the phone while one of the gorgeous waitresses clears up the mess. Luke, who's at least feigning indifference to my conversation, orders me another, even though I mouth at him not to bother.

'I was getting carried away myself,' complains Chris. 'But you scared the shit out of me.'

'I'm sorry.'

I seem to have spent the entire day apologising to Chris.

'Say something,' he demands.

'Like what?'

'Something to get the image of you and a broken glass out of my mind so that I can finish this off.'

I groan. Silently. Luke has wandered to the end of the bar. Maybe he's settling the tab.

'I wish you were inside me,' I say rapidly. 'Melting me.

The way you do. Moving with me . . .' I've never felt less like talking about sex in my life.

I can hear Chris's breath, faster and faster.

'I want to hold every part of you,' I say as I gaze at the cathedral. 'Explore you . . .'

Luke is starting to walk back to our table. He has a bowl of mixed nuts in his hand.

'With my tongue,' I add quickly.

Chris is moaning and I'm hot with embarrassment. I hear a long-drawn-out breath from my fiancé and I exhale slowly too. I add a bit of a moan for good measure.

'That was great,' says Chris. 'For you too?'

'Of course. You're the best.'

'I was thinking that if you ever have to go away in the future, we could set up mirroring on the phones and use FaceTime and watch ourselves on TV.'

Luke sits down opposite me and I smile at him.

'What a brilliant idea.' Thank God he didn't think of it sooner. 'You'll have to show me how to do that, though. You know how crap I am at technology.'

Luke raises an eyebrow and I know that he knows I haven't been talking about technology.

'I'd better get back to the party,' says Chris. 'I don't want them looking for me.'

'Enjoy yourself,' I say. 'I'll probably go to sleep now.'

'You must be tired.' He laughs. My lack of ability to drop off as quickly as he does astonishes him.

'Worth staying up for.'

'Totally,' he says.

'I love you.'

'Love you Lots.'

I end the call, then I take an enormous swig from the glass the waitress has just placed in front of me and sit down again.

'Aren't mobile phones great?' Luke speaks idly. 'No matter where you are, you can be close to someone.'

'Indeed.'

'Pity we didn't have them when we were younger.'

I blink a few times before agreeing with him.

'I'm sorry I didn't call,' says Luke.

After we'd said goodbye, I went into the house, poked my head around the living room door, said good night to Mum and went straight to my room, ignoring her questions about where I'd been. I didn't want the magic to wear off by talking about it to her. Because it had been magical. The unspoken words between us, the brief touch of his lips on my cheek. Magic and promise and everything to look forward to.

I thought of how the rest of my life with Luke might be. Easy and uncomplicated. We both liked the same things. Neither of us cared too much for expensive possessions. Perhaps, I thought, we would backpack the world together, finding mountain villages with whitewashed houses and sleepy town squares; or we might spend some time trekking along a rugged coastline and buying fish from a boat; or simply find a sun-kissed valley where we would stay forever because all that mattered was that we were together. In my rose-tinted vision of the future, everything was bathed in a warm glow of happiness and contentment. All I wanted was to be with Luke and for him to want to be with me.

Even though I was tired, I had no intention of going to sleep. If I was asleep, I wasn't reliving the memory of his

119

body close to mine, of our fingers touching as we took popcorn from our shared bucket in the cinema. I wouldn't be remembering his smile as he wiped tomato ketchup from my chin in McDonald's. Or the way he put his arm protectively around me as we walked from the bus stop. I relived these moments over and over again as I lay on my back, and told myself that I was glad to be more than just Luke's friend. And I imagined what the touch of his lips on mine would be like. I still had that to look forward to. Maybe it was good that he hadn't kissed me. Maybe it was nice to hug that expectation close.

It was about four in the morning when I heard the noise of people on the road outside. Murmuring voices and then the sound of a car door – no, I thought, the sliding doors of a van – being opened. And more talk and noise. I kneeled up on my bed and peered between the slats of the venetian blinds on my window.

The van was a Ford Transit and it was parked in front of the Evanses' house. Mr Evans was walking down their pathway carrying an enormous box, which he then loaded into the van. Mrs Evans followed with a suitcase. I had no idea what was going on, but I thought that perhaps they were getting rid of some of their stuff. Although why they needed to do it at four in the morning, I simply didn't know. I kept watching as they brought more and more things out of the house. Kyle and Jordan were helping, but I didn't see any sign of Wayne or Luke. And then, a while later, I did. Both of them came out of the house dressed in jeans and fleeces and got into the van, along with their parents and their brothers. Mr Evans then started it up and drove away.

I was bemused. Where on earth were they going with a van full of things at this hour of the morning? I lay down in my bed again and thought about it. It took a while before I concluded that they'd headed off to a car boot sale somewhere. It was the only explanation that made any sense. Though I felt sorry for Luke, who wasn't a morning person but who'd obviously been dragged along to help. I hoped he wouldn't be too tired to call for me tomorrow. Because tomorrow was when my life with him would properly start.

Luke hadn't said when he'd call for me the next day, and so I spent the morning in a state of jittery anticipation. Mum, who'd finally seen my new hairstyle, kept looking curiously at me and asking me why I'd had it done. She liked it, she said, but it changed me completely. Meanwhile Julia, to whom I'd given a brief account of my night out, remarked that I was like a lovesick child and told me that I needed to learn to treat 'em mean and keep 'em keen. 'He'll get very tired of you if you're overeager,' she advised me. 'You've got to retain a sense of mystery.' Which was all very well, I thought, but this was Luke Evans. There was nothing about me he didn't already know!

I kept an eye out for the return of the white van all day, because I knew Luke couldn't call me until he was home, but by five in the evening there was still no sign of it, and I was getting worried. What if there had been some awful accident? What if Richard had crashed the van and Luke was lying injured in hospital unable to talk to me? Worrying about me worrying about him. Or, even worse, unconscious and unable to worry about anything.

At six o'clock, and with no sign of the van, I pulled on a

jacket and walked over to Luke's house myself. I reasoned that I might have missed their return and that Richard could have dropped off the family before taking the van back to wherever he'd rented it. I wasn't sure that I should have come – after all, Luke had said he'd call me – but I couldn't hang around at home wondering forever. So I stood on the doorstep as I'd done so many times before, and rang the bell. I could hear it echoing down the hallway as I waited for someone to answer. But there was only silence. No sounds of doors opening, of music leaking from another room, of Mrs Evans's high heels tapping on the tiled hallway floor. Just total silence.

What on earth had happened? Where the hell were they?

I stood hesitantly on the doorstep for another minute. Then I went home.

All the old hurt has come back, and even though I know Luke wasn't to blame, I still wish he'd tried to get in touch. I want to make some kind of flippant remark, ask him what he's talking about, say that I don't need an apology from him, but for some reason I can't speak.

He's looking at me and I think he's going to apologise again, but in the end he simply asks if it was my fiancé on the phone. I toy with the idea of saying no, that I was having an erotic conversation with a complete stranger, but I don't. I nod instead.

'How long have you known him?' asks Luke.

'A year and a half.'

'And he's the one?'

'Yes.' I speak firmly. Obviously in terms of our relationship, today has been a bad one for Chris and me, but one bad day doesn't make up a lifetime, and we've shared lots and lots of good ones. I know that Chris loves me because he's proved it time and time again. He proved it when we went for a walk in the Dublin mountains and I cut my foot on a piece of glass and he carried me for three kilometres on his back. He proved it on my last birthday, when he presented me with a gorgeous silver heart on a chain – the one I wore to this morning's breakfast meeting because I think it's lucky. And he proved it on the Friday he told me to meet him at the clinic and he brought me to the exclusive and gorgeous Sugar Loaf Lodge hotel for a night of pampering and passion (he'd packed an overnight bag for me too, with beautiful new lingerie). He's a good, good man and I'm glad I have him in my life.

'You're lucky,' says Luke. 'It's great to find the right person.'

'Yes, I am,' I agree. 'Chris and I love each other. He's never let me down.'

Luke says nothing. He shells a pistachio nut from the bowl on the table.

'But I did,' he says eventually.

I shouldn't let him think this. I know he wouldn't have deliberately done anything to hurt me. Yet I'm still not ready to talk about it.

So I ignore his comment and ask instead how his parents are.

'Divorced,' he replies.

'Oh.'

'No big surprise,' he says. 'They'd grown apart. How about yours?'

'Still together,' I tell him. 'They're like two peas in a pod as they travel the world and have fun on special seniors' deals.'

He laughs.

'I always liked your mum and dad,' he said. 'They were good together.'

'They still are,' I concede.

'And your sister?' he asks. 'Julia?'

'She's married with two boys. She lives in Canada.'

He looks surprised.

'She went there for a couple of years, met a man from Vancouver and that was that.'

'Does she like it?'

'She lives in a fabulous house just outside the city, has two adorable sons, and Jeff is a great guy. I think she's very happy.'

'Have you visited?'

'Not yet. But hopefully one day soon. How about your brothers?'

'Kyle married a girl from Manchester. He moved there and has three children. Jordan lives with his partner in Torrevieja, on the east coast. She's Irish. Wayne is in Australia. He works as a fitness instructor.'

That doesn't surprise me. Wayne was the fittest of the Evans boys. He used to spend all his free time in the gym.

'My father owns a nightclub,' Luke continues. 'Apparently it's very successful. But everything he's done over the last few years has been successful.'

I say nothing.

'Mum divides her time between Marbella and wherever else she decides she wants to be. She's a hard woman to pin down these days. She has a very busy life and there are a lot of people in it, including men. She's told me that she's no intention of being exclusive with any of them, because these days she's out for fun and not marriage. It's a bit of a jolt to hear your mother say something like that, but as long as she's happy . . .'

'And you?' I ask. 'Where do you live?'

'I have a studio apartment in Marbella,' replies Luke. 'But I travel a lot around Spain.'

My eyes are fixed on him.

'That TV programme was bullshit.' He's suddenly angry.

I want to believe him. But I keep thinking of his rich friends and the Aston Martin and his dad who runs a nightclub. And I don't know what to say.

Chapter 10

Concierto de Aranjuez: Allegro – Narciso Yepes

The gossip started on Blackwater Terrace before the news actually broke. The story was that the Evanses were in deep financial trouble and that they'd skipped the country before their house was repossessed. The truth was that Richard Evans had been running a Ponzi scheme and he'd got out before it was exposed. Nobody in Blackwater Terrace had ever heard of a Ponzi scheme back then, but years later, when the financial crisis hit the country, everyone realised that Luke's dad had been ahead of the game.

Because of all the stuff the Evanses had, we assumed – if we'd thought about it at all, which I'm pretty sure nobody did – that he was simply very successful at what he did, and very well paid. But selling insurance wasn't well paid; insurance salespeople made most of their money by commission. And Richard Evans had apparently decided that he could do a lot better by diverting some of his clients' funds to his own account. Not that he said he was doing that, of course. What happened was that whenever he was selling a policy, he would talk to the client about the cheapest option, and then give them the chance to invest more money in what he called a high-yield product as well. Very few people asked how this high-yield product could give them such a great rate on their savings. People like Richard Evans get away with it because so many of us want to believe that we're getting a great deal. That we're somehow smarter than the next person. But, like every Ponzi scheme, all Mr Evans was doing was using the money from new clients to pay clients who needed funds back. As long as he had new money coming into his scheme, he was all right. And he was all right for a long time, because he was very, very persuasive. It turned out that almost everyone on Blackwater Terrace had invested with him. The only people who hadn't were Mum and Dad, and old Mr Dawkins at number 40, who was as tight as they come and who died leaving two hundred thousand euros in the credit union and a ten-year-old Ford in his driveway.

The Evanses fled because the scheme had begun to unravel. Even though I pored over the papers at the time, I didn't entirely understand the intricacies of it all. And I've forgotten a lot of it now, although some of the newspaper articles are still burned into my memory. But the bottom line was that Mr Evans knew it was all going to come crashing down, and the family sneaked out of the house at four in the morning before the police caught up with him.

According to a later TV documentary on Irish criminals living it up in the sun, they took a ferry to Holyhead and then another from Portsmouth to Santander. Then they drove to Marbella, where Mr Evans used the money he'd conned out of hard-working people to buy a luxury villa and a pub. The programme went out a few years after the Evanses had left, and they weren't a major part of it, because there were other criminals who'd bought pubs or nightclubs or set up businesses in the south of Spain who were far more successful (if that's the right word) than our former neighbours. But there was a shot of the luxury villa and another of the pub, and a moment when the reporter accosted Richard Evans on the pavement. Mr Evans brushed by him with a muttered 'no comment' before dodging into a building and closing the door behind him.

Over the years, I've seen other programmes about what reports describe as the soft underbelly of crime on the Costa, and the Evans name has popped up in a number of them. But the more recent programmes have concentrated on drug gangs and property developers gone bust, and on successful Spanish investigations, not on almost-forgotten swindlers like Richard Evans.

'That TV programme was bullshit,' repeats Luke. His eyes are hard, his face taut.

'I don't know which TV programme you're talking about,' I say. 'There was more than one. But I guess there must be a grain of truth, whichever it was.'

Luke's shoulders slump and he runs his finger around the rim of his glass.

'It made us look as though we were all part of Dad's great plan. That we were a family of effing master criminals.'

I know the programme he means now. It's the one that reported that, in addition to the pub, Richard had opened an estate agency staffed by his wife and sons. I watched it wondering if they'd show a shot of Luke, but when the cameras went into the agency it was Murielle who was behind the desk. She looked as amazing as ever. The only difference in her was her chest. I'm sure it was new. It was certainly more impressively stacked than I remembered. Murielle dealt brilliantly with the reporters, saying that the agency was well respected and extremely profitable and deflecting all their questions about her husband with a wave of her hand and a rattle of the collection of gold bracelets that adorned her wrists.

I don't want to get into an argument with Luke about the truth or otherwise of TV documentaries. But I do want to know what happened the night they left. I want to know how much he knew about his father's activities. And I want to know why he never tried to get in touch with me. I don't, of course, want him to think it matters to me. It doesn't. Not any more. It took time, but eventually I accepted that the life I'd dreamed of having with him – backpacking, finding fishing villages and whitewashed towns – was gone forever.

'I never felt comfortable with Dad and his work, you know that,' says Luke after a moment. 'I hated the way it was so all-encompassing. I told him that he didn't need to work so much. Hell, Carly, you know how I felt about all the things we had. That we didn't really need them. That it wasn't worth all the hard work. Not, of course, that it was exactly hard work for Dad when he was . . .'

I feel sorry for Luke as he speaks, even though for a long time I was angry with him. I was angry because he should have told me. We were supposed to be best friends.

'When I got home that night, all our things were packed.' Luke isn't looking at me directly; he's staring into the distance, reliving it. 'I wanted to know what was happening, and Mum and Dad said that Dad was in some trouble and that we needed to get away so that he could clear his name.' He swallows, then takes a sip of the mojito. 'I couldn't believe it. It was like Dundalk all over again. That's why we left to come to Dublin, you know.'

'Your dad was running a Ponzi scheme there too?' I'm shocked. There was no mention of it in the TV programme.

'No, no. But there was an issue in the company he worked for. Apparently he was rounding odd amounts in money received and putting the difference into another account. It wasn't a lot of money but it was wrong. The company told him to leave or they'd prosecute. He always said that it had been a mistake, that he'd set up that account to deal with errors, and I believed him back then.'

I nod. Mr Evans was always eminently believable. That was his skill.

'Anyway, Mum said we were going to Spain, which would be an enormous adventure, and that we'd have a better life.'

'What about your brothers?' I ask. 'Kyle must have been – what – nineteen, twenty back then. Surely he didn't need to leave?'

'Dad wanted the family together, out of reach of the authorities. Besides, Kyle was thrilled with the idea of living in Spain. We'd been there on holidays before and he loved it. So did everyone else.'

'And you?'

'I didn't want to go,' he says. 'At least . . . not without saying goodbye to you.'

But he didn't say goodbye to me, did he?

'Mum said I couldn't talk to you. That we couldn't leave a trail. That people couldn't know where we were. She kept saying how important it was. Even when we arrived in Spain, she wouldn't let us ring home.'

'You could've, though,' I remark. 'You could've gone to a pay phone and called me.'

'I desperately wanted to, but I was afraid,' admits Luke. 'The way Mum and Dad told it, there were people out to get us. And if we made a single mistake, a single phone call, Dad wouldn't be able to clear his name.'

'At what point did you realise that he didn't have a name to clear?' I wince as I say the words, because they sound harsh and uncaring. But Richard Evans had been harsh and uncaring when he'd swindled the neighbours, none of whom could afford to lose money to him.

'I think I always knew.' Luke looks tired now, and his shoulders slump still further. I want to put my arms around him. I want to hold him close to me and tell him not to worry. Like he used to do for me when I was upset about things at school. But I don't. I simply listen as he continues to speak. 'We had so much, you know, and it was at a time when people didn't have a lot. We seemed to be lucky. No matter what we wanted, we got it. Dad kept saying it was because he was a top man in his company, but I'd hear him on the phone to his supervisor sometimes and I'd wonder how it was that someone as successful as him still had a supervisor. There was something off about it, you know? I just didn't want to find out exactly what it was.'

'And what was it like, hiding out in Spain?'

Luke looks embarrassed.

'Our villa was lovely. Not as big and luxurious as that TV programme made it out to be, but way better than Blackwater Terrace. Dad used a lot of his money to buy the pub, fit it out, all that sort of thing. Of course the people who came into the pub . . .' He sighs. 'To the holidaymakers it was

131

just a pub, but to the people who lived there . . . The regulars got to know that everything wasn't exactly above board. Dad was involved in some shady deals in Spain too. Actually, I think that's how he got the estate agency. I was pleased about that, though, because it seemed a far more legitimate sort of business. And it turned out to be hugely successful, because he sold it and made a genuine fortune before the bottom fell out of the market.'

'Did you work there?'

'During my holidays,' he admits. 'I was quite good at it. I liked showing houses to people.'

'Didn't any of you worry about what he'd done in the past?'

'He never admitted it. He always said he'd been set up. That it wasn't how people were making it out. You say he didn't have a name to clear, but whenever we talked about it – which wasn't very often – he'd say that one day people would know he wasn't a cheat.'

'He was, though?' I make it a question, not a statement. Because maybe a terrible injustice was done to Richard Evans. Although Mr and Mrs O'Connell, who still live next door to my parents and who lost the fifty grand they gave him to invest, wouldn't think so.

'Oh of course he was!' cries Luke. 'Dad is a con man. He always was and always will be. At least,' he corrects himself, 'he doesn't exactly con people any more. He moves in different circles these days. But if there's a suspect deal to be done, a short cut to getting money, Dad will be there doing it. He can't help himself.'

'What about the money he took?'

'What about it?' asks Luke. 'I don't know how much it was or who it was from.'

132

I mention that fifty grand of it was from the O'Connells, and he looks uncomfortable. Mrs O'Connell used to give us ice creams on hot days. She was lovely.

'When I eventually realised that Dad wasn't the innocent party, I was gutted,' says Luke. 'But I didn't cop that until we'd been in Spain for a few years. Maybe I was naive. But who wants their father to be a con man? Who believes it?'

He's right. We love the people we love despite everything. We want to believe the best of them.

'All I ever assumed was that he had his priorities wrong,' says Luke. 'He thought things were more important than people. Everyone in my family did. Me – well, I'm the opposite. I like people. I always have.'

'Did you ever think of me?' I ask the question casually as I swirl the ice cubes around my glass with the straw.

'All the time!' cries Luke. 'I thought about the fact that we'd said good night and I didn't know that I was really saying goodbye. I desperately wanted to call you. To talk to you. But I was terrified that someone would trace the call, find out where we were and come after my dad. I realise how stupid that sounds now, but back then I believed what my parents were telling me. By the time I knew exactly what had happened . . . well, things had moved on, hadn't they? There was no point trying to get in touch with you. There was all that stuff in the papers. The TV programme had been broadcast and made it seem like every one of us knew what was going on. I didn't think you'd want to know me. Your parents certainly wouldn't have wanted you to be involved with me, would they?'

I shake my head slowly. He's right. Mum and Dad were appalled when the whole thing came out. Mum said that she'd always known there was something not quite right about that family and Dad congratulated himself on seeing through Richard Evans and keeping the O'Keeffe family savings safe and secure. Mum also made it her mission to remind Julia that she'd disapproved of Kyle Evans too. Julia, not unreasonably, reminded her of my friendship with Luke – although she didn't say anything about the fact that my last night with him had been a date – and Mum simply remarked that it was different and that he'd been a decent boy. To me, Julia simply said that there were plenty more fish in the sea and that at least he hadn't had a chance to break my heart. As well as which, she told me, I'd got a nice new haircut out of it so I had to look on the positive side. There was no point in me telling her that my heart was already broken.

'It's all in the past now,' says Luke. 'I've put it behind me. I do my own thing.'

But had his own thing, whatever it is, come about because he'd lived a privileged life thanks to other people's money? Not that he could help that, I suppose. But what about now? What about the rich friends with the Aston Martins and flashy apartments? I know I'm being judgemental, and that his friends seem genuine and sincere, but Richard Evans seemed sincere to the people he swindled. And I don't know anything about his friends really.

'I went to college in Malaga,' Luke continues, when he realises I'm not saying anything. 'I studied philosophy. I think it helped me cope.'

'And do you make a good living as a philosopher?' I know there's an edge to my voice, but I can't help it.

'That's not what I do,' says Luke. 'I work for a foundation now.'

'What sort of foundation?'

'It helps disadvantaged children to stay in education.'

Just as I was beginning to harden my heart against him, he brings out the big guns. Working for a charitable organisation is a pretty good way of redeeming yourself. Dorothea Bennett would approve. Though it's a bit weird that, like the Bennetts, Luke is a charity hound, and I'm still the only one involved in filthy commerce.

'You must do well if you can drive around in an Aston Martin.' I'm not sure I entirely believe him. Nobody working in the charitable sector can afford a flashy car.

'The Aston belongs to the founder of the trust,' he says. 'I already told you it wasn't mine. He's a businessman who made his money in trading oil. He was in Seville for the *feria* and he left the Aston here when he decided to go back to Monaco by private jet. I knew I'd be around so I said I'd pick it up and drive it back to Barcelona, where he has a base.'

'Right.' It sounds glamorous, though. Oil industry. Seville. Monaco. Barcelona. Aston Martins. Private jets. A long, long way from Blackwater Terrace.

'I don't live off my father's money, if that's what you're thinking,' says Luke. 'We're not close. In fact our relationship is almost non-existent. Not that it should matter to you.' There's an edge in his voice too, and I know that my body language has been negative and disapproving. I don't blame him for being sensitive. I've been holding back from him all day because of my prejudices about his father. And because I've been nursing my broken heart for eighteen years. Well, that's not strictly correct, of course. It didn't take eighteen years for me to stop expecting to see him on the street and making up scenarios in which he called me from his hideaway in Spain and I fled to be with him. I have to admit that I do think of him every time I visit my parents and drive past the Evanses' old house on Blackwater Terrace, but I've long since stopped thinking about my lost love as some kind of Shakespearean tragedy. Grown-up emotions are a lot less intense than teenage crushes, or whatever it was that Luke and I had. However, I can't help remembering now how I felt back then, and I know I'm also holding back from him because he seems so rich and happy when I suppose I had some mad notion that he was still nursing a broken heart over me. I know that's daft. Maybe I haven't grown up as much as I thought.

Anyway, Luke has been lovely to me today. And I can't blame him for what happened when we were fifteen. If my parents had uprooted us from our home and told us not to say a word to anyone, I would have done what they said. Especially if I thought I was helping my dad in the process.

'I'm sorry,' says Luke now. 'I think I've put a bit of a dampener on your evening.'

'No you haven't,' I tell him. 'You've cleared the air. It probably needed to be cleared anyway.'

'Probably,' agrees Luke. 'I wish I'd tried to contact you before. I wish I hadn't been so silly as to believe everything my parents told me.'

'Oh for heaven's sake, you were just a kid,' I say. 'Of course you believed them. I would've too. Anyway, we've both moved on from being silly teenagers, haven't we?'

'That's true. You've done really well for yourself, Carly.'

'Not bad.' I want him to know I'm successful. I want him to know that I made the most of my talents.

'From what you said earlier, you're a star performer for the company you work for.'

'I wouldn't go that far. But I do well,' I agree.

'You've made a success of your life. I'm delighted for you.'

I've made a success of my life because, after Luke had gone, I threw myself completely and utterly into my schoolwork. I used my memory to my best advantage. The way I saw it, the only person in the world who could make me happy was myself. The only person I could depend on was myself too. Indirectly, I suppose, I am who I am because of him.

Ever since I bumped into him at the hotel, I've felt as though I'm on the back foot. But now I have the upper hand. Because my story is straightforward and good. I've done well. I have a great job. I'm going to marry a fantastic man. And my parents are the kind of people who don't even tell white lies.

'So can we put my family's chequered past behind us?' There's still a trace of anxiety in his voice. It must be hard for him. I don't want him to feel bad.

'Of course,' I say.

Luke gives a relieved sigh and orders another couple of mojitos. And even though I've really had enough alcohol for tonight, I don't say no.

Not surprisingly, I'm tipsy by the time I finish the cocktail. I'm finding it hard to keep my eyes open and I know I'm slurring my words ever so slightly. I tell Luke that I've had enough and he agrees that it's time to go. I wobble on my heels as I stand up and he steadies me by holding on to my arm. He keeps a grip on me as we walk to the lift and emerge at street level again.

My feet are hurting. The shoes were a terrible choice. They're rubbing my already tender ankles as well as the tops of my toes. Every step is sheer agony and I'm sure Luke thinks I'm drunker than I really am because of the way I'm hobbling. He's holding my arm very tightly while I concentrate on not yelping from the pain of my feet.

When we reach the apartment building I immediately take off the shoes. The cool tiles are like balm to my burning soles.

'I never took you for a tortured high-heels girl,' Luke remarks. 'I seem to remember it was sensible brogues for you.'

I snort with laughter and he grins. We both get into the tiny lift. Without my shoes, I only come halfway up to his shoulder. I resist the temptation to lean against him. I'm exhausted, and it would be lovely, but I stand upright, glad that I've freed myself from the slavery of the shoes.

When we get inside the apartment, he looks at my feet and gasps in horror.

'They're not that bad,' I tell him as I inspect the blisters.

'They're awful,' he insists. 'You need to put something on them. I'm sure Anita has plasters in her . . . her . . . *botequín.*'

I frown, and he looks frustrated.

'Medicine chest.' The words finally come to him and he looks rueful. 'Sometimes I forget the English for things,' he tells me. 'That's when I think I should go home.'

'Have you ever been back?'

He shakes his head as he walks towards the main bathroom.

'No,' he calls back to me. 'I've made my life here and there's nothing for me to go back to.'

138

Me, I think. You could've come back for me when you were old enough. I give myself a mental shake and wonder if it's the passion of the flamenco and the alcohol in the mojitos that's making my thoughts veer towards the melodramatic. Why on earth would Luke even consider coming back for me? We were childhood friends, that's all.

'Here you are.' He walks back into the room with a large white plastic box and opens it to reveal an eclectic assortment of pills, bandages and plasters. I wonder if Anita is a hypochondriac.

'The Spanish love their medicines,' Luke tells me as he takes out a packet of specialist blister plasters and begins to unwrap one. I protest feebly that I can't take all Anita's plasters, and he scoffs at me.

'She'll be thrilled to know that they were used,' he assures me. 'Anyhow, I'll replace them. Now give me your foot.'

His fingers are warm on my skin as he applies the plaster, smoothing it so that it's stuck firmly in place.

'Other one,' he says, and I comply.

'What about your toes?' He surveys the damage. 'They look a bit raw to me.'

I don't need a plaster on every toe, even if Anita's extensive stash could probably provide one.

'They'll be fine. I'll wear tights and my ballet pumps tomorrow.'

'Sure?'

'Yes. Thanks.'

'You're welcome.'

I'm no longer tipsy, but my heart is beating faster, which always happens when I drink too much.

'Well, look, I'd better go to bed.' I realise that I have to

139

speak because we've been standing looking at each other for what seems like forever without uttering a word.

'And I'll put the *botequín* back in place,' says Luke. 'Good night, Carlotta.'

'Good night.'

There's an awkward moment when neither of us moves. Then he kisses me quickly, once on each cheek, and I go to my bedroom.

The bed is super-comfortable. The sheets are crisp and the pillowcase cool. But I'm hot. It's from the cocktails. I always break into a sweat when I drink too much. It also keeps me awake, which is frustrating, because I think alcohol should knock you out, not leave you tossing and turning and – in my case tonight – being very aware that Luke Evans is in the other room.

I turn over and bash the plump pillow so that there's a hollow for my head. I don't care that Luke is next door. It doesn't matter. It really doesn't. It's just – well, this entire situation is weird. I don't know how to deal with it. I mean, I'm dealing with it fine, I've been polite and sociable and I've behaved perfectly well, but I still wish I hadn't missed the train.

It takes me forever to fall asleep. When I do, I'm back at school again, waiting for Luke to meet me at the gate before we walk home. But he doesn't show. And a wave of disappointment washes over me. I depend on Luke at school. He makes it all worthwhile.

I know it's morning when I wake up, because there's a finger of sunlight poking its way through a narrow gap in the shutters. I rub my eyes and then move my head experimentally from side to side. My eyes are a little bit dry, and so is my tongue, but I don't have a headache. I sit up and check the time on my mobile. It's nearly ten o'clock.

Ten o'clock! For the second time in as many days I push the covers back and leap out of bed. What in God's name is happening to me? I never, ever sleep till ten o'clock! I open the shutters completely and sunlight floods the room. The sky is a perfect blue with not even a wisp of cloud. I open the window too, and the scent of orange blossom drifts on the warm air. I think that it would be lovely to live here and wake up to blue skies and orange blossom every day, then I tell myself that it's probably hell in the hot days of summer and that spending one night in a city isn't the same as being a part of it. I should know that by now. I've stayed in enough of them over the years.

I step under the shower in the en suite and wonder if Luke is up. He usen't to be a morning person, but maybe he's changed. If he's still asleep, I'll just sneak out of the apartment and get a cab to the train station. Hopefully with better luck than yesterday. Definitely with better luck, as there's no chance of rain today.

I get dressed in one of my suits. Normally I prefer casual clothes for travelling, but I want to be the efficient, business-like me today. I want Luke to see that I'm not an incompetent wreck who misses trains, gets drunk and wears the wrong shoes. Speaking of which . . . I can't wear pumps with this skirt and jacket. I rummage in my case and find a comfortable, if boring, pair of court shoes with a mid heel. They're my fallback shoes. They go with anything and they never give me blisters.

As soon as I open the bedroom door, I'm hit by the aroma

of fresh coffee. I'm drawn to it like a parched traveller in the desert to an oasis. Luke is in the kitchen, fiddling with a complicated machine.

'Anita got this from Italy,' he says. 'It's brilliant, but you have to do everything exactly right.'

'You can work it, though. You made coffee yesterday.'

'Yesterday's was instant,' he confesses. 'I like the real thing in the morning.'

'So do I.'

I move from the door of the kitchen so that I can look more closely at the machine. It has dials and buttons and levers and is a far cry from the Pixie Nespresso that I have at home. But Luke seems to be managing OK.

'Strong or medium?' he asks. 'Espresso, latte, cappuccino?'

'A medium Americano would be nice.'

'Cold milk on the side?' he asks. 'It's not fresh, it's UHT.'

I wrinkle my nose. 'Black is better.'

Luke makes the coffee and we both go through to the living room, where he opens the double doors to the balcony.

'I feel like someone in an art house movie,' I comment as we sit at the bistro table on the balcony overlooking the city.

'Beats a fry-up on Blackwater Terrace,' says Luke.

I make a face. 'That depends. Sometimes sausage, bacon, beans, tomato and mushrooms is just the thing.'

'With black and white pudding?'

'Ugh, not for me. The rest of it, though . . .'

'We used to have a fry-up on Saturday mornings,' says Luke. 'When we first came to Marbella, we'd go to one of the seafront cafés on Saturdays instead. Quite a few of them do the full English.'

'I like fruit and yoghurt,' I say. 'And when I fall off the wagon, I add in a Danish or toast and marmalade.'

'You never ate junk food.' And then, like me, he remembers the first time we met, because he asks me about it and I nod in agreement with him as he recounts it perfectly.

'I thought you were very self-possessed back then,' says Luke.

'I wasn't.'

'You had a certain something,' he tells me. 'I liked you straight away. And then, of course, you were super-clever with that memory of yours. Is it still as good as ever?'

'Pretty much.'

'You were such a cool person to know.'

'Not really.' All the same, it's nice that he thought I was cool.

'Still, we had fun together.'

I nod in agreement.

'Maybe it was just as well it never went any further,' he remarks. 'We'd have split up eventually and it wouldn't have been the same afterwards.'

Perhaps we wouldn't have split up. Perhaps we would've been those childhood sweethearts who stay together forever. In years to come we might have been on a TV programme telling the world how we'd managed to stay married for more than fifty years or something. We could have had a perfect life together.

I'm being silly. It's over. I have a perfect life now.

I pick up my phone from where I left it on the table and send a text to Chris.

Morning, I type. *Hope the head isn't too bad.*

There's no reply. He's probably still in bed, sleeping off Dorothea's party.

'What time's your train?' asks Luke.

'Two,' I tell him. My flight isn't until half eight, but I'm not taking any chances today.

'So you've still time to spend in Seville with me,' says Luke.

'A little,' I agree. 'But I'm sure you must be busy. You've a wedding to go to.'

'Not till this evening,' he reminds me. 'Tell you what, why don't I bring you for a drive. You can see a little of the countryside?'

'In the Aston?' Part of me wants to say yes simply because I loved being in the Aston, but I don't want him to feel that he has to look after me. Most of the time I can pretty well look after myself.

'It's the only car around.' Luke grins.

'Won't your employer mind?'

'No,' says Luke. 'He likes it being driven. There's a nice little town just outside the city that's worth a visit.'

I hesitate. I'm not entirely sure about Luke. In many ways he's as lovely as I remember, but a lot has happened since then, and I really don't know him any more. I'm conflicted, and he sees this.

'If you'd rather just hang around by yourself until you go to the train station, that's absolutely fine,' he says. 'I can meet up with my friends.'

But what's the point of sitting here and just waiting? How many opportunities will I ever have to be driven round the south of Spain in a gorgeous car? I check my mobile. Still no reply from Chris.

'OK,' I say. 'Let me get all my stuff together so that we don't have to come back here.'

'Perfect.'

I go back into the bedroom and put my bits and pieces into my suitcase. I look at the bed doubtfully. I'm not sure if I should strip it, but I don't like leaving a bundle of sheets in the corner of the room. So in the end I just plump up the pillows and straighten the duvet. I spritz them with my Jo Malone too. The room looks as neat and tidy as when I first saw it.

Luke is standing in the lounge, car keys in his hand. We leave the apartment, make another journey in the tiny lift (I'm squashed up against him again) and then get into the car. My heart is in my mouth as we negotiate the car park and drive up the ramp to the street, but Luke manages without scratching the gleaming paintwork of the Aston. And then we're outside and heading for the outskirts of the city.

I like driving more than being driven. I love my red Mini Cooper. It's easy to drive and to park and I like the quirkiness of the big dials and the retro buttons that you have to press hard to make things happen. Chris drives a Volvo, all Swedish and safe and without my Mini's effervescent personality. But very, very comfortable.

Nothing, though, can hold a candle to the Aston. We're in the suburbs now and heading towards the open road. As we leave the buildings behind us, Luke opens the throttle and the Aston surges forward. I can hardly contain myself. Luke shoots me an amused glance and goes a little faster.

A little over half an hour later we arrive at Fuente del Rio. There are car parking spaces alongside the river, which forms an arc around half of the town, and Luke slides the Aston into one of them. When we get out, I can hear the roar of

145

the water as it streams over a series of man-made steps cut into the riverbed.

'There's a spring further up,' explains Luke. 'That's the *fuente*. *Fuente* also means fountain, and there's a gorgeous one in the square, which is where we're going.'

The town is pedestrianised, he tells me as we walk along narrow streets bordered by traditional whitewashed houses with wrought-iron grilles and balconies at their upper windows. Everyone has to park in designated areas away from their homes. This is hardly surprising, as it would be a feat of driving skill to get a car up some of these roads anyway. As we arrive at the cobbled square, I can see why they've banned cars there too. It's not very big, but it's absolutely beautiful. The fountain in the centre sends jets of water sparkling high into the air at regular intervals. The ubiquitous orange trees are here and there are hanging baskets of flowers on every upstairs balcony, as well as tubs of multicoloured blooms placed around the square itself. The scent is intoxicating. There are two bars, one either side of the square. Luke leads me to one of them.

'There isn't exactly competition between them,' he says. 'They're both owned by the same family. Great food here too. *Hola*.' The waiter arrives and Luke orders coffees for both of us. I'm drinking too much damn coffee with him, I think. I'll be wired to the moon.

The coffee is excellent, and the waiter has also brought us some slices of baguette and individual servings of Nutella.

'You used to like it,' says Luke as I exclaim in surprise.

The first time I tasted Nutella was in the Evanses' house. Mum would never have bought anything as decadent as chocolate spread. Jam and marmalade, yes. But chocolate on bread – she'd sooner cut her hand off. When Murielle Evans offered me a piece of bread with it one day (Luke and I were doing maths homework together), I looked at it sceptically. And then I tasted it and was lost.

It's my guilty pleasure nowadays, an ever-present jar at the back of the fridge. Any time I'm feeling down, or whenever I want to give myself a special treat, I nip around the corner to the local Centra, buy a fresh bread roll and smother it with Nutella. And I'm transported back to that day with Luke, when we'd finished the maths and then sat companionably watching cartoons on their huge TV. It's not that I didn't get all that at home with Mum and Dad and Julia, but this was me doing my own thing with someone I liked.

'So are you going to have some?' asks Luke.

I open one of the servings, take a piece of bread and spread it liberally with Nutella. I sip the coffee. The sun is warm on my shoulders, the fountain rippling in the background. This is the most peaceful place I've ever been in my life.

'Anita's grandmother was born here,' says Luke. 'The family moved to Seville when she was a baby. Years later, when he'd made his money, her father bought back the original family home. They come here for weekend breaks.'

'How nice,' I say.

'It's cute. I wouldn't live in it,' he adds. 'The house is too small and too dark for me, but that was how they made them back then.'

'And did you come here with Anita when you and she were going out?' I shouldn't ask the question, but I can't help myself.

'Once or twice.'

I don't really want to think of him with his girlfriend,

wandering around the town hand in hand, eating just-baked bread and Nutella together and going back to make love in some quaint country house. But I do anyway. I can't help feeling a bit jealous, which is totally irrational. After all, she's marrying someone else today. And, very soon I'll also be marrying someone else!

'Anyway, when people talk about the real Spain, they're talking about places like this,' says Luke. 'Although these days all the houses are modernised inside and Fuente tries to be self-sufficient energy-wise. There's a solar farm just outside the town that meets a lot of the energy needs. And the river provides some too.'

'Seriously?'

'Absolutely. It's all very ecofriendly.'

'Progress is good,' I tell him. 'Especially when it's the sort of progress that you don't really see.'

'More coffee?'

I hadn't realised I'd finished the cup, nor that I'd stuffed my face with another slice of bread.

'I'd better not. I go a bit gaga with caffeine.'

'Let's walk.'

He brings me for a stroll around the town, which is really only the square, a few streets, a small park and the river. I wouldn't want to live here, but I can see how it would be a perfect romantic hideaway.

'C'mon so,' says Luke eventually. 'I'd better get you back. Don't want you to miss your train two days in a row.'

I get into the car.

I look back at the town.

It's a pity to have to leave it.

*   *   *

'Tell me about the organisation you work for,' I say as we hit the open road again.

'It supports children in education,' Luke tells me. 'We help them to stay in school in cases where otherwise family circumstances would force them to leave, and we partner projects that work with disadvantaged communities and help them to provide educational facilities for their children.'

How much more altruistic could he get? Once again I think of myself as the cuckoo in a nest of charity-working people. Dorothea would love him. Perhaps I should try to introduce him to Pen. Or Lisa.

'How did you become involved?'

'Through a friend of a friend of . . . my dad's.'

I shoot a look at him, but his eyes are fixed on the road ahead.

'Nasir is a great guy,' says Luke. 'I said he made his money in oil, which is true, but oil futures and trading, not getting it out of the ground. He's a financier, puts deals together. But he's also very philanthropic. He believes that education is everything.'

'Sounds good.' I nod in agreement.

'It is, though there's always more to be done. We have fantastic volunteers and the PR and fund-raising staff are amazing. I prefer to keep in the background, to be honest, though I enjoy negotiating with our sponsors.'

'I like negotiations too,' I agree. 'Although mine would be a lot less humanitarian than yours.'

'I spend a lot of time dealing with applications for funding, too,' Luke elaborates. 'What happens is that other social projects come to us to see if we can help with cash flow. We have to make sure it's a sustainable project and that there will be long-term benefits.'

I nod again, even though I doubt that Luke sees it. He's still concentrating on the road. I'm not really surprised he ended up working for some kind of charitable organisation. He was always better at giving things away than keeping them for himself. That was the big difference between him and the rest of his family. Maybe it still is.

We lapse into silence and then Luke turns on the radio. The music, more classical guitar, is vaguely familiar. It's slow and haunting and seems to embrace the warmth of the sun on the vine-clad hills through which we're driving. Like the flamenco, it reaches inside of me in a way I wasn't expecting and wraps itself around my soul.

It seems like an age since I was presenting to the board of Ecologistics. To be honest, it feels like a different life. A different me. Because ever since then, I've been the girl who sleeps late, who wants to dance flamenco in a red dress, who has coffee and Nutella in a village square and who's moved almost to tears by a random piece of music. Of course, I remind myself, I'm also the girl who had cocktails on a rooftop bar and who is – even now – being driven in one of the most gorgeous cars in the entire world. I haven't become some kind of hippy-freaky sobbing vegetarian. I've just been . . . different. And I don't know if that's because of Luke or because every once in a while, everyone needs to be someone else.

We've reached the outskirts of Seville and I glance at my watch. It's almost quarter to two. I told Luke that the train left at two, but it actually departs at a quarter past. I wanted some leeway in case something happened. I can't afford to miss it again.

'Don't worry,' says Luke. 'I'll get you there in plenty of time.'

'I wasn't worried,' I tell him.

He smiles, and a moment later he's pulling in to the train station. He parks the car, gets out and then takes my case from the boot. Already people are shooting admiring glances at the Aston.

'I'll come in with you,' says Luke. 'Make sure you don't miss it.'

I fess up about the time and he grins.

'I knew that. I checked the timetable earlier.'

'Why didn't you say?'

'I didn't want you to think I doubted you. You used to hate it when I never took you at your word.'

I say nothing.

In the glorious sunshine it's less chaotic outside the station than it was yesterday. We walk the length of the concourse to the platform where, once again, the gleaming white train is waiting. They haven't started boarding yet. This time, I'm early.

'Coffee?' suggests Luke, and I shake my head. The heady brew from Fuente del Rio is still working its way through my system. I might have allowed myself to be soothed into silence by the music earlier, but I'm far from relaxed. So all we do is stand side by side as a short queue begins to form.

'It's like assembly at school,' he remarks, and I laugh. Even though there's been an occasional frisson of tension between us, it's also proved remarkably easy being with him. We're still friends. We should stay in touch.

Finally the Renfe employees arrive and open the gate. The queue moves forward and I take my ticket out of my bag.

'Well,' I say to Luke. 'Thank you so much for everything.

For letting me stay in Anita's apartment. For bringing me out last night. For today's trip. It was all wonderful.'

'You're very welcome.'

I'm about to ask him for his phone number, but I hesitate. We can't really be friends. Not in our current lives.

'I'm so glad we bumped into each other,' adds Luke.

'Me too.'

It's been wonderful, to be honest, but we're different people now. I twirl my engagement ring on my finger. He notices.

'Good luck with the wedding,' he says. 'I hope you'll be very happy together.'

'We will. And you enjoy the one you're going to today.'

'I'm sure it'll be fun.'

Most of the other passengers have passed through the gate by now. I have to go too. At least this time we know we're saying goodbye.

I give him a hug as I say the word, and he hugs me in return. The memories come flooding back. I don't care that I was only a kid. He was my best friend and, even though I never really thought about it until the day before he left, I loved him. We look at each other and I know he's remembering too. His eyes are fixed on mine and I can't break away from him. He kisses me on the cheek. I kiss him on the cheek. He kisses me on the other cheek. I do nothing, just explore his face with my eyes, and then he kisses me on the lips.

I wasn't expecting this. I didn't know that my entire body would be overcome by passion. I never guessed that I could want something, someone, so much. I'm melting in his arms and I don't want it to stop. I hold him tighter and tighter and he keeps me close to him. I know that this is

152

one perfect moment in my life. That even if I meet a better kisser, I will never have a better kiss.

'*Perdonen.*'

The voice of the train employee breaks the bubble that has surrounded us. Luke loosens his grip on me and I begin to breathe again.

'*Perdonen.*' I don't understand her but I know what she is saying. That the gate is about to close so that the train can leave on time. But I can't go. Not now. Not after that kiss.

'Your train,' says Luke.

'I know.'

'You don't want to miss it, do you?'

I look at him in confusion. Doesn't he want me to stay? Doesn't he want me to come to the wedding with him? Doesn't he want . . . and then I come back to earth and I realise that this has been a wonderful interlude but that's all. Because Luke has his life and I have mine, and I'm already in love with Chris Bennett and I'm getting married to him very soon. And that I might have been a different person today and yesterday but tomorrow I am going to be myself again.

'*Señores?*' The employee looks at us expectantly.

'Goodbye, Luke.' I wriggle from his arms and hand my ticket to the woman standing at the gate. And then I walk down the platform and get on the train.

Almost immediately, it begins to move away.

As we begin to pick up speed, my phone rings. For a split second I think it's Luke, and then I remember that we haven't exchanged phone numbers. Besides, it's Chris's ringtone.

'Hi.' My head is still in the kiss and it's not fair that I'm thinking how Chris has never kissed me like that. It was a one-off, a mad moment. It wasn't real. 'How're you?'

'Hung-over.' Chris groans. 'After we talked, I went back to the party and got into a conversation with Patrick Reilly. Well, you know what he's like . . .' He continues to talk, and I'm listening, but at the same time I'm running the tips of my fingers over my lips. They feel like they're swollen. For the first time in my life, I think, I might have pouty lips. And that's without having to buy expensive potions that sting but don't really do anything.

'. . . sorry you weren't there,' finishes Chris.

Huh? What did he say?

'I'm sorry too.' It's a gamble and it half pays off.

'I know. But it would've been good to have you to watch my back with Patrick.'

Patrick, who is one of Chris's former colleagues, fancies me. Well, maybe that's not it exactly, but he always flirts with me and Chris doesn't mind because it means that he can extricate himself from Patrick, who is a massive bore. This means that I'm left with him, but it's never for long because I've perfected the art of smiling sweetly and telling him that I really have to go now.

'You're OK to pick me up tonight?' I ask.

'I will be by the time you get in,' says Chris. 'Though it's just as well I don't have surgery tomorrow. It takes me too long to completely recover from an alcohol-fuelled night these days.'

If he'd had surgery, Chris wouldn't have got drunk at his mother's birthday party. He's too professional for that. He knows it and so do I.

'Are you going to stay with me tonight?' I need him to. I need to be back in my own life with the man I love now.

'Of course I am.'

'I'm looking forward to being home.'

'Yes.' Chris's voice softens. 'And I'm looking forward to having you home. It's been a long time.'

I've never been parted from him for as long as this before. Yesterday, after the meeting, I'd been counting down the hours until my return. Now . . . now it's a new countdown. I run my fingers over my lips again.

'Love you Lots,' he adds.

I love him too. I don't know what came over me earlier. I should never have allowed Luke to kiss me. I should never have kissed him back. But it happened, and it shocked me, and I have to forget about it. Which I will.

The train is now travelling away from Seville at 245 kph.

And I know that's a good thing.

Chapter 11

Entre Dos Aguas (Between Two Waters) – José de Córdoba

I am, of course, way too early for my flight but I go directly from the train station to the airport and settle down with a magazine to pass the time. Yet I can't get Luke Evans and that kiss out of my head. If he'd kissed me like that when I was fifteen, I'd never have got over him. And if he'd felt the same way, maybe he wouldn't have gone. Or perhaps he would have defied his parents and phoned me. Everything might have been totally different.

I remind myself that a kiss is just a sensation. A reaction. Chemicals. Pheromones. It's not important because Luke isn't important. Besides, if it had been as great as I'm imagining, I wouldn't have got on the train, and Luke wouldn't have let me go. I have to get my head around the fact that this was a random moment. It shouldn't even have happened.

In the past I've been scathing about my male colleagues who engage in a bit of offside behaviour when they're away. My firm view is that they should think of their wives or girlfriends and that falling for the charms of an unknown girl for one night is both tawdry and disrespectful. For all my puritanical views, it seems I'm as bad as they are. I've been disrespectful of Chris. And regardless of the past, Luke Evans is a virtual stranger! Even though I haven't slept with him . . . I exhale slowly and thank God I didn't sleep with him. Because I don't know if I could ever get over the guilt. Not when a simple kiss has reduced me to a near wreck.

But it isn't just the kiss, wonderful though it was. It's how I felt with Luke. Relaxed, happy, as though we were still best friends. As though we still knew everything we needed to know about each other. Which is stupid, of course, because we know nothing about each other any more, nothing about our lives apart.

How could I have kissed him? What on earth was I thinking?

I feel that my guilt must be branded across my forehead, but when I walk into the Arrivals hall at Dublin airport, Chris doesn't recoil from me in shocked disgust. He greets me at the barrier, kisses me quickly on the cheek and leads me to the car park. He hasn't picked up any guilty vibes from my still tender lips. He's busy feeding coins into the ticket machine, loading my case into the boot of the Volvo and chatting away about Dorothea's party. His hangover, he says, has gone. But it was the worst he's ever had.

'So how was your unexpected night in Seville?' he asks.

'I would've preferred to be here,' I reply. 'Was your mother really angry with me?'

'Angry?' He turns on to the motorway. 'She wasn't angry. Disappointed, of course.'

'Did she say anything?'

'Like what?'

'That I was undependable? That I didn't care?'

'Don't be silly.'

And yet he doesn't say she didn't. I bet she did. I know that's how she thinks of me. And she's right, because I couldn't be depended upon and because last night I didn't actually care that I was missing her party. I was too busy watching flamenco and knocking back mojitos to care. I'm a horrible, horrible person.

'Tired?'

'A bit.'

'Never mind. Home soon.'

Things will be different when we're home. I'll be back in my life again. And I'll remember what's really important to me.

Chris has already been to my house. The lights are on, music is playing and there's a bottle of champagne on ice on the dining room table.

'Welcome home,' he says. 'I've missed you.'

And before I have time to do anything else, his arms are around me and he's sliding my jacket from my shoulders. Two passionate kisses from two different men in the same day wasn't in any of my life plans! And yet it's happening. I've clearly been hiding my wanton hussy light under a bushel all this time. However, it's my fiancé's kiss that's the important one. I've missed him all the time I was away. I've missed the scent of him and the familiarity of him, the comfort of him. And the passion, too. Different, obviously, from Luke's passion. But passion all the same. In fact Chris is currently being passionate enough to practically undress me in the kitchen.

'Upstairs, I think.' I gasp the words and he nods briefly, then picks me up and carries me to the bedroom. It's all very caveman and proprietorial, but it's nice too. It's good to know that he wants me so much.

Our lovemaking is quick and breathless, and afterwards, lying in the tangle of sheets, I tell myself that in Seville, for the briefest of times, I stepped out of my real life. And now it's time to step back in again. There's no other life you're meant to lead. There's only the one you have. Everyone makes mistakes. The important thing is not to let them define you. I can't let my silliness with Luke Evans mess with my head. And I won't.

Chris goes downstairs and returns with the champagne. We drink a glass and he says that he probably should have poured it over me and drunk it from my body.

'Which sounds good in principle,' I remark, 'but in practice would probably be very messy and a desperate waste of champagne.'

'I know.' Chris tops up my glass 'That's why I didn't do it.'

'I'm surprised you can drink anything if you had a hangover today.'

'Hair of the dog,' he says. 'After the Solpadeine.'

'I'm sure it's not good for you.'

'Every so often we all have to do something that's not good for us.'

Absolutely. He got drunk. I kissed a man. Now both of us are recovering.

Chris falls asleep before his glass is empty. I take it from his fingers and put it on the locker. Then I get out of bed and pull on my fluffy bathrobe. He's out for the count. I retrieve my suitcase and bring it upstairs. I unpack my clothes, hanging my suits in the wardrobe and bundling laundry into the basket to be dealt with later. Chris is snoring gently, undisturbed by any sounds I'm making. I think about getting into bed, but I'm wide awake. I know there's no chance of falling asleep and so I go into the bathroom and run a bath. I tip in some of my favourite bath oil and then lower my body into it. It's peaceful and relaxing but I'm as wide awake as ever.

I stop myself from wondering if Luke is too.

I'm definitely not the woman who sleeps for hours any more, because, after finally getting into bed and nodding off at around four, I open my eyes at seven o'clock and I'm instantly awake again. Chris is buried deep beneath the duvet and I get out of bed without disturbing him. He has a late start to his clinic this morning and there's no need for him to be up yet. I leave a note on the table telling him I'll call him later and thanking him again for picking me up last night and having champagne waiting. I feel a rush of affection for him as I think of him setting up the champagne and putting on the music before driving out to the airport. I'm lucky to have him.

I'm out of the house and in the office before eight. Cadogan Consulting is conveniently located on the opposite side of the quays to Chris's clinic. Sive's office isn't far from the clinic either – sometimes it seems to me that we inhabit a village, not a city. I'll call Sive later, try to meet up with her for lunch. Maybe I can unload some of the guilt I still feel on her. She's good at putting things in perspective.

But right now I go into Dirk's office and accept his congratulations on the Ecologistics contract. We talk about the plan that's been devised for them, and then we have a general chat about current and prospective clients, after which he hands me a report to read.

'I have to give a talk about this next week,' he says. 'Could you go through it and paraphrase it for me?'

I nod, although I'd rather be driving through the countryside of Andalucia than reading turgid reports. Dirk has this idea that I can speed-read my way through things no matter how often I tell him I can't. He gets it from the movies or TV shows he's seen where people with photographic memories glance at a sheet of paper and instantly recall every word. It doesn't matter how many times I tell him it doesn't work like that, I'm still the one who gets the heavy reading. But I do remember it. That's the thing.

On the way back to my own office, I stop at the coffee machine. Ian McKenzie, one of my colleagues, is ahead of me, and he congratulates me on the Ecologistics account. Ian and I were both in the running for it and I know that, more than anyone, his feelings are divided over my success. I thank him for his good wishes and ask about his own clients. He wastes ten minutes of my time telling me what a good job he's doing for them and I'm glad to escape to my desk with my coffee.

I sit there with the report in front of me, but I don't read it. I sip my coffee and gaze out of the window. I have a slender view of the river and I can see the sparkle of the sun on the gunmetal water. The music that was playing in the car as Luke drove me to the train station is now playing in my head. I can't seem to dislodge it. It keeps bringing me back to the twisting roads of Fuente del Rio. I can practically smell the leather of the Aston Martin and I have the feeling that if I turn around I'll see Luke beside me.

I haul myself back to the present. I take a large gulp of coffee and open the report. Every so often I'm interrupted by colleagues who drop in to give me the thumbs-up on Ecologistics. I know that, like Ian, their congratulations are tempered by their own desire to beat my ass into the ground when it comes to securing contracts for Cadogan. It's a competitive environment to work in and I'm perfectly aware that although getting new business is always welcomed, many of my co-workers are also seething at the fact that it was me, not them, who landed it. I feel the same way when someone else brings in a major account. Pleased, but a bit jealous too. It's pathetic, but I can't help it. I wonder if all businesses are like this or if it's just Cadogan. Dorothea might have a point about filthy commerce if that's the case.

I finish reading the report, most of which I can now remember perfectly, and call up my diary. I check my schedule for the rest of the month. Lots of internal meetings are already pencilled in, which makes me groan. Many business-people (mainly men, it has to be said) like meetings because it makes them feel important. They thrive on being round a table with lots of others, fighting to have their voice heard and generally talking for the sake of it. I don't. I like a relaxed environment where anything that needs to be discussed is discussed, and then we get on with the rest of the day. But it never seems to work out like that. The other reason I don't like big, formal meetings is that I'm still afraid of being found out. Of not being able to hold my own. Of letting the sister-hood down.

It's not that I'm the complete opposite of Dorothea, a dyed-in-the-wool feminist who believes that we should be breaking through that glass ceiling at every available opportunity. You have to choose your battles and decide what's right for you. But the truth is that the majority of the business world is still horribly misogynistic, and any woman who believes otherwise is deluding herself.

Normally I don't care about the unfairness of it all. Today I'm wondering if it's actually worth it. I pick up the phone to my ball-breaking female friend.

'How'd it go?' asks Sive. 'Did you wow them all with your brilliance?'

'Not sure about the brilliance part, but we got the business,' I reply.

'Well done you,' says Sive. 'I had every confidence.'

'I wasn't all that convinced that the bilingual presentation would work,' I confess. 'But they were really happy with it, even though I felt a total fraud.'

'Who cares?' Sive has the kind of confidence that I still lack. 'You got the deal, that was the main thing. But more importantly . . .' her voice becomes less brisk and more confidential, 'how did Dorothea's party go?'

My friend is fully up to speed on my fragile relationship with my future mother-in-law. She was the one who suggested the enormous bouquet of flowers.

'Ah, well.' I proceed to tell her about missing the train and, like everyone who knows me, she's totally shocked.

'I can't believe you slept during the day,' she says for about the fifth time. 'It's just not you, Carlotta.'

'I know.'

'Did Chris freak out?'

'He was understanding,' I say. 'Supposedly Dorothea was understanding too.'

'Hah!' Sive is unconvinced. 'As if.'

'I know. He so wants to believe that we get on.'

'One day you're going to have to point out the impossibility of that to him.'

'I keep thinking that maybe one day we will.'

She snorts. She's never met Dorothea, but I've spoken enough about her for Sive to know that a warm and loving relationship between the two of us is never going to happen.

'How are you fixed for lunch?' I ask. 'I want to give you all the gory globetrotting details.'

Sive likes hearing about business negotiations. She prefers watching programmes like *Newsnight* and *Question Time* to *Strictly Come Dancing* and *X Factor*. I'm not a *Strictly* or *X Factor* girl myself, but political programmes either bore me to tears or leave me shouting at the TV screen in frustration. My relaxation TV of choice is cookery shows. Maybe it's because I know that decent cooking is something I'll never be able to do myself. My planner is full of *Masterchef* and *Bake Off* programmes for my nights in.

'Tied up all week,' she says cheerfully. 'How about a bite to eat? Wednesday evening? At mine?'

'Sounds great,' I say.

'Can't wait,' she tells me. 'It's ages since we met.'

With a bit of luck I'll have got over my stupidity by the time I see Sive and we won't have to talk about Luke Evans at all.

Chris rings later in the afternoon, when I'm doing a second read-through of the mind-numbing report. He tells me that he's arranged for us to see Dorothea tonight, so that I can apologise in person for missing her party. I knew that sooner or later I'd have to do this and I suppose it's better to get it over and done with, although I'd planned a quiet evening in to catch up on my housework. It's not that I'm a domestic goddess or anything like it, but whenever I come home after being away, I indulge in a bout of intense cleaning. Sive says that I'm nesting, making the place my own again, and maybe she's right. I can't help thinking a couple of hours with Mr Sheen and a cloth is preferable to a couple of hours at the sharp end of Dorothea's tongue. But maybe she really does understand. Maybe she'll be nice.

Chapter 12

Serenata Española (Spanish Serenade) – Pepe Romero

Dorothea's two-storey over-basement house is typical of Rathgar's elegant red-brick buildings. The garden is enclosed by plain railings and filled with a variety of evergreen shrubs. The steps up to the door are worn from age, and lead to a tiled porch area. You can tell from the shining brass letterbox and knocker that the interior of the house is going to be equally well maintained, and it is.

When Chris opens the door, we walk into the carpeted hallway. The entire house is carpeted, which seems odd in these days of wood floors and rugs, but it generates a feeling of warmth and luxury. My fiancé then ushers me into the front room, which is the family's living area. This room connects with a formal dining room to the rear, which in turn leads to the large, surprisingly modern kitchen which Dorothea had installed when Pen took up residence in the self-contained basement flat below

Chris leaves me alone while he goes in search of his mother. Dorothea spends a lot of her free time in a south-facing first-floor room which is her private domain. I was allowed in there once – there's a reclining chair and a wall-mounted TV, as well as a small desk with a computer. Dorothea is very computer literate, and she spends a lot of her time posting comments on the online stories of a wide variety of news sources. Her username is Swordof Justice, which I once remarked sounded like an al-Qaeda alias. She didn't think it was funny. The walls of Dorothea's den are covered in framed photos, mainly of family and friends in younger years. There's also a fairly large bookshelf laden with worthy literary novels – although in the brief moment I had to check it out, I spotted the *Fifty Shades of Grey* trilogy nestling between Salman Rushdie and J. M. Coetzee. The idea of Dorothea as a submissive is just too hard to picture, although seeing the erotic novels made me think of the Sword of Justice in a whole new light.

In contrast to her hideaway, the room I'm in is decorated with an eye to visitors, with dark blue wallpaper, wing-backed chairs and occasional tables containing her *objets d'art*. There are oil paintings on the walls and the drapes at the windows are heavy velvet. There's a large mirror in an ornate gilt frame over the mantelpiece. A nod to the fact that people actually sit in here is the TV in the corner, but it's the only modern thing in the room. I always sit down as soon as possible so that I don't accidentally knock over a piece from her priceless china collection. I often think that it must be really weird for Chris to come from this elegant house to my own cheerfully modern home. He's never said anything about the difference and I've never asked him.

After about five minutes, which I spend staring at the empty grate, recalling some of the report I read earlier just to be sure it's fixed in my mind, Dorothea walks into the room. She looks serene and elegant in an aquamarine Louise Kennedy dress and matching cardigan. She's followed by Chris and Pen. Dorothea gives me a polite hello and Pen offers an equally polite smile.

'Where's Lisa?' I ask, although as soon as the words are out of my mouth I realise that the first thing I should have done was wish Dorothea a belated happy birthday.

'She went back to London this morning,' says Pen.

'I'm sorry to have missed her,' I say. 'And I'm so sorry, Dorothea, to have missed your party. I brought you this.' I delve into my bag and take out the enormous bottle of Chanel I picked up for her at Madrid Barajas airport. I know she likes it.

'How thoughtful,' says Dorothea as she unwraps it. 'Another perfume.'

Don't tell me everyone bought her Chanel. Have people no imagination!

She leaves it on the mantelpiece and then opens the door to the dining room. It's dominated by a long mahogany table, which has been set for four. I'm reminded of *Downton Abbey* or any of those Agatha Christie movies set in grand old houses. Dorothea's is obviously a lower-key affair, but the atmosphere is still the same.

I hadn't realised we were going to eat at Dorothea's, but as I haven't had anything since a wrap at lunchtime, my stomach rumbles at the anticipation of food.

The table is far too big for four people, but we're sitting close together. Pen brings in an enormous pot of mussels and a large bowl of salad. My rumbling stomach is disappointed. I don't like mussels, or any kind of shellfish. Chris knows this but I'm not sure Dorothea does. I spoon a couple on to my plate for show, then help myself to the salad and a slice of brown bread from the basket in front of me.

'Was it a late night in the end?' I ask, moving the pot so that my plate is hidden from her.

'Of course,' she replies. 'It was so wonderful to have my family and friends all together in my home, I didn't want it to end.'

I nod as I glance around. You'd never think there'd been a party here. The place is pristine. I say so.

'We had the cleaners in,' says Pen.

'Already?' She's an efficient woman, I have to concede that. 'And impressive that you've managed to get dinner organised tonight too. Thank you.'

Dorothea shoots me a look that says I'm laying it on a bit thick.

'Did you enjoy your party?' I opt for a simple, safe question.

'It was a memorable night,' Dorothea says. 'Though Chris missed a lovely moment when a very old friend and I did a tango together.'

A tango! I can't imagine Dorothea lost in the passion of a tango.

'He was on the phone to you,' Dorothea adds.

'I was trying hard to keep in touch,' I explain.

'A bit difficult given that you were two thousand kilometres away,' remarks Dorothea.

'I know.' There's no point in making flippant remarks about the world being a smaller place these days or technology bringing us closer. She doesn't care. She just wants to make me feel bad. Thing is, I don't any more. It's over and done with.

'So tell us about your jaunt around the world,' says Pen.

'I was working,' I remind her. 'It wasn't a jaunt.'

'Still – you were in Rio, weren't you? That must have been lovely.'

'Buenos Aires,' I amend. 'It was surprisingly cold.'

'We've had some lovely weather,' says Dorothea.

'I'm glad to be home.'

'I didn't think your job would take you away for so long,' she says.

'It doesn't usually. But we were trying to do our best for the client. It's a great contract to win and the company is very pleased with me.' I can't help boasting a little.

'Did you get much free time?' she asks.

I think about the unexpected time in Seville and I feel my face flame. But Dorothea doesn't seem to notice as I say that I was too busy to have free time.

'You won't be able to stay away for weeks when you're married,' she tells me. 'You can't leave your husband at the drop of a hat.'

I shoot a glance at Chris and I'm glad to see that he looks amused. I raise an eyebrow at him and he joins the conversation.

'If Carlotta has to go away, she has to go away,' he says mildly. 'But it's highly unlikely she'll have any more trips like that in the future. It was because her client has offices overseas that she had to go to South America.'

'And Europe,' adds Pen.

'Mostly I just get stuck with Ireland and the UK,' I remind them. 'It's usually the men who bag the exotic locations.'

Although, like I've said before, going abroad on business isn't really exotic. You don't get to go with friends and you don't get to do the things you'd do if you were on holiday. To be honest, it's a chore. Very few people realise that.

'That's a good thing,' says Dorothea. 'When you're married, you'll have to be a greater support to Chris.'

The old bat is only saying this sort of sexist stuff to rile me. I've learned not to rise to the bait, so I tell her that Chris and I are mutually supportive of each other.

'Nevertheless, his career is undoubtedly more important than yours.'

She never shuts up about it. The great Chris Bennett, sight-saver extraordinaire, will always be far more important than me. I already know that. He *is* a brilliant ophthalmologist. He *is* more important than me. I just don't need her to ram it down my throat.

'Give it a rest, Mum,' says Chris. 'Lottie works hard and she deserves her success.'

'Can you call it a success when all you do is lose people their jobs?' asks Pen.

'You don't always have to be so down on what I do!' I exclaim. 'When companies have to streamline their staff, it's because they've let it all get out of control. That's not a reason to treat me as though I was some kind of satanic figure raining hell down on everyone I meet.'

'There's no need to get hysterical,' says Dorothea. 'We all realise how vital your role apparently is.'

I'm grinding my teeth. I try to stop, because my doctor told me ages ago that my interrupted sleep might be caused by my teeth-grinding. Which I'm not completely convinced about, but still. I wonder if it's always going to be like this. If she'll ever accept me as the girl her only son has chosen. And then I remember that I'm not a girl, I'm a grown woman who is respected by her friends and colleagues and I don't need Dorothea's approval at all. And I think that maybe it was a good thing I wasn't at her stupid party where I might have had too much to drink and told her some home truths.

'What was Seville like?' asks Pen. 'I've always wanted to go there.'

I'm grateful to her for diverting the conversation, although remembering Seville is a slippery slope that leads me to the kiss at Santa Justa station. But I tell them that it was lovely and I talk about the cathedral and the bell tower and the way the sky changed from grey to blue in an instant. As I talk, I'm there again.

'So are you all right?' Pen looks at me. 'You weren't badly injured in the car crash or anything?'

I don't know how serious Chris made it out to be.

'A little shaken up.' I rub the back of my neck. 'And I'm a bit sore too. But I'm sure it's fine.'

'You should see a doctor,' says Dorothea. 'Whiplash can be extremely debilitating.' She goes on to tell a long story about a friend who had her neck in a brace for months. 'You should have made a report to the police.'

'I was rushing for the train.' At least I'm on confident ground here. 'I didn't have time.'

'Fleeing the scene of an accident.' Chris speaks with mock severity and I look rueful.

'Finished?' asks Pen.

We all nod and she stands up.

'Let me help.' I don't want her to see my uneaten mussels, so I quickly put Chris's plate on top of mine. In my haste I knock over a glass of wine, which soaks both me and the tablecloth.

For crying out loud, I think. I'm a successful, competent woman. Why do I only do stupid things in front of someone who dislikes me as much as Dorothea? I apologise profusely.

'You idiot.' But Chris's words are amused, not annoyed. 'You've ruined your blouse.'

It's red silk and it's now a mess.

'I'll get you something else to wear,' says Pen.

'There's no need . . .'

'Yes there is.' She picks up the plates and carries them into the kitchen. I follow her down the stairs and through the door that leads to her basement flat. I've never been in here before and I'm surprised to see that, like the kitchen but not the rest of the house, it's modern and spartan. More modern than my own home, for sure. There are no girlie touches – no pink fluffy cushions or swagged curtains. No candles or fairy lights. The sofa is black leather with matching leather cushions, the windows have slatted venetian blinds and the lights are recessed into the ceiling, although there's a stainless-steel reading lamp arching over the sofa.

'Wait here.' Pen opens another door while I slide my soaked blouse from my shoulders. I can't remember the last time I knocked over a glass of wine. I'm usually very careful about things like that.

Pen returns a moment later with a plain white T-shirt, which she offers me. I put it on. Pen is a size bigger than me, but it's fine.

'Thanks,' I say.

'Happy to help.'

I feel I should say something else, something funny and confiding so that we can bond over my clumsiness, but she's

173

so like Dorothea that I can't come up with anything at all. Instead I simply pick up my blouse.

'Leave it,' says Pen. 'It can go to the laundry along with the tablecloth and everything else.'

'The laundry?' I look at her in surprise. 'Do laundries still exist? It's fine, I'll wash it at home.'

'Mum uses a laundry service,' she says. 'So you might as well avail yourself of it.'

I don't want Dorothea laundering my blouse. I tell Pen that I'll get it cleaned at the dry cleaner's near the office. She shrugs and hands me a plastic bag for the blouse and walks out of the basement. I follow her back into the kitchen again.

'Was your mum very upset that I didn't make her party?' I ask as she picks up one of the plates we brought in earlier and begins to empty the shells into a bin.

'Truthfully, I don't think it bothered her.' Pen's honesty hurts, even though I'd comforted myself by thinking that Dorothea wouldn't have cared much about my absence. 'It was frustrating that we had to rearrange the bouquet ceremony.'

Bouquet ceremony! What is it with these people? Chucking some flowers at Dorothea was hardly the same as negotiating a peace treaty, for heaven's sake. Or making an important presentation at the crack of dawn. Why do they have to make such a big deal about everything? Why does Pen have to sound exactly like her mother? I wonder if she means to. I realise that I don't know Chris's younger sister at all. Does she believe the same things as Dorothea? Did she really care about the bouquet?

'*Buenos días, señores.*' The opening words are still in my head,

174

along with the slide showing a picture of the Ecologistics head office. '*Me llamo Carlotta O'Keeffe.*'

'And Chris was very upset,' adds Pen as she slices an apple tart.

'So was I,' I tell her. 'I nearly had a heart attack running for the damn train and I was in a complete frazzle for the rest of the day.'

'You? Frazzled?' Pen looks at me in disbelief. 'I really don't think so.'

'Why wouldn't I be?' I demand. 'I didn't want to be stuck in Seville for the night.'

'You would've preferred to be here?'

'Of course.'

Pen places a slice of apple tart in the exact centre of the delicate china plate she's taken out of a cupboard.

'I didn't think you liked us very much,' she says.

'Why on earth would you think that?'

'The way you look at Mum.'

'Huh?'

'All condescending and arrogant.'

'What!'

'You look down on her because she was a stay-at-home mother and you look down on Lisa and me because we don't have high-flying careers like you.'

'You're joking, right? I look down on you? It's your mum who thinks you're all too good for me. She thinks Chris is marrying beneath him. That my job is worthless in comparison to his.' The words tumble out of my mouth.

'Nonsense,' says Pen. I suddenly realise how like Dorothea she looks as well as sounds. She has the same narrow face and high cheekbones, and if she put her straight-cut shoulder-length hair up into the chignon that Dorothea habitually wears, they'd be even more alike. There's a quiet confidence about the Bennetts and their place in the world that I simply don't have, and it intimidates me in a way that a group of directors around a board table doesn't.

'Every time you walk into this house you want to boss us around. Make us more efficient. You do the same to Chris,' she continues, fixing me with a stare from her blue-grey eyes.

'I do not!'

'You look at us as though we're lazy employees.'

I don't. I really don't.

'None of us thought you'd turn up to Mum's party, and we were right.'

'None of you?' I'm aghast. 'Chris didn't either?'

'He had his doubts. After all, you heading off on that so-called business trip for three weeks was very bad timing.'

'I had to go,' I say. 'It's my job.'

'Well, we thought you should've been more supportive of Chris. And Mum.'

OK, this is ridiculous. I'm totally supportive of Chris. As he was of me having to go abroad. At least, I thought he was.

'Amanda supported him more,' says Pen.

Chris never talks about Amanda. I've never talked about my previous boyfriends to him either. We don't ask. We're more mature than that.

'But they split up,' I counter. 'So it didn't come to much, did it?'

Pen tosses her head dismissively. She's a really difficult person. All the Bennett women are difficult. Maybe that's why they don't have men in their lives. This thought comforts me immensely. I'm about to speak again when Pen picks up two plates and walks off towards the dining room, leaving me no option but to follow her.

Chris and Dorothea are talking about people at the party, people I don't know. They break off long enough for Chris to say that I look good in Pen's T-shirt and then Dorothea restarts their conversation. I listen, although inside I'm mulling over Pen's remarks. They can't possibly be intimidated by me, can they? I'm too small to be intimidating! That's why I wear skyscraper heels in the office.

As I look at Pen, demurely passing the plates around, I decide that, like her mother, she enjoys riling me. I jab my fork into my slice of apple pie. Maybe I'm not supportive of the female coven of Bennetts, but I'm very supportive of Chris. And his past with Amanda doesn't matter, just as my past with Luke (such as it was) doesn't matter either. The important thing is that we're together now and we love each other. And what I need to remember is that it's him I'm marrying. Not his damn mother. Or his sisters!

It's late by the time Chris and I leave Dorothea's, and neither of us speaks much on the journey back to Harold's Cross. There's not much time for talk anyway; it's less than ten minutes door to door.

Once we're inside, I put the kettle on and pop a slice of bread in the toaster. Despite the generous slice of apple tart, I'm starving. Salad and brown bread wasn't enough for dinner.

'D'you want some?' I ask Chris, and he shakes his head.

'I'm sure she didn't mean to serve mussels,' he says.

I ignore that comment and pour boiling water over the tea bag.

'Really, Lottie.' He puts his arms around me. 'She's thoughtless, that's all.'

'She thinks I'm arrogant and condescending.'

'What?'

I've thrown him; he's completely taken aback.

'Pen as much as said so.'

'Pen did?' He sounds incredulous.

'When I was changing into the T-shirt. She lectured me about my responsibilities to the Bennett family.'

Chris laughs.

'It's not funny,' I say. 'She told me that you all doubted I'd make it to Dorothea's party.'

'You were cutting it fine,' he reminds me. 'And . . . we were right. You didn't.'

'Even you thought so?' I'm really upset by this. He should've had faith in me. Admittedly, it would've been misplaced, but missing the train wasn't my fault.

'I just thought something might happen. And it did.'

I hate them being proved right about me. Partly right, at any rate. Because I don't look down on them. I just don't understand them! And they clearly don't understand me.

'Nonsense,' says Chris when I tell him this. 'We all have different views on things. But we get on fine.'

'I'm not sure your mum even wants to get on fine with me,' I mutter.

'She's not that bad.'

'Isn't she?' I begin buttering the toast. 'I'm worried that she's going to be the mother-in-law from hell.'

'Lottie!'

I turn to him and I know my anxiety is etched on my face.

178

'Really,' I say. 'Her attitude towards me tonight was frigid. She's pissed off at me for missing her party. She doesn't think I'm a suitable wife for you and she tried to poison me with mussels.'

Chris looks at me as though I'm a cranky toddler. 'She was disappointed about the party,' he says. 'She's an old-fashioned woman. She thinks that women should put their husbands' careers before their own. She's trying to understand yours, but it's not in her DNA. And she's not a demonstrative woman. She finds it difficult with people she doesn't know very well.'

'She knows me well enough by now,' I protest. 'We've been together for a year and a half!'

'That's a very short time in the life of someone who's seventy,' he reminds me. 'Honestly, Lottie, she does like you. She just needs time to let her warmth come through.'

'I suppose you're right.' I stuff some hot buttery toast in my mouth. 'And I suppose the main thing is that you love me.'

'Of course I do,' says Chris and kisses me on the nape of the neck.

I love him too.

I just want to feel secure in my life again. I want to forget about the past.

Chapter 13

Cantos de España (Songs of Spain) – Julian Bream

Wednesday is a convenient day to meet Sive, because Chris
works late on Wednesdays and I don't have to choose between
my friend and my fiancé. It's not like Chris and I live in each
other's pockets or anything, but I like to put him first when
I can. At the same time, I can talk to Sive about stuff I
wouldn't dream of mentioning to Chris. And the latest events
in my life fall very firmly into the category of girl talk.

She lives in Clontarf. On the north side of the city, Clontarf
is a kind of mirror image of Dorothea's Rathgar, another one
of those leafy suburbs with red-brick houses and big gardens.
Unlike Rathgar, there isn't a bustling village; instead Clontarf
has views over Dublin Bay. Sive and Natasha live in a house
five minutes from the seafront, and from the attic bedroom
you can just about make out the silver sheen of the water.

Sive rents the house, which is in a small enclave built in
the last ten years. The houses are smaller than their red-brick
neighbours and have patio yards rather than gracious gardens.
She and Adrian, her ex-husband, used to own an older home
nearby, but when they split up it had to be sold. It wasn't a

good time to sell: prices were on the way down and their house was at the higher end of the market, which was being hit hard. The estate agent insisted that there was still value in good homes and told them not to panic, but Sive, being both intelligent and pragmatic, said he was talking nonsense and made him put it on the market at 75K less than he was suggesting. He was horrified, but she'd done the right thing, because the house sold in less than a month. Although they didn't have any money left over after repaying their mortgage, they didn't have crushing debts either, which made them fairly unique among a lot of divorcing couples at the time. Didn't make it any easier emotionally, I suppose, but at least the lack of negative equity made things a little easier than they might otherwise have been.

As I stand on the doorstep, I think that at least this time I'll be able to eat whatever's on offer. Sive has never tried to poison me with shellfish or anything else I don't like. I also think that when I'm married I'll have to do a bit of upskilling on the home-cooking front myself. I can't depend on the unwatched episodes of *Masterchef* for inspiration, and it's embarrassing to spend so much time eating other people's food. I've never asked Dorothea or Sive to my house for dinner. But given that my current talents can only be described as adequate at best, it's not any great loss from their point of view. Still, I need to brush up on my domestic goddess credentials. Maybe I'll buy a few Nigella books. Even if I never use them, I can leave them artfully displayed around the place as I dish up heated meals from Avoca or other upmarket food halls.

Natasha answers the door, hugs me and then drags me into the kitchen, where Sive is emptying the dishwasher. I give her the bottle of wine I brought with me, and hand my god-daughter the T-shirt I bought for her in Argentina and a decorative mantilla comb I picked up in the hotel gift shop when I first arrived in Seville. Then I help Sive put away the crockery. I know where everything goes. Bramblewood is like my second home.

'It's just quiche and salad tonight,' says Sive. 'I picked the quiche up from the deli. I didn't get out of the office until late.'

'Sounds good to me,' I say, although the food is always better when Sive cooks it herself, because she's the kind of person who does everything brilliantly. Even though we have regular conversations about how scared we are that someone will discover we're winging it at work, I know she only agrees with me in order to boost my self-esteem. Nothing scares Sive. If she wasn't my best friend, I'd feel totally inadequate beside her, because she combines a properly high-powered career with raising Natasha and running her house faultlessly. I said this once and she gave me a wry smile and told me that she clearly wasn't adequate enough for Adrian, which sort of stopped me in my tracks. Nowadays I compliment her on things but I never make comparisons. She *is* amazing, though, no matter what she thinks herself.

'Please fix this in my hair.' Natasha gives me the comb and I work her long dark tresses into a coil, which I then secure. Given that my own hair has been short for years now, I'm no longer familiar with updos, but the assistant in the hotel shop showed me how to style around the comb and allowed me to practise on a doll that she kept for that very purpose.

'You look lovely,' says Sive. 'Dad will be very impressed.'

'I'm having a sleepover with him tonight,' Natasha tells me as she looks at her reflection in the mirror and then twirls around. 'I look like a princess.'

'You do indeed,' I say.

'She's a very lucky girl,' says Sive. 'Extra time with Dad, and presents from Carlotta.'

'You just want me out of the house so's you can have a gossip without worrying that I'm listening.'

I grin at my god-daughter's words and Sive gives her an exasperated look.

'It's true,' says Natasha. 'But I don't mind. Dad says I can watch all the *Toy Story* movies. Though honestly I think he likes them more than me. He's such a kid.'

'It's a school night,' Sive reminds her as I stifle another grin. 'You can watch one movie and then you have to go to bed.'

Natasha makes a face and then runs to the door as the bell sounds. When she comes back into the kitchen, she's followed by Adrian.

He's a handsome man. He's always had that brooding, soulful look about him, which these days he accentuates by leaving a few days' worth of stubble on his cheeks. He wears leather jackets and well-cut jeans and most women fancy him like crazy. Hard not to. But the truth is that he broke Sive's heart, and I won't ever forget that.

He leans against the worktop and turns his smouldering dark eyes in my direction. Honestly, the man is sex on legs. It's no wonder that he attracts women like a mobile magnet. He hooked Sive early in our college days and somehow it never mattered to her that he didn't have the same drive for success that she did. In fact, they're polar opposites in many ways.

Unlike Sive, who works really hard and has a good lifestyle as a result, Adrian wants the lifestyle without the hard work. He seems to think he's entitled to it. Shortly after Natasha was born, he quit his job at a travel company to be a stay-at-home parent and a writer. Even though I'm single and childless, I'm well aware that looking after kids can be very hard work – I've babysat Natasha lots of times when Sive has been at business functions – so I don't for a second deny that Adrian put in a lot of effort to be a really good dad, and still does. However I always felt that he played the house-husband as a tortured creative soul a little too often. He allowed Sive to feel bad about being at work all day and not being around for their daughter as much as he was. And because she's a woman and women feel guilty about everything, she perpetually felt that she wasn't pulling her weight at home. So at the weekends she would go into a frenzy of home baking and preparing dinners for the week ahead, which Adrian simply had to heat up every evening. Yet him staying at home really was the ideal solution. She earned vastly more than him, and he wanted to devote time to writing the sci-fi trilogy that he often said would be a sure-fire best-seller as well as a quick route to Hollywood. In fairness, he dreams big, although we're still waiting to see either a printed manuscript or a Hollywood deal. Thing is, even if I can't forgive him, I still like Adrian. It's impossible not to. But he certainly knows how to push Sive's buttons.

'So how are things with you, Carlotta?' he asks me. 'Any excitement in your life?'

'Lottie was away for ages,' says Natasha. 'All over the world. She bought me this for my hair – look!' She indicates the mantilla comb. 'And a T-shirt.'

'I hope you said thank you.'

Like I said, he's a good dad. He turns to me.

'Business or pleasure?'

'Business,' I reply.

'You career girls.' He gives a theatrical sigh. 'Always trying to prove yourselves.'

'Carlotta doesn't need to prove anything,' says Sive, who's polishing wine glasses. 'She brought in a great contract for her firm.'

'I'm surrounded by alpha females,' says Adrian. 'It's exhausting. I hope Chris knows what he's letting himself in for.'

Sive obviously still feels responsible in some way for her ex-husband, because she answers on my behalf, saying that Chris is lucky to have found me.

'And are you going to continue on at the coal face, or do you intend to be a hothouse mother instead?' he asks me.

'Give me a chance,' I say mildly. 'I'm not even married yet and you're imagining a whole family.'

Sometimes when I see how Sive beats herself up over Natasha, I wonder if I'll ever have a child myself. I don't think there's a mother in the world who doesn't want to do the very best job possible and who doesn't blame herself if she thinks that her standards have dropped even a smidgen. And I've become a perfectionist. What if I'm not a perfect mother? I need to think about it all very, very carefully.

That was the one thing in her life plan that Sive got wrong. In our college years we often talked about motherhood, and we both agreed that sometime in your early thirties was the optimum time.

'Although,' Sive once said, 'you do run the risk of failing to get pregnant at all.'

I think about that too, sometimes. It's so unfair that the prime time in a woman's working life is also her prime time for getting pregnant. Our biological clocks are just time bombs ticking away inside us. Sive's pregnancy, in her twenties, was unplanned. Now, even though she sometimes wonders if it would be good for Natasha to have a brother or sister, she doesn't have the time either for meeting men or for having babies.

'I'm sure you'll be an alpha mother, just like Sive,' says Adrian.

She ignores him and takes some plates out of the cupboard.

'How's the screenplay coming along?' I ask Adrian.

'Brilliantly,' he replies. 'My agent says that he has interest in it.'

He utters the word 'agent' with relish. I know it makes him feel important.

'I look forward to seeing it on the big screen.' I'm being sarcastic but I can't help it. He can be such a plonker sometimes. Thing is, I saw through him at college. I don't know why Sive never did.

They married when Natasha was two, and as far as our group of friends was concerned, they were a thoroughly modern couple. We wanted to believe that he was comfortable with being at home and we loved that he was actually writing a book, even if it was sci-fi, which some of us secretly believed wasn't real fiction at all. We (I suppose I'm only talking about the females here) also loved that Sive was powering ahead in her career and leaving most of us standing. We reckoned she was proving that even if you couldn't have it all, with the right attitude you could have a lot of it. And even though I knew about Sive's ball of guilt, I never let on that she was anything other than a hundred per cent pleased with her choices.

'But it all went horribly downhill from there,' Sive says in our maudlin moments when we mull over our ten worst decisions, or top five mistakes or whatever. 'Everything would've been fine if we hadn't tied the knot.'

I don't know about that. Their marriage broke up because Adrian had an affair. He blamed Sive because she was out so often. She said to me that he might have had a point. It took a lot of heated discussion over many bottles of wine to make her see that he was doing that classic male thing of making a woman feel responsible for something bad that he'd done. I reminded her that he could have talked to her about it instead of jumping into bed with someone else, and although she agreed with me, I know that she still felt partly to blame.

She wanted to forgive him, but in the end she couldn't. As far as she was concerned she couldn't trust him any more. She told me that it served her right for believing the hype, for thinking she was the one person who could have it all. I told her not to be stupid.

'Maybe he's right,' Sive says sometimes when she's revisiting it all with me. 'Maybe if I hadn't been so determined to get ahead, to prove myself, Adrian wouldn't have had the affair and everything would've turned out OK.'

I normally shrug when she says this. I try never to diss Adrian in front of her, but I think he was happy to hang on to Sive's coat tails when it suited him and then justified his affair by saying that she didn't look after him properly. I suppose some people would say that Adrian was no different from the stereotypical bored housewife who has an affair, but I've never supported bored housewives having affairs either.

Although they were eventually fairly civilised about everything, Sive still wonders what she could have done differently. She asks if she couldn't have tried harder to trust Adrian again. She worries that a broken marriage is damaging to Natasha.

I usually tell her that when trust is gone, there's no way back, and that Natasha is a well-adjusted girl who has adapted well to changed circumstances. But I know that Sive feels she failed as a wife and that she's constantly afraid that she'll fail as a mother, no matter how much evidence there is to the contrary.

It's not just me who wants to be perfect. All women do, and when we're not, we blame ourselves.

These days, Sive and Adrian manage to make things work, which is the most important thing. And Natasha is quite happy to go home with him tonight, leaving my friend and me to an evening alone. Sive heats up two slices of quiche in the microwave, takes some mixed salad out of the fridge and pours two glasses of wine.

'So tell me about your business deal,' she says as she sits down opposite me.

I give her a brief summary of my three weeks of hard work, and we clink glasses to celebrate landing the account.

'I'm delighted it worked out for you,' she says.

'Me too. It gets tiring being on the move all the time, so I'm glad it was worthwhile.'

'And you missed Dorothea's party because of it.' Her voice is laden with sympathy. She knows everything there is to know about my future mother-in-law. 'I can't believe you overslept. It's so not you.'

'It must have been jet lag,' I say.

'I didn't think you got jet lag, Miss Four-Hours-a-Night.'

'I sleep more than four hours a night,' I protest. 'Just not very well.'

'I suppose it's a case of every cloud and all that,' she says. 'I'm betting that a night in a luxury hotel in Seville was probably more fun than Dorothea's party anyway.'

'I'm sure it would have been.' I have to come clean to Sive. I've been aching to tell her ever since I stepped into the house. 'But I didn't stay in a hotel.'

'Huh?'

I give her the whole story then: the meeting with Luke, the Aston Martin, the apartment in the old quarter of the city, the night at the flamenco . . . and all the time her eyes are growing wider and wider. I stop before getting to the trip to Fuente del Rio.

'Let me get this straight,' she says. 'You run into an old boyfriend by chance. You go out with him. You spend the night with him and you don't say a word to Chris about it. Not that I'm surprised.' There's a hint of disapproval in her voice. I guess I'd expected that.

'It's not how it seems.'

'Oh my God, Carlotta!' This time her eyes are like dinner plates, they're open so wide. 'Adrian said that to me when I found out about Annette!'

Annette was the woman he had the affair with. She's since been replaced by . . . oh, there have been a few, so I'm not sure who the latest is. Sive's one request is that none of Adrian's women are there when Natasha stays over.

'I didn't sleep with him,' I protest. 'I need to explain . . .'

'Let's get more comfortable.' She picks up the wine bottle. 'This requires deep consideration.'

When we're ensconced in the light-filled annexe room off the kitchen, she refills our glasses and motions me to continue.

'The only time you ever mentioned Luke to me was years ago and you were totally dismissive of him,' she says.

Of course I was. I'd explained my relationship after we watched one of the Costa crime TV documentaries together. I'd told her we were neighbours and friends and that we'd gone out together once. I hadn't said anything about my heart being ripped out.

'Because we were just kids back then.'

'But . . .?' She looks at me quizzically and I run my finger around the rim of my glass.

'But . . .' I sigh. I confess that for a long time I felt cheated that Luke and I had been parted, that I dreamed of the sort of life we'd have lived together and it was hard to let it go. I mention that he's turned into a very attractive man, and then I say I was feeling hurt by Chris's annoyance over me missing the train and that—

'I thought you said you didn't sleep with him,' she interrupts me.

'I didn't. However . . .' My voice trails off and I remember the kiss at the train station. And it's as though he's here with me again, his lips pressed against mine, his arms tightly around me. The best kiss of my life.

'Carlotta?'

'It was . . . unexpected. We had time to spare before I left. He took me to this lovely mountain village. We had coffee and Nutella. He brought me to the train station. He kissed me goodbye.'

She's staring at me.

'I always wondered what it would have been like to be kissed by him,' I admit. 'I wondered if it would've made a difference.'

190

Her eyes haven't left my face.

'It was amazing,' I admit. 'I've never been kissed like that in my life before.'

She says nothing.

'It was like something out of a dream.' I'm rambling now, filling the silence with words, and I'm not sure it's a good idea to keep talking. But I do. 'Magical,' I add.

'Magical?' She's sceptical.

'Oh, I don't know.' I sigh. 'Maybe it was because I was away; maybe it was just the air in Seville or something. But in the league table of kisses, it's in the number one spot by a distance.'

She's still staring at me.

I lower my eyes and take a sip of wine.

'So what next?' she demands.

'Oh God, nothing!' I put my glass on the small table in front of me. 'Nothing next. It was a kiss, that's all. A great kiss. A magnificent kiss.' My casual smile is more wobbly than I wanted. 'The king of kisses. But that's all it was.'

'And yet you're sitting here telling me all about it and looking as though you're the heroine in a bodice-ripper.'

I don't say anything about having felt as though I was slotting into the life I should have had with Luke. Of wanting to be a flamenco dancer. I know that's nonsense.

'I'd had a lot of mojitos the night before,' I say, as though that explains everything.

'Thank God it was only the drink!' She runs her fingers through her fair hair. 'Because I was thinking there for a minute that you wanted to abandon Chris, rush back to Luke and tell him you've been waiting for him all your life.'

'I have to admit . . .'

'Jeez, Carlotta! You didn't seriously think of it, did you?'

'Not seriously,' I say. 'Not really. It was just . . . it was weird, Sive, you know? Someone you haven't seen of or thought of in years, and then they turn up out of the blue, and they're better than you ever imagined – and they look after you and it's a great night and a great morning and you feel . . . oh, I don't know. That this is how it could have been. Should have been, maybe. But then you realise it was a moment. Nothing more. All the same, it knocked me a bit.'

'So you're not in touch with this Luke guy now?'

'No. We didn't exchange numbers or anything. Besides,' I add, 'he could've been spinning me a line about working for that charity. He could be still connected to his family.'

'And is that what bothers you most? His family? Not wrapping yourself around him in public?' She's incredulous.

His family has nothing to do with how I feel about Luke. How I felt. Especially since he hardly ever sees his father now. I try to explain this, but I don't think I succeed. Sive still has a bemused expression on her face.

'If you thought that Luke was pure as the driven snow, would you want to keep in touch with him?' she asks. 'Is it only because of his dad that you have doubts?'

'No.' My answer is swift.

'So basically you just feel bad about kissing him.'

'Yes.'

'Because if Chris did the same, you'd be furious with him.'

'Yes.'

'But you've no intention of ever seeing Luke again.'

'No.'

192

'He's not going to come looking for you and you're not going looking for him.'

'Of course not.'

'In that case,' says Sive, 'I guess you have to invoke the Lambay Rules and chalk it up to experience.'

The guys in work follow the Lambay Rules all the time. They mean that what happens outside Ireland stays outside Ireland.

'You think?'

'Forget about it,' she advises. 'You made a mistake. It wasn't the worst mistake in the world. You didn't sleep with the guy. A kiss is just a kiss.'

'But you're right. If Chris kissed Amanda, I'd be incandescent with rage.' I don't want to be let off so easily. I want Sive to be as disappointed in me as I feel I should be in myself.

'Let's hope he doesn't.'

I grimace. 'It makes me such a hypocrite, doesn't it?'

'Cut yourself a bit of slack.' Her voice is suddenly warmer and more sympathetic. 'It was the end of a stressful time. Your defences were low.'

'I still wouldn't accept that as an excuse from Chris.'

'What do you want me to say?' she asks. 'That you should tell him everything?'

I can hear the horror in her voice.

'I've been thinking about it,' I tell her. 'But I know that'd only make things worse.'

'You bet it would!' she exclaims. 'You might feel marginally better for a nanosecond, and for what? For coming clean and hurting him? Why would you do that? Let it go, Lottie.'

193

'You're right.' I nod approvingly. 'I know how I feel. I love Chris. He's the best thing that ever happened to me. And we're a good couple.'

'Despite Dorothea?' Sive grins.

'Despite Dorothea,' I say, and hold out my glass for another refill.

Chapter 14

Diablo Rojo (Red Devil) – Rodrigo y Gabriela

Some time after sunset, we move from the annexe to the living room, taking the nearly empty bottle of wine with us. We've just polished it off when the doorbell rings. Sive gets up quickly to answer it while I gaze unseeingly into the unlit fire and allow my mind to drift. I tell myself that Sive is right and I should stop beating myself up over a simple mistake. And then I think that I do that all the time, not just in my personal life. If I get something wrong at work, I worry myself to death over that too. So my problem is getting things out of proportion. Not kissing Luke Evans. I'm feeling pleased with my reasoning when Sive walks back into the room. She's followed by a tall man, and as I uncurl from the armchair, I realise with a shock that I know him.

'Carlotta.' Sive looks both pleased and slightly apprehensive. 'This is Kieran. Kieran, this is my friend Carlotta.'

'Kieran.' I can't believe that another man from my past has suddenly reappeared unexpectedly. Why is this happening to me? Although in Kieran's case I don't want to be dragged into a life with him in it. And I've clearly been mistaken about Sive's busy life if she's managed to hook up with Kieran McDonagh.

'You know each other?' Sive is astonished.

'We were colleagues,' says Kieran as he keeps his eyes fixed on mine. 'A few years ago.'

'Who would've believed it!' exclaims Sive in evident pleasure.

'Who would've?' I ask.

Like I've said before, Dublin is a small town for all that it's also a capital city. It's over three years since I've seen Kieran, and I haven't thought about him once in all that time, which is, quite honestly, a good thing.

We used to work together in another consultancy firm. A bigger one than Cadogan, where there was an even greater tendency for colleagues to knife you in the back in order to further their own careers. Nevertheless, it was a prestigious company and a good name to have on my CV. I was lucky to have got a job there.

Kieran joined the year before I did, and because of that considered himself senior to me, even though we were both junior consultants working in the same division. I never took much notice of him because I was too busy concentrating on doing my job well. Most women I know concentrate on doing their jobs well, which means that sometimes they're blinded to the office politics around them. Our male colleagues, by contrast, are nearly always on top of the political situation, and far more interested in positioning themselves favourably than actually getting the job done. I realise that's a sweeping generalisation, but in my experience, it's true. I'm better at it now, but I was utterly hopeless then. However, Kieran was the ultimate politician, always trying to put himself in the frame for high-profile projects and talking himself up whenever he had the opportunity. He was supremely self-confident and certain about his position in the firm.

We had our first run-in the day he had a meeting with new prospective clients in one of the meeting rooms on our floor. I was reading through a restructuring proposal for another client when Kieran came out of the meeting room and strode across the office to my desk.

'Carlotta, I need tea and biscuits for four inside,' he said.

I stared at him.

'Quickly,' he added. 'I don't have all day.'

'I'm busy,' I told him politely. 'I promised Bernard I'd have this finished by three. And I'm not here to make tea. Why don't you ask Sarah or Anna?'

Sarah and Anna were the two PAs on our floor who looked after the admin work but who were also the providers of tea and coffee whenever we had clients in to the office.

'They're not around,' said Kieran.

'I'm busy,' I repeated.

'Oh for God's sake,' said Kieran. 'Just do it.'

'Why don't you ask Philip?' I glanced towards the meeting room. Philip O'Brien's desk was immediately outside it. Kieran had had to walk past Philip as well as two other men before arriving at my desk. Besides which, Philip was the company's most recent hire, and therefore the most junior member of staff. I knew that Kieran was asking me to make tea because I was the only woman available. But I wasn't available. I was as busy as Philip, John and Brian. Busier, in fact.

'I'm not asking Philip,' said Kieran.

'Why? What's he doing that's so urgent?'

'Look, just make the goddam tea.' Kieran was sounding pissed off now.

'Do it yourself,' I said. 'You could've picked the bloody leaves in the amount of time you've spent talking to me about it.'

'I'm not asking you to make tea,' said Kieran. 'I'm telling you.'

'Last time I looked, you weren't my boss,' I told him. 'Bernard is. And I'm working on this report for him.'

'Make the tea.'

'No.'

The two of us were glaring at each other, and I'm not sure how things would have eventually turned out, but at that moment the door of the lift opened and Sarah stepped out. Kieran looked from me to her and back again. Then he asked Sarah to make the tea.

'Don't think I've forgotten,' he said to me as he turned and went back to the meeting room.

My heart was pounding and my palms were damp. I knew that my three male colleagues were watching me. I picked up a pen and started to make notes on the file in front of me. Not surprisingly, the notes made no sense whatsoever.

After his meeting, Kieran came back to my desk.

'If you ever make a show of me like that again, you'll be sorry,' he said.

'If you ever ask me to make tea again, so will you,' I replied.

Even though I'd been shaking at the time, I put the whole incident out of my head. I put Kieran out of my head too. I didn't think he was worth the trouble. A few days afterwards, I spent the morning in the company vault, trying to trace some paperwork that Bernard wanted. It was real grunt work, and as I searched through the mounds of files, I wondered if this was what I'd slaved over my degree for. A primary school child could have looked for the papers, I thought. I should be doing something more interesting. That was when I started to wonder if, being the only female junior consultant, I was getting the shittier jobs. Just as I was beginning to feel particularly hard done by, I found the paperwork. I ran up the back stairs of the building (I'd made a pact with myself to use the stairs instead of the lift to work off the weight I was gaining owing to the fact that I was existing on takeaway food) and opened the fire door on to the third floor. John and Brian were leaning over Philip's desk, looking at his computer and laughing. They didn't notice me walking up behind them. Which meant they didn't have time to minimise the image they were looking at.

'What the—' I couldn't believe my eyes at first. And then I looked at them. They were simultaneously shamefaced and defiant.

'Which one of you did that?'

The thing about being one of the few women on a male-dominated team is that you walk a fine line between knowing when to get annoyed about something and when to laugh it off. I could see why it might be amusing for them, but this wasn't something I could laugh off.

Because Philip had a picture file open on his desk. The picture was of the body of a glamour model. I don't know who first coined the term 'glamour' for girls who are photographed topless for tabloid newspapers or men's magazines. It doesn't seem in the slightest bit glamorous to me. And this photograph wasn't exactly glamorous either. The model was wearing a pearl necklace, a tiny white lace thong and matching white lace fingerless mittens. She was, as the newspaper or magazine would say, curvaceous. She was stretched out on a leopard-skin rug. I probably wouldn't have looked twice at her – although I was uncomfortable that the guys were perusing soft porn photos in the office – except for one thing. The model had been Photoshopped. The face that was looking out from the photograph was mine.

'Who did that?' I asked again.

'Ah, Carlotta, it was just a bit of a giggle.' Philip minimised the photograph.

He shouldn't have.

There was another one behind it. And in this one a man was standing beside her. Me. Her. The glamour model. His back was to the camera, but he was naked. And someone had added a caption that said, 'If you won't make the tea, then make me happy!'

I know my mouth opened and closed, but I really and truly couldn't speak.

'Shit,' muttered Brian.

'It's a joke,' said Philip.

I was fighting the urge to cry. And to be sick. My face was flaming with embarrassment and the general feeling of discomfort any woman would feel when looking at a naked picture of herself (even if it was Photoshopped) along with three of her colleagues. It was demeaning.

'Which one of you . . . you . . . shitheads thought this was a good idea for a joke?' I finally managed to spit the words out.

'It's harmless,' John said. 'It's just—'

'It's not fucking harmless.' I rarely swear at work. I don't think it helps. So hearing it from me had a much greater effect than from someone else.

The rest of the staff could see there was something going on now. But just as necks were being craned in our direction, Philip closed the second picture.

'C'mon, Carlotta,' he said. 'You've got to take a joke, roll with the punches.'

And then the lift doors opened and Kieran McDonagh walked out. The three men looked at him. He looked at us. And I realised that he was the one who'd Photoshopped the picture.

'You shower of bastards,' I said, and walked away from them.

I left the paperwork I'd brought from the vault on Bernard's desk and then I walked out of the office building. It was located close to St Stephen's Green, so I went into the park and sat on one of the benches. My heart was thumping in my chest.

Today I would deal with it differently. I'd go immediately to Alexa, our head of human resources, and make an official complaint. I wouldn't care that some of the guys would think I was overreacting. I wouldn't care that they'd call me a frigid bitch who couldn't take a joke. I wouldn't care how much trouble it would cause. Even an un-Photoshopped picture of a woman like that has no place in the office environment. How can you possibly be seen as an equal if someone objectifies you? You can't. No point trying to say you can. It's impossible. So now I know what to do. Then, I didn't.

I sat in the park for over an hour. Every time I thought I felt well enough to go back into the office and stood up, my legs crumpled beneath me. I just didn't know how to face them. Sure, the body wasn't mine. One of them was bound to make that comment sooner or later. That I'd nothing to worry about. They weren't my boobs on display. (They'd probably make some kind of unfavourable comparison about their relative merits, too.) But that was missing the point entirely.

I didn't go back at all that day. I went home to the studio flat I was renting and I went to bed. I wished I could talk to Sive about it, but it was around the time her relationship with Adrian was breaking up. She'd gone away with Natasha for a week and I wasn't going to add to her burdens by offloading my problems on her. I was going to have to deal with this issue myself. The only thing was, I couldn't decide the best thing to do.

I think that in the end I chose the wrong option. I went in the following day and I acted as though nothing had happened at all. The three stooges, as I'd christened them, gave me sheepish smiles, but when they realised that I didn't seem to be making an issue out of it, they got on with their day and didn't take any notice of me. Nor did Kieran McDonagh. Actually, the one good thing about the entire episode was that Kieran actively ignored me.

And then, two days later, I worked late.

Bernard had given me more to do on the paperwork I'd found for him. Apparently the client was talking about taking an action against us for bad advice. I had to check back over old decisions that had been made and find who'd authorised them and a whole heap of other things to bolster our case. Bernard was hoping that we would be able to bury it under a blizzard of information, and the way I was going, it looked like we might.

I'd been glued to my desk all afternoon and didn't even look up until after seven. I seemed to be the only one left in the office, which was a bit unusual as people generally liked to hang around late to show how much the job meant to them. But there was a soccer match or rugby match or something on that night, which probably explained the empty seats on the third floor.

I knew I'd need another couple of hours to finish with the file, so I got up from my desk and went to the cubbyhole of a kitchen where a kettle, a fridge and a microwave were available to all the staff. I was pouring hot water into a mug when I suddenly noticed Kieran standing in the doorway behind me. Almost at once my legs began to shake. I don't know if it was because I was so angry with him, or because having him so close kind of scared me. But I tried not to let any emotion show. I stirred the coffee and picked up the mug. Kieran was still blocking the doorway.

'Excuse me,' I said.

'Make me a cup of tea,' said Kieran.

Now, every part of me was shaking. I held tightly on to the mug so that my trembling hands didn't cause the coffee to spill.

'No,' I said.

'I really thought I'd done enough,' said Kieran.

'You did more than enough,' I told him, suddenly and definitely angry. 'You disgust me.'

'Oh, lighten up,' he said. 'You can't take a joke. You couldn't take one then and you can't take one now.'

'If you're referring to that disgusting photograph, there was no joke involved,' I said.

'Of course there was.'

203

'Not the way I see it.'

'That's the problem with you career girls,' he complained. 'Tight-arsed.'

'Get out of my way,' I said again.

'Come on, Carlotta,' said Kieran. 'Give me a break here. I'm trying to be nice.'

'I don't think that'll ever work,' I said.

'Yup,' he said. 'A tight-arsed bitch. Maybe I can do something to change that for you.'

I don't know what he planned to do. All I know is that he leaned forward as though he was going to kiss me. I yelped, dropped the mug and head-butted him right in the centre of his face. So dead centre, in fact, that the top of my head connected with his nose. The next thing I knew he'd reeled away from me, his hands covering it, blood pumping from between his fingers.

'You bitch!' he gasped. 'I'll fucking kill you.'

I dodged past him and out of the kitchen. I ran to my desk, grabbed my bag and then clattered down the stairs and out of the office. My heart was pounding and my legs were trembling. I hailed the first taxi I saw and climbed into the back seat. I don't think I exhaled until I was halfway home.

I paid the taxi driver and let myself into the house. And then I threw up into the kitchen sink.

Now Kieran holds out his hand and I don't have any choice other than to take it.

'I didn't think we'd ever meet again.' I can feel the pressure of his fingers around mine. 'How have things been?'

'Not bad,' I say as I slide my hand from his. 'And you?'

I can't believe we're talking politely to each other.

204

'Oh, I'm working in media now,' he tells me.

'Great.'

I'd heard about his change of job. He didn't leave the company until after me. The day after the altercation, I rang the headhunters who'd got me the position in the first place and told them I wanted a change. My timing was perfect. Cadogan were looking for people and I got an interview the following week. A month later I was working for them and I couldn't have been happier.

'I didn't know for sure Kieran would call tonight,' says Sive as she motions for us both to sit down. 'I told him my best friend would be here and he wanted to meet you.'

'You did?' I wonder what went through his mind when he heard I was Sive's friend. I'm surprised he showed up at all; obviously he hasn't told her anything about our past working relationship.

'Why wouldn't I want to meet Sive's best friend?' His tone is jocular. 'I didn't say anything to her because I wasn't a hundred per cent sure it really would be you. She called you Lottie, and of course you always insisted on Carlotta in the office. Besides, I wanted to surprise you.'

He's certainly done that. And it's not a nice surprise.

'You guys are . . . an item?' I look enquiringly at her.

'We met the day after you headed off on your travels,' says Sive.

I'm horror-struck. I hate to think that she's in any way involved with that man. OK, I have to admit that, after a while, I did wonder if I'd made a mountain out of a molehill. Yes, the Photoshopping had been a tacky thing to do. But it wasn't the worst that could happen, was it? And yet I'd felt both defiled and humiliated afterwards. Thing is, I never got around to telling Sive about it. My problems seemed trivial in comparison to her deteriorating relationship with Adrian, which hadn't improved after her return from her break with Natasha. As well as not wanting to bother her with it, I also felt too ashamed of how I'd dealt with it – or rather not dealt with it – to want to talk about it. The only good part had been seeing Kieran coming into the office the day after the head-butting incident with a swollen nose and two bruised eyes. He said it had happened playing rugby. And when I told Sive I was leaving to move to Cadogan, she thought of it as a good career move. I didn't want to say that I'd felt forced into leaving. I wanted to think that things had worked out for the best.

So what do I tell her now? If anything?

'Have you introduced Kieran to Natasha?' I ask.

'Not yet. It's early days.'

That's something. I'll tell her when he goes, and I'm pretty sure she'll never see him again. Sive's very big into respect in the workplace, and Kieran's behaviour was, at the very least, disrespectful.

But he doesn't go. He stretches out in one of the armchairs as though he belongs there. All I'm thinking now is that I should be the one to leave, because I don't want to spend a minute more in his company than I have to. But I'm damned if I'm walking out yet.

Nevertheless, it's me who eventually gets up to go first. It's after eleven, I'm tired and I'm stressed about the entire situation. I call a cab and Sive walks to the front door with me.

'How serious are you about him?' I ask.

'It's early days, but I like him,' she replies. 'And he's independent.'

She means financially independent. I know she always worries about Adrian's uncertain cash flow.

'That's something,' I say cautiously.

'Is there any history between you?' Her eyes narrow and I know she's caught the atmosphere between Kieran and me.

'Not that sort of history,' I tell her. 'Nothing . . . Ah, sure, we'll talk about him another time.' The taxi has arrived and I give Sive a hug. 'Let's do lunch soon.' I can't talk to her on the doorstep with him in the house.

'OK.' She's looking at me with a hint of puzzlement.

'I'll call.'

'OK,' she repeats.

I get into the taxi and head for home.

It's my first night on my own since I came back from Seville. When I get into the house, I kick off my shoes and flop on to the sofa. I'm still thinking about Sive and Kieran and wondering how I'd react if she told me that Chris had been responsible for a similar situation. Freak out, I guess. But it's hard to imagine, because Chris just isn't that sort of person. He's totally respectful of the women he works with. He has to be. It's a tight team in the eye clinic. Besides, those women are professionals.

I was a professional too. I *am* a professional. It's just different in an office environment. Maybe Dorothea has a point after all. Maybe everything to do with commerce gets tainted eventually.

I have to tell Sive about it. But I don't know how I'm going to do it. Do I make a joke of it? Would I be able to? Because even now, years later, it has the power to hurt me. To make me feel inadequate. Despite getting the Cadogan job, my confidence suffered dramatically. It took me a long time to recover. Sometimes I wonder if I ever really have.

Bloody men, I think. Nothing but trouble.

My phone rings.

It's Chris, and he tells me that he's on the way over.

'Now?' I look at my watch. It's nearly midnight.

'I've missed you,' he says. 'I want to be with you.'

To be perfectly honest, the way I'm feeling now, I don't want to see him. I'm too angry with men in general to want to have to tell one of them that I love him. Besides, I was looking forward to a night alone in bed. I sleep better on my own. And with what's going on in my head right now, I'm finding it difficult to clear space for Chris. Although it would probably be a good idea for him to be with me. Maybe what I need is to be in bed with my fiancé's arm around me to banish all thoughts of Kieran McDonagh – who has at least dislodged Luke Evans from my mind!

So I tell him that I can't wait for him to come over.

Twenty minutes later he's at the house, and despite what I thought earlier, I'm glad. Because I know what a good, decent man he is. In fact I'm so glad to see him that he's hardly in the door when I kiss him.

'Well, well,' he says. 'What's got into you?'

'I love you,' I say.

I love that he's not Kieran McDonagh. I love that he's not Luke Evans. I love that I can always trust him to be there for me and do the right thing. We go to the bedroom and get ready for bed. When I clamber in beside him, he puts his arms around me and draws me close. I think we're going to make love and I lie patiently in the crook of his arm. Then I realise he's fallen asleep. So much for my charms!

I slide out from his embrace and look at him. He's very handsome. I'm a lucky girl. I kiss him on the forehead and snuggle down beside him.

He gives the gentlest of snores and rolls over. I lie on my back and stare at the ceiling. Then I start counting sheep.

Chapter 15

Faena (Chore) – flamenco version

At two thirty in the morning, unable to sleep, I leave my fiancé in the bed and go downstairs. I make myself a cup of hot chocolate, then take a sliced loaf out of the bread bin. I open the fridge and reach for the highest shelf. My fingers close around the jar of Nutella. I unscrew it and slather two slices of bread with it. Then I sit down with my hot chocolate and Nutella and open my laptop.

I revise a letter that I plan to send to Antonio Reyes in the morning. It's just about a time frame for some of the reforms he needs to implement, but I want to make sure it's absolutely right. I usually type my letters straight away, while I'm thinking of the most important things, and then look at them again later, when I know I'll remember other bits and pieces I want to add. That's when I try to make them less snappy and more friendly too. When I first compose them, all I'm thinking of is what needs to be dealt with. Second time round I try to think of the person reading them. I take a look at a financial spreadsheet one of my other clients has sent. I can see that some of the numbers are significantly different to the estimates the client suggested a few weeks ago, and I make some notes about them. Then, with every possible scrap of work dealt with, I open my personal mailbox.

There are loads of emails. I haven't had time to go through them since I got back from my travels, but it hasn't bothered me too much because I left an auto-reply for any real people saying to call me if it was urgent.

One that I definitely will want to look at is from the Sorrento Bay. That's the hotel where we've booked our wedding reception. I told Luke Evans that nothing except the vows was important in a wedding, but I wasn't being entirely truthful with him. The location matters too. After all, it's nice to have somewhere beautiful to celebrate those vows, and the Sorrento Bay was an absolute find. It's a gem of a quaint old building overlooking Dublin Bay. And their wedding package is absolutely top-notch. One of the reasons I'm totally stress-free – smug, actually – about my wedding day is that I know the Sorrento Bay has everything under control. I click to open the email and I nearly choke on my slice of bread. Apparently the Sorrento Bay is no longer available for our reception due to unexpected and urgent structural works. I read it again in case I misread it the first time, but I didn't. Urgent structural works? When did the management discover that the place was falling down around them? And why the hell didn't they ring me as my out-of-office reply requested?

The email, which was sent while I was in Argentina, says that they have provisionally moved our booking to another hotel nearby, and asks that I contact them as soon as possible if I have any issues or need further information.

Of course I have issues and need further information! Yet I keep reading and rereading it as though the message will change. I'm wondering if it's a sign. I don't actually believe in astrology, fortune-telling, guiding spirits, guardian angels or any of that stuff, but coming after the week I've had, I'm absolutely thunderstruck. I can't help feeling that somebody somewhere is telling me something, but I manage to gather myself together enough to realise that all I'm being told is that there's a major crisis about my wedding venue. I'm supposed to be good in a crisis. What I need to happen, and what eventually does, is that I click into my management mode.

They can't simply shift my wedding reception to another location without talking to me first. I open the link to the substitute hotel and study the website. On the face of it, it doesn't look too bad, but the building isn't half as charming as the Sorrento Bay, and when I browse photos of the interior I know that it just isn't me. Or Chris. This is a perfectly presentable hotel, but it's missing the ambience of the one we originally chose. Once again I have to stifle the voice inside my head that's muttering about it being a terrible omen.

I try to be detached about it as I comfort-eat bread and Nutella and look at the rooms, which don't have the puffed-up pillows and comfy-looking beds of the Sorrento Bay that I liked so much, but I feel myself begin to panic. We were lucky to get the hotel in the first place, and there's not a hope in hell of us managing to get anywhere as good at this late stage. We might be stuck with the alternative no matter how much I hate the idea. When I called the Sorrento Bay in January this year and asked for a September weekend date, the wedding co-ordinator asked which year as though it were perfectly reasonable to assume it could be in 2030. She was sort of shocked when she realised I was talking about a date nine months away and told me that I was extremely lucky that they had one free day. Every other weekend in September was already booked. Our date was Friday the 13th. Which, I tell myself angrily, is very definitely not bad luck. Or a sign. Or an omen. Or anything.

I will solve this. I realise my solve rate on personal matters hasn't been very good lately, but this will be fixed somehow. Chris and I will have the wedding we planned. And the venue will have to be at least as good as the Sorrento Bay.

I'm tempted to run upstairs and wake him, but despite the urgency of the crisis I know he won't want to talk about hotels at three in the morning. So I swallow the last piece of bread, grit my teeth and bang out a snappy response to the email, saying that I'm not a bit happy and asking why they didn't have the courtesy to tell me about this major development by phone. I hit send before I read it back because I don't care how the person reading it feels. Then I go back to bed. Chris is still sleeping. I'll wait till I've heard back from the Sorrento Bay before I break the news to him.

As I sit at my desk the following morning, I can't help thinking that since going to Seville my life seems to be spinning out of control. Oversleeping. The car crash. The missed train. The kiss with Luke Evans. Then there was the edgy dinner with Dorothea and Pen at which I clumsily knocked over the glass of wine, the sudden appearance of Kieran McDonagh in Sive's life, and now the disaster of the wedding venue. All of these things are combining to make me feel panicked and uneasy. And making me think about bad luck and trouble.

I pull my laptop towards me and check the work I did in the middle of the night. I send the letter to Antonio and I'm just about to look at those financial statements again when Dirk walks into the office and sits down in front of me.

'Busy?' he asks.

I look up from the laptop. 'I always have time for you.'

'Thanks for giving me a great breakdown of that report,' he says. 'My talk went really well.'

'No problem.' I'm relieved that something, somewhere has gone according to plan.

'I wanted to talk to you about the conference.' Dirk pulls his chair closer.

This pushes any remnants of personal issues out of my mind completely.

Cadogan Consulting has a major conference every year for our clients and for people we want to be our clients, and it's one of the most important events on our corporate calendar. We bring in inspirational speakers and follow them up with lots of corporate schmoozing.

Dirk tells me about this year's speakers and then he says that he'd like me to give the 'How Great We Are' talk. I look at him in surprise. It's one of the welcoming talks on the first day and Dirk usually gives it himself.

'I've given it a few times,' he corrects me when I say this. 'But not every time. I'm going to do the after-dinner talk this year, which is why I think it's a good idea for someone I can depend on to kick things off.'

Take that, ominous signs! Go to hell, bad luck and trouble! This is everything falling back into place again. Dirk asking me to speak is a major honour and a massive opportunity. I'm delighted he's chosen me instead of Ian, who casually mentioned to me yesterday that he and Dirk were going golfing together this week. I smiled brightly at him and told him to have fun, but the male golfing clique is a real pain. The guys bond over the greens and the women have to suck it up.

'Are you sure you want me to do it?' I say, and then I get annoyed with myself, because I can't afford to show any doubts in front of my boss. 'Not that I don't want to, of course,' I add hastily.

'It would be too much for me to give the opening address *and* the after-dinner talk,' he says. 'Besides, it's good for our image to have one of our strong women start things off.'

I'm glad he thinks I'm a strong woman, while at the same time noting that my presence is designed to enhance our corporate image. I'm being hung out as the token woman, I guess. And yet I'm not a token. I'm good. And that's really why Dirk is asking me.

'I'd be delighted,' I say in what I hope is my confident, professional voice.

'Excellent,' says Dirk.

'Do I write it, or is it a collaborative effort?' I ask.

'Oh, I'll leave it up to you,' says Dirk. 'I'll get Fiona to email you a copy of last year's. But you know the buttons we have to press. Our longevity. Our impartiality. Our professionalism. Our commitment to client satisfaction . . . that kind of thing.'

215

'Great,' I say. 'Thanks for your confidence in me.'

'You're welcome,' says Dirk. 'Let's face it, Carlotta, you stood up in front of a roomful of people and spoke to them in a language you didn't understand, and they still signed with us. So even if you get up there and spout gobbledegook, you'll make an impression.'

I'm not sure how to take that. But I smile at him all the same.

'I understood what I was saying in Seville,' I tell him. 'I made sure I knew what each slide was about. I just wouldn't be able to put all those words together in a different context.'

'What would happen if you were transported to Madrid now?' he asks. 'Would you be able to talk to anyone?'

'Only if I wanted to tell them that we have very specific key performance indicators in place to monitor the progress of our plan,' I reply.

He laughs, and so do I. I like Dirk, even though, like everyone else at Cadogan, his main priority is himself.

'Anything else on your plate?' he asks.

'Client reviews,' I tell him. 'But I have some new prospects coming to see me next week, so fingers crossed.'

'Sounds good.' He nods approvingly. 'As soon as you've got your talk together, you can run it by me so's I can cut out all the terrible bits.'

'Sure.' I yawn suddenly and cover my mouth with my hand.

'Are you all right?' He looks at me quizzically, a sudden note of concern in his voice.

'Of course I am.'

'You look a bit peaky,' he observes. 'Hope it's not all becoming too much for you.'

I can't afford to look peaky. I don't want him thinking that I can't hack it, not after him giving me the chance to speak at the conference. I explain that I haven't had much sleep since finishing with Ecologistics.

'Probably all those time zones,' I finish. 'Messes with the body clock.'

'Hmm. Well, get plenty of zzzs at the weekend,' he says. 'We need you in top form.'

Dirk leaves my office and my phone rings. It's the wedding planner. She insists that she called and left a message on my voicemail as soon as the problem arose. When I didn't get back, she says, she assumed that I was happy with the switch.

'I'm not,' I tell her, wondering if I accidentally deleted the voice message. My phone was filled with voicemails every day while I was away. Unlikely and annoying though it is, I could have missed one. I can't say that to Chris, though.

'The Dalkey Heights is a very good hotel,' she says. 'And they're pushing out the boat to make sure that all the relocated weddings go off without a hitch. The menu you've chosen is unchanged. The drinks reception is unchanged. All that's moved is the venue.'

'The venue is the most important thing,' I point out. 'I have to visit personally.'

'Well, you need to go soon,' she informs me. 'Otherwise you'll lose your deposit.'

'Excuse me?' I'm incredulous. 'You're the people who've messed up, not me.'

'But we said you had to get back to us before—'

'I was away,' I interrupt her. 'I didn't get your message.'

'That's hardly my fault. But,' she adds, 'we realise that

this is an inconvenience and we want your day to be special. So we'll work hard to make sure that it is.'

I want to shout at her that it's more than a bloody inconvenience. Instead I agree that I'll go out to the Dalkey Heights within the next couple of days and let them know what Chris and I want to do.

I didn't tell him about it this morning. I left before he was out of the shower. But I guess I'm going to have to tell him now. He won't be happy. He's a perfectionist too. And he hates having his plans changed.

But before I have time to call him, I receive a text from my mother telling me that she and Dad will be arriving in Dublin the following morning and asking me if I'll be able to stock the house with some fresh milk, bread and a few other bits and pieces. Even though I rarely take personal time away from the office I send a reply saying that it's no problem, and telling them I'll pick them up at the airport. Almost at once another text comes back to say that they can get a taxi, but I know they like being collected from their trips, and eventually Mum agrees, saying they're looking forward to being home and seeing me again.

We haven't seen each other since before I set off on my Ecologistics mission. I usually drop in once every couple of weeks, although as my visits have to fit in with their silver surfer active lifestyles, I sometimes feel that they simply schedule time for me so's I don't feel neglected. Truthfully, though, I love the fact that they've embraced their retirement years and are getting the most they can out of life. When I was younger I always thought that they were boring and repressed. I sometimes wondered how on earth they'd managed to meet each other, marry and have children, because they seemed to be so unaware of everything around them, locked into their narrow world of the house in Mum's case, and the factory in Dad's. In reality it was me who was unaware of the adult world they inhabited, cocooned in my teenage self-obsession. Until I left college and started working myself, I never really appreciated my parents.

It's too late to phone Chris now because he'll have started his clinic, so I send him a text to tell him I'll be at Blackwater Terrace that evening but will see him tomorrow. That won't bother him as he'd planned to be at Dorothea's anyway, but now I can't decide whether to break the bad news later or wait until I see him tomorrow. It's not something I need to worry about immediately, so I put my head down and work my way through the financial statements.

And at six thirty, when I've finished the last of them, I allow the other stuff to come to the surface again. The most problematic of all isn't really the catastrophe of my wedding venue, which, let's face it, will get sorted eventually; I'm really more concerned about Kieran and Sive. I fervently wish I'd told her about the incident with Kieran when it first happened because it seems wrong to tell her now, even though I feel she should know the kind of man he is. Thing is, maybe he's *not* that kind of man any more. Maybe he's turned into a totally PC decent guy. And yet . . . I'll never like him. However, I haven't a clue how to even broach the subject with my friend. Maybe it's one of those things that I'd be better off never mentioning. Maybe I only want to tell her to make myself feel better. I don't think so, but I don't trust myself either. I worry and worry about the situation but I can't come up with a solution that doesn't involve me thinking

219

that I'm making a big mistake. I wonder if I should ask Chris for advice. The problem with that, though, would be having to say what Kieran had done to me and what I'd (inadvertently) done to him. Because if we ever meet up it would be awkward for everyone. Besides, I've more important things to worry Chris about. I feel like I'm a walking repository of bad news. With no clue how to break it.

I sigh deeply and lean back in my comfortable leather chair. I stop thinking about Chris and Sive and Kieran and I think about me. However, the problem with thinking about me is that I think about me in Seville. It's the default thing that takes over my mind when I'm not thinking about anything else. And all my concerns simply disappear in the memories of the narrow streets, the vibrant flamenco and the heat of the city. The images are as vivid as they were when I was living them. I can see the crispness of the colours, hear the ripple of the river and taste . . . I can taste Luke's lips on mine. That memory overpowers everything else and leaves me breathless behind my desk.

I don't know what to do about this. I'm used to remembering facts, not emotions. I'm not sure I can cope with feeling his lips on mine over and over again, sensing the way my body melted into his, remembering the touch of his hand on my back. It's exhilarating and frightening, welcome and unwanted all at the same time.

I open my eyes and wake my laptop from sleep. Then I type 'Luke Evans' into Google. I deliberately haven't done it before because looking him up implies that I want to know about him. And although I do, I know I shouldn't. But I can't stop myself.

There are pages and pages of hits about an actor called

Luke Evans who is quite famous and has been in some major movies. There are a couple of other Luke Evanses too, but not my Luke. I snort. Loudly. He's not my Luke. He was never my Luke! I try to remember if he told me the name of the charitable institution he worked for, or of the wealthy founder, but alcohol blurs my ability to retain information and I can't recall anything. I type 'Luke Evans foundation' but that doesn't help either. I try 'foundation Marbella' and 'foundation Barcelona', because I think I vaguely remember him saying that was where the founder was located (at least when he wasn't in Monaco). But there's nothing for Marbella and all of the Barcelona hits direct to the football club and its charitable work.

I wonder if Luke has a Facebook account. I don't have one myself. I'm not a social media sort of person, which, I guess, is unusual these days but it's not my thing. Besides, Cadogan Consulting is very conscious of its image, and although it doesn't stop employees from using social media, it encourages us to be mindful of our responsibilities towards our employer when we're using it. I don't like the idea of any of my clients being able to see a status update in which I'm ranting about something, or a photo of me looking anything less than a groomed businesswoman. I prefer to keep my rants private and my working self professional. However, I type 'Luke Evans Facebook' into the search box. It's impossible to know if any of the results that show up are the Luke I'm interested in, but at first glance most of them seem to be the actor again. I'll have to see one of his movies!

I try a different tack, and type 'Richard Evans' instead. Then I add 'fraud' and press go.

There are hundreds of hits. Even though it happened such

a long time ago, there are links to more recent newspaper articles about Irish crime and the Costa del Sol. Most of them only mention Richard as part of a wider story, but there's one profile piece that recounts his exploits in Ireland and the family's dash to Marbella. Apparently there was talk about making a movie out of it. Straight to DVD I'd've thought. I don't know how much of a story there is to tell. There's a picture of the family home in the hills, a shot of the estate agency and then . . . My eyes widen. It's a picture of Luke and his father standing beside a Mercedes convertible, with a view of the sea behind them. Richard's arm is across Luke's shoulder.

Luke is about twenty in the photograph. He's wearing a Tommy Hilfiger baseball cap pulled low over his forehead. His polo shirt, loose over a pair of Bermuda shorts, is Hilfiger too. The caption on the piece says that Richard Evans and his son Luke were at a fund-raiser to help local children held in the Four Green Fields pub. There's a tiny inset photo of the pub too, but it's the main picture I'm staring at. While I was at college in Dublin, struggling to pay my way, Luke was dressing in designer gear, attending fund-raisers and driving around in a Mercedes with his dad, the Costa criminal. Luke who isn't supposed to like material things and who told me he now works for a charity himself.

Well, that could be perfectly true. There's no reason to doubt him. Yet it's hard to see him side by side with his father looking happy. I think I want to believe that he hated every moment of his life in Marbella. That he was miserable without me and an unwilling participant in his new life. But there's a smile on his face in the photo.

I close the laptop. I don't know why I'm doing this. I've

no need to look up Luke Evans. I feel bad enough about the whole thing already. All I'm doing is prolonging the agony. I have to forget it, forget him.

Only problem is, I'm someone who remembers. Not forgets.

Chapter 16

Canción de la Luna (Moonsong) – flamenco version

Blackwater Terrace these days is nothing like it was when I was growing up. Back then most of the houses had front gardens and the owners parked their cars on the street outside. Now, almost everyone has paved over the garden so that they can fit two cars in it. And many of them also have a third on the road. Mum and Dad had their garden paved too, although they left a small maple tree in the corner. Their decision was based on maintenance rather than on parking availability, because Dad hated mowing the lawn, and as Mum always considered it one of his chores, our garden was never exactly a landscaper's dream. They share a car, a Ford Focus, which is currently neatly parked behind the double gate. I pull up, get out and lock the Mini. Then I carry my shopping bag of supplies up to the house. As I put my key in the door, I can hear the ringing of the landline echoing through the house. I push the door open and hurry into the kitchen, but I'm too late to answer the phone. I'm not overly worried about it. It was probably a cold caller trying to get my parents to switch their phone, electricity, TV or gas provider. These days, the people you want to call you use your mobile number. I don't even have a landline. Just like everything from my childhood days, things change.

The house has changed inside too. When Dad took the early retirement package, he used the lump sum to renovate it completely. Whereas before it was divided into three rooms – a kitchen, living room and dining room – now the entire downstairs is open-plan. It makes everywhere seem much bigger, although it's still not that large.

I put milk, eggs and a butter spread into the fridge, along with a bottle of wine. Then I put bread in the bread bin and biscuits in the biscuit barrel, and walk upstairs.

It doesn't feel like the house I grew up in here either. As part of the renovations, my parents had an en suite bathroom added to their room and installed a huge jacuzzi bath in the main bathroom. Mum jokes about them sitting in it together with glasses of bubbly and I try hard not to allow that particular picture to lodge in my mind for too long.

I push open the door to my old bedroom. Because I'm the youngest, I was stuck with the box room. The name, in this case, is apt. The room is shaped like a shoebox, long and narrow. There's just space for a single bed, a single wardrobe and a chest of drawers. (I didn't have a chest of drawers back in the day. I had a fold-up desk.) The walls have been painted in soft cream. The duvet cover and pillowcases are cream and pink. It's pretty and girlie in a way that it never was when I had it.

I look out of the window. If I lean forward and crane my neck, I can see the Evanses' house. I don't know who lives there now. About a year after they disappeared, the bank put it up for sale. It took a long time to sell, even at the reduced price they were asking, because people were wary about living in the ex-home of a master criminal. Richard Evans wasn't, of course, an actual master criminal, but he was as good as it got in Blackwater Terrace. I can see that, like all the houses on the street, the windows and doors have been replaced. The current owners have also repaved the front garden. When Mr Evans did it, it was in red cobblelock. Now the paving is a soft yellow sandstone. It looks better.

I sit on my old bed – well, it's not my old bed, but it's in the same place as my old bed – and despite all the changes to the house and my room, I'm suddenly fifteen again. I'm remembering the days after the Evanses disappeared, when the Gardai came and interviewed people in the street.

They interviewed me.

They called to the house one Friday afternoon, shortly after I'd returned from school. I was in my room, changing from my navy uniform into jeans and a sweatshirt, when I heard the knock at the door and saw the squad car outside. There was a murmur of conversation and then my mother called up to me, telling me to get downstairs right away.

The garda who spoke to me was quite young. He was friendly and approachable and he did his best to put me at my ease, but how could I feel anything other than anxiety when a man in uniform was asking me about Luke and his family. He asked if Luke had said anything to me about them going away. I shook my head, unable to speak. I was almost sure that their leaving was just as much of a shock to Luke as it was to me. But the way the garda phrased the question made me wonder if Luke had been aware of it all the time. If I'd been taken for a fool by him, like everyone else had been fooled by his dad.

The interview with the garda ended up with me in floods of tears. Mum eventually stopped it, saying that there was no need for them to upset me and putting her arm around me in a way that I normally didn't let her do any more. Even after they'd gone she kept holding me, telling me that everything would be OK. Then she asked me if I'd known anything.

'I said no to the police and I was telling the truth!' I looked at her indignantly.

'I know, I know.' Her tone was comforting. 'I just wondered if Luke had said anything to make you think—'

'The garda asked me that too!' I cried. 'He said nothing. Nothing at all. Either he didn't know himself or . . .'

Or he didn't care about me, I thought. He'd never cared about me. And he was the same as the rest of the Evanses after all.

As I leave the house, I see Mrs O'Connell walking up the street. She's a few years older than Mum, but, like Mum, she seems younger now than she ever did when I was a teenager. Which is some weird kind of space-time thing obviously. Back then, Norah O'Connell's black hair was sprinkled with grey. These days it's a gentle toasted brunette. She smiles at me as she reaches the gate.

'Carlotta,' she says. 'It's lovely to see you. You're looking well. Are your parents home?'

'Not till tomorrow.' I explain about stocking up the house, and she nods.

'And how's Julia?'

'Great,' I say. 'Happy.'

'Well, it's not such a big thing these days, going abroad, is it?' says Norah. 'Not with the Skype and the Facebook and the Twitter and all the ways you can keep in touch. Sure, half the time you wouldn't know where in the world people are.'

I grin. 'You're right.'

'And listen to me, when are you and the boyfriend tying the knot?' She looks down at my engagement ring with interest. She hasn't seen it before but I know she's aware of my engagement. She and Mum are good friends, having lived on Blackwater Terrace since both of them arrived as young brides.

'September,' I reply, clamping down on the sudden feeling of helplessness that engulfs me as I remember the disaster that is the hotel situation.

'Lovely,' she says. 'I hope you'll be very happy. Your mum tells me he's a surgeon.'

Mum is proud of the fact that I landed someone in the medical profession. Her favourite TV shows are *ER* and *Grey's Anatomy*.

'Chris is an ophthalmic surgeon,' I clarify, in case Norah has visions of him up to his armpits in blood and guts.

'Oh, isn't that great,' says Norah. 'Such a fantastic thing, to be able to help people with their sight. You must be very proud of him.'

'I am.'

'And he's a lucky lad to be getting you,' Norah adds.

'Thank you,' I say. And then to be polite I add, 'How's Mr O'Connell?'

'Not too bad,' says Norah. 'A bit of trouble with the ticker but they're keeping it under control. God love him, though, they've made him give up on the fry-ups and the greasy food. Not that I cook greasy food,' she adds hastily, 'but Stan loved his fry-ups. Ah well, at least he's still with us, thank God.'

I don't think Stan O'Connell is that old. Early seventies perhaps.

'Anyway, that incident with Richard Evans didn't kill him, so I don't suppose anything will,' says Norah.

I'm taken aback by her mentioning the subject.

'You lost money, didn't you?' I say.

'Wiped us out.' Norah's face is grim. 'Every last penny.'

'I'm so sorry.'

'Nothing to do with you, girl,' says Norah. 'Though you were very friendly with young Luke, weren't you? Poor boy, with a family like that he's probably gone off the rails himself, no matter that he seemed a decent enough lad. I saw the TV programme, you know. *Costa Criminals*. And the gorgeous villa he'd bought. With our money! Stan nearly had a heart attack watching it.'

'I'm not surprised.'

'But God is good,' continues Norah. 'And in the end we did all right for ourselves. Won a little bit of money on the lottery. Bought a house and sold it before the property crash. So we got it back.'

'Well done.' I hadn't known that.

'And a bit more,' says Norah with satisfaction. 'I say to Stan that maybe we wouldn't have won anything if God hadn't known we'd been fleeced.'

I'm not a big believer in God, but I sometimes think that for people who do believe, good things happen. Yet that shouldn't be the case, should it? Because if God is all-loving, he should love everyone equally. I've had this conversation with Dorothea, who's a regular churchgoer. She ties me up in knots so that when she's finished I'm not sure what I believe.

'I'd better get going, Mrs O'Connell.' I'm not able to call her Norah even though I'm an adult now; it would be too weird.

'I'm sure you've better things to do than stand around all day gossiping with me,' she agrees. 'Your mum is very proud of you, you know. She says you've got a great job.'

I feel pleased that Mum boasts about me to the neighbours.

'But I suppose it'll have to take a bit of a back seat when you get married,' continues Norah. 'You'll be wanting to start a family, won't you? Now that you're over thirty, it's not a good idea to leave it too late. Dodgy eggs, you see.'

I don't make any comment on Norah's assessment of my eggs but simply say that we'll wait and see how things go.

'You can't do that,' she says. 'Not at your age. You've got to get to it.'

I stifle a giggle. 'I'm sure we'll do our best.'

'Don't laugh at me, young lady.' Norah shakes her head. 'You girls think you can have it all, but you can't.'

She's probably right about that, I think, as I get back into the car. None of us can have it all. No matter how hard we try.

I don't mind taking time off from work to pick my parents up at the airport. I've almost finished my speech for the conference and I'm up to date with the stack of reviews on my desk. So I have a clear conscience as I stand in the Arrivals hall and wait for them to appear.

They walk out side by side pushing a trolley. They look well and not a bit tired from their transatlantic flight. I wave at them and they veer towards me. I give Dad a hug and Mum a kiss and lead them to the car park.

'Julia's in great form,' Mum says as she settles into the back seat. 'And the boys are adorable.'

It's been three years since I've seen my sister and her family face to face. But we keep in regular contact and I don't feel as though she's that far away at all.

'We had a wonderful time in Vancouver.' Dad takes up the conversation after Mum finally stops filling me in on how fantastic Hank and Shaun, my two nephews, are, and what a wonderful husband Jeff is to my sister. 'It's a lovely city, well worth a visit. You should go yourself sometime, Carlotta.'

'I might.'

'With all the globetrotting you have to do, you'd imagine the company would send you on a bit of a jolly to Canada,' says Mum.

'I don't travel abroad that much, but when I do it's not a jolly,' I remind her.

'Ah, sure you have to have some time to enjoy yourself,' says Mum. 'What about this last trip? You were all over Europe and then South America. Don't tell me you didn't have at least one night of fun in all that time.'

I feel my face redden, and my grip tightens on the steering wheel.

'Honestly, it's not about fun,' I say. 'It's about getting the job done.'

'Well that's a very sad state of affairs,' she informs me. 'And you're not getting the most out of that job if you're being straight with me.'

'You can get fun out of anything,' Dad says.

'It's not that I don't enjoy myself.' Obviously I can't have my parents thinking I'm a total loser, even if they do boast about me to the neighbours. 'Of course I do. It's just that work comes first.'

'And you're right that it's important,' agrees Mum. 'But surely when you get to the position you're in, you have minions to do the boring things for you.'

I know what she means. When I was on the very bottom rung of the ladder I thought the same way. That life would be easy when I had people below me. But the truth is, it gets harder. You have more responsibility. I explain this to her.

'So what about all these companies where you hear about the chief executive heading off on expenses-paid golf trips and stuff like that?' she demands. 'Sounds like they're on jollies to me.'

I concede the point about golf, which is, of course, the holy grail of corporate entertainment and which is dominated by men.

'Does Chris play golf?' she asks.

'Sometimes,' I reply. 'He's not obsessed about it, though.'

'I bet he missed you while you were away,' she says.

'Of course he did.'

'He's a dote.' Her tone is complacent. 'And the good thing is he lets you do what you want.'

'Excuse me?' I glance at her. 'He *lets* me?'

'You know what I mean,' she says. 'You're headstrong, Carlotta. Not all men can put up with headstrong women, you know.'

'Well thanks for thinking he has to put up with me!'

'Oh, get off your high horse,' she says. 'I'm saying he understands you. It's good to find someone who understands you.'

I didn't realise I'm the kind of person who needs to be understood and put up with. I've always thought of myself as kind of relaxed and easy-going. I accept that when it comes to my career I want to do well. But I'm not some sort of Cruella de Vil, for heaven's sake!

'I'm very grateful that both my girls have found the right man,' continues Mum, as she makes herself more comfortable in the seat. 'It's a pity she's so far away from us, but Julia's got a great life. You know she's doing this job-sharing thing so she only has to work three days a week. That means she has plenty of time for Jeff and the boys as well as all the clubs she's a member of. She does ice-skating and tennis and all sorts.'

'Good for her.'

'Jeff has been promoted,' Mum adds. 'That's why she took the job-share, to give her more free time for the boys. It works out great for them.'

Jeff is some kind of technician in an environmental company. I've no idea what he actually does.

'Are you suggesting I should abandon my career to support Chris?' I keep my tone mild.

Mum looks doubtful. 'I can't ever see you doing that,' she says. 'Julia enjoys working, but you . . .'

'What?' I ask.

'It's part of you,' she replies. 'You're my driven daughter. You never stop wanting more.'

'You like to test yourself.' Dad's voice startles me. Because he hasn't been contributing to the conversation I assumed he'd nodded off in the back seat. 'You're never happy.'

'Of course I'm happy!'

'I mean, you keep having to try new things,' he says. 'Like I said, test yourself.'

I wonder if my parents talk about me when I'm not around. Ask themselves why it is I keep pushing the limits of my comfort zone. To be honest, I sometimes ask myself that question too.

We're almost at Blackwater Terrace now.

'You'll come in for some tea,' says Mum as I turn on to the road.

I'd factored that in to my time away from the office this morning. She'd never forgive me if I didn't have tea.

So fifteen minutes later we're sitting around the table, feasting on the chocolate Kimberleys I bought yesterday. When we were children, Kimberleys, with their ginger flavour and sugared sponge filling, were an absolute treat. I don't think the chocolate versions were available back then. Probably just as well. Along with the Green & Black's and the Nutella, they're another guilty chocolate pleasure.

Mum and Dad fill me in on stories about their Canadian adventure, as they call it, and I listen and nod and say that I'll have to get over there to see Julia myself some day soon. It might be a nice holiday for Chris and me after we're married. He and Jeff can do male bonding stuff and me and my sister will natter away about what it's like being a married woman in today's world. And I'll be relaxed and chilled out in my happy and successful life.

Chapter 17

Un Diálogo (A Conversation) – Jaime Guiscafre

I get back to the office by one and I've only just sat down behind my desk when my phone buzzes. It's Sive, asking if I want to meet up for lunch. Even though I've spent the morning away I agree, because I forgot to buy a sandwich earlier, and despite the tea and chocolate Kimberley I know I'll be hungry sooner rather than later. Before she hangs up, and because it's been bubbling up inside me, I vent a little about the hotel.

'They can't do that,' she says.

'They have. But what other option is there?' I ask. 'Besides, I don't want the happiest day of my life ruined by the building coming down on top of us. It'd put a dampener on things, don't you think?'

'When are you going to look at the alternative?'

'I should've gone already. I haven't had the time.'

'How about now?' she asks.

'Now?' I'm taken aback.

'Why not? We could have lunch there. Unless you and Chris want to go together.'

'He's entrusting it to me,' I say slowly. 'You could really come now? You have the time?'

Normally Sive has a fuller diary than I do.

'Today I have,' she says. 'I'm ahead of myself on our current liquidation and I was thinking that it would be nice to have some down time.'

Now I'm shocked. Sive never talks about down time. My parents would be even more horrified by her devotion to work than they are by mine.

I think of what Mum said about having more fun and letting other people carry the can, and I think that I could do that for the rest of the day. Let them carry the can, that is. I'm not expecting the hotel viewing to be much fun, although maybe I'm doing them a total injustice and I'll be delighted by it.

So I say OK to Sive, gather my things, tell Verity – the PA I share with Ian and another colleague – that I'll be out again for a few hours but am contactable on my mobile, and meet Sive in the car park of my building.

She's looking great, because she's softened her usual don't-mess-with-me business look by wearing her caramel-blonde hair loose. And her face is less strained than usual.

'Natasha is staying with Adrian tonight,' she tells me as she gets into the car. 'His mum is up from Carlow and wanted to see her. So I said she could have a sleepover.'

Sive is great about giving Joan, Adrian's mum, access to her only grandchild. In fact she was great through the entire separation. She was fair but firm, and even when Adrian got particularly stroppy with her she never lost her cool.

'What's the point?' she used to say. 'We'll work it out

eventually. There's no point in becoming an emotional wreck over it. He's hurt me enough as it is.'

I don't know how she managed to keep her temper in check when he was being such a twat, but she did. She was a role model for divorcing women everywhere!

I put the car into gear and we head off. Traffic is heavy, but as soon as I catch sight of the sea I begin to smile. I love the way the sunlight breaks upon the water and shatters into a million sparkles. I love the sense of infinity the sea brings, the knowledge that this water joins up with all of the other water on the planet, connecting everything. That's why I was pleased to have our wedding reception in a hotel over-looking the sea. I say this to Sive, who grins.

'You're such an idiot,' she says. But she's laughing with me, not at me.

I laugh too. We're playing hookey today, and it feels good.

It takes us just under three quarters of an hour to reach the hotel. During the drive I've agreed with Sive that I won't make any snap judgements about it and that I'll give it a fair chance. Just because it isn't my first choice doesn't mean it won't be perfectly acceptable. As I bring the car to a stop outside, I confess that it's the loss of control that I don't like most of all. The fact that having made a decision, someone else has changed it.

'I know,' she says.

'I mean, as I told Lu— um, as I've said a million times, the day isn't important. And it's not.'

'Excuse me?' She turns to look at me. 'It's not important?'

I should stop saying this. People get the wrong idea.

'I mean – the venue isn't the important thing. What's

important is the vows that Chris and I are going to make.'
I know I sound idealistic. And I'm not really an idealist. I'm
a pragmatist.

'I agree that the vows are the critical moment,' says Sive,
'but for heaven's sake, Carlotta, every girl dreams of a perfect
romantic wedding.'

'I never did.' I open the car door.

'Never?'

I shake my head. I'm telling the truth. Even though I
want my wedding to be lovely and memorable, and for
everything to go without a hitch, the kind of fairy-tale
wedding that many girls seem to want was never high on my
list. For starters, white isn't my best colour. It sort of drains
me. Red is better. But all fairy-tale dresses have to be white,
don't they? Plus, I don't like a fuss. I don't like being the
centre of attention and I absolutely hate having my photo
taken. When Chris and I got engaged and we started to talk
about the wedding, the only dream I had was for something
small and private. Chris was surprised – maybe lots of men
think women want the whole princess-for-a-day thing – but
he was delighted I thought that way because he wanted
something low-key and intimate too, so both of us were
happy.

However, when I told Mum I wanted a small, private
ceremony she went ballistic.

'Julia's was the small, private wedding,' she cried. 'It had
to be because so few of Jeff's relatives could make it over. I
wanted something a bit flashier for you. And,' she added
fiercely, 'I don't want Dorothea Bennett thinking that the
O'Keeffes can't put on a big splash for their daughter.'

She'd met Dorothea by that stage. Chris and I had

organised a 'getting to know you' dinner in a stylish restaurant off Grafton Street and I know Mum felt a little out of her depth. She and Dad don't do fine dining, mainly because they like friendly restaurants where nobody bats an eye if you ask for a well-done steak, and the food comes with gravy, not jus.

It was a meal at which Dorothea tried to assert a certain amount of moral superiority and my parents – specifically my mum – wouldn't let her. If it hadn't mattered to me that it go off peacefully, I would have egged Mum on in the point-scoring contest, but as it was I was terrified that one of them would say something to send the other off in a huff, and so I ended up with terrible indigestion.

I hadn't realised before, though, that Mum had wanted blinging weddings for her daughters and felt let down by Julia's. I thought of all the times she'd made sacrifices for me and my sister when we were young so that we could have a good education and do what we wanted with our lives, and so I decided to give her her dream and have a big bash at a hotel. I told her to invite as many people as she wanted. Chris was totally taken aback by my about-turn, but when I explained it to him he was stoical about it. That's why I love him. He understands stuff like this.

'I suppose my mother will appreciate something a bit bigger too,' he observed. 'She has a lot of friends she wanted to invite and if we go the whole hog she can. All the same, it's not what I would have chosen.'

But then we found the Sorrento Bay and he decided that the hotel's charm and elegance made it an ideal location, and suddenly our wedding was a big deal after all but at least we were both in agreement about it all.

As Sive and I stand outside the Dalkey Heights, I cross my fingers and hope for the best.

Sive walks up the steps ahead of me and pushes open the glass doors. I put the fact that the Sorrento Bay has lovely old-fashioned wooden doors to the back of my mind. Doors are doors, I remind myself. They're a means of getting in and out of a place. That's all.

I walk past the enormous beech table that takes up a lot of the modern reception area. There's a large vase of flowers in the centre. I deliberately don't look to see how fresh they are. I remind myself that I might like control but I'm not a control freak. I head to the reception desk and ask to speak to Anji, the events co-ordinator.

'She's out for a few minutes,' the receptionist tells me. 'She'll be back really soon. D'you want to have a drink or anything?'

'No thanks.' I shake my head. 'We'll just have a look around if that's OK.'

'Sure. Weddings are held in the Green Room. Anji will catch up with you.'

Sive and I follow the signs that lead us through the hotel. The Green Room is at the back and I'm getting hopeful that it will, at least, overlook the sea. But then I realise that I was being silly. It's named the Green Room because it overlooks the garden.

And because it's channelling green. Green wallpaper, green drapes, green carpet. Different shades, but all green. And the thing is, the view through the windows is green too. Trees, shrubs and grass.

'Don't say it.' Sive knows what I'm thinking. 'It's not a bad-size room.'

240

That's true. It's big and square and will easily hold whatever number we eventually agree on. If anything, it might be a bit spacious.

'It's sunny,' she adds.

Which is a plus, I suppose. For sea views it would have to be facing east and it wouldn't get as much light. But the room at the Sorrento Bay was bright, despite the easterly aspect.

'It's a bit . . . soulless,' she concedes.

And that's the problem. The Sorrento Bay oozed elegance and atmosphere. This place is hotel-by-numbers. It's like any of the anonymous hotels I've stayed in when I've been on business. It's not a personal place and no matter how much I've said the venue doesn't matter, I realise it does. I'm about to say this to Sive when Anji, tall and striking with long black hair, comes into the room, introduces herself and starts to tell me how the Dalkey Heights will give me the wedding experience of a lifetime.

'The menus have been compiled from the Sorrento Bay,' she says. 'You won't even notice the difference. Except,' she adds brightly, 'we anticipate that your day will be even better than you expected.'

Realising that I'm not saying anything at all, Sive starts asking questions and Anji does a good job of answering them. She's pleasant and helpful and I like her. But not her hotel.

'Anything else?' She looks at me when Sive has finished.

I shake my head.

'We look forward to seeing you in September,' she says. 'And don't worry that it's Friday the thirteenth. All your bad luck has already happened. And we at the Dalkey Heights want to turn that into a good thing for you.'

I don't tell her that I'm not a believer in good or bad

luck, signs or omens; just in things happening the way they're supposed to. Usually if something isn't right I say so straight away. I don't pretend. But Anji is so bright and bubbly and relentlessly positive that I can't bring myself to complain. So I tell her I'll be in touch and then Sive and I leave.

'I'm cancelling,' I say as we get into the car.

'Oh Lottie, it's not that bad.'

'Compared to the Sorrento Bay it's a kip.'

'Don't be silly. It's clean and it's bright and I'm sure they'll do a good job.'

'It has no soul.'

'But it has a major advantage.'

'What?'

'It's not going to fall down. And that room is fine. All you need is plenty of white flowers to offset the green.'

Sive is in full interior-decorating mode now. She suggests more things to make the room feel brighter and more elegant and every one of them is a good idea.

'There's only one thing making me feel you have a point,' I say eventually.

'And that is?'

'We haven't a hope in hell of anywhere else.' My tone is gloomy. I'm gloomy. Despite my lack of belief in signs, I can't help thinking this is a bad one. But what other option do I have? I can't tell Mum and Dad that we're back to the restaurant and thirty people. Not after she's worked herself into a frenzy of excitement about my big day, as she insists on calling it. It would break her heart. Besides, the Dalkey Heights is perfectly adequate. If a little heavy on the green. I hope Chris will think so too.

*　*　*

242

It's now way past lunchtime and both of us are starving. I don't really want to spend any more time in the hotel and suggest we go to one of the many pubs and cafés in the village. Sive agrees, and ten minutes later we're sitting in a charming pub ordering open sandwiches.

'Weddings are all about compromise,' Sive says as she grinds black pepper over her prawns on brown bread.

'We *did* compromise,' I remind her. 'I agreed to a hotel bash to keep my parents happy. So did Chris.'

'Were both of you seriously contemplating a quick nip into the registry office and lunch in a restaurant afterwards?' she asks.

I tell her that she's making it sound rushed and thoughtless and not, as we'd imagined, sophisticated and tasteful.

'We would have picked a really good restaurant,' I say. 'And we wouldn't have had to choose months in advance!'

'I didn't exactly get the wedding I wanted either, did I?' she asks.

'Yours was lovely,' I protest.

'Oh, I know it all went well and everyone had a good time but . . . to be honest with you, I did have that glittering dream.'

'Your wedding *was* glittering,' I remind her.

'And pared-down,' she says. 'Adrian and I were broke, remember?'

'It's not about money.'

'I know, I know. All the same . . . Does it sound awful that I wanted the huge white dress?'

I shake my head. 'You have the face and the body for it,' I tell her. 'But you looked stunning anyway. And way more comfortable than me.'

Sive's wedding dress was calf-length silk and she'd picked it up in a Monsoon sale for less than a hundred euros. She'd worn it with delicate sandals and flowers in her hair and she'd looked absolutely radiant. My bridesmaid's dress was a sleek cerise number. It too had been in the sale and was half a size too small for me. I could barely breathe thanks to the variety of body-shaping underwear necessary to maintain the svelte look that it deserved.

'Slinky was stylish back then.' She's apologetic.

'I still have a drawer full of Spanx and stuff,' I confess. 'The Spanx are handy but the only time I've used the rest was when I decided to wear a fitted dress to a medical do of Chris's and I realised that I was bulging in the wrong places.'

'And did it work out?'

'Well, there wasn't room to eat a thing but two of the so-called eminent specialists patted me on the bum,' I tell her. 'Cheeky pups.'

'There's a case of that at our company,' she says suddenly.

'Of what? Bum-patting?'

'Pinching,' she clarifies. 'Which we have to treat as assault.'

Immediately I think of Kieran. This is the perfect time to tell her. Because if she thinks that pinching someone's bum is assault, she'll also have to admit that Photoshopping someone's face on to the nearly naked body of a glamour model is a kind of assault too. Of course, head-butting the perpetrator is also assault. In a way it was lucky that neither of us took things any further. I can think that now, with the benefit of time. All the same, I wish Kieran McDonagh had just pinched my arse. It would be easier to bring it up in this conversation.

244

'What would you do,' I begin cautiously, 'if someone you worked with . . .' I pause, not entirely sure how to proceed. 'Circulated personal photos of you,' I eventually say.

'In the office?' She looks at me in surprise. 'Has someone tried that at Cadogan?'

'Not that I know of,' I reply.

Her look is curious now. 'Do you mean . . . sort of compromising photos?'

'Yes.'

'You'll have to tell me what this is all about when you can.' She grins. 'Sounds intriguing. But to answer your question, I'd report whoever it was like a shot.'

So if she'd been the Photoshopped model, she would have reported Kieran. Yet I'm still uncertain about telling her. Sive's not a stupid woman and if she's with him now he must have changed for the better. All the same, it's wrong to keep it a secret from her. I hesitate as I try to gather my thoughts, and then her phone rings.

'Hi.' Her voice has softened and for a moment I think it's Natasha who's called. But then she starts talking and I realise it's Kieran himself.

'Sure,' she says. 'Yes. It'll be fun. I can't wait.'

He asks her something else and she tells him that she's out of the office with me, looking at wedding venues. He says something else and she nods as though he can see her. Then she finishes the call.

'Kieran,' she says unnecessarily.

'I guessed.'

I have to tell her. I really do. But she sounded so happy talking to him. And I've realised that her new, casual look is for him. He's good for her. I can't mess it up when there were no consequences to what happened between us. Other than that both of us ended up changing jobs. I'm wrong to chicken out but I do and I ask how he is.

'Actually, I was wondering . . .' Sive looks at me enquiringly. 'Would you and Chris like to come to dinner with us some evening next week?'

Normally, given my own lack of ability in the kitchen, I love people asking me to dinner. But I don't want to go to dinner with Sive and Kieran. Nevertheless I tell her that I can't wait.

Sometimes you tell white lies, even to your best friend.

I hope I haven't made a terrible mistake.

Chapter 18

Concierto de Aranjuez: Adagio – Narciso Yepes

I don't entirely play hookey from work. I get back at four and I close the door of my office and finish my speech for the conference. I know I'll eventually make some changes to it but I do a quick run-through out loud anyway. It's twenty minutes long and, even if I say so myself, it's practically perfect. I know I'm going to do a good job with this.

Dirk walks in just as I finish. He asks what I've been up to today and I fill him in. He tells me he's emailed me with info about a prospective client he wants me to talk to. It's a sporting organisation that needs a new direction and I think it'll be an interesting project.

'No travel this time,' says Dirk. 'Unless you think Belfast is an exotic destination.'

I smile. 'I'm quite happy to stay on the island of Ireland for a while,' I tell him.

He looks at me thoughtfully for a moment and then asks how much personal time I'm taking after my wedding. I reply that Chris and I are going to the Maldives for three weeks.

'Lucky you,' he says. 'Three weeks of lying on the beach sipping cocktails.'

'I need to use up my annual leave,' I remind him. 'You called me out on that last year.'

'So I did.' He grimaces.

'And you've often said that rested employees are more productive employees.' My tone is innocent.

'All perfectly true,' he concedes. 'Can't imagine the place without you for that long, though.'

'You were without me while I worked on Ecologistics,' I say.

'Missed you then too.'

'You say the nicest things.'

'It's true,' says Dirk. 'You're good to work with, Carlotta. You've got drive and determination and they're great qualities to have in a woman.'

'Great qualities to have in a man too, I imagine,' I say.

'That depends.' He makes a face. 'Sometimes it can go over the top and you get all sorts of big-swinging-dick stuff going on.'

'Someone tilting at your crown?' I ask.

'Boardroom battles,' he tells me.

'But you're the grandson of the founder,' I point out. 'They can't defeat you.'

'We never say can't here,' Dirk reminds me.

'I don't believe you could possibly be shafted.'

'Nothing's impossible,' he observes. 'Ah well, they can't do a thing when we're continuing to get accounts like Ecologistics. So keep up the good work, Carlotta. And wow them at the conference.'

'I'll do my best.'

'Good woman.'

And he walks out of the office.

I mull over his comments after he's gone. I'm surprised at his confidences. Dirk is usually the aloof CEO of the company. He must be feeling the pressure to mention anything at all to me. Cadogan Consulting isn't normally the place for people to have doubts. Least of all the man in charge.

I glance at my computer and see that, while Dirk has been talking to me, I've received ten emails. One is from Anji at the Dalkey Heights confirming the wedding plans. And one is from Antonio Reyes, with information about how things are progressing at Ecologistics. As I read his perfect English, I'm transported back to Seville again.

My phone rings.

'What time will you be home tonight?' asks Chris.

And now I'm back in Dublin. Thankfully.

'Seven-ish,' I reply.

'Any food in?'

It's a regular question. My fridge can either be crammed with food close to its best-before date, or empty except for milk and the Nutella jar.

'Not a lot,' I admit.

'Takeaway?'

'Sounds good. What time are you planning to come by?'

'I've just arrived now.'

'I thought you weren't finishing till late tonight.'

'Last-minute cancellation,' he says. 'So I decided to take advantage and sneak off early.'

'Lucky you. In that case, relax and put your feet up,' I tell him.

'I will. Text me when you're leaving and I'll ring in the takeaway order.'

'Thanks.'

I end the call. I like the idea that I'll be arriving home to food on the table. We all need looking after at some time in our lives.

When I get into the car an hour later, I text Chris and then switch on the radio. As I drive along the quays I'm startled to hear the same haunting melody I was listening to when Luke Evans drove me back from Fuente del Rio. I know I don't believe in omens, but I can't help thinking that there's something weird about suddenly hearing it again. It jolts me back to the sweep of the road, the bruised purple of the mountains and the perfect blue of the sky. I can feel the charge of the atmosphere, the feeling that there was something unseen and unspoken between us. And I remember the flamenco dancer as she whirled and spun on the stage in front of me. It's amazing how music can put you into a different time and place. I don't even notice the journey I'm now taking, and I can't believe I'm turning into my street already.

I've arrived at the same time as the takeaway. I pay the delivery man and carry the bag of hot food (Bangkok duck for Chris, pok pok for me) into the house. Chris is watching TV, his feet propped on the small coffee table in front of him. When he sees me he removes them and looks guilty. Despite my invitation to put his feet up, he knows I didn't mean on the table. I have a bit of a thing about feet anywhere I might also put food or drink. I say nothing and simply get some plates and forks from the kitchen before divvying up the meal.

'I need this,' says Chris as he takes the plate. 'Hell of a day despite the early finish.'

He goes on to tell me how one of the nurses managed to mess up a fluorescein angiography, which resulted in the yellowish dye used in the procedure being sprayed all around the treatment room, as well as over the nurse and the patient. The angiography allows the ophthalmologist to check a patient's retina, but the woman concerned was so upset by what happened that she refused to allow them to carry on and insisted on going home.

'She'll have to come back, though,' I say.

'Maybe not to us.' Chris jabs moodily at his duck. 'If we can't do something as simple as that without turning her into a walking tangerine, I don't blame her for thinking we're too incompetent to look after her vision. And she needs looking after.'

Chris doesn't just do laser eye surgery to enhance vision. He deals with lots of different eye problems too.

'She'll get over it,' I assure him.

'Hmm.'

We eat in silence for a few minutes and then, risking making him even grumpier, I tell him about the Sorrento Bay. He's not just grumpy about it, he's absolutely furious. Fortunately his fury is directed towards the hotel and its apparent lack of maintenance programme rather than me and the fact that I didn't listen to their call. After he's finished sounding off about it, he asks what I think of the alternative. I give him my honest view, that it's not a patch on the Sorrento Bay but that it's adequate and has the added advantage of being structurally sound.

'Adequate?' He stares at me. 'We want more than adequate, Carlotta.'

'Maybe I'm being a bit harsh,' I say. 'It's fine. It's just not the Sorrento Bay.'

'Why don't we forget the whole big wedding thing and go back to our original plan?' he asks.

I don't tell him that the same thought had occurred to me because I've already decided that I'm not letting Mum down by changing things. So I waffle on about it being what both our mothers want and then I remind him that the wedding is only a few months away and of the impossibility of getting another venue in that time.

'We'd get a restaurant,' he says. 'Like we wanted all along.'

'You know my mum has her heart set on a big do,' I remind him. 'I can't let her down.'

'I feel like I'm compromising my principles as well as on the hotel,' he protests.

I repeat Sive's comments about weddings being all about compromise anyway.

'I suppose you're right.' His grumpiness has returned. But it's better than fury.

I clear away the forks and the plates and make some coffee. Chris takes his Kindle from his bag and begins to read. A few minutes later I sit down beside him and open my book. I don't use my iPad to read for pleasure. Nor do I have a dedicated e-reader. I'm not sure I ever will. I like books. I like the weight of them in my hand, the smell of them and the look of the font on the printed page. When I first said this to Chris he agreed with me, but then he added that he liked the convenience of the Kindle. He's right, I know. But I don't think I could ever feel affection for an electronic gadget. Whereas the well-thumbed copies of my favourite books are like the warm embrace of a good friend.

Either way, though, my fiancé and I are sitting together in companionable silence. And after the news I had to break today, I reckon it's a good result.

Chris is asleep in the bed beside me. Once again I'm lying on my back, my eyes wide open, the Spanish music going round and round in my head as it has been all night. I'm back with the flamenco dancers, remembering how they stamped their feet and moved their arms and brought their passion alive. I remember that they made me feel passionate and alive too, and I'm wondering what would have happened if, when Luke and I had returned to the apartment together, I'd given in to my desire to be passionate then. Because it had been there. Dampened down. Shut out. Hidden away. But there all the same.

I felt guilty then, but I feel worse now, lying beside a man I know I love, thinking about someone else. The problem is that I can't help wondering how it could have been. I don't want to. I really don't. But I do.

Usually I can put unwanted thoughts and memories into a closed-off part of my mind, where they remain until I need them or until they fade into insignificance. I'd managed that with the part of my teenage past that had contained Luke, but now those memories have spilled back into my consciousness, and they haven't faded at all. They're just as fresh as they were eighteen years ago.

The rational part of me knows without a doubt that I've turned Luke into a kind of fantasy figure. The person who would have been perfect if he hadn't been stolen from me. The rational part of me also knows that the thoughts I've been having – ones in which Luke and I were never parted and we lived happily ever after together – are complete nonsense. And yet I simply can't get rid of them no matter how often I tell myself that we were too young and that it wouldn't have worked out. What if we weren't? What if it had?

But how could it have been any better than what I have? Because my life has turned out fine without Luke Evans. I've done the things I wanted to do. I've got a great job, I work with interesting people, I have good friends. And I have Chris, who's the absolutely perfect man for me.

So why on earth do I keep on thinking of what might have been? Especially as we were kids and so what might have been would probably have amounted to a bit of a fumble in the back lane behind my house before Luke moved on to someone else. He was the popular one, after all.

Damn it, I think. Nobody walks a straight line, getting everything they want, everything they expected. But does the rest of the world spend the night-time hours beating themselves up over it?

I roll over on to my side and put my arm around Chris. He mumbles in his sleep and moves away from me, because it's warm tonight and my body close to his is making both of us too hot. I roll away again and the Spanish music I'd heard earlier, the music that transports me back to Fuente del Rio, takes over my brain once more. I hate it when the only sound in your head is the one melody over and over, even though, in this case, the Arabic undertones and mesmerising rhythms are utterly beguiling. I'm searching for the memory of it, annoyed that my usually reliable recall isn't working. Maybe remembering what it was called would make it go away.

I push the duvet from my body and slide out of bed. I grab my iPhone and, closing the bedroom door behind me, I go downstairs. I tap the app on my phone and start to hum the music.

I'm not a great singer, but I can hold a tune. And so when I hum the Spanish music, the app identifies it as the Concierto de Aranjuez. And suddenly the memories flood back with total clarity. I can't understand why they didn't come before. I first heard it sitting beside my dad. We were watching a movie. It was a few months after the Evanses had left, and I know that because Dad made a comment about our video recorder being bought from an honest day's work, unlike the top-of-the-range model Richard Evans had. The movie was bittersweet and I cried when they played the music because it was so beautiful. Now that I remember, I can close my eyes and see the video box and the name of the movie. *Brassed Off.* Ewan McGregor. Pete Postlethwaite. Tara Fitzgerald. Nominated for a BAFTA. It's perfectly clear in my mind. They called it the Concierto de Orange Juice.

I find the brass band arrangement on iTunes and I listen to it. I'm back in the living room of Blackwater Terrace, sitting beside my dad, watching the movie. I remember enjoying his company because we rarely did things together. He worked long shifts at the factory and when he was home he was usually occupied with DIY jobs around the house.

That afternoon, I recall, he'd put up new shelves in my bedroom.

He was a good dad. Still is.

One day Chris will be too.

I close my iPhone before the music ends.

Chapter 19

Villanesca – Narciso Yepes

Chris and I usually spend one evening a week with Dorothea. Since missing her birthday party I've put in extra effort whenever I'm with her, and I think it's paying off, because her smile when we turn up for our next visit is warmer than usual, and she actually puts her hand on my shoulder as she ushers me into the living room.

'How are you feeling?' she asks as I sit down.

'Fine.' Actually, I'm feeling slightly freaked out by her new-found chumminess. 'And how are you?'

She says she's fine too and immediately asks if I have any news on wedding venues.

I can't blame her if she thinks the cock-up is all my fault. Which, despite her friendly tone, I'm sure she does.

'We don't really have any choice but to go with the alternative hotel,' I reply. 'But I'm sure it'll be fine.'

'Nevertheless, every girl wants the perfect wedding,' Dorothea says.

What's this obsession with perfect weddings? Why am I the only woman in the world who thinks that as long as the bride and groom end up as husband and wife, everything else is pretty much unimportant? I realise that's the complete opposite of how I felt when I first read the Sorrento Bay's email and then visited the Dalkey Heights, but I was being irrational then. I'm back to my old self now.

'I want you to have the perfect wedding,' she continues.

There's a brief moment when I think she's going to add 'to someone else' to her sentence, but she doesn't.

'I've been talking to Chris about it,' she says.

I glance at him. His expression is sheepish.

'And he's in agreement with me.'

His expression changes to one of 'what else could I do?'.

'We'll have it here.'

I hear the words but it takes a few seconds for their meaning to filter through to me. Dorothea is talking about having our wedding reception in her house! And Chris agrees! Is he mad? Is she?

'That's very sweet of you,' I say when I'm able to speak. 'But I don't think—'

'It's absolutely no trouble at all.' She gets up and goes to her old-fashioned sideboard. There's a big blue ring-binder on it which she brings over to me. 'I've done some investigation, made enquiries, got some quotes. You'll save a fortune, by the way, and have a much better experience.'

The binder is packed with information, neatly filed in see-through plastic inserts. She's clearly spent hours on it.

'Chris?' I look at my fiancé.

'I was doubtful at first,' he says. 'But Mum makes some good points.'

'Why didn't you talk to me about it?' I ask.

'Mum wanted to surprise you.'

I bet she did. She wanted to spring it on me so I couldn't say no. But of course I can say no. My whole career is based around being the kind of person who can say no.

'And the thing is . . .' Chris looks at me, and I can see a hint of eagerness in his eyes, 'although we can still ask the same number of people, it'll be more like what we wanted at the start. A more intimate setting.'

He has a point. Oh crap.

'You and I can work out the finer details,' Dorothea tells me. 'We'll have fun.'

She's got to be kidding.

But she's not. And Chris wants this, I can see it. Not just for her, but for him. I turn the pages in the blue binder. Dorothea has done an immense amount of work already. But still. My wedding. In her house! I know I didn't want perfection, but this . . .

'Carlotta?' says Chris.

I take a deep breath. 'I can't think of anything better,' I say. 'Dorothea, you're a genius.'

They both look at me with approval.

I've just taken one for the team.

The following week, Chris and I make it to Sive's for dinner. Even though I've been dreading it, my obsession with being punctual means that we are actually far too early, so Chris insists on driving along the coast road and sitting in the car overlooking the sea until nearer the time.

The silence between us is companionable. Ever since the change in venue for our wedding reception, he's been in really good form – pleased, I think, that Dorothea is so engaged with the process and pleased that I've allowed her to be. I haven't had a choice about that. She's already sending me about five emails a day. Nevertheless, despite my own mother's pursed lips when I broke the news, I feel that I've done the right thing. It's a kind of penance, I think, for Seville.

I wish I hadn't thought of Seville again, but it's like my brain is hyper-aware at the moment. It doesn't take much to bring the vine-clad hills and cornflower-blue skies bubbling to the surface. And every time I imagine them, I want to be there. Which, I think, must mean that I'm under more stress than usual in my day-to-day life. Because that's when we dream of escape, isn't it? When things are getting a bit much. I shouldn't be stressed, because everything at work is going great and this whole wedding thing is under someone else's control, but still . . . I stare at the green water of Dublin Bay and tell myself that these feelings are only temporary. Everything in life is temporary.

Chris starts the engine. The stress could be to do with this damn dinner. Seeing Kieran McDonagh. Pretending I don't care that he's going out with my best friend when every time I think about them together I want to scream. I'm not looking forward to the next few hours at all.

We arrive an acceptable five minutes late. Kieran is already in the living room, and once again he greets me with a wary look. I introduce Chris, and after the two men shake hands they immediately start talking sport, even though Chris isn't really the sporty type. I sometimes wonder what men would talk about if sport didn't exist. It's the only conversational opener I know that works for all of them.

Sive and I leave them to it and go into the kitchen.

'Can I do anything to help?' I'm watching her arrange salad leaves on plates.

'Not a thing,' she says cheerfully. 'All under control.'

'As ever.'

She shoots me a glance.

'Everything OK?' she asks.

'Of course.'

'Sure?'

Why is she asking this? Don't I look OK? Don't I sound OK?

I tell her that I'm fine and then ask about my god-daughter.

'She's having another sleepover tonight,' Sive tells me. 'With one of her friends this time. When did that become so popular?'

I look at her blankly.

'They do it all the time,' Sive explains. 'Last weekend three of Natasha's friends stayed here. They closeted themselves in her room and spent the night giggling and whispering, and I'm sure none of it was good.'

I grin. 'They were probably ripping some other poor girl's reputation to shreds.'

'I know,' wails Sive. 'Girls can be so awful to each other.'

'On the other hand, they might just have been trying out make-up and stuff.'

'They're only eight.' Sive sighs. 'They shouldn't even be thinking about make-up. But yes, it was all about doing their nails. Natasha painted hers in blue glitter.'

I make a face.

'Better than pink glitter,' says Sive. 'This pink tyranny for girls does my head in. Natasha was the only one wearing yellow jammies. The rest of them were in a million shades of pink.'

While we've been talking, she's taken individual vegetable

261

tarts from the oven, placed them on the plates and drizzled them with a dressing. I help her carry the plates to the dining area, where Kieran opens a bottle of wine. He fills my glass but Chris says he won't have anything because he's driving. Kieran looks disappointed.

'It's a really good wine,' he says.

'I know.' Chris has seen the label. 'But I'll stick with water. I don't want to get the shakes when I'm operating on someone's eye.'

That's enough to turn the conversation to laser eye surgery. Kieran asks if Chris's clinic does deals for friends. Chris says that the surgery's rates are very competitive and that you get what you pay for. I kind of like that he slaps Kieran down, even though he does it with great charm.

We start to eat. I'm sitting beside Chris and opposite Sive, but I keep glancing at Kieran. Twice now our eyes have met and I've looked hurriedly away. Actually, what I'm straining to see is if there's a bump or anything on his nose. A permanent scar from its encounter with my head.

Then Chris turns to Sive and asks her about work and her plans for the summer.

'Haven't made any holiday plans yet,' says Sive. 'Natasha and I need to fit in with what Adrian wants, of course. But I'm thinking it would be nice for us to go somewhere warm, so that I turn up at your wedding with a golden glow.' She turns to Kieran. 'They're getting married in September and heading to the Maldives afterwards.'

'Yes, you said earlier.'

I don't like to think that Sive and Kieran have been discussing me and Chris. I don't like to think of my name being mentioned at all between them!

'Did Carlotta fill you in on our reception?' Chris asks Sive, and she looks at him in surprise.

He tells her about the switch to Dorothea's house and her eyes widen while I smile broadly to show I'm delighted by this turn of events.

'I'm sure it'll be wonderful,' says Sive, who has correctly interpreted my beam as a grimace.

'Mum is very excited,' Chris confides. 'She's drawing up lists of approved caterers and decorators as we speak.'

Sive shoots me a sympathetic look.

'Dorothea's party was a great success,' I tell her. 'I have utmost faith in her.'

'And so you should.' Chris nods. 'Mum's looking forward to lots of girl time with Lottie.'

I take a sip of wine. Sive's look is even more sympathetic this time.

'It'll be great fun,' she says solemnly.

'When – and if – I get married . . .' Kieran shoots a complicit look at Sive, 'it'll be a no-expense-spared event in a five-star location.'

Christ almighty! Men never talk about their potential wedding day. Never. Kieran and Sive can't have discussed marriage yet. They hardly know each other.

'Dorothea's house is wonderful,' Sive tells him. 'It's a five-star location in itself.'

'Where does she live?'

'Rathgar.' It's Chris who answers.

'Oh, that's OK then.'

For the first time since I've known Dorothea, I'm offended on her behalf. Kieran is speaking as though it actually matters where her house is, as though if it were somewhere else – Blackwater Terrace, for example – it would be totally unsuitable. The only thing that matters is that it's where Chris and I are having our reception.

'I'm glad you think so,' says Chris.

I can tell by his voice that he's annoyed, and I don't blame him. I squeeze his hand and we share a look of complete understanding.

Sive begins to clear the starter plates and disappears into the kitchen. Kieran follows her.

'Is it me?' asks Chris when he's gone. 'Or is that guy a complete dickhead?'

'Utter,' I agree.

'Have you said this to her?'

'No,' I admit. 'She seems to like him.'

'I don't know what's wrong with her,' says Chris. 'She's a smart woman. Maybe it's just that the marketplace for single mothers in their thirties is a bit limited.'

'Chris!' Even though Sive already said as much herself, it sounds sort of desperate coming from him.

'Sive's a good catch,' he says. 'I'd just hate that asshole to be the one who catches her. I don't know what the hell she sees in him.'

Neither do I. We're in complete agreement about that.

Sive returns to the dining room carrying a dish of roasted vegetables, which she puts on the table. Then, while she goes for more side dishes, Kieran places plates of pan-fried sword-fish with lime sauce in front of us. Chris says that it looks delicious and Kieran tells us that he was the one who made the sauce, so any complaints should go to him, not Sive. Although, he adds as he drops a kiss on to her golden hair, she supervised. I picture them preparing the meal in perfect

264

harmony, side by side, and a lump of swordfish gets stuck halfway down my throat. I splutter, cough and gulp water from my glass before I finally manage to swallow it.

'Are you OK?' asks Sive.

'I'm so sorry,' I gasp. 'Went down the wrong way.' I finish the glass of water as I wait for my breathing to return to normal, then excuse myself and go to the bathroom, where I reapply my lipstick and wonder what to do about my best friend and the man I head-butted.

He's in the hallway when I emerge, and I jump like a startled rabbit.

'I just wanted a quick word,' he says.

'What sort of word?' I can hear Chris and Sive talking in the dining room. She laughs at something he says.

'I know you two are best friends and I know women are hot-wired to share every blasted thing with each other,' he says. 'But what happened between us – well, I don't want you telling her and making it out to be more than it was.'

I stare at him.

'It was just a bit of fun between two colleagues,' he says.

This is where I should say the things I should have said years ago. But I'm unable to speak.

'You got the wrong end of the stick, that's all,' he says.

I'm still speechless.

'So don't try to fuck it up between me and Sive. Because if you do . . .' he shakes his head, 'you'll be sorry.'

I'll be sorry? Me? Why? There's nothing he can say or do to make me sorry. He's the one who'll be sorry when she finds out what a douche he is. And I'm about to tell him this when he walks away, back into the kitchen, where I hear him call to Sive that he's found the bottled water.

I realise that I'm shaking. It's with fury.

When I return to the dining room, everyone's joking about some new comedy on TV. I play around with my food but I'm not hungry any more and Sive has to ask if I'm finished because everyone else has cleared their plates while I've left half my fish.

'Scarred by the near-death experience,' I joke feebly. 'Sorry.'

'It's fruit compote for dessert,' she says. 'You'll manage that.'

I just about do and then she goes to make coffee. She stops at her iPod dock to change the music and I can hardly believe it when the ethereal melody of the Concierto de Aranjuez fills the room. It's like I'm being haunted by this one piece of music. Although right now it's calming and soothing, and it pushes me into that other life where I'm enveloped by orange blossom and warm air. I suddenly think that if Luke and I had been together I'd never have met Kieran McDonagh in the first place. But then I might not have met Sive either. Or Chris, who's continuing to be civil to Kieran even though I can hear an almost imperceptible irritation in his voice as he speaks.

I'm sure if I'd lived the life with Luke I'd conjured up there would have been horrible days too. Nothing is ever as perfect as we want it to be. And we can't go back. Yet at this moment I'd love to be in Seville. Or Fuente del Rio. Away from worrying about Sive and Kieran. Away from Dorothea and her daily emails. Away from Cadogan Consulting. Even away from Chris.

Suddenly it strikes me and I almost gasp out loud – has Sive told Kieran about Luke? Is it something he thinks he can hold over me? Is that why he thinks I'd be sorry? If I tell Sive about him, will he tell Chris about Luke?

I think the time has come to tell Chris myself. Bottom line, it was all perfectly innocent. Well, at least until the kiss, but even then we walked away. I said goodbye. Nothing else happened. I can say that with perfect honesty. But I'm not sure I can talk about snippets of music and the life I didn't lead. I don't know if my wonderful fiancé would understand that.

I wipe my brow and take a couple of deep breaths. I'm getting myself into a tizzy for nothing. Sive wouldn't have said a word to Kieran; she's the soul of discretion. And no matter what, Kieran can't mess up my relationship with either Chris or Sive. If it came down to it, both of them would believe me over him any day. Wouldn't they?

Although I have to face up to the fact that I cheated on Chris and kept secrets from Sive. OK, not cheated, I tell myself as the music builds to a crescendo. Not the way people usually mean. Because of that kiss, I've simply wondered about what could have been. And every bride does that, doesn't she? Everyone gets a fit of nerves. That's what I had in Seville. A fit of nerves. That doesn't alter the fact that I love Chris. I know I do. He's a good man.

Maybe he's too damn good for me.

I get up from the table and follow Sive into the kitchen, offering once again to help.

'I guess I know what's wrong now,' she says.

Immediately I think that she's heard part of the conversation between me and Kieran and she's got the completely wrong idea of what went on between us, and I look at her with a frozen expression on my face.

'Dorothea's house for the wedding!' Sive hasn't noticed how distracted I am. 'Nightmare.'

I heave a sigh of relief. A few days ago I wouldn't have thought that a wedding reception at Dorothea's would be a source of relief to me but it's a sign of how utterly demented I am tonight that it is.

'It's a generous offer.' At least I can speak again. That's something.

'Seriously, Lottie,' she says. 'Isn't it doing your head in?'

'Of course it is.' The music has changed. It's still Spanish guitar but at least it doesn't have the same effect on me as the Concierto. I'm able to concentrate on my surroundings again. 'But what can I do about it?' I ask. 'I truly didn't like the Dalkey Heights, no matter how lovely Anji was. So this is a good alternative.'

'Hmm.'

'It is,' I protest.

'You look wrecked,' she says. 'And I'm not surprised.'

I feel wrecked. Though it's not Dorothea's fault.

'I'll make it work,' I say.

'Just as well you didn't want a dream wedding then, isn't it?' she remarks. 'How's it going so far? Has she taken over?'

I tell her about the daily emails. Which come with pre-prepared answers anyway.

'Oh, Lottie.'

'I'm doing it for Chris. He's been great about everything. He even rang Anji with the bad news. She wanted to keep the deposit but he managed to get it back. He's really good at that sort of thing.'

'You're good at that sort of thing too,' she says.

'I'm supposed to be,' I concede. 'But I was glad to have Chris do the dirty work for me this time.'

'Men have their uses,' says Sive, and she grins broadly. I

really and truly hope she's not going to confide in me about the uses she has for Kieran. I have to head this off at the pass.

'You really like Kieran?' I put a blue espresso cup on a matching saucer.

'He's different,' says Sive. 'He knows what he wants. He's his own man.'

'Unlike Adrian.'

'Precisely.'

Maybe he really thought that Photoshopping that picture was a joke. Maybe his behaviour towards me was completely out of character. Maybe I unwittingly provoked him. Perhaps he accosted me outside the bathroom because he was afraid I'd poison Sive against him even though he's become a wonderful, sensitive human being. I'm aware that I'm making excuses for him now, because even though I'm sure I should tell her, I really don't want to. I'm such a coward.

I'm a coward about everything, I tell myself, as I think about Luke again. I'm not someone who should be giving advice to anyone. I'm the one who needs advice.

'Sive?'

'Yes?'

'Am I doing the right thing?'

She looks at me in absolute astonishment.

'What d'you mean?'

The words tumble from me in a rush. I babble incoherently about the Concierto de Aranjuez, the passion of the flamenco, Fuente del Rio and driving through the mountains with Luke Evans. I don't mention the kiss but I do talk about the feeling of being in the wrong life, that everything I've done has been a mistake, and her expression becomes more and more bewildered as I speak.

'For heaven's sake, Carlotta,' she says when I finally finish. 'You're surely not trying to make some huge personal crisis out of the playlist on my iPod, are you?'

I look miserably at her. 'It's not the playlist,' I say. 'It's everything.'

'If you've got doubts about Chris and your wedding, you've got to tell him. You're not being fair to him otherwise.' Her voice is firm and I guess it's the tone she uses when she walks into companies and tells them the game is up.

'I love him and I want to marry him, but I'm afraid.'

'Of what?' she demands. 'That there's something better out there? There isn't, Lottie. You should know that.'

'There doesn't have to be something better, but how do I know Chris is still the right man for me?'

'Why in earth wouldn't he be?' She stares at me. 'Carlotta! This Luke bozo has been in touch, has he?'

I shake my head.

'So what's the problem? Is it someone else?'

'No!'

'What then?'

'I want to be sure I'm doing the right thing.'

She looks at me sympathetically. 'This is nerves, Carlotta. That's all.'

I feel a surge of relief. 'That's what I thought too. But . . . Luke—'

'Bloody Luke,' she cries. 'Get a grip, Carlotta!'

'It's not his fault.'

She stares at me. 'But it's because of him.'

I shrug helplessly.

'How long did you spend with him?' she demands.

I look at her in puzzlement before reckoning that all in

all, over one night in Seville and the time at Fuente del Rio, it was about twelve hours.

'And you're prepared to let twelve bloody hours ruin your entire life!' She looks at me in disbelief.

'I don't want to ruin my life, of course I don't. But . . .'

'But what? You think there might be something between you and Luke?'

'No. Not really.'

'Not really?' She's horrified. 'But maybe?'

I shrug despairingly. I don't know, that's the problem. I'm usually so certain about everything in my life, but right now I'm totally confused.

'It's like I was someone else when I was with him,' I say. 'Someone different.' I think of the flamenco dancer. 'Someone free.'

'Jesus, Lottie.' I can see the incredulity in her eyes.

'I know it's daft.'

She says nothing for a moment, then she sighs deeply.

'Maybe you should go to Spain. Meet this Luke guy. Work it out. I'll come with you and hold your hand.' She grins.

I stare at her in disbelief.

'You can't marry Chris if you're having doubts,' she says.

'I can't destroy what I have on the basis of a few hours with someone I once knew either,' I object.

'Yes, but perhaps you need to meet him again. See for yourself that you're building this out of all proportion. Have him laugh in your face. Then you can come home and get married just like you were supposed to.'

'If I find him – and I don't know how I'll do that – what if we fall into each other's arms and decide that we want to be together forever?'

'I'm betting a hundred per cent that's not going to happen. You had an intense experience, like a soppy holiday romance, and it's messed with your head, that's all. And remember, Lottie, in all those programmes about women falling for men they meet abroad, the men have usually forgotten them before their return flight has even left the ground.'

She's right about that. It doesn't make it any easier, though.

'And I keep it all a secret from Chris?'

'If you talk to Chris, the only thing you can do is say you want to postpone the wedding. And no one postpones weddings. They just split up. I can't believe you want to split up with the man who's absolutely perfect for you.'

'Oh, Sive . . .'

'I don't approve,' she tells me, and then her voice softens. 'But I don't want you to ruin your life just because you're having a meltdown.'

'You're a really good friend,' I say.

'I know.' She smiles. 'And you were a really good friend when I was having such a hard time with Adrian. The least I can do is return the favour. Besides, I could do with a mini-break in the sun myself. Anyhow I'm pretty sure every-thing will turn out OK for you and Chris. You just need to prove to yourself how damn lucky you are to have him.'

'Any chance of those coffees appearing before we get wrinkles in here!' It's Kieran's voice that interrupts us.

'On the way,' she calls.

'Thank you.' Just sharing my neuroses has made me feel better already. I almost say there's no need to go to Spain at all, but she's already picked up the tray and walked out of the kitchen.

* * *

272

I'm quiet on the drive home, and it's Chris who eventually says that he's very fond of Sive but he never wants to see Kieran McDonagh again.

'I'm glad you think that,' I say. 'Because I don't want to see him either.'

'I don't know why she's so taken in by him.' Chris sounds genuinely puzzled. 'He talks the talk with all the sweetheart and pet and darling stuff, but it doesn't sound right at all.'

It's nauseating actually.

'It's as though she's some kind of fifties housewife,' he continues. 'Which would be marginally understandable if she was a brainless bimbo and he was a captain of industry or something, but it's quite clear that he's intellectually way below her.'

And yet she seems to be crazy about him. In the same way she was crazy about Adrian, who was streets behind her too. Although, as we observed earlier, at least Kieran earns his own money.

'When he talked about the sort of wedding he hoped to have, I nearly fell off my chair,' I say. 'I don't want to think of them as a couple. I'm hoping it's all a mad fling as far as Sive is concerned.'

'Do single mothers have flings?' he asks as we cross the bridge over the Liffey and turn up the quays. 'I thought it was all about finding someone who fits into your life.'

'I don't know.' And I don't. When Sive and I talk about men, it's usually about them as competitors in the office, not as partners at home. She has a lot of experience of them as competitors, but in any other sense she's a novice. After all, she was barely twenty when she met Adrian, and as she told me then, her relationships before him had all been brief and

273

juvenile. She's never been madly keen to find a replacement for him, although she admits that if the right man came along she'd count herself very lucky indeed, believing as she does that most of them are losers. Which makes it such a pity that she's been taken in by someone who I'd firmly put in that category.

'Oh well, let's hope she cops on eventually,' says Chris.

Maybe I can talk some sense into her when we go to Spain.

Maybe she thinks that's when she can talk some sense into me.

Chapter 20

Foc (Fire) – Rodrigo y Gabriela

A blast of warm air hits us as we step out of the terminal building at Malaga airport, and it's as though I've suddenly been wrapped in a welcoming hug. I'm not sure, of course, that I deserve any welcoming hugs, because the last couple of weeks have been a total nightmare and the burden of guilt gets heavier every day. This morning, when Chris told me to have a great hen weekend with Sive, I nearly backed out of it altogether, but I couldn't desert her at the airport, not after she'd gone to all the trouble of arranging everything and not after she'd already had to talk me out of abandoning the plan!

The Monday following dinner at her home, she'd called me to agree the dates for our trip. Away from the music that had lured me into thinking that I was surrounded by signs and omens, I told her I was having a change of heart. That I was never going to find a better man than Chris and it was just a case of pre-wedding nerves.

'We said this before,' she reminded me. 'What we need to do is prove it. Otherwise it'll always be there, nagging you. Every time you have a disagreement you'll be thinking "what if". Better to deal with it now.'

Even though she might have been right, I wanted her to change her mind, but she was firm and determined and I think she really does want me to find Luke and be humiliated by him. Which is what will happen. So she went ahead with the holiday plans, and despite the fact that I've spent the last few days going through wedding preparations with Dorothea, we're on our way to Marbella, which is where Luke said he lived. I haven't actually figured out how I'll react if I don't find him. Which is the most likely scenario.

When the cab pulls up outside the hotel, Sive suddenly turns to me and says that it's a long time since we've been away together, and that no matter what, we'll have a good time. I hope we do. I wish this was a proper hen weekend and not an occasion for me to make a fool of myself. And what if I don't? What if I meet Luke and he sweeps me into his arms and tells me he's always loved me? What happens then?

Sive was right about me having a meltdown. And she's right to drag me to Spain too, because I realise this whole thing was simply about me being girlie and silly and wanting some kind of secret romance. Faced with Luke Evans in the cold light of day, no matter how he reacts to me, I know I'll be happy about the choices I've made.

We walk into the hotel reception area. The Girasol is small and boutiquey, a couple of streets back from the beach. It's lovely, the sort of place I'd wanted to stay in Seville, beautifully modernised, but oozing Andalucian charm.

After checking us in, the receptionist calls a porter, who leads us across an internal courtyard dotted with bistro tables to the opposite wing of the hotel. Our rooms, next door to each other, both have high vaulted ceilings with fans turning lazily over enormous beds. Huge french doors open from each room on to a pretty garden stocked with hibiscus and bougainvillea. There's a tall palm tree in the centre which shades the grass from the full glare of the sun.

'Good choice,' I tell her as we stand in the garden.

'Nothing but the best,' she says in satisfaction. 'The only way to have a meltdown is surrounded by luxury.'

I nod approvingly. 'Will I be all right at the end of it?'

Her expression is unexpectedly serious. 'I sure hope so,' she replies. 'I don't want you to do something really stupid, Carlotta.'

Neither do I. But I do think it's a good idea to put it into perspective. It's important to know that every time I've dreamed of Luke and of Spain, it's been just that. A dream. Not reality. Never reality.

'We'll talk over dinner,' says Sive as she turns back towards her room. 'I don't know about you, but I need to have a shower and freshen up.'

I nod.

'How about we meet in the courtyard at seven thirty,' she suggests. 'I'm sure we could have a drink there. Then we'll head out and see what the eating options are.'

I agree to this and return to my room, where I unpack my bag, set my toiletries on the shelf in the bathroom then step under a tepid shower. I can't quite believe I'm here. Or that I'm looking for Luke. And I still don't know what will happen when I eventually find him. Somehow I'm sure I will, even though I've no idea where he lives or works.

* * *

The courtyard is shaded as the sun slides lower in the sky, but it's still warm. There's something about sitting at a table outdoors that makes me feel content, even if I'm also a mental wreck. Eating and drinking outdoors is good for the soul, and my soul certainly needs something good going on.

We're having tapas to go with the glasses of Rioja that we ordered. We haven't decided if olives and dates wrapped in bacon is enough for an actual meal, but right now I'm more in the mood for picking at food than sitting down to anything substantial. I nibble at one of the dates while Sive contents herself with the olives.

'So,' she says, when we're suitably settled. 'Let's put our plan together. Have you worked out how we're going to find this guy?'

'I have a sort of plan,' I admit. 'But it's not very detailed. Thing is, I couldn't find anything about Luke Evans on the internet.'

'He's difficult to track down all right,' she agrees.

'You tried?' I'm startled.

'You hardly think I'm abandoning my daughter and my job for a weekend to search for someone without at least having done some spadework,' she says. 'Give me credit.'

I should've known she'd do her research.

'And how did you get on?' I ask.

If she's managed to find him when I couldn't, I'll feel really stupid. But her expression is one of frustration as she speaks.

'He's pretty much ungoogleable,' she replies. 'You're right about his web presence. You'd imagine that someone who works for a charitable foundation would have something more substantial. Always provided he *does* work for a charitable foundation.'

278

I swallow the date I've been chewing and wash it down with Rioja.

'You think it's a lie?'

'I don't know what to think,' she says. 'It's no skin off his nose to say what he likes to you. He won't have been expecting to see you again, after all. You did say goodbye.'

She's trying hard not to sound censorious, but once again she's pointing out that Luke hasn't come looking for me.

'He told me he was an admin person,' I remind her. 'So maybe there's no need for his name to be all over the place.'

'Perhaps if you knew the name of the foundation or the charity or whatever we'd be able to trace him anyway,' she says.

'I'm sorry.' I look at her helplessly. 'I didn't ask. I wasn't thinking that I would ever be trying to find him.'

'Pity you aren't on Facebook,' she remarks. 'There's no hiding there.'

'Maybe he isn't either,' I point out. 'And you can't blame someone for wanting to keep a low profile on the net. It's a total invasion of privacy.'

Sive doesn't have quite the same view. She's highlighted on her company website and there are lots of links to talks she's given at various seminars, or quotes from her about well-known liquidation cases. She also has Facebook and Twitter accounts. She says that sometimes social media is her only leisure-time activity.

'Whatever,' she says now.

I can't let it go. 'Not everyone is all over the web,' I protest. 'That doesn't mean anything.'

I can see she's not convinced, that she thinks Luke's lack of profile is suspicious, but she says nothing.

'Here's everything I've got.' I take out my iPad and show her the saved searches I've made; they include information about the Four Green Fields pub, which still apparently exists, and a picture of Murielle in the estate agency. The picture doesn't give any information about where the agency is, but I thought we could ask around. There can't be that many Irish people running estate agencies here, can there? I also searched for 'Richard Evans nightclub', because Luke mentioned that his father owned one, but although there are loads of nightclubs in Marbella, his name hasn't come up in connection with any of them.

'Nevertheless, the nightclub might be a good starting point,' says Sive thoughtfully. 'If Evans senior's a bit of a player around town, I'm sure someone will know which club he owns.'

'I thought the pub might be a better start,' I say.

'On the basis that we probably won't go clubbing tonight, I suppose you're right. But the club is definitely a good option for tomorrow.'

I can't help laughing, and she looks at me curiously.

'I never thought I'd be back clubbing,' I say. 'I wasn't great at it first time round.'

She grins. 'Every good hen night has a nightclub in it.'

'I suppose so.' I lean back in my chair. 'You really do think I'm crazy, don't you?'

'Certifiable.' Her tone is so reasonable it makes her words seem even more precise. 'You love Chris, you know you do. Until a few weeks ago you were absolutely sure you were doing the right thing. He's done nothing that should make you change your mind. But everyone has a time in their life when they go off the rails a bit. All we need is a bit of damage limitation.'

She's a great friend.

'I'm sorry I've dragged you into it,' I say.

'Hey, we're having a holiday.' She looks cheerfully at me. 'It's ages since I've had a girlie break. So I'm looking on the bright side of your wrong-life fantasy. I'm pretty sure you won't be changing history.'

Luke and I always thought time-travel storylines were silly. He said it was incredibly arrogant to think that you could change history. Or that the timeline you were in was wrong. 'It is how it is,' he used to say whenever *Star Trek* or any other sci-fi programme showed characters wanting to 'fix' the present. 'It's not up to them to try to change it back. Who knows what other lives they'll mess up.'

I agreed with him then. I still agree with him.

But I'm not trying to change anything, am I? I've come here to prove the point. That nothing can be changed. We are who we are and I'll never be a flamenco dancer with a red dress whirling around my body. I'm a tight-suited, cool-headed velvet assassin. I always will be.

Despite the fact that we stay up talking until the early hours, we're both at the breakfast bar by eight thirty the following morning, and ready to embark on our mission to find Luke a half-hour later. The streets around the hotel are fairly quiet at this time of day, although when we cut through towards the beach we see that there are towels draped over sunbeds in the universal 'occupied' sign.

'I'd like to spend at least a couple of hours on one of those,' remarks Sive, and I promise her that we'll devote some time towards proper holiday things like topping up our suntans. Although topping up isn't the word. Both of us are pale and interesting given that our skin hasn't really been exposed to the sun so far this year, so it'll be more a case of remedial action than anything else.

According to the map I downloaded earlier, the Four Green Fields is about a kilometre away. It doesn't face directly to the sea, but is in one of the nearby side streets. Sive and I walk briskly along the promenade, past seafront cafés busy with people having breakfast, and finally climb some steps leading to the street where we hope we'll see the pub.

Which we do. It's decked out in the dark wood and small windows that are a feature of some Irish pubs abroad, but has a cheery green and white striped awning shading the outside pavement area, where the tables are tall barrels with high stools beside them.

I recognise the pub, not just from the info I got when I searched for it, but from the tiny photo I saw in the article about Richard's fund-raiser. The one in which he had his arm around Luke. It must have been taken on the promenade behind us.

'Are you all right?' Sive looks curiously at me.

'Yes, fine,' I reply. 'I just . . . it's weird, you know. Thinking of Luke living here while I was back in Dublin.'

'Was their home nearby?'

'I don't know,' I admit. 'He said it was nice.'

'Most of the houses here are,' she observes. 'I'm sure they weren't cheap, even eighteen years ago.'

The pub is small and dark inside, with a selection of Irish signposts and the ubiquitous Guinness mirror on the wall. After we order a couple of glasses of water we ask the barman, a genial man from the north of England, if he knows Richard Evans.

He doesn't, having bought the pub from someone else, but he tells us that he thinks Richard's nightclub is in Puerto Banus, and it's called Chances.

We thank him for the information and emerge into the sunlight, immediately taking out our sunglasses because it's much brighter now than it was earlier.

'At least we know the nightclub to go to,' says Sive. 'Means we don't have to hop from one to another.'

'I never planned to hop from nightclub to nightclub,' I tell her.

She laughs. 'Come on. Next stop the estate agencies.'

We have less luck here. Nobody seems to know of Murielle Evans, although in one place the agent tells us that he thinks she might have an agency in Fuengirola. Or perhaps Torremolinos. He's pretty certain that she doesn't operate out of Marbella. We thank him and flop into the wicker seats of the nearest bar. We're both hot and thirsty by now.

'This looking for someone stuff is hard work,' I say. 'And not as easy as you'd think.'

'I'm not traipsing around Torremolinos looking for estate agents,' says Sive. 'We've barely scratched the surface of them here. It's still a national pastime, owning property! You'd think the financial crisis never happened.'

It's true that there are a lot of estate agents around. It's also true that without knowing where Murielle's is, we have a very limited chance of finding her agency. I googled her name before we left too. There were a few hits but none of the photos were of the woman I knew.

'In any event,' says Sive after two orange juices arrive for us, 'she could've moved on from estate agency in the same way that Richard moved on from owning a pub.'

'I guess so.'

'It doesn't matter,' she tells me. 'We know the nightclub. Crank up the iPad and let's check it out.'

There's no Chances nightclub in Puerto Banus. We look at each other doubtfully. Bill, the barman, had seemed pretty definite.

'You'd imagine if he opened a nightclub there'd be some mention of it,' says Sive.

'Maybe there was in a local paper but it never made any search engine,' I say. 'Let's try something else.'

I input a number of different spellings of Chances, and strike it lucky on the third attempt. I open the link that takes me to Chanzes – the hottest, hippest night spot in Puerto Banus – and show it to Sive.

'Wow,' she says.

As well she might. The website shows lots of internal shots of mirrored walls, waterfall chandeliers and deep upholstered banquettes. In fact, I think, it's a blinged-up, supersized version of Richard and Murielle's home at Blackwater Terrace. Mum used to call it showy.

'Sounds like the place to be,' Sive adds.

I've never been one for nightclubs, and this looks like my worst nightmare. But if it's a way to find Luke . . . I shudder suddenly. What if I see him cuddling up to some woman?

'But that's what you need, isn't it?' asks Sive when I say this. 'For him to be living the high life, strutting his stuff with a woman on each arm and laughing hysterically when you come looking for him like a love-struck teenager.'

Well, I know that's sort of the plan, but it's heavy on the humiliation factor. I decide that what I really want is for him to say that he hasn't stopped thinking about me and that he should never have kissed me and that he's really sorry. I want to be able to forgive him and tell him that I'm in love with someone else.

I want to hurt him. Bloody hell, I realise with a sense of complete shock, is that what it was all along? Do I want him to feel some of the misery I felt as a fifteen-year-old? To take belated revenge for having been left behind without a word? If so, I'm an even more mixed-up person than I thought.

'Do you ever google yourself?' Sive realises that I'm not going to answer her previous question.

It's called egosurfing and everyone does it. I do it too. But I do it with a different objective. To make sure that there's as little out there about me as possible. Like I said, I don't want prospective or current clients seeing stuff about me that I don't want them to see. So I know, even as I type my own name into the search box, that there'll be very few hits.

'Which means he might have found it just as hard to find me,' I point out as I show her the meagre results.

'He knows where you live,' she says. 'He could've started there.'

I hadn't even thought that he could have called my parents' house. Which he hasn't done. Because that's something they definitely would've told me.

Sive sees the expression on my face.

'Maybe he forgot the number,' she says.

I haven't forgotten his. Even if I didn't have a phenomenal memory I wouldn't have forgotten it. It's a pity there were no mobile phones back then. Or Facebook. Or Twitter. We'd never have lost touch and I wouldn't be in the state I'm in now.

'Anyway, do you want to go to the club tonight?' she asks.

I do. And I don't. I'm here to find him and terrified of finding him. For as long as I don't, he's my secret unrequited love. My snippet of romance. My very own *Brief Encounter*.

'I'll take that as a yes.' Sive is back in management mode.

'Sive?'

'What?'

'Am I making a terrible mistake?'

'I'm here so it doesn't turn out that way.' She winks at me and gets up from the chair.

I'm glad we're in this together.

There are still some sunbeds available on the beach. We decide that we need to do some proper holidaymaking before our sleuthing. So we pay for the loungers and then Sive offers to stay with them while I hightail it back to the hotel to pick up some swimsuits, suncream and towels. I buy a couple of gossip magazines in the shop next door and then join her back at the beach.

'I know sunbathing isn't the main reason for being in Spain,' she says as she rubs cream into her stomach. 'But I badly needed some time away.'

'We should do it more often,' I agree.

'If you decide that you're going to live with Luke for the rest of your life, this might be an everyday occurrence for you,' she says.

Deciding to live with Luke isn't why we're here. We've come so that I can be sure that I don't.

Sive knows I'm thinking this and she opens her magazine. But I'm not going to rise to the bait. I stretch out on the sunbed and open the second magazine. I'm asleep before I find out if some celebrity I've never heard of has broken up with her husband of six weeks or not.

We spend the rest of the day reading, dozing and drinking water to stay hydrated and don't leave the beach until the dying rays of the sun slide beneath the sea. Then we return to the Girasol and get ourselves ready for a late night. Mindful of the clubbing, I choose a filmy dress that I bought two or three years ago but hardly ever get to wear. It's short, peach lace and organza, and not at all the sort of dress I usually go for, but it's the closest to a sexy nightclub outfit I have. I wear it with high heels and a selection of gold costume jewellery. Instead of my sparkly clips, I pin one with a gold butterfly in my hair.

'Lovely,' says Sive when we meet in the hotel lobby. She's wearing a multicoloured floral dress that shows off her long legs.

It's a short cab ride to Puerto Banus. We ask the driver to leave us at the marina, although we know that Chanzes is set back a little from the sea. But we're here to eat first because we know it'll be late before the nightclub opens. Before eating we stroll around the shops. Puerto Banus is full of designer boutiques and I can imagine Murielle spending lots of time flitting from Vuitton to Armani, Versace and Ferragamo. Even before labels were a big thing, Murielle always described her clothes by who'd designed them. I remember telling her that I really liked a pair of jeans she was wearing (my mum never wore jeans back then), and Murielle flashed a huge smile at me and said 'Cerruti' even though I had no idea who or what Cerruti was or why Murielle was so pleased about him. Or her. I'm still not big into labels although I spend a lot of money on my work outfits. But Marbella is probably label heaven for Luke's mum.

Both Sive and I are more up for going to bed than staying out by the time we decide we should head for Chanzes, which is a ten-minute walk from the restaurant where we've had calamari and salad. We hear it before we see it, a big square building that seems to be mainly glass, bathed in purple light. There's a queue to get past the purple and silver rope that bars the entrance and I don't know on what basis people are being allowed in. I'm not sure that we'll make it because everyone in the queue – male and female – seems to be stunningly beautiful. Manufactured beauty, Sive whispers as we stand in line, and I guess that's true, at least as far as the girls' boobs are concerned, because there are a lot of perfect round globes straining at the flimsiest of tops. Sive and I are definitely overdressed, even though we're showing a lot more boob and thigh than usual ourselves.

But we're let in all the same. We discover that there are three levels to Chanzes. The ground floor, which is the main bar and dance area, is ultra-modern in design, all steel and glass and strobe lighting, which reflects off the mirrored walls I recognise from the website; one level up there's a cocktail lounge that seems to open on to an outside terrace; the second floor is off limits to us as it's for VIPs only. But we don't need to be with the VIPs, and both the cocktail bar and the dance bar are amazing. The club is filling up and the dance floor is becoming a seething mass of gyrating bronze limbs and blonde hair. It's also extremely loud. I suggest to Sive that we should head to the cocktail bar and stay there. We discover that it does indeed open to an outside terrace, which is slightly less manic than the interior, where one wall is bathed in pink light from massive crystal chandeliers and black and white film of the jet set in the sixties flickers on the one opposite. The whole thing reeks of money and decadence. It's completely over-the-top and breathtaking and I feel totally out of place among a crowd of people who seem blasé about it all.

Sive orders Bellinis, which we drink standing at a high glass-topped table while we people-watch. There's no real opportunity to talk because the music, though not quite as loud as downstairs, makes conversation difficult. Anyway, I'm not sure what we'd say – we're too busy gawping at the fabulous women and even more fabulous men. We must be giving off some kind of stay-away vibe, because nobody makes a move on us or tries to get us to dance. Not even the men (and women) who we realise work for the club because they are all wearing the same type of outfit. Slim-fitting trousers and open white shirts for the men, gold lamé bikini tops, the shortest of gold skirts and dominatrix heels for the women.

I'm totally dazed by it all, but the cocktails aren't half bad and there's a certain wonderment in being so completely out of my comfort zone. I've been to cocktail bars before, of course – part of working for Cadogan involves entertaining clients – but never anything like this. Besides, on those occasions I'm very aware that I'm not out for a fun night and I generally nurse one drink for the duration.

We're not quite into the spirit of it but getting there when I suddenly see him. He's wearing a white suit, which could look kind of seventies but actually, teamed with a casual blue T-shirt, is surprisingly on trend and is exactly right for where we are. He's different to how I remember. His head is shaved and there's some designer stubble on his cheeks. His eyes are older, more worldly. But he's still Richard Evans. Luke's dad. And he has a girl on his arm. I presume it's obligatory for nightclub owners to have girls on their arms.

She is, of course, young and extremely beautiful. She has the kind of dark, lustrous tresses that you see in advertisements for the latest sleek and shiny hair-care products. There's so much of it that I'm pretty sure she's wearing extensions. Her skin is smooth and flawless; her make-up enhances her expressive eyes and red, pouting lips. She's wearing a short black dress and shoes with heels so high that I don't know how she can stand on them. But she can, and she looks amazing. It doesn't matter if her beauty is natural or cosmetic. She's by far the loveliest (and sexiest) woman in the place.

It's a very different world from Blackwater Terrace and Richard Evans going down the pub with Murielle for a night out. Hogan's was our local, not that I frequented it much because back then it was a dark suburban pub with threadbare seats and a carpet that never seemed properly clean. It's since been upgraded to a gastro-pub with Scandinavian blond furniture and wooden floors, and Mum and Dad go there every Sunday for lunch. But in my mind it remains gloomy and poky.

I can't take my eyes off Richard. I'm wondering if he's had a facelift because he looks remarkably fit for a man who must be in his sixties. It used to be a bit sad for guys in their sixties to hang around nightclubs. Maybe it still is. But obviously not if you're the owner.

Sive has seen me staring at him and she looks at me quizzically. I mouth his name at her and her eyes widen.

'Handsome,' she mouths back.

I nod.

'Does Luke look anything like him?'

'Better looking.'

Her eyes widen even more.

'Now I understand.'

'Huh?'

'Sweetie, that man is gorgeous. No wonder you kissed his son.'

'I didn't kiss Luke because of his looks,' I tell her, and she gives me a sceptical glance. She turns back towards Richard and the glamorous girl and I can see the cogs turning in her brain. She's thinking that with me and Luke it's all about sex. It has to be. And maybe she's thinking that coming here was a bad idea after all.

Eventually she looks at me again.

'You going to go over to him?' she asks.

I can feel my heart pounding in my chest. I used to sit in the same kitchen as this man. I used to watch TV in the same room as him. He used to go to the same pub as my dad. But now they're worlds apart. And I don't know him any more.

'Carlotta?' Sive digs me in the ribs. 'He's going to the VIP lounge. You want to get him before then.'

The VIP lounge is accessed by a small glass lift watched over by a burly security guard. Even as I stand, paralysed, Richard and his girlfriend get into the lift and are whisked upstairs.

'I'm sure if you go over and say who you are he'll let you go up,' says Sive.

'You think?'

Richard Evans, this Richard Evans, wouldn't even remember

me. And even if he did, would he want to see me? Someone from a place he's left far behind.

'If you won't, I will,' says Sive. 'I didn't come here to be overawed by a man with a criminal past.'

'Oh, Sive . . .' I look anxiously at her. 'I can't. I just can't.'

'Do you want to find out about Luke or not?' She's properly angry with me now, her blue eyes hard and unforgiving. 'You're having your mid-life meltdown because of him! You've lied to Chris about your reasons for coming here, and now that you're within spitting distance of someone who can help you sort it all out, you've got cold feet?' Her voice rises with righteous indignation.

She's right about the cold feet. And everything else. I take a deep breath and then swallow the Bellini in one gulp. Sive downs hers too and we walk across the cocktail bar to the lift.

I try to explain to the security guard that I'm an old friend of Richard's, but he either can't hear me or doesn't understand me. In any event all he keeps doing is shaking his head at me. It's Sive who loses patience with both of us. She opens her bag, takes out a business card and writes on the back of it, *Carlotta O'Keeffe, friend of your son Luke, wants to see you.* She gives it to the security guard and gestures at him to bring it to the VIP lounge. He's hesitant at first, but then he calls over one of the gorgeous men in the tight trousers and hands the card to him. The gorgeous man disappears, and a few minutes later the security man presses his earbud closer to his ear and looks at us in some astonishment.

He opens the door to the lift and we step inside.

Another security man faces us when the doors open again. He escorts us through the VIP lounge (the decor of which is black and silver) and brings us into a smaller room. It's also slightly brighter although the lighting is still very subdued, and I can see Richard Evans sitting in a big upholstered chair. There's no sign of the model girlfriend.

As we walk in, he stands up.

'Carlotta O'Keeffe,' he says. 'Luke's little Carly. Well, well, well.'

'Mr Evans.' I feel silly calling him Mr Evans like I did when I was a teenager, but it would seem all wrong to call him Richard. Like it's wrong for him to call me Luke's Carly. He only ever called me Carlotta back in the day.

'How are you?' he asks. 'I wouldn't have recognised you. You've changed.'

'I'm older,' I say and he grins.

'And sexier.'

I'm blushing. I can't help it. He's my childhood friend's dad and an ageing nightclub owner, and even if he's still handsome, his trousers are too tight!

'And you are?' He turns to Sive and his eyes run up and down her body.

She introduces herself.

'You're both very welcome to Chanzes,' he says. 'I hope you're having a good time.' He takes out his mobile phone and taps on it for a moment.

'It's very impressive,' I remark.

The door to the room opens and another beautiful girl, this time with masses of long blonde hair, walks in. She's carrying a silver bucket containing a bottle of champagne. She goes to a shelf, takes down three glasses, opens the bottle and pours the drink. She hands a glass to each of us.

'Cheers,' says Richard Evans.

'Cheers.'

It's funny how you do things automatically sometimes, whether it's to be polite, or because you're not sure what else to do. It feels ridiculous to be sitting here drinking champagne with this man, but that's what I'm doing. It's good champagne, too.

'We're here to ask about Luke.' Sive has obviously decided that she needs to take control of the situation. 'We're looking for him.'

'Luke?'

'Your son,' she says briskly.

'You and Luke were such good friends, weren't you?' He ignores Sive and looks at me.

'Until you left,' I say. 'Until you ran away.'

'It was a difficult time,' says Richard Evans. 'But it was the only thing I could do. And Carlotta, not everything you heard about me was true.'

Even if it wasn't, he still fleeced the O'Connells. I know that for a fact.

'I'm not interested in any of that,' I say. 'All I want to do is contact Luke.'

'Why?' asks Richard.

'Because I . . . Look, it doesn't matter why. I just want to get in touch with him,' I say. 'So if you could give me a number, I'd appreciate it.'

Richard throws back his champagne and refills his glass.

'What makes you think I know where Luke is?'

'You're his father,' I say. 'And if you don't know, then perhaps you can give me the number of someone who does.'

Nervous though I was at the start, I'm quite bolshie now. I'm not afraid of Richard Evans. Or overawed by him. Or anything. I just want to find Luke.

'I'm sorry, Carlotta, I can't do any of those things.' Richard leans back in his chair. 'I've cut my ties with the past.'

'Luke isn't your past,' I say. 'He's your son.'

'Luke has made it perfectly clear that he doesn't see me as much of a father figure,' Richard says. 'He has no interest in being with me; quite frankly, he's his own man these days. He's an adult. You can choose your friends but not your family, blah blah. His choice.'

'But he lives here,' I protest. 'In Marbella. You must know where he is. What he does.'

'I don't,' says Richard. 'We haven't been in touch for years. I tried, he didn't. I respect his choices. Besides, we were never that close.'

So Luke was telling the truth about that. I look at Sive, who shrugs.

'What about his mother?' she asks Richard. 'Could she help us, d'you think?'

'My ex-wife does her own thing too,' says Richard. 'I haven't a clue where she is either. In fairness to Murielle, she stuck with me through the bad times. Stayed for some of the good times. But now she's got a new man and a new life. I don't see her or talk to her.'

'Does she still have the estate agency?' asks Sive.

'You've really done your research, haven't you?' Richard looks at her thoughtfully. 'No, she doesn't. She sold up. And I have no idea where she is because I don't keep tabs on my exes. I do know that she spends a lot of her time in South America. With the new man. Who's younger than me.

Younger than her as a matter of fact. But then she always was a bit of a cougar.'

I can't go to South America in search of Luke's mother. If I can't find him, I doubt I can find her.

'Oh well,' I say. 'It was worth a shot. Thanks for your time, Mr Evans.'

Bolshie or not, I still feel like I'm a kid when I'm talking to him, which is a bit mad.

'What's with this sudden interest in Luke?' he asks. 'Blackwater Terrace was a long time ago.'

'It's not important,' I say. 'I just . . . well . . . it doesn't matter. But if you are in touch with him ever . . .' The thought has just occurred to me. 'Please don't say I was here.'

He gives me a puzzled look. 'Why not?'

'It was a bit of a spur-of-the-moment thing to look for him,' I say. 'But now I'm thinking the past should stay in the past.'

'I couldn't agree with you more,' says Richard, while Sive shoots a sideways look at me.

I'm sure she's wondering about my sudden desire for the past to stay where it is, while the man who swindled the neighbours certainly doesn't want his younger days revisited.

'We'd better go,' I tell him.

'It's early,' he protests. 'We've a great new DJ coming in shortly. And I'll give you some VIP passes.'

'No thanks.' I shake my head.

'Still not really the party sort, are you?' He smiles at me. 'You were always a bit nerdy, Carlotta.'

I don't reply.

'And have you done well out of the nerdiness?' he asks. 'You could remember stuff, couldn't you? Luke was always very impressed by that. Actually, we all were. I remember thinking you'd be a good person to bring to a casino.'

He did? He had visions of me counting cards or something? Even back then?

I must look as surprised as I feel, because he laughs.

'I thought about getting into the casino game myself,' he says. 'It's very lucrative because nobody, not even you, can beat the house. But the nightclubs are my thing. It's nice when you find your thing.'

Even if it's funded by other people's money. I don't say this out loud. I don't want to insult him, which is daft. Nevertheless, it's really hard to believe that Richard Evans swindled anyone. He's so damn charming. He always was and he always will be. He can't help himself. But he's hardly a salutary lesson about crime never paying. As yet another gorgeous girl walks into the room, it seems that, for Luke's father, it has paid very well indeed.

Chapter 21

**Recuerdos de la Alhambra (Memories of the Alhambra)
– Pepe Romero**

We leave the nightclub and get into a cab without saying a word. Although Puerto Banus is still heaving with people, it's quieter back at the hotel, where the only person around seems to be the receptionist. I don't want to go to my room despite the fact that it's the early hours of the morning, and I ask if the bar is open.

'I can get you a drink if you wish,' says the receptionist. 'What would you like?'

Sive suggests gin and tonics, which both of us usually order only when we're really stressed. We sit in the comfortable lounge area and wait for the drinks. When they come, they're heavy on the gin and light on the tonic. I gasp at the taste of the alcohol, but I welcome it. The receptionist also leaves a small dish of olives on the table. They make me feel less of a lush.

'Well, that was instructive,' says Sive, popping one into her mouth. 'What a man.'

'You say that in admiration? Horror? Disgust?'

'Not admiration,' says Sive. 'Fascination maybe. He's very determined, isn't he?'

I nod. 'He was always like that. That's why we all thought he was so successful.'

'He has a presence, all right. And if Luke is anything like that . . .'

'Luke is nothing like his father,' I say. 'Nothing at all.'

'But you said he was better looking.'

'That's different. He is. He's also a lot younger. Obviously.'

Sive grins. 'If he gives off those power vibes, though, I can see what your problem is.'

'He doesn't. Luke is much gentler.'

'And yet he has a hold over you. Just like I imagine Richard could have a hold over people,' muses Sive. 'A sort of animal magnetism.'

That's not the vibe I got from Luke. Though in fairness, his kiss was pure magnetism.

'Do you believe him when he says he hasn't kept in touch with Luke?' I ask.

She considers this for a moment, then nods. 'I think it's very possible. The man clearly carved out a particular life for himself. If his family didn't approve or fit in – and let's face it, how many first wives and children would fit in with the siren we saw on his arm – then I can quite easily see him leaving them all behind.'

'They're family, though,' I object. 'I know Luke told me he didn't see much of his dad either, but surely they at least keep in touch.'

'Your family does,' Sive agrees. 'Because that's the sort of people you are. Loads don't. I think it's a shame; because I have so few relatives, I think it would be lovely to have more, but on the other hand, if there's someone in your family who drives you nuts, what's the point?'

'So no joy from Richard, no joy from Murielle and no sign of Luke.' I take a large gulp of gin. 'It's not gone well, has it?'

'Not in the finding Luke sense.' Sive nods. 'What's next?'

'Richard made me feel like I was fifteen again,' I admit. 'And he's right, Sive. *You're* right. Luke is out of my life. I don't need to see him to know that. I don't need for him to laugh at me. I was just chasing rainbows.'

'More like storm clouds,' she says.

I high-five her. And we order another round of gin and tonics.

I don't know what time it was when we went to bed, but when I open my eyes I wish I'd kept them shut. My head is pounding and my mouth is desert dry. I ease myself into a seated position and take a generous swig from the bottle of Evian water beside my bed. I half open the shutters, grimacing at the shaft of light that slices through the bedroom, then pad into the en suite and stand under the shower for at least fifteen minutes. Chris, when he's hung-over, does a very macho hot-shower-followed-by-cold-shower regime, but I'm too cowardly for that. My shower is tepid. I feel marginally better after it, and then I get dressed in a light top and pair of shorts before opening the shutters completely and reaching for my sunglasses as the light floods the room. I check my phone and realise that it's nine o'clock. I can't really call it sleeping late, as I suspect I probably passed out in an alcohol-induced coma as soon as I got to the room. So it was more of a drunken stupor than a refreshing night's slumber. I'm pretty sure that Sive won't be up yet and so I sit on the patio outside my room, rehydrating with the bottle of water and half reading another of the gossip magazines I bought.

It's about an hour later when she opens her own patio doors and steps into the garden.

'Hi,' I say.

'Don't.' She lifts her sunglasses to show two bloodshot eyes, blinks rapidly and drops them to her nose again.

'Don't what?'

'Speak too loudly.' She groans. 'What were we thinking? How many of those damn G&Ts did we have?'

It might have been four. But the measures were huge. So in terms of what we're used to, it was probably off the scale.

'I think I'm going to die,' she moans. 'Right here. Right now.'

'Oh dear.'

'Don't tell me you feel all right?'

I explain that my tepid shower and consumption of almost a litre of water has helped considerably and that I'm thinking a spot of breakfast will finish my recovery. She shudders. Breakfast is not on her agenda, she informs me. Lying on her bed is. She suggests I get something and return in a few hours, when she hopes that Solpadeine and a darkened room will have done their magic.

'Are you sure?'

'Sweetie, I can't even stand,' she says. 'I have to go back to bed.'

I leave her to it.

They've finished serving breakfast in the hotel, so I head to a café on the corner of the street for some coffee and pastries. It's a traditional whitewashed building with tables set beneath the jacaranda trees on the pavement outside. As I sit down, I wish that every Monday morning had time for coffee at a sunny pavement café. It's far removed from a tepid mug of instant muck at your desk. Or a tasteless cup of filter coffee at a morning meeting. There are meetings going on at this café too, though. Local people dressed in suits are chatting animatedly and sharing images on iPads or phones. There's even occasional paperwork being passed about too.

I take out my own phone and check my emails. Nothing important, but a few things that will need my attention in the morning. I do realise that by taking the entire day off today, ahead of three weeks' honeymoon later in the year, I'm being incredibly blasé about my job. But it's been worth it.

It's been worth it because last night, amid the gin and tonics, I suddenly realised how out of proportion I'd let this whole thing with Luke get. Maybe meeting Richard Evans had kick-started my brain again. Maybe I really and truly realised that the past was the past and needed to be left there. Maybe I was just so drunk I reconnected with everything that was important to me. But whatever it was, I told Sive that I was very definitely over Luke and that I didn't need to see him to know I was ready to marry Chris, and that I couldn't wait to get home and throw myself into the wedding preparations.

'Really?' Sive looked at me out of a half-closed eye.

'Absolutely.' I repeated my assertions at least another half a dozen times, then texted Chris to tell him how much I loved him. Fortunately the text alert didn't wake him up, because he didn't reply with a 'for God's sake woman it's four in the morning' response, which would have been totally justified.

I've only just remembered that text and lack of reply, and so, while I wait for my Americano and croissant to arrive, I phone him now.

'Hello,' he says.

He doesn't answer his phone by saying 'Bennett' any more. That's why I love him. He listens to me.

'I just wanted to say that I love you,' I tell him.

'I'm glad to hear it. How did your hen weekend go?'

'We got smashed last night,' I confess.

'I guessed that when I saw your text. I didn't reply because I thought you might be in a coma.' He laughs to show that he was joking about the coma.

'I think I was, to be honest. We had cocktails. And gin. I hope I didn't wake you in the middle of the night.'

'No. I was out for the count. I saw it this morning. Mum had me looking at seating arrangements all evening.'

'She didn't! We were supposed to be doing that this week.'

'This was only provisional seating,' says Chris. 'Apparently the invitations haven't gone out yet.'

'Six weeks beforehand is plenty of time,' I tell him. 'She's just being a bit paranoid.'

'Whatever you say.'

'I'm right about this.' I make myself sound my most authoritative. 'I looked it up online.'

'I knew that between you, you and Mum would work it out.' He sounds pleased.

'We will.'

'Got to go,' he says, over the sound of someone calling his name. 'I'll see you later.'

'OK. You have my flight details?'

'Yes.'

'Love you.'

He doesn't reply, clearly already caught up in whatever issue he has to deal with.

I tip some sugar into my coffee. I rarely take sugar, but I need the energy boost today. I'm going to go on a strict detox when we get home and I'm going to focus all my attention on my upcoming nuptials. I feel quite grown-up and sensible as I say this to myself. As though the personal me has suddenly caught up with the professional me. But I also feel girlie and excited and decide that I'll organise a shopping expedition and book hair and make-up and do all the sort of things that brides-to-be are supposed to do. For me and Sive and Natasha, who's also going to be a bridesmaid.

Right now, I can't wait to get married to Chris and for it to be the best day of my life. I want to wear a gorgeous dress and have a fun reception (or at least as fun as possible given the venue) and I want Mum and Dad to enjoy themselves and be proud of me. What the hell, I don't really mind that Dorothea will undoubtedly take it over. She's a mum too, after all. If I'm making my parents happy and proud, I want her to be happy and proud too. She'll want everything to go without a hitch because it's in her home, and that suits me just fine. For once we'll be singing off the same hymn sheet.

I'm not hearing the Concierto de Aranjuez in my head any more. I've no desire to be a flamenco dancer. I want to go home and I want to be me again. I'm glad I came here but even gladder that I didn't humiliate myself.

I see the woman out of the corner of my eye. I don't immediately recognise her, because she's wearing a white shirt-dress with a narrow plaited belt over a pair of taupe shorts, and not the ultra-fitted black number of last night. Her sandals, though high-heeled, are significantly lower than the shoes she was wearing then too. It's her flowing, glossy hair with its shades of tawny and bitter chocolate that I recognise straight away, and how I know that she's the woman I saw with Richard Evans. I pick up my sunglasses and put them on as I watch her walk to the corner of the street. That's where she raises her hand and waves, and that's where Luke Evans emerges from a tall, narrow building and she wraps her arms around him and kisses him on the cheek.

I watch as they walk down the street together, his fair head and her dark one close together, animated in whatever conversation they're having. And then they turn the corner and out of my sight. My heart is thumping and my head is pounding again.

And that's it. That's my humiliation right in front of me after all. Luke and his father both know this girl. So whatever Richard said about them not being in contact can't be true. And Luke has kissed her. Well, strictly speaking, she's kissed him, but he didn't recoil from her in horror and I doubt, somehow, that's it's the first time she's kissed him. I know nothing about Luke and his life. Nothing at all. And yet I was prepared to jeopardise everything I had just because he made me feel special again.

I've had a lucky, lucky escape.

I fumble in my bag for my purse and take out more than enough cash to pay for my coffee and croissant. I leave the café and walk over to the tall, narrow building. I look at the brass name plates on the wall. I read them all – corporate names, and triple-barrelled Spanish names, and long phone numbers. None of them are Luke Evans. None of them refer to children or charity. None of them mean anything to me.

I walk to the end of the street and turn the same corner as Luke and the girl. They're nowhere to be seen. And that's a good thing. Because the Luke I once knew is someone else completely. He's made his choices. I've made mine. It's time to move on.

I don't tell Sive that I saw him. When I get back to the hotel, she's sitting in the dim lobby wearing her sunglasses, a glass of water in front of her. She tells me that she's fragile but functional and that she could probably manage coffee and a pastry. And so we go back to the café, where I order another Americano and where I anxiously scan the passers-by in case Luke reappears. Not that it matters to me at this point, of course. I'd already got myself back on track before I saw him and the girl and before I realised that Richard Evans probably lied about not keeping in touch with Luke, and Luke probably lied about whatever it is that he does, and the girl – well, goodness only knows who she is and where she fits in, but she's certainly close to both of them.

I'm relieved when we get up to leave. I'm even more relieved when we check out of the hotel and get into a taxi for the airport. I've closed the door on whatever history I had with the Evans family. My future is what's important now. The life I'm going to live. The life I'll be happy in.

The airport personnel have arrived at the gate and are getting themselves ready to board the passengers when my phone rings.

'Hi, Chris.'

'Lottie, I have a bit of a crisis on my hands.'

'What's the matter?'

'I'm at Mum's,' he says. 'She fell off a chair.'

I think I've misheard. How could she have fallen off a chair? And how has it become a crisis?

'She was standing on it. Measuring the height of the wall.' He sounds both exasperated and anxious. 'Something to do with the wedding. She slipped and fell and she's probably broken something in her arm. Maybe her leg too.'

'Oh Chris, that's awful. How is she?'

'Waiting for an ambulance,' he says. 'But I'm ringing you now because we'll end up in A&E and I don't know how long we'll be there. So I can't pick you up tonight.'

'Don't worry about me,' I say. 'I can get a cab. I hope she's all right.'

'I got a shock when she called,' admitted Chris.

'Poor Dorothea. Poor you.'

'I'll phone or text and let you know how things go,' he says. 'I don't know if they'll keep her in. She has private health care but I'm not sure what hospital we'll end up going to and if they'll have beds available . . .' He breaks off. 'The ambulance is here now. Got to go.'

'No problem. Talk later.'

'Bye,' he says, and ends the call.

The arrangement had been that Chris would drop Sive back to her house before crossing the river to mine, but as that's now out of the question, we begin to make our way directly to the taxi rank after we've walked through the terminal building in Dublin. Neither of us is fazed by not being met at the airport – we're both used to business travel and stalking off the plane and into a taxi. But we've only gone a few metres when we hear Sive's name being called and we look around.

Kieran has come to meet her even though she'd already told him that Chris would be there. But as he wraps her in a bear hug, he tells her that he wanted to bring her home himself. She looks very pleased to see him and I try not to look too uncomfortable while they say how much they've missed each other. The subject of Kieran didn't come up at all during our Spanish visit. It was all about me. It shouldn't have been. I should've made time for her too. I'm a terrible friend. I've been horrendously self-centred for the last few weeks. I need to get over myself.

'Where's your fiancé?' Kieran looks enquiringly at me and Sive is the one to explain about Dorothea's accident.

'Do you want a lift as far as Sive's?' he asks.

I shake my head and remind her that it's not the quickest way to my house. I say it's just as easy to get a cab.

'Are you sure, Lottie?' asks Sive. 'I mean, you can call one from mine and—'

'And there's a whole rank of them outside,' I interrupt. 'Honestly, Sive, it's no bother.'

She looks at me uncertainly for a moment and then nods.

'It was a great few days,' she says. 'Thanks for asking me.' There isn't a hint of anything in her voice to suggest that we've had anything other than a girls' weekend away. Nothing to make me feel that I'd been selfish and stupid. No hint of the fact that she was looking out for me the whole time.

'Thanks for coming,' I say. 'And see you soon. Lunch maybe?'

'Don't forget you have to arrange our bridesmaids' excursion,' she reminds me. 'Natasha will explode if you leave it much longer.'

'I won't,' I promise. 'I'll get on it first thing in the morning.'

'Great,' she says. 'Hope Dorothea's OK.'

'I'm sure she will be.' I give her a wry smile, then walk away from them to get my taxi.

Chapter 22

Anoche (Last Night) – Juan Carlos Quintero

I call Chris from the cab.

'Lottie,' he says as he answers the phone.

'How's Dorothea?' I ask.

'Finally being looked after.' He sounds exhausted and I'm not surprised. A&E is always stressful.

'Do you want me to come over?'

'To the hospital?' He sounds surprised.

'Or to Dorothea's.'

'Thanks for offering, but it's fairly chaotic here, and I'm not sure what time Mum will be released, so there's no point in you heading to Rathgar.'

He's right. I'd only be in the way at the hospital and, of course, I don't have the keys to Dorothea's house so I can't wait for them there. Besides, it could be a very long wait.

'I'll call you tomorrow,' he adds.

'Tell Dorothea that I'm thinking of her,' I say.

'I will.' His voice is warm. 'Thanks, Lottie.'

'Talk tomorrow.'

I end the call as the taxi pulls up outside my house.

I let myself in and stand in the darkened hall. I'm sort of relieved that I don't have to head to the hospital or to Dorothea's, because I'm suddenly exhausted. I feel like I've run a marathon and all I want to do is collapse into a chair. I haul my bag upstairs and leave it in the bedroom and then go back down again because, tired though I am, I'm suddenly hungry.

I like that everything in the kitchen is exactly how I left it – my favourite red mug upturned on the draining board, the iron on the worktop where I left it to cool after dealing with the stack of work blouses piled on a chair. I find ironing them therapeutic. It's the only domestic chore I'm any good at. Maybe because it requires precision, and I'm good at that.

The few pieces of fruit in the bowl in the middle of the table are looking a bit tired and I tip them into the bin. I open the freezer and take out a loaf of bread, and pop a slice into the toaster. Then I make myself a latte. I know that coffee isn't really a good idea; I actually want to sleep, but even though I'm tired, I'm too edgy to go to bed. This happens to me all the time when I'm working on a big project for Cadogan. No matter how tired I am, the ideas chase themselves around in my brain and keep me awake. Although obviously tonight it's not Cadogan keeping me awake.

The toast pops out of the toaster and I spread a dollop of Nutella on it. Then I take it and the latte outside because it's warm in the house. Not as warm as Spain but warmer than I expected. I sip the coffee standing in my yard. Or patio, as the estate agent who sold the house described it. Shortly after moving in, I bought a small outside table and a couple of chairs and I envisaged spending many evenings enjoying a cool glass of wine and soaking up the evening sun in a kind of sophisticated urban way, but of course I've hardly ever done that. The yard doesn't get as much evening sun as I expected and it's normally too chilly in the shade to linger over glasses of wine. But tonight it's positively balmy and I sit at the table with my toast and coffee. Although the sky is clear, it's impossible to see the stars because of the light pollution from the city. (Gazing at the night stars was another of my pre-ownership fantasies.) But I'm quite content sitting here with the hum of the traffic for company.

I'm glad Sive and I went to Spain. I've achieved what I wanted. Closure on the whole Luke Evans scenario. I know that I'll always harbour some kind of residual feelings for him – maybe everyone does with their first crush – but now I can put him out of my mind forever.

I get up suddenly and fetch my iPhone from inside. I think about texting Sive to thank her again for putting up with my madness. She's the best friend a girl could have. I have the message composed before I remember that she's gone home with Kieran McDonagh and she probably doesn't want messages from me disturbing her.

A knot forms in my stomach when I think of them together. I wish we'd talked about him while we were away. Much as I needed to be saved from myself, Sive needs to be saved from Kieran McDonagh.

I delete the message, then open iTunes and do a search for the Concierto de Aranjuez. There are lots of different versions but I download the first one I see. I press play, and the haunting melody fills the night air. It's important to me to be able to listen to it without feeling like I should be somewhere else. Nevertheless, as I stare at the sky, I still can't help thinking of Fuente del Rio and Luke Evans and speeding through the mountains in the Aston Martin. I think of how close to him I felt then, of how he made me feel,and I can't believe he's not the man I wanted him to be.

I silence the phone. I'm never going to listen to the Concierto de Aranjuez again. Although it evokes memories of Luke, it also rekindles the passion in my soul and a longing in my heart. Not for him. Just for my life to be different. Less precision. More passion.

I know it's nonsense. Chris and I share plenty of passion – we have phone sex, for heaven's sake! And I'm passionate about being a management consultant too. Although perhaps it would sometimes be nice to be the girl in the red dress, stamping my feet and clicking my castanets instead of wielding my iPhone and my PowerPoint presentation.

I close my eyes and I'm back in Seville. I can feel the warmth of the air and the heat of Luke's body as we stood together in the lift. I can feel the fire of his lips on mine and my arms gripping him tightly, and I know that I didn't want to let him go.

My coffee is going cold in front of me. I can't finish it. I can't finish the toast either. I can't do anything other than think that I'm supposed to have found closure but I haven't. Because even though Luke Evans will never be a part of my life again, he's destroyed the life I had. I've known it from the moment he kissed me, yet only now do I accept it. Nothing happens without consequences. And the consequences of that moment in Santa Justa station are more wide-reaching than

I ever imagined. Dammit, I think, as I watch a shooting star streak across the night sky. If I was going to allow Luke Evans to wreck everything, I should've made it worth my while! I should've just slept with him and found out what it was like.

I exhale slowly and wonder if this is truly the conclusion I've come to. Am I really thinking of breaking it off with Chris to be on my own? Am I allowing my past to destroy my future?

I get up and go into the house. My A4 notebook, where I jot down all my work ideas, is on the table. I pick it up, along with one of my brightly coloured pens, and go outside again. When I work with clients I often tell them to write down the pros and cons of their important decisions so that they have a flow chart leading them to a certain conclusion. I'm going to do my own flow chart now.

I write Luke's name at the top left-hand corner of one sheet, and Chris's on the right. Beneath Luke's I write: *passion, kiss, longing, desire.* And then I write *hopeless.* And *liar.* Beneath Chris's I write: *love, sharing, understanding, togetherness.* And then *compatible.* And *safe.*

On paper, Chris and I are perfect. But we don't live our lives on paper. We live them in the real world, where things are messy and complicated and can't be solved by coloured pens and flow charts. I tear out the page and crumple it up.

But I can't erase how I feel.

And Chris deserves better than someone like me.

After a sleepless night, I get up at six thirty and have the quickest of showers, not bothering to wash my hair, before getting dressed in one of my plain black suits. Chris thinks my black suits, along with the white blouse I usually wear with them, make me look like a solicitor. I think they make me look efficient. I pull on my patterned tights and high-heeled court shoes, run a brush through my hair, add a couple of clips and then head for the car.

The traffic hasn't had a chance to build up too much, so I'm in the office by 7.15.

'Carlotta.' Dirk joins me about five minutes later. 'Nice holiday?'

I have to gather myself to answer him sensibly. My head isn't in the business environment at all. I protest that I only took one day off.

'Ah, but I missed you.' Dirk grins at me.

It's a relief to be with someone who has no interest in my personal life.

'What's up?' I use my most professional voice for the question, and push thoughts of Luke, Chris and passionate music out of my head.

'Quite a lot, actually.'

'Oh?' I feel an anxious jolt in the pit of my stomach. What now?

'I'm leaving Dublin,' he tells me.

'Dirk!' I search his face for signs of anxiousness or worry as I remember his concerns about power struggles within the company and his own position as a result. 'D'you want to leave? Or has this been forced on you?'

He looks complacent. 'It wasn't forced on me.'

He would say that, wouldn't he? Men do. They never admit to being squeezed out or sideways or anything. Women are different. We confess to each other that we've been stabbed in the back or passed over or whatever. But men – they take the ball and start running, spinning the story to their advantage.

But Dirk seems to be telling the truth. The company is setting up a division in Cape Town and he's going to head it up. It's a big promotion for him and he'll be moving there a few weeks after our conference.

'Who'll be taking over?' I ask him.

He gives me an appraising look. 'The king is dead, long live the king?'

'Don't be silly. I'm sorry you're going. But your replacement will set the tone for our work here and—'

'And it's a good question to ask. I don't know yet. In fact nobody outside the group management team knows anything about Cape Town. I told you because I know I can trust you, Carlotta.'

'Thank you.' I'm flattered. Although having the soon-to-be-ex-CEO trusting me isn't as useful as having the next CEO trust me.

'I've always trusted you,' says Dirk. 'I like working with you. You're a straight person.'

Hmm. Well. Not always. Not when it comes to my personal life. Personally, I'm a deceitful . . . Oh well. Professionally, though, I'm as straight as they come.

'You'll keep it under your hat for the time being, won't you?'

'Of course. I'm still astonished you told me.'

'I had to tell someone.' He looks slightly embarrassed.

Dirk is unmarried. He doesn't have family in Ireland. But he has friends.

'There's no one close enough.' He seems to have read my thoughts. 'You and I – well, we've always got on. Talked about things.'

That's true. I'm always conscious that Dirk is my boss but I'm never afraid to tell it to him like it is. As a consequence, he's shared titbits of office gossip with me in the past. But this is different. This is huge.

'When I know who's taking over I'll tell you,' he says. And then he gives me a knowing smile. 'It'll allow you to set yourself up, Carlotta. For better things.'

I look at him. I know what he's hinting. That in the inevitable reshuffle of responsibilities that comes with a new boss, there will be opportunities. I need to be ready to stake my claim to them. And I will be. Because I don't have to think about being the married woman in the office any more. I won't be that woman. Even though I'm still wearing my beautiful engagement ring, I won't be marrying Chris. I love him too much and not enough to go ahead with it. I just have to tell him.

'Do a good job at the conference,' he says. 'Let them see you shine.'

'Did you know before?' I ask. 'Is that why you wanted me to give the opening address?'

'I didn't know. But it was possible.'

'Thank you.' I smile at him. In corporate politics you get used to being shafted. It's not often that you get a leg up. But Dirk has definitely given me one.

'You're worth it, Carlotta,' he says. 'You deserve the best shot.'

'Thank you,' I say again.

He leaves the office and I sip my almost cold coffee.

Changes in Cadogan.

I'll be ready. I've nothing else to distract me.

Chris eventually texts to say that Dorothea is home again. She has a broken wrist and a sprained ankle. She's been lucky, it could've been a lot worse, but I realise that this is bad enough for a seventy-year-old woman, even if she is made of steel. I phone Chris and ask him what his plans are for the day. He says that his schedule is in disarray because of having to be at the hospital. He tells me he'll call me when he has a better idea of how he's fixed. I ask him if anyone is with Dorothea now and he says that Pen has taken the day off. But he thanks me for worrying about his mother and for suggesting that I might be able to be with her. I didn't actually suggest that, but I guess I sort of implied it by asking if she was alone. Chris now thinks I'm a lovely person. I hope he's good with disillusionment.

I turn my attention back to my work and stay engrossed until Ian McKenzie puts his head around the door and asks me about the Cadogan conference. He wants to know how many of my clients are coming and I say I haven't seen the latest list of acceptances so I don't know. All of Ian's major accounts will be putting in an appearance, it seems, and he says that they're looking forward to the sessions.

'How's the speech going?' he asks.

'Pretty well,' I reply.

'Hope you do a good job,' he says.

'I will.'

He's irritating, is Ian. And he's behind the curve because he doesn't know about Dirk. I hug that piece of knowledge to myself as I tell him that I'm going to get a sandwich – even though I'm still not hungry. But I head to the café and buy a takeaway roll to eat at my desk. Like all the rolls they do at the café, it's very tasty, but with every bite some of the filling slides off the bread and on to the glossy wood. If – when – I get promoted, I'll have to forgo the kind of rolls that make a mess. It wouldn't look good for junior staff to find an executive consultant – the next level up for me – surrounded by tomato and egg.

I dispose of the remains of my roll in the bin, clean the desk and wipe my hands on a paper napkin. My phone beeps and it's Sive saying that she really enjoyed our time away and it's awful being back at her desk. She adds that Natasha is super-excited about our planned shopping expedition for bridesmaids' dresses. I don't reply. I have to talk to Chris before talking to Sive. Besides, my friend will be gobsmacked by my sudden change of heart.

I used to be boringly predictable. Now I'm anything but. Even to myself.

Chapter 23

Fantasía (Fantasy) – Pepe Romano

It's nearly five when Chris calls me to ask if I could sit with Dorothea for a while. Pen has to go out and he won't be home till seven, and she needs someone to be there. I feel such a fraud talking to him, even though I don't mind staying with Dorothea until he arrives. I imagine she's a lot frailer and less domineering since her fall.

I arrive at her house a little after six. Pen lets me in and says that she can't hang around, so I'm alone with Dorothea straight away. Weirdly, knowing that I won't be part of her family in the future makes me far more relaxed about being here. She's sitting in one of the high-backed armchairs, her arm in a sling and her bandaged ankle resting on a brocade footstool. I can see strain etched on her face, but nonetheless she looks almost regal in her Chanel suit and gold jewellery and not half as frail as I'd imagined.

'You must have had a terrible fright,' I say as I sit opposite her.

'I don't remember much about it,' she admits. 'One minute I was on the chair, the next I was on the floor.'

'Chris said you were measuring the wall. What on earth for?'

'Oh, I was thinking of some tall indoor plants for the wedding,' she says. 'I wanted to see exactly how high they'd reach.'

And for that she's now got a broken arm and a sprained ankle. When there won't be a wedding at all. I swallow hard. I'm not going tell her that her injuries have been in vain. Not yet.

'The wedding file is on the sideboard,' she says. 'Bring it over and we'll go through it.'

I look around and see the binder, which has doubled in size since I was last here. I bring it to her.

'I've printed out your proposed guest list,' she says. 'I thought I might ask one or two more of my friends. They'd enjoy the day.'

It's irrelevant, but even if it wasn't, I couldn't say no.

'And I downloaded the sample music from the musicians from iTunes.' She looks pleased with herself. 'I didn't know how to do that before, but it's quite simple, isn't it?'

I nod.

'Have you bought your dress yet?'

She knows I haven't. I say that I'm planning a big day out with Sive and Natasha soon.

'At least you know how to dress,' she says.

I look at her in surprise.

'You're always well turned out. Not like some girls.'

I don't know who the some girls are and what they wear that Dorothea disapproves of. Short skirts? Skimpy tops? How come she's suddenly approving of me?

'So the one thing I'm not worried about is you looking ridiculous,' she continues.

321

'You haven't paid any deposits or anything yet, have you?' I ask.

'No, because I haven't made any final choices.' She smiles suddenly. 'It's all very exciting, isn't it?'

I can't believe she's excited about it now, when she was so frigid about it before. I feel terrible not saying anything to her as she chats away happily about menus and guests lists and her new-found ability to use iTunes. I can't help thinking that her organisation of my wedding would have been flawless.

I'm glad when Chris finally arrives, even though my stomach is a tight ball of tension from keeping my terrible secret from his mother. At least it's not because she's been horrible and icy towards me like she normally is.

He's brought Indian takeaway, which is the only takeaway food that Dorothea will eat.

'Given her crocked arm, it has to be something she can manage with a fork,' he tells me as he goes into the kitchen. 'I'll organise it, you stay here.'

My heart is thudding. I can't tell Chris I'm breaking up with him over an Indian takeaway!

'Come and get it!' he calls after a few moments.

We don't eat in the living room in front of the telly, like normal people. Dorothea doesn't believe in TV dinners. We go into the elegant dining room, where Chris has divvied up the rogan josh and chicken makhani on to Dorothea's fine china plates.

We talk a bit about the events of the previous night and we all agree that she was lucky it wasn't worse. Then she tells Chris about her plans for the wedding and he shoots me sympathetic glances. I know he's afraid I'll freak out about her micromanagement of everything, and if it was all going to happen, I probably would. But as it is, I simply say that all Dorothea's ideas are great ones. His eyes open wide at that, but she looks pleased and I think I've finally found a way to get on with her, which is just to tell her how wonderful she is. And I guess she is wonderful in a way. She's not letting a broken wrist and sprained ankle hold her back.

Chris begins to debate the music situation with his mother, suggesting that a female DJ who's a friend of Pen's might be a good compromise for dancing music. I'm startled by this because I didn't know that Pen knew DJs of any sex or that Chris would have even spoken to her about wedding arrangements.

'Pen assures me she's fantastic,' he adds.

If there was going to be a wedding I'd be feeling totally blindsided by all the Bennett involvement. But as with Dorothea, I just say that it sounds like a good idea. Which makes Chris look curiously at me.

'You don't want to go and hear her?' he asks.

'Not if you think she's the right person,' I reply.

Dorothea looks sternly at Chris. 'Carlotta is far too busy to bother herself with details,' she says. 'She understands the nature of delegation.'

Dorothea. My new best friend.

'It'll be a wonderful day,' Chris assures me.

'I know.'

It would be. The Bennetts have it all under control. If only I had.

After dinner we return to the living room, where the TV is eventually switched on so that Dorothea can watch a repeat of *Midsomer Murders*. She's a big fan of John Nettles and those English country crime dramas. I find it hard to suspend my disbelief at the fact that there can be so many murders in such a small area, but Dorothea insists that rural communities are hotbeds of crimes of passion. The Chief Justice apparently presided over quite a few murder cases in his career, so she feels she's an expert. Her other favoured viewing, not surprisingly, is any kind of legal drama. I bought her a box set of *Rumpole of the Bailey* for Christmas, which I thought was a very appropriate gift, although I don't think she's watched any of them yet.

Chris and I sit side by side on the sofa. Obviously I can't relax, but he stretches his feet out in front of him. The episode of the drama seems to go on forever, and by the end, I think the body count is around eight.

'If eight people were murdered in a country village you wouldn't be able to move for Sky News and assorted other channels cluttering up the place,' I observe as Barnaby and his cohorts round up the murderer at a local fete.

'I abhor twenty-four-hour news,' says Dorothea. 'They make a drama out of everything.'

I can't really disagree with her there. On a slow news day the most awful dross gets enough airtime to make it seem like imminent disaster.

'I'd better go.' I get up from the sofa. 'Thanks for a lovely evening, Dorothea.'

'Drive safely,' she tells me. 'Girls on their own out at night are fodder for criminals.'

She should watch less crime drama. Really.

Chris walks me to the car. I should say something to him now, but just as I couldn't break up with him over Indian takeaway, I find it hard to do it in the middle of the darkened street.

'You and Mum seem to be getting on like a house on fire,' he says. 'I was afraid you'd lock horns over wedding details.'

This is the ideal opening. We've just arrived at my car. There was no space in front of Dorothea's house so I had to park at the corner of her street.

'We need to talk about the wedding.' I've finally said it.

'I know,' says Chris. 'Tomorrow. When I'm not so stressed out by work and Mum and everything.'

I'm about to say 'no, we need to talk now', but I can see that he's tired. And, coward that I am, I'm thinking that another twenty-four hours would help me too. I can practise what I'm going to say. I'll write it down and memorise it, just like my talks for work. So that I don't mess it up.

'It wasn't your fault the Sorrento Bay had to close,' he says.

'I should have been on top of it sooner,' I tell him.

'It'll all work out in the end,' he says.

He kisses me. It's a friendly kiss. I lean my head on his chest for a moment. And then he says he has to go. He doesn't want to leave Dorothea on her own. 'But I might call later,' he adds. 'For . . . you know.'

What's one more deception? I ask myself as I start the engine and think about faking phone sex again.

Chapter 24

Almoraima – José de Córdoba

It seems that finding a time to break up is just as hard as finding the right time to propose to someone. After we got engaged, Chris told me that he'd been trying to work the conversation around to it for ages, but he never seemed to find the perfect moment. Even in the restaurant, with everything organised, he wasn't sure he was doing it the right way. I know exactly how he feels. I can't simply blurt it out, yet I don't know how to set the scene. It's really difficult.

I know he's going to be hurt no matter what I say, but I want to have the conversation in the right setting. I need to be thoughtful about it. I want to get it right.

Unfortunately, circumstances aren't on my side. He doesn't phone me until the morning because he spends most of the night sitting up with Dorothea, who has refused to take either the sleeping pills or the painkillers the doctor has prescribed on the basis that she's never needed them before, and who can't sleep as a result. At least it means I don't have to fake phone sex. Then he has to make an urgent unplanned trip to Seattle to look at some new laser machine because Edward, his colleague who had planned to go, has perforated an eardrum and can't fly.

He's back later today, but I won't be able to speak to him because it's the Cadogan conference and I can't have anything in my head other than my talk and our clients. It's madly frustrating, although I'm having to push that to one side, because right now, the conference has to take priority.

A number of Cadogan's senior management from various offices have come along and we're all pretty sure that our new CEO is among them. I need to make a good impression on them if I want to continue to climb the corporate ladder. And if my personal life has gone to hell in a handcart, my professional life will be even more important to me, so yes, I want to climb that ladder. I want to go as high as I possibly can.

Despite the fact that I'm word perfect for my speech, I'm nervous as I make my way to the large meeting room. Shaking with nerves actually, even though I'm doing my best to radiate an aura of serenity. I'm visualising the words I've written on the page, mentally reading them, getting the inflexions right. I'm not afraid of forgetting it, but I am afraid of not seeming professional enough, even though today I'm wearing my sharpest of sharp suits, an unforgivingly slim-fitting Louise Kennedy in midnight blue. I've teamed the suit with navy shoes and a white blouse, which I think gives me a kick-ass look, despite the fact that I have a sparkly clip in my hair. I thought about leaving it off, but it's become a sort of trademark for me and I'd feel lost without it.

The technical people are in the meeting room, checking that the sound level is correct and that the visuals are working. Dirk Cadogan walks in and pats me on the shoulder.

'Ready to rock and roll?' he asks.

'As I'll ever be.'

'I'm expecting great things,' Dirk says, and I give him a half-smile in return. He looks at his watch. Fifteen minutes to go. 'We'll start rounding them up shortly. You shouldn't be here until they've all taken their seats. We want you to make a dramatic entrance.'

I tell him it's not a Hollywood premiere. But we've already agreed on how things will work, and the plan is that I walk out to a full room, not sit at the front like a teacher waiting for the pupils to file in.

So I go to the Ladies', check my make-up, check the suit for any stray bits of fluff and then sit in a little anteroom while I wait for our guests to take their seats. Then, at a signal from one of the techies, I stride into the room and up to the front.

I'm looking at a sea of men who are also in navy-blue suits. And then I pick out the women, most dark-suited like me, but one in vibrant red. I thought about red for today too, but in the end decided to blend in rather than stand out. Being a woman sets you apart anyway. It doesn't matter how many women do well in business, we're still in a minority. But at least I'm here. Giving the welcome speech. Aiming to go higher.

I take a deep breath and begin. The words flow easily and smoothly, just like I practised. I speak about Cadogan, its past and its future and the successes we've had. I thank the clients who have been with us for a long time, I welcome the new ones, I tell those who aren't yet with us that I hope we get the chance to show what we can do for them. And then I introduce Steve Redmond, Dirk's number two (and

328

therefore another possibility for his job), who's making the first presentation.

Steve is an engaging man, but it suddenly occurs to me that I did a better job with my speech than he's doing now. I know I have the advantage of memory, but even so, I was fluent, clear and competent. I didn't stumble or hesitate as Steve occasionally does. I was as pretty close to perfect as it was possible to be.

Hopefully this means that I have secured further respect and kudos in Cadogan. I'm going to need professional respect when I've no personal life worth speaking of any more.

My job now is simply to mingle again, and that's what I'm doing when I feel the touch of a hand on my shoulder and I turn to see Antonio Reyes. I knew he'd be here, of course. I'd seen his name on the guest list.

'Hello, Carlotta,' he says.

'Antonio. It's good to see you.'

'You too,' he says as he gives me a courtesy kiss. 'You gave a good speech.'

'Thank you,' I say. 'But it's easy when I'm talking about a good company.'

'Well said.' Antonio laughs. 'And true. The plan you devised for us is working.'

'I saw the updates,' I tell him. 'You're moving fast.'

'We have to,' he says. 'Without change, Ecologistics doesn't have a future.'

I nod. That's what I try to explain to Dorothea. That what we do really does help. That with our advice, businesses that might otherwise have failed can succeed. But she doesn't see companies as individual people working together. As far as she's concerned, they're evil capitalists who don't deserve to do well.

'I hope you have a very long future ahead of you,' I say.

'I hope so too. In fact, I know we do. We lost our way for a time, but you showed us how to get back to where we want to be.'

I'm pleased at that.

'My board was very impressed with you, Carlotta.'

His pronunciation of my name makes it sound very seductive.

'I'm glad to hear that.'

'We think you would be an asset to our company.'

An asset to his company? I stare at him. Is he – is he actually headhunting me? At our own conference?

He obviously sees the surprise in my face.

'Maybe this is not the time or place to discuss this,' he says. 'But perhaps after dinner?'

We've arranged a dinner for our clients at Dublin Castle. All the Cadogan people will be there.

'Perhaps.'

He nods. 'Good. I will talk to you then.'

And he moves away, leaving me staring after him.

If the conference centre was modern and bright, Dublin Castle brings a historical perspective to our clients, although the cobblestones of the impressive courtyard make walking in high heels a bit of a nightmare. But inside, the room is wonderful and the tables are elegantly presented.

I'm sitting with a group of our newest clients, a group that includes Antonio Reyes. It's my job to keep the conversational ball rolling, and so I lob a few different topics at them and they eventually run with golf, which is a tried and tested subject and generally allows everyone to express a view.

330

Before today's conference I read the sports pages for a week so that I was totally up to date over the issues of whether Europe or America have the better golfers, or if Sir Alex Ferguson was the best football manager of all time, or if Brian O'Driscoll is a true legend in rugby.

My personal sporting activity is very much of the couch-potato variety. My gym membership works out at about forty euros a visit because I'm so erratic, although because of the wedding I've tried to get there a bit more often over the last few weeks. I suppose I'll be grateful for the toned body when Chris is hating me.

I'm planning to tell him the day after tomorrow, when the conference is over and my time is my own again. I know that our life together (soon to be apart) should be more important than Cadogan Consulting, but right now it can't be. The day after tomorrow is definitely the day, though, because I can't put it off forever. Besides, Sive wants to know about our shopping expedition. It's out of a sense of respect to Chris that I don't share my plan with my closest female friend, even though I probably should. After all, she knows more about the whole situation than Chris anyway. But it seems wrong to me. Still, Natasha in particular is getting very anxious about her dress. I'm going to have to buy her something to make up for it. As a way of saying sorry, you won't be a bridesmaid after all.

'. . . Ryder Cup captain. What do you think, Carlotta?' Antonio Reyes looks at me and I have to drag my mind back from broken engagements to the conversation around me. Even though I've been in my own world, I've still been listening with half an ear to the talk about the brilliance of European Ryder Cup captains over the past number of years, and so I agree with him that José María Olazábal was a great captain, even though I actually think he was probably just the luckiest.

They start comparing golf courses and I can't really participate in this because I've never stepped on one in my life. There's a golf outing tomorrow, but I won't be part of it. Perhaps I should take it up. Especially if I get promoted in the changes that will shortly take place in Dublin. Maybe that's what I can do with all the spare time I'll have on my hands now that I won't be getting married and supporting Chris and having babies like people expect.

After the meal we all disperse to different tables. I guess it's networking for both us and our guests, but by now it's all fairly laid-back. I'm feeling more relaxed about everything when Antonio approaches me again.

'So,' he says. 'About the idea of you working for my company.'

'I appreciate you wanting to talk to me, but this is still probably not entirely appropriate.' I glance across the room at Dirk Cadogan, who's in deep conversation with Ian McKenzie and Charles Hanson, from the London office. Is Charles in the frame for the CEO position? He's the deputy in London so it's possible. If so, it would be better for me to be there talking to them and not allowing Ian to monopolise them.

'It's a good opportunity,' says Antonio, and I forget about my rivals and look enquiringly at him. He tells me that they need someone to oversee the implementation of their changes throughout Europe. It's an important job. In fact, as he describes it, it would be more influential than any I could get at Cadogan.

'You would be based in Seville, but there would be a lot of travel in Europe,' explains Antonio. 'Occasionally to our Latin American offices too. Well, you would have guessed that.'

Seville again, I think. The flamenco. The music. The passion.

The possibility, no matter how remote, that one day I'd bump into Luke Evans again.

I can't move to Seville. My home is here and so is my future career. I say this to Antonio and I remind him that, despite my performance at the presentation, I can't even speak Spanish.

'I still find that hard to believe,' he says.

'It's true, though.'

'But you would be quick to learn.'

'Probably,' I agree. 'Nevertheless, Antonio, interesting as your offer is, I can't consider relocation right now.'

'These days nobody is chained to one place,' says Antonio. 'We are all in touch, everywhere we go. All I ask is that you think about it,' he adds. 'We – the board and I – we were very, very impressed with you.'

It's nice to think that I impressed them, no question. And as I reapply my lippy in the Ladies' afterwards, I realise that I'm pleased to have been approached by him like this. It's always nice to be headhunted, and it proves that no matter how crap I am at managing my life sometimes, I must be doing something right.

Which is a relief.

Chapter 25

Juan Loco (Mad John) – Rodrigo y Gabriela

It's late by the time I get home. The clients stayed social-
ising until well after midnight. In the case of Antonio Reyes,
I guess that's normal, since Seville seemed to be at its
buzziest then. It was almost two before he returned to his
hotel. At that point, the majority of our guests had gone
and only a few diehards were talking about going on to
other venues. They're the ones who aren't going to tomorrow's golf outing. It's an early start because they're being
picked up from their hotels before being driven to Mount
Juliet, a two-hour drive away. Right now I'm glad I'm not
a golfer and happy to be holding the fort at the office
instead. I won't really need to be on top form given that
so many of our clients will be living it large on the golf
course, but I want to be prepared for any eventuality. And
it's been a long day. I'm tired and I'm really hopeful of
falling asleep as soon as my head hits the pillow for a change.

I'm yawning as the cab pulls up outside my house. I pay
the driver and get out, and then realise, with some surprise,
that Chris's Volvo is parked nearby. I don't know why he

called around when he must be exhausted from his trip away and when he knew that I was at the conference all day. The last thing I want to do is break it off between us at half-two in the morning, but I can't pretend any longer.

I push open the door. He's stretched out on the sofa, his eyes closed. The TV is on a shopping channel, which means he must have fallen asleep ages ago, because he's never watched a shopping channel in his life. I wonder if he's so soundly asleep that he won't even hear me.

I walk quietly into the kitchen and then I stop. My eyes widen in horror. Because on the table is a sheet of paper. It was once crumpled, but now it's smoothed out. It's the sheet of paper on which I did my Chris v. Luke flow chart.

Shit.

I take a deep breath and am trying to think how I'm going to play this when Chris walks into the room.

'Hello,' he says.

'Hi.' I whirl around. He's rubbing his eyes. 'I wasn't expecting you here.'

'I hadn't planned on it.' His voice is sleepy but there's a hard undertone to it. 'But then I thought it would be nice to see you after being away. I forgot about your conference.'

My eyes are dragged back to the paper.

'I knocked over the bin,' he says. 'I was picking stuff up when I saw my name on this. I suppose you'll say I shouldn't have looked at it, but I couldn't help it.'

I don't speak.

'Luke Evans?' His words are like ice cubes rattling into an empty glass.

I paint a smile on to my face and then try a dismissive laugh.

'The guy who used to live near me in Blackwater Terrace,' I say. 'You remember him?'

'No,' says Chris.

'I know I mentioned him. We were friends.'

'Looks like you were more than that. *Are* more than that.'

'Not exactly. Not at all,' I say.

'In that case, what's all this about?' He jabs a finger at the page. 'And why is he – as well as being passionate and God knows what else – a hopeless liar?'

I didn't mean Luke was a hopeless liar. I meant he was a liar and we were hopeless.

'It's just silliness.' I sit down at the table. Chris does likewise. 'I . . .' I have to think how to put this. I suppose it doesn't matter, but I couldn't bear him to completely hate me. 'I met him,' I admit.

'When?'

'In Spain.'

'With Sive? On your girlie weekend?' He's incredulous.

'I didn't meet him with Sive,' I say. 'It was when I was stuck in Seville.'

It takes Chris a moment to process this information.

'What are you saying?' he asks. 'You met this guy and you deliberately missed my mother's party to be with him? For . . .' he smoothes the page and holds it up in front of him, 'passion and longing and desire and kisses? You set it all up and you deceived me?'

I feel sick.

'So it's actually you who's the liar – and a cheat,' he adds, his voice full of contempt.

'God, no!' I cry. 'It wasn't like that at all. It was totally random. I missed the train, just like I told you, and then I bumped into Luke purely by chance.'

'And then what? You realised you've been lusting after him all your life? You decided to rush into bed with him? Because . . .' he waves the paper in front of me, 'what I'm seeing here is some kind of sexual encounter. And I'd like to know what happened between you that you didn't think worth mentioning to me.'

This is not going well. I'm being painted into a corner of my own making.

'There was no sex!' I cry. 'It wasn't like that at all. It was . . .'

I remember the heat of the flamenco and the coolness of the mojitos. I think about the aromatic coffee and sensual music of Fuente del Rio. And then I think about Luke's lips on mine. I swallow hard a couple of times, but my throat is completely dry and my voice comes out as a croak.

'I was stuck at the train station and he invited me to meet some friends of his later that night and we went to flamenco and it was just a bit of fun.'

'Flamenco? When I phoned, you said you were watching flamenco. You were with him?'

'There was a crowd of us,' I say.

'But he was the only one you knew.'

'Yes.'

'You didn't tell me you were with anyone.'

'No. I didn't.'

'And afterwards?'

'Nothing,' I say. 'Absolutely nothing.'

'Don't lie to me, Carlotta.' His words are like a whip

337

cracking through the air. 'You might have decided to take me for a fool, but I'm not that stupid.'

'Nothing happened,' I repeated. 'He saw me off on the train and I'll admit that he kissed me goodbye. But everyone kisses everyone goodbye in Spain.'

'To be polite,' says Chris.

I'm back in the painted corner again.

'It was a bit more . . . than it should have been.'

I feel better now. I know I haven't told him the full story, but I have confessed to the kiss. And that's the most important part, after all.

'You liked it?'

'It was . . . When we were younger, when I knew him, he never kissed me. I'd always wondered.'

'And now you know,' says Chris. 'And what you know is that this Luke person is passionate. Whereas I, the man you're supposed to be marrying, am just loving and compatible. And safe. Which from where I'm standing sounds like a criticism, not a compliment.'

'It *is* a compliment!' I cry. 'We just—'

'Just what? Just need to spice it up with other people? Is that what you think? Is that what you want? A threesome to make it a bit more exciting? With this . . . this childhood Don Juan?'

'I admit that I was foolish. I'm glad you know about it, because I've been consumed by guilt and I wanted to talk to you anyway—'

'That's supposed to make it all right?' he interrupts me. 'That you feel bad about cheating on me?'

'I didn't cheat.'

'I told you not to lie to me, Carlotta.'

338

'Honestly,' I said. 'It was just a kiss. And then I got on the train and came home and I haven't heard from him since.'

'Why is that?' he asks.

'Because he has a life,' I say. 'Same as me. It was a moment of . . . of . . . oh, whatever it was, it was just a moment!'

'He probably has a wife and a family in that life,' says Chris. 'That's what makes him a liar.'

I shake my head. Luke would have told me if he was married. He'd no reason not to. He knew I was engaged, after all. And then I remember the beautiful girl and I don't know what to think.

'Do you take me for a complete fool?' Chris is looking at me furiously.

'No!'

'Yet you expect me to believe that there's nothing between you and this . . . Luke Evans.'

'There isn't.'

'But you went back to Seville with Sive.'

'We went to Marbella, not Seville.'

He says nothing, and I know that I have to come clean.

'But he lives in Marbella,' I admit. 'I was feeling . . . uncertain. I needed to see him. To be sure.'

'And you never said a word to me. You allowed me to think you were going off with your best friend for a few days of sun. You didn't say you were having doubts. That you wanted to trade in compatible for passion and lying.'

'Chris, it wasn't like that.'

'It was exactly like that,' he says. 'You went looking for some kind of sexual adventure but you were keeping your options open. Making sure that you had a fallback. Me.'

'That's not true,' I say, even though it more or less is.

'And what happened?' asks Chris. 'Did this Luke Evans give you the cold shoulder? Or was Sive there simply for cover so you could keep on having passionate moments? How many of them were there, by the way? And should I get checked out for diseases?'

'Chris! No, of course not. I didn't even meet Luke in Marbella. Me and Sive just had a holiday.' I don't know exactly why I'm still not telling him the complete truth. After all, I'm going to break up with him. That's been the plan ever since I came home. To break up because my heart isn't in the right place. And yet I feel I have to defend myself to him. To fight, almost, for what we had, even if we can't have it any more.

'Was she in on this?' he asks.

'She thought I was crazy,' I tell him. 'And she didn't approve of anything. But she's my friend.'

'I thought she was my friend too. I didn't think she'd stand by while you—'

'Did absolutely nothing,' I say.

'Yet you wrote this.' He crumples up the page again and flings it across the room.

'I needed to sort it out in my head,' I explain.

'Bullshit!'

'Really, Chris.'

'And so is it sorted?' he demands. 'Am I supposed to be grateful you're still with me? That somehow you've found out he's a liar and a cheat? Is that it?'

I'm agonised here. I really am. I don't know what to say.

'But you're not still with me, are you?' He's looking at me, realisation dawning in his eyes. 'You're not with me at all. I'm not enough for you any more.'

'It's not that exactly,' I say.

'Oh, come on, Carlotta. It is that exactly. You saw this old – old boyfriend, and suddenly you decided that I was a mistake.'

'It's not you,' I tell him miserably.

'Trot out a few clichés, why don't you?' he says. 'Make yourself feel better.'

'I can't make myself feel better. I feel awful.'

'Good.'

'Please,' I say eventually. 'I'm really sorry.'

'So am I,' he says. 'I'm sorry I believed in you. I'm sorry I thought you were the one for the rest of my life. That I invested in you. That I cared about you. When all I am to you is a substitute for some sordid affair.'

'That's not true.'

'Of course it is. Were you ever planning to tell me about Luke Evans? This master of passion? The man you're lusting after – thinking about – when you're in bed with me?'

'Chris—'

'But why would you? Why ruin everything? Why not get married to good old dependable, compatible Chris and keep your fantasy life going? And then head over to Spain for a touch of passion whenever you want it? Have the best of both worlds?'

'No, no,' I say. 'I tried to tell you—'

'You did? Because since you've come back from Marbella, I haven't heard any requests to talk about our future. In fact, all I'm aware of is that you came to my mother's house and discussed our wedding plans without saying a word. You were happy to make a fool out of her too.'

'I said we needed to talk, but you had to go to Seattle and—'

'You sicken me, Carlotta,' he says. 'You really do. You don't care about anyone but yourself. Certainly not me or my mother. Or Sive, otherwise you wouldn't have made her a party to this deception.'

'Oh, Chris . . .'

'Don't,' he says. 'Don't say something that will make me more disappointed in you than I already am.'

'I never intended to hurt you.'

'And that makes it all right?' He snorts. 'I believed in you, Carlotta. I loved you. I wanted to marry you.'

'I wanted to marry you too,' I say.

'But that's not going to happen,' he says. 'Because I wouldn't dream of marrying a deceitful, cheating . . .' He stops and looks at me through narrowed eyes.

'And you don't want to marry me either, do you? You don't want me to forgive you and tell you that it's all right.'

'I want you to forgive me,' I say.

'No,' says Chris. 'You lied to me. You made a fool of me. I won't forgive you. Ever.'

It's nothing more than I deserve, I suppose.

'I never want to see you again,' says Chris.

I can't blame him for that.

'You've every right to be angry with me,' I say.

'I suppose this is the sort of guff you learn in corporate consulting,' he says. 'Admit some kind of liability, apologise for it. Try to move on. Well, I don't know if you've admitted everything to me, and I don't know if you're sorry about it or just sorry you got caught. But what I do know is that we have to move on. So that's what I'm doing. On and out of your life, Carlotta.'

He picks up his car keys, which are on the counter.

'Chris . . .'

'Don't talk to me,' he says. 'Just don't.'

And what is there to say, after all? He's managed to break up with me before I broke up with him. Maybe that's a good thing. But I can't believe it's happened in the middle of the night, in my own kitchen.

'I'm sorry,' I whisper one more time.

We're looking at each other, and I've never seen his eyes so hard and so angry.

And then I slide my beautiful diamond solitaire from my finger and put it on the table. Chris looks at it and at me. He picks it up and puts it in the pocket of his jacket.

'Goodbye,' he says.

I remain immobile in the kitchen while he walks out of the room. I hear the front door open and close behind him.

I'm on my own.

That's what happens when you try to meddle with the timeline.

Chapter 26

Por el Camino (For the Road) – José de Córdoba

I sit at the table long after Chris has gone and look at the thin white line on my finger where my engagement ring used to be. I rub it gently, as though it will magic the ring back into place. I can't believe it's all over. That it's happened like this, so quickly and so unexpectedly. Well, OK, hardly unexpectedly, but this isn't how I planned it. I never even considered that Chris would see what I'd written. I'd thrown that piece of paper away! I should have torn it into little pieces. And I can only imagine how he felt. I never wanted to hurt him. I love him. Not enough, after all, to marry him. But enough to want him to be happy.

I wonder if my ideas about love are screwed up. I thought it was all about being compatible with someone, of knowing that you are there for each other. I'm sure that's what it's supposed to be. It's not as though Chris and I didn't have our passionate moments. We did. But I've traded it all in for a memory of rhythmic music, swirling red dresses and burning lips on mine. I'm certifiable. I really am.

It's nearly five before I go to bed. I crawl beneath the

duvet and lie there with my eyes closed but not sleeping until the alarm goes off. I'm bone weary when I get up again. Things always seem better in the morning, and with the sun shining into my bathroom window I tell myself that this was how things were meant to be. I just wish it felt like that.

There's an eerie calm to the office when I arrive, thanks to the fact that most of the senior staff are on the golf course. I sit at my desk and drink my Americano in its takeaway cup. I check my diary, deal with my full inbox of emails and do some prep work for the following week. Then I allow my mind to wander back to more important things.

I have to tell people about my broken engagement. Sive first. Then my parents. Then my friends and colleagues. And Julia. God, I think, Julia will go nuts! She's booked flights for the family to come to Ireland for a wedding that isn't going to happen. She's not going to be happy about that.

And although I think the only person who'll eventually be happy about it is Dorothea, I feel bad about the fact that her incredible organisational work was for nothing, and that all the thanks she got from me was a night in A&E.

It's a mess, I think miserably, and it's a mess of my own making.

I open my email program and click on 'compose new'. Maybe Sive will have some advice for me. Whatever it is, this time I'll follow it.

Her advice is to call over that evening, which I do.

Natasha opens the door and hugs me and says that it's lovely to see me and then starts chattering about her brides-maid's dress. She's seen one, she says, in a magazine. It's pink and princessy and lovely. Sive, who has come into the hallway behind her, winces. Obviously she hasn't yet told Natasha that there's not going to be a wedding after all. I don't tell her either. I push my hands into the pockets of the loose trousers I'm wearing so that my god-daughter doesn't notice the lack of engagement ring.

The three of us sit and chat for a while and then Sive tells Natasha it's time for bed. Natasha spends an obligatory ten minutes or so moaning about it, but eventually she leaves us to our own devices and Sive demands to know what happened between me and Chris.

So I tell her, and her expression changes from horrified to sympathetic to exasperated and horrified again.

'And there's no chance he will actually forgive you and have you back?' she asks.

'The thing is . . .' I speak slowly, 'I was going to end it anyway.'

'What?' She looks at me in disbelief. 'I thought you'd decided that this whole Luke Evans thing was a ridiculous fantasy. I thought after Marbella you were OK about it all.'

'I was,' I say. 'But . . .' I launch into a rambling explanation that includes music and kisses and not loving Chris enough, while she looks at me with despair in her eyes.

'So you don't love him at all?'

'I do,' I say. 'But it's not enough any more.' I also tell her about seeing Luke with the girl from the nightclub, and her eyes open even wider.

'Carlotta, you're out of your mind. You want the impossible. You want a guy who doesn't love you – who's probably lied to you – to sweep you off your feet. While you've rejected the man who does.'

'I know how stupid I must seem to you,' I say. 'But I can't pretend that it's all OK with Chris when it isn't.'

'So what are you planning to do?' she asks. 'Go back to Marbella again? Camp outside this building and waylay Luke? Demand an explanation about Miss Beautiful? Ask him to leave her – and his dad – for you?'

I don't even try to defend him. I shake my head.

'What then?'

'Nothing,' I say. 'I'm doing nothing. Which is the right thing. I'm not going to marry Chris because what we have – had – isn't right for me any more. I'm not going to make a fool of myself in Spain. I'm going to let it all wash over me and get on with my life, and one day hopefully I'll meet a brilliant kisser who can put both Chris and Luke out of my head forever.'

'Oh, Carlotta.'

'What else can I do?' I ask. 'I thought everything was perfect with me and Chris. But it can't have been, Sive, because otherwise meeting Luke wouldn't have affected me the way it did. I would've been able to dismiss him easily.'

'What if you never do?' she asks.

'I don't know.'

'You can't live your whole life wanting the unattainable.'

I shrug.

'You're making a big mistake,' says Sive.

'I've already made it,' I tell her. 'Now I have to live with it.'

'I can't understand it,' she says.

'What?'

'How you allowed yourself to make such a complete tit of things. You don't, as a rule.'

She's right. I normally act with my head and not my heart.

It's why I've been so successful. It's clearly the better way to be, because acting with my heart has brought nothing but misery. And yet . . . quite suddenly the knot in my stomach loosens just a little and I feel an unaccustomed sense of relief. As though, quite literally, a weight has been lifted from my shoulders. I realise that I've done the right thing. Even if it means being miserable. Because marrying Chris would have been a terrible, terrible mistake.

'How can you say that?' demands Sive when I say this. 'Chris is a fantastic guy.'

'I know,' I say. 'But he's just not for me.'

She sighs.

'I'm sorry,' I say. 'I know you and Natasha were looking forward to the big day.'

'That's the least of my worries.'

I nod. 'All the same, Natasha will be very disappointed.'

'Better she's disappointed than you're married to the wrong man,' says Sive. 'It's just that I still can't believe he's the wrong man, Lottie. I really can't.'

'I wish he wasn't.'

'However, it's your life and you know what's best.' She says this in a tone that clearly implies she still thinks I'm a candidate for the funny farm.

'I probably don't know what's best,' I admit. 'But I do know a big mistake when I see it. And I don't want to make it.'

'Oh well.' She gives me a sympathetic smile. 'At least I won't have to share my divorce tips with you.'

'No.' I smile too.

'C'mon,' she says. 'Let's make a dent in this bottle of wine. I think we both need it.'

*   *   *

We're on our second glass, and reminiscing about our college days, when her phone rings. Her voice softens as she answers and I know it's Kieran McDonagh. I get up and go into the kitchen while she's talking to him. Five minutes later she comes looking for me.

'You didn't have to leave,' she says. 'It wasn't a private conversation. Though Kieran was surprised to hear about you and Chris.'

'You told him!'

'Of course. It's not a secret, after all.'

The idea of Sive and Kieran picking over the shards of my relationship makes me shudder, though now I don't have to worry about him telling Chris about Luke.

'OK, so it's time to tell me exactly what your problem with Kieran is,' she says, and I know I haven't managed to disguise how I feel. A spasm of anxiety hits my stomach and the knot returns, tighter than ever.

'What d'you mean?' I try to keep my voice light.

'God almighty, Carlotta, you're making it very obvious that there's some issue there. Did something happen when you worked together?'

I'm not sure I can take any more emotional drama. Besides, she's been a rock to me and I can't destroy her happiness in return.

She walks back into the living room and I follow her.

'I need to know.' She sounds less like my best friend now and more like the corporate mogul she is. I have to say something. Eventually, the best that I can come up with is that she can do better.

'Excuse me?' She raises her eyebrows so far they disappear behind her hair.

'He's not as smart or as clever as you.'

'Very few people are.'

It's a statement of fact, not a boast.

'I don't want to see you making a mistake.'

'Lottie, I'm a single parent. I've already made my mistake.'

'Another one, then,' I say.

'Why are you so convinced that Kieran is a mistake?'

'He . . . he thinks too much of himself. And he . . . he's a bit of a misogynist.'

'A misogynist!' She laughs. 'Sweetie, he sends me flowers. He brings me to lovely restaurants for dinner. That's hardly the behaviour of a man who dislikes women.'

'Maybe not dislikes,' I say. 'Maybe he just doesn't see them as equals.'

'Carlotta O'Keeffe! What are you talking about?'

Her expression is truly puzzled. And a little bit anxious. I can't lie to her, even by omission. Look where that left me with Chris. So I tell her the truth. I tell her what happened. I speak quickly and breathlessly and she stares at me, a look of horror on her face.

'I didn't want to tell you this,' I say when I'm finished. 'But it's been eating me up.'

'Oh for heaven's sake!' she exclaims. 'I can't believe you got your knickers in a twist over a little joke.'

I stare at her. It wasn't a little joke. It was horrible. I say as much.

'Why didn't you just make the damn tea in the first place?' she demands. 'Why do you always have to turn everything into such a big deal?'

'What?' I'm completely taken aback. Sive wouldn't have made the tea either.

'I can see it. Him asking. You getting all high and mighty. Pissing him off.'

'Sive! You know what happens in offices. You know you have to draw a line in the sand.'

'You could've made the tea,' she says.

'No,' I say. 'I couldn't. But me not making it didn't give him the right to Photoshop that picture. You said yourself that passing around inappropriate pictures was wrong.'

'You didn't give me a context. Everything's different in context.'

'Sive, he put my face on the head of a woman wearing nothing more than a thong and a necklace!' I cry. 'As well as another awful picture with a naked man. That's the only context you need.'

'You head-butted him,' she counters. 'You broke his nose.'

'He's lucky it was only his nose!' I'm as angry as she is now. 'I didn't know what he was about to do. He could've tried to . . . well, I don't know.'

She's looking at me, fury in her eyes.

'What are you trying to accuse him of?'

'Nothing! Nothing! It was – I felt threatened by him, that's all.'

'Yet you say nothing until tonight. Until you're here in a flap about your own relationship,' she says. 'But that's typical, isn't it, Carlotta?'

'What d'you mean?' I'm staring at her in bemusement.

'It's always been you, hasn't it? You weren't stupid enough to get pregnant and married when you were too young to know what you were doing. You weren't the one whose husband had an affair. You weren't the one who was fleeced in a divorce. You've just sailed through life doing better and better until you found Chris. And now that you've made a mistake and it's not going according to plan, you want to mess with my happiness too.'

I can't believe what she's saying. I can't believe she believes it either.

'It's always been so bloody easy for you,' she continues. 'You only have to think of yourself. You can do what you want, when you want. And now it's come back to bite you on the arse. You were thinking of yourself when you got involved with Luke Evans, and when you agreed to go to Spain to look for him, and then when you changed your mind while you were there . . . *and* when you wrote whatever garbage you wrote in your stupid notebook. You're totally thoughtless. You always have been and always will be.'

'Sive, this is nonsense.' My voice is shaky. I've never fought with my best friend before and I don't want to now. But I seem to have stirred up a hornets' nest without ever meaning to. 'You asked me about Kieran and I told you. I'm not expecting you to change your relationship with him because of me.'

'You're not?' Her tone is scathing. 'You've just told me that a man I love assaulted you. You think it's all right for me to be dating someone like that?'

'Oh, Sive . . .'

'Don't oh Sive me.' I've never seen her so angry. 'Just don't. Don't pretend that you care when you're just jealous!'

'You're totally wrong.' I'm shocked. I've never known Sive to be like this before. She's normally even more cool and rational than me. She can't really believe what she's saying.

'Kieran is great to me. And great to Natasha. She really likes him.'

'I'm sure he is. People change.'

How often have I thought that over the past few weeks? And how often have I wondered if it's true?

'So you're retracting what you said?'

'Look, what happened happened. You asked, I told you. I find it hard to like Kieran after my experience of him, but I accept that he's in your life and he must have changed for you to have him there. Especially because of Natasha. I'm really sorry I upset you, though. I wouldn't want to do that.'

Sive says nothing for a moment. Then she drains her glass.

'I'll accept your apology. But I don't want to talk to you any more, Carlotta. Not today. Not ever.'

I get up and go.

In the last twenty-four hours I've managed to turn both the man I was going to marry and my friend against me. And I'm not sure that either of them will ever forget it. Or forgive me.

Chapter 27

Zapateado (Tap Dance) – Julian Bream

I'm completely rattled by my encounter with Sive. I knew she'd be upset, but I thought it would be with Kieran, not with me. In the days following my visit to her, I don't hear from her at all. I'm not sure what to do. I'm hoping that she'll eventually get in touch, because I'm afraid to try to contact her. I don't want to annoy her further.

All I'm doing is upsetting people right now. My parents are also aghast over the break-up. Like me, they still can't quite believe it's happened. I called to see them the day after I visited Sive. I was still shaken up and I blurted the news of my broken engagement almost as soon as I was in the door.

'What happened?' asked my mother. 'What on earth did you do?'

Even though it's all my fault, I can't help noticing that she obviously thinks so too. I don't go into details with her. I just say that we agreed it wouldn't work out after all.

'But why?' wailed Mum. 'I thought you two got on so well. If it's because that woman has taken over your wedding . . .'

'It's nothing to do with his mother,' I told her.

'If he did anything to hurt you . . .' Dad sounded angry.

'Not at all,' I said quickly. 'In fact it's more about me. So please don't blame him.'

'Oh, Lottie.' Mum sniffed. 'I thought I didn't have to worry about either of my girls any more.'

'Ah, now Mona, don't be getting so fussed,' said Dad. 'Lottie is a sensible girl. You don't have to worry about her.'

'I worry about my girls all the time,' she told him.

I decided not to point out to her that she was contradicting herself.

'I thought it would be nice to have you settled,' she said. 'I know you're happy with your career and everything, but . . . well, when it comes down to it, what's the point of great stuff if you can't share it with someone?'

'Better not to share it at all than to share with the wrong person,' observed Dad.

I gave him a watery smile.

'Have you told Julia yet?' asked Mum. 'What about all her plans?'

'I haven't said anything, but I hope she can cancel her arrangements without losing any money,' I said. 'Or perhaps she might come to see you anyway.'

Of course she's only just seen them. They're not long back from their own trip.

'Maybe,' said Dad, even though I know he was only saying it to make me feel better.

'I'm sorry,' I told them. 'I'm sorry for messing up.'

'Ah, Lottie.' Mum got up and put her arms around me, hugging me to her like she did when I was a kid. 'You haven't messed up. I'd rather you change your mind now than after the wedding.'

'I know.' My words were muffled against her chest. 'It's still awful, though.'

'I'm sure you'll find the right person eventually,' she said as she stroked my head. 'Though when you're a perfectionist like you, it's a lot harder.'

I laughed. I couldn't help it.

'What?' She sounded hurt.

'Nothing.' I straightened up, grabbed a bit of kitchen towel and blew my nose. 'I didn't realise I was at a disadvantage.'

'You *are* a perfectionist.' I could hear an exasperated tone to her voice. 'You always were. It makes things difficult for you.'

'No it doesn't.' But maybe it does. Maybe your mother is always right.

'At least we won't have to be lorded over by that witch of a mother of his.' Mum always finds a crumb of comfort in things. 'I wasn't looking forward to the reception in her house, to be perfectly honest with you.'

'Actually,' I admitted, 'she was doing a great job of arranging everything. Even with her broken wrist. She was even quite nice to me about it. Doubt she'll ever be nice to me again.'

'Small mercies.' Dad grinned.

I stayed with my parents for another hour. Both of them made a big fuss of me before I left and told me over and over that it was better to have done the deed now than to realise I'd made a terrible mistake later. I was grateful to them for not probing too deeply into things, although I have a feeling that Mum will start inviting me to concerts and art exhibitions and other social events again, as she did before I met Chris. She doesn't really like to think of me living alone. And when I go out with her, she always mentions unmarried sons of people she knows, as though there's the faintest chance I'll hook up with any of them.

When I finally Skype Julia, she's already heard the news from Mum and she's as shocked as our parents.

'I'm sorry about your flight,' I tell her, after going through the litany of questions about why. 'If you can't change it, perhaps you could—'

'It's a flexi fare and I can,' says Julia. 'Which is lucky, because I was going to do a web fare, which I couldn't change. But . . .'

But what? But she already knew that I wasn't going to marry Chris? She guessed before I ever did?

'Of course not,' she says when I ask her. 'I did wonder about the two of you, all the same. You were a bit too . . . too power couple.'

'I beg your pardon?' I'm completely taken aback by her comment. Most people say how great we are. Were.

'You the corporate mogul. Him the successful eye surgeon. It never fitted my picture of you, Lottie.'

'Which part? Me being a corporate mogul? Me being married?'

'The whole successful lifestyle,' she says.

'Huh.' I'm taken aback. 'What's wrong with having a successful lifestyle?'

'Nothing,' she says. 'Only you were never so . . . so driven when you were younger. And with him you were.'

'That's nonsense,' I object. 'I always wanted to do well. If you remember,' I add waspishly, 'I was usually top of the class in school.'

She laughs. 'I know, memory girl. But like you said to me back then, it was just regurgitating facts.'

I concede that point but add that my career has gone from strength to strength and that's through hard work, not just memorising things.

'Sure it is,' she says. 'Mum and Dad are really proud of you. So am I, if it comes to that. But it's like . . . oh, I dunno, Lottie, it's like since you met Chris you seem to think that you have to work extra hard just to prove a point.'

'That's not true,' I tell her. 'I'm working extra hard because I like what I do.'

'I thought it might be to prove you were good enough for him and his bat of a mother.'

Julia never met Dorothea. But my ex-future-mother-in-law has been a topic of conversation in our family ever since the dinner in the posh restaurant off Grafton Street. However, my sister has a point. I'm competitive at heart. I like putting myself up against my colleagues and doing well. And it was always important to me that Chris didn't think of himself as the only one in our relationship with a great job. Possibly my thinking was warped.

'Anyway,' she continues, 'I might use the flights to come over at Christmas with Jeff and the kids instead.'

'That would work for you?' It would be nice to see them at Christmas. And I'd have more time to be with them than at my wedding.

'Christmas will be more fun than September anyway,' says Julia.

I'm assuming that she doesn't actually mean my wedding wouldn't have been fun.

'When I see you, I'll want the full gory details,' she warns.

'I promise I'll tell you at Christmas.'

'It's a long time to wait to find out why my little sister dumped her perfect fiancé at the altar,' she says glumly.

'It wasn't at the altar,' I remind her.

'Practically.' She's not interested in the distinction. 'Hey, why don't you visit us here? It'd do you good to get away.'

'I don't need to get away. I went to Spain with Sive, remember!'

I didn't tell Julia why we went. She assumed it was the fabled girlie weekend.

'That doesn't count. You need a break now. You've cancelled your wedding. You must be shattered.'

I am. But I tell her that I have to keep going.

'Oh don't be so silly,' she says. 'Nobody has to keep going. Take some time out, for heaven's sake. Come here. Tell me all about it.'

'You don't need to know all about it.'

'I do. I can advise you.'

The last time Julia advised me about anything, it was about my make-up on the night I went out with Luke.

'I give good advice,' she says when I don't speak. 'And maybe for once in your life you'll listen to me.'

'Nothing can change what's happened,' I say.

'C'mon,' she says. 'I saw you through the Luke Evans crisis, didn't I? And that other guy you broke up with – Gavin whatsisname?'

I'd forgotten Gavin Curran. We'd been going out together for about six months when I first went to college, but he broke it off with me just before the exams. It was the timing more than the actual break-up that upset me then, and I remind Julia of this.

'Maybe,' she agrees. 'But what about Luke? That really shook you.'

I keep my voice very steady as I say that Luke was an entirely different thing.

'I used to wonder,' says Julia, 'if you two would've stayed together. You were like two little peas in a pod. Well, not physically, I suppose – you're dark and he's fair – but the two of you used to sit on the wall outside the house, remember? Side by side.'

'I remember.'

'What a thing that was, though! I never would've believed it of Richard Evans. I wonder did they ever get him?'

'I don't think so.'

'Probably living the high life,' says Julia.

I can't believe she's banging on about the Evanses now. It's the first time she's mentioned them since it happened. I don't say anything, but fortunately Julia has switched to talking about other neighbours on Blackwater Terrace and I've managed to compose myself by the time she gets around to me again.

'So what d'you think, Lottie? D'you want to visit us? We'd love to see you.'

'Maybe,' I say. 'Give me a few days to think about it.'

It might not be a bad idea, I think after we finish our call. It might be good for me to get away from Ireland for a while. Out of the eye of the storm.

In the meantime, though, I throw myself into work. I'm in the office at seven every morning and I don't leave before seven in the evening. I'm on top of everything and carrying out my job with ruthless efficiency. I draw up plans for clients that are equally efficient and equally ruthless. I work the support staff endlessly. I'm not the velvet assassin. I'm just the assassin.

I hear the gossip, of course, and it's that I'm angling for a top job after Dirk leaves for South Africa. I don't care what people think. I'm pouring my heart and soul into what I do because I know this is something I'm good at.

By the end of the week I've cleared my desk completely, I have a diary that's carefully weighted between new and existing business and I'm also up to speed on what my colleagues have been doing because I've read and memorised every single office memo that's been emailed to me.

If I can't be lucky in love, I think, I'll be lucky in my career. It's the one thing I can depend on.

Dirk drops in at five o'clock and eases himself into the visitor's chair.

'Everything OK?' he asks.

'Absolutely, why?'

'I've had more emails from you in the last week than in the last three months combined,' he says.

'Lots of stuff to be sorted before you leave,' I tell him. 'I realise not everything is urgent, but I do need you to look over the Winterburn proposal. And the hotel chain strategy.'

'I'm sure my successor will be able to do that,' he says.

'You know who it's going to be?'

'Actually, I do,' says Dirk. He lowers his voice even though nobody can hear us. 'Joost van Aken from the Netherlands office.'

'Oh.' I've met Joost. He's older than Dirk. More traditional. But he has a fearsome reputation.

'You'll work well with him.'

'You think?'

'He'll like your efficiency.' Dirk smiles. 'He's big into getting things done on the spot.

'What's happening to Steve?' I ask.

Steve Redmond had been the Dublin office's pick for Dirk's successor, although I'd ruled him out. A decent man, but not ruthless enough.

'He'll remain as is,' replies Dirk.

'And Ian?'

'It'll be up to Joost to name his team,' says Dirk.

'Fair enough.' I'd like to think that I have a good chance of promotion. But I'm one of the youngest. And a woman.

'I've given you a glowing recommendation,' Dirk says.

'Thanks. You've probably given all of us glowing recommendations.'

'I mean it,' he says.

I feel a sudden surge of affection for Dirk. We've never been anything other than professional with each other, but right now I'd like to give him a hug.

'Other matters now,' says Dirk, crossing his legs. 'Is the rumour true?'

'What rumour?'

'That you've dumped the eye doctor.'

'He's an ophthalmic surgeon.' I make the correction automatically. 'And yes, the wedding is off.'

He flashes me a look of sympathy before he asks what happened.

'He changed his mind,' I say.

'Why?'

'I wasn't the person he thought.'

Now he's looking at me quizzically.

'And the why doesn't matter,' I say. 'The outcome is the same.'

'I'm sorry, Carlotta.'

'I'm not.' I keep my voice steady. 'It gives me more time for the firm.'

He laughs. 'Nobody ever dies saying they wished they'd spent more time in the office,' he reminds me.

'Just as well I do a lot of my work outside it.' My voice is light-hearted, to show that I'm not upset, either by talking about Chris or by my boss's comment.

'Are you OK?' he asks.

'Of course I am.'

'It's very late for a change of heart,' says Dirk.

'Never too late,' I tell him. 'And just as well we decided before we actually said "I do".'

'Indeed.' He nods. 'Nevertheless, it's still a bit of a trauma, isn't it?'

'Not at all.' I'm firm and decisive. 'I was upset, naturally. But it's for the best.'

'What about your honeymoon?' asks Dirk. 'The Bahamas or something, wasn't it?'

'Maldives.'

Chris emailed me two days ago to say that he'd cancelled it. In the email he also confirmed that Dorothea had cancelled the string quartet, the marquee, the flowers and the caterers. She hadn't got round to booking Pen's DJ friend for the dance music. He also said that her arm and her ankle were both healing well. I didn't know if he was blaming me for the fact that she'd been injured in the first place or implying that her recovery had speeded up because of my departure from their lives.

'Going anywhere else instead?' asks Dirk.

'Actually I'm thinking of visiting my sister.' Suddenly it seems the right thing to do. 'Just a week. Sooner than the honeymoon was meant to be.'

'She's in Vancouver, isn't she?'

Dirk remembers personal stuff about his staff.

'That's right.'

'Nice city,' he says. 'Do you good to have a break, Carlotta.'

'Perhaps.'

'Definitely,' he says. 'Before Joost starts. Get yourself in shape.'

'Am I out of it?'

'You've been beyond efficient all week. But I know everything isn't right,' says Dirk. 'Take the time. It'll do you good.'

As soon as he leaves the office, I book my flight.

Chapter 28

Romance de los Pinos (Romance of the Pines) – Pepe Romero

I send Sive an email telling her I'm visiting Julia, but I still haven't heard back from her by the time I land in Vancouver. I can't believe that Kieran McDonagh has come between me and my best friend. I thought he was out of my life forever. But then I thought Luke Evans was out of my life forever too, and somehow I've allowed him to come between me and the man I was supposed to marry. I haven't really got my head around either of these things yet. I'm hoping that being seven thousand kilometres away from everything that's bothering me will help me put things into a certain amount of perspective.

It's six thirty in the evening and my body clock thinks it's half-one in the morning, but I'm not in the slightest bit tired and I'm excited to see Julia, Jeff and the two boys waiting to greet me. Hank actually runs to me and grabs me around the knees. I'm surprised he remembers me, because he was only three the last time I saw him. Shaun, who was a baby and is now three himself, hangs back, holding on to Jeff's jeans and hiding his face.

'Auntie Lottie.' Hank beams at me.

'Hello, Hank.' I bend down and ruffle his hair, and then I remember how much I hated adults doing that to me. So I give him a pat across the shoulders and tell him that he's grown incredibly since I last saw him, which is the truth. 'And hello, Jules.' I give my sister a hug. She looks as beautiful as ever and not at all like a harassed mother of two children. But then, according to Mum, she's living the good life and not harassed in the slightest.

'Hiya, sis.' She hugs me back.

Jeff hugs me too, and Shaun, suddenly losing his shyness, asks if I can carry him to the car.

'Don't even think about it,' advises Jeff. 'He weighs a ton.' He picks up his son and swings him on to his back. 'There y'go, big fella,' he says. 'You don't want to kill your auntie before she even gets home, do you?'

Shaun squeals, Hank giggles and we make our way into the Canadian sunshine. The sky is clear and blue and the breeze is warm.

We pile into a huge 4x4 that swallows up the family and my luggage, and Jeff heads out of the airport and towards their home. Jeff and Julia live in Deep Cove, in north Vancouver, which is close to the city while still giving the impression of being part of the great outdoors. Julia, like me, is a city girl born and bred, so the wilds of the Rockies wouldn't exactly be her thing, although Jeff comes from a small town in the middle of nowhere. Their rancher-style house, near the waterfront and with views of the mountains, is a perfect compromise, especially as it's on a huge plot almost surrounded by pine trees.

I know everything about the house and its location even

though I've never been here before. Given the amount of photos, information and web links that Julia has sent since she moved there, I feel I've visited already. All the same, nothing has prepared me for the scent of the pine and the crispness of the air when I step out of the 4x4.

'It's lovely,' I tell her.

She smiles proudly, and the boys (both of whom seem to be my new best friends) drag me up the path and into the house. It's huge inside, open plan, with big windows looking out over the garden and towards the water beyond. The boys insist on showing me their rooms – also huge – and then want me to come outside with them to bounce on their trampoline.

'Carlotta is exhausted,' Julia informs them. 'She's been up for hours. We're going to have something to eat and then she'll want to go to bed.'

I haven't got the energy for trampolining, but I'm wide awake, so when Jeff suggests throwing some steaks on the outside grill, I'm all for it. And that's how it is that on a night I imagined would be spent panicking over wedding arrangements with my fiancé, I'm actually sitting outdoors with a cold beer eating steaks in Canada.

I do, however, sleep like the proverbial log when I go to bed. I don't even wake up when the rest of the family does, and you'd think that two small boys would be enough to rouse even the deepest sleeper, let alone someone like me who normally jumps up at the slightest sound. It's nearly nine before I potter downstairs in the spotted blue pyjamas and matching slippers I bought specially for this trip. (Most of my nightwear, when I bother to put it on at all, is a bit too risqué for a family with young boys!)

Julia's already dressed and sitting at the wooden table that stretches the length of her kitchen. She's wearing pale green capri pants and a sleeveless top. Her hair is bunched into a ponytail and she looks at least fifteen years younger than she is.

'How do you do it?' I ask as I pour myself some aromatic coffee.

'Luck,' she tells me. 'And genetics.'

'Hmm. I wish I knew which ancestor it was. I'd give her a good talking-to for not being more generous.'

'Ah, you look great yourself,' says my sister loyally. 'A bit peaky at the moment, but that's to be expected.'

'I'd have thought that if anyone should be peaky it's the mother of two irrepressible kids.' I look around. 'Where are they?'

'Summer camp,' replies Julia.

'There are camps for three-year-olds?'

'Camp is probably pushing it,' she says. 'It's only a two-day outdoor activity one. Mainly based around tiring them out. Shaun went on one earlier this summer, which he loved, and this is a follow-on. Meantime Hank is doing a soccer camp all this week.'

'Proper soccer? Not American football?'

'Of course. He's quite good, actually.'

'Are they out all day?'

'Till mid afternoon.'

'Did you bring them? I didn't hear you leave. I didn't hear a thing this morning.'

She laughs. 'Jeff did. They're on his way to work so it wasn't a problem.'

Her husband is a paragon.

'Why is it when men do the littlest thing for the family, like bring the kids places, people are so impressed? But with women it's just expected?' demands Julia when I say this.

I look shamefaced. She's right. I lost sight of my inner feminist for a moment. I'm no better than Kieran McDonagh expecting a woman to make his tea.

'Anyway,' says Julia. 'The men of the house are all busy till about four, when the camps finish. So we have lots of time to talk. No holding back, Lottie. You have to tell me everything.'

'Would you mind if I waited until I'm washed and dressed and properly awake before I bare my soul?' I ask.

'Not at all,' she says. 'Help yourself to some brekkie. Woman cannot live on coffee alone, even though that's a particularly nice blend. There's an array of stuff in the fridge, or I can make pancakes with maple syrup if you like.'

I decline the offer of pancakes even though I crave a sugar hit, and virtuously choose my old reliables of fruit and yoghurt instead. Julia and I spend a pleasant half-hour or so sitting at the table and chatting about nothing in particular while I devour the fruit and nurse another cup of coffee. After I've showered and dressed, Julia suggests that I might like to see a bit of the city, so she brings me to Granville Island, which is about half an hour's drive away. The island is buzzy and touristy, full of artisan shops and restaurants, and we browse happily in the public market, where I buy some trinkets for Natasha. I wonder when, or indeed if, I'll be able to give them to her. Whether the rift between Sive and me means that I won't be seeing much of my god-daughter in the future. I feel a stab of pain at the thought. I add a glass bead bracelet for Sive to my purchases. I can't believe that we won't regain our friendship. But I do wonder if we'll ever be as close as we were before.

When I'm finished browsing and buying, Julia says we should have something to eat. I'm not hungry, but I know that it's time for her to quiz me about the disaster area that is my life.

She picks a restaurant with a rooftop terrace and views across the city, and we settle in for what I reckon is going to be a grand inquisition. But Julia doesn't ask too many questions; she just lets me tell the story, and her expression barely changes from the compassionate one she wore when she first asked me what went wrong.

'Wow,' she says when I've finished. 'You've been living the life, haven't you? And Luke Evans. Who would've believed he'd turn up again?'

'I know.'

'If it were anyone else I'd be shocked. But Luke. Makes all the difference.'

'Well it certainly made all the difference in me thinking for a second that there was something between us,' I admit. 'Anyone else and it would've been goodbye and good luck. But Luke . . .'

'It's like fate,' says Julia.

'The wrong sort of fate,' I remind her. 'It all went pear-shaped, don't forget. Just because of a simple kiss.'

'Oh Lottie.' She looks at me in disbelief. 'It's way more than a kiss. You already know as much.'

Yes, but not in the way she thinks. Only because it messed everything up.

'From the moment you saw him, you said you kept imagining how things could've been different,' Julia points out.

'And instead of thinking that your life was great the way it was, you started thinking of how it might have been with Luke.'

I frown.

'You wouldn't have wondered about that for more than ten seconds if you were happy with Chris,' says Julia. 'So bottom line is you've made the right choice.'

'I *was* perfectly happy with Chris,' I object.

'Really?'

'I was going to get married to him!' I cry. 'I must have been happy. I must have loved him.'

Julia says nothing.

'If I didn't,' I say with a hint of desperation, 'then I know nothing at all about love.'

'Why didn't you approach Luke when you saw him in Marbella?' she asks.

'Because he was with another girl,' I say immediately, and then I frown at Julia's gaze. 'What?'

'The answer to that is "because I knew I loved Chris",' she says.

'That too!' I cry.

'Are you sure . . .' she's picking her words carefully here, 'are you sure that you didn't just see Chris as a good option all along?'

'Well of course he was. We made it work together. We were right for each other. That's why we were getting married, for heaven's sake!'

'You don't have to explain to me why you got engaged,' says Julia. 'All I want to know is what you're going to do next.'

'I haven't the faintest idea.' I sigh. 'Well, I suppose I'll just get on with my job and hope for the best.'

'Ah, lookit.' Suddenly my sister has lost her Canadian intonation and sounds exactly like herself again. 'You'll be better before you're twice married.'

It was my mother's favourite expression when we were kids. She still uses it. I can't help laughing. It's the first time I've done that in goodness knows how long.

Julia and Jeff leave no stone unturned in their quest for me to have a good time in Canada. We take in a tour of the city, two visits to the theatre (I can't remember the last time I went back in Dublin; I'm clearly a total philistine), some time out with the boys at Kitsalano beach and Stanley Park, and a day trip into the mountains, where I get in touch with my great outdoors self and come home utterly exhausted. Once again I fall asleep as soon as my head hits the pillow, which is simply magical. But more important than the trips and excursions is the time I spend with my sister and her family, getting to know them in a way I haven't before.

Jeff is probably the nicest man on the planet. He's kind and gentle, even though he's a big guy and has that rugged outdoor look about him. But he treats Julia like a princess and he's brilliant with the two boys. My nephews are fun to be with and I reckon they're probably the reason I'm sleeping so well at night, because they carry me along on the wave of boundless energy that only children possess. They are both individual people with their own personalities – Hank is impetuous and fearless whereas Shaun is more thoughtful and precise – and they make me feel like a kid myself. During my time in Vancouver, we camp out in the back garden, do a barbecue for Jeff and Julia and play endless games of baseball, which is basically rounders, something I was crap at in school. I haven't improved any over the years and even Shaun, who can hardly hold the bat, is more co-ordinated than I am. By the end of my stay I've lost three kilos and that's entirely thanks to the children, because on the flip side, I've been eating like a horse. Jeff isn't a man who skimps on his food and Julia provides him with everything he wants. As for my nephews, well, they just seem to hoover it up.

'You're so lucky,' I tell my sister on the last night when we're sitting in her swing chair on the outside deck. 'You have a great marriage, lovely kids, a one-in-a-million husband and you keep the whole show on the road while looking like someone just out of school herself.'

'Bullshit.' Julia's had a couple of glasses of wine and she's more woozy than normal.

'Not bullshit,' I say. 'You've got it right, Jules.'

'I agree with you that I'm lucky with Jeff and the boys, but I have to work at my marriage, Carlotta. Sometimes Jeff gets sent off to other parts of the country for weeks at a time and I have to cope with everything on my own. Which is fine, but that doesn't leave much time for myself. For doing things I want to do.'

'Like what?' I swing the chair idly.

'I don't know,' she says. 'It's just – I always thought I'd be someone.'

'You are,' I say. 'You're Jeff's wife, the boys' mum and my sister.'

'My point exactly.' She stops the chair swinging by allowing her foot to scrape the wooden beams beneath. 'I'm somebody's something. But there are times I need to be me.'

'But you're living a fantastic life.' I wave my arm at the

373

expanse of garden and the star-studded sky above us. 'This is wonderful.'

'It isn't always,' she says. 'I had to make this life for myself. I didn't know anybody when I came here and they didn't know me. Getting work was hard, and then having the kids without any family around was even harder.'

'Jeff's folks . . .'

'Are a six-hour drive away,' says Julia.

'But you're happy.' I want her to be happy. I need her to be happy. It's important that someone is living a perfect life.

'Of course,' she says. 'It's just . . . you have to work hard to make yourself happy sometimes. It doesn't just come along.'

She has a point. I can spend the rest of my life being miserable that things haven't worked out the way I wanted; or I can be happy that I avoided making a terrible mistake. Although it's still hard for me to imagine that Chris would have been a terrible mistake.

'D'you ever want to come home?' I ask her. 'Would that make you happier?'

'I think of it sometimes,' she admits. 'But I've made my own home here. And most of the time I'm fine. I'd like it to be more about me occasionally, that's all. I guess all moms think that.'

'Probably,' I agree.

'I envied you, you know.'

I look at her, startled.

'Your big important job. Jetting round the place. Going to meetings and stuff.'

I laugh. 'I'm not that important. Most of the time I'm on a red-eye to London, which is as far from jet-setting as you can get. And as for meetings – I hate them. It's a difficult task picking the one useful nugget out of a storm of hot air.'

'You do it for yourself, though,' she says. 'That's what I envy.'

'Bloody hell,' I say. 'Are we the kind of sisters who want to swap lives?'

'Would you?' she asks. 'If you could switch with me and have all this, would you?'

It takes me longer than I thought to answer.

'To be honest, I'm not sure. If I had a husband like Jeff and kids like Hank and Shaun . . .' I give her a shamefaced look. 'I wouldn't be able to look after them like you, though. I'd probably make a balls of it.'

'How were you imagining things with Chris would work out?'

'I thought it would be perfect.'

'And what did you think you'd have with Luke?'

'When?' I ask. 'When I was fifteen or when he kissed me?'

'You thought of having a life with him when he kissed you?'

'When we were fifteen, I couldn't imagine a life without him,' I say. 'One of the things that made me nervous about going out with him was thinking that one day we might split up. I didn't want to lose his friendship. But I did anyway. I know that teenagers are completely melodramatic about what happens to them, but even so, I found it difficult to let myself care about someone that way again.'

'Not even Chris?'

'I thought what I had with Chris was more grown-up,' I admit. 'But when Luke kissed me, all that stuff came back. How I felt. How I wanted to be with him forever. All emotion and no common sense. It was stuff I'd never allowed myself to grow out of.'

'What if you were never meant to?'

'Y'see, that's what I kept thinking!' I look at my sister. 'That's partly why I went back to Spain. But Sive was absolutely right. It wasn't just about me. It was about him too. And don't forget that after he kissed me, he didn't ask me not to go.'

'You didn't try to stay.'

'Julia!' I can't believe the direction this conversation is taking. 'Do you really think I was right to . . . to want to see him again?'

'I don't know,' she says. 'All I know is that from the day you met him to the day he left, you were the happiest I've ever known you.'

'I was happy with Chris too,' I point out. 'And it was an adult relationship. Not puppy love.'

'Luke Evans was the sweetest kid.'

'Lord God, Julia, you sound like you fancied him yourself!'

'A bit too young for me.' She grins. 'But the best-looking of that family by a long streak.'

'He's still a looker,' I admit. 'But there's the simple matter of the girl I saw him with. I don't know how she fits into the picture. Especially given that she was in the nightclub with his dad.'

'Are you honestly trying to tell me you think Luke and his father are having a relationship with the same girl?' Julia is scathing.

'It's just that she knows both of them. It means that there's a connection between them. And that bothers me.'

376

'For heaven's sake, Lottie, the man is his father. And I'm pretty sure that Luke and Richard Evans aren't sharing the same woman.'

I shrug.

'You're just looking for a reason to be angry with him,' she says.

'There are plenty of reasons to be angry with the Evanses,' I tell her. 'Scamming half the neighbourhood for starters! But I suppose with Luke . . . well, I was angry with him when I saw him again. Because he looked great. Because he was driving an Aston Martin. Because his friends were rich.'

'So what?' she says. 'Jeff and I have rich friends. You go to corporate functions with rich people. They're not all bad.'

'None of my clients are wanted by the police,' I point out. 'At least not as far as I know.'

'That's probably a good thing,' she deadpans.

'I can't bear to think that he became part of it all,' I confess.

'And yet you still went looking for him in Marbella.'

'Sive persuaded me it would be the right thing to do. That he'd be horrified to see me and that I'd snap out of it when I saw him too. I convinced myself she was right. But I suppose it wasn't until I saw him with that woman in the street that I realised just how stupid I was being.'

'Do you really think he's sharing a girlfriend with his father?' Julia's tone is disbelieving.

'It doesn't seem like him,' I admit.

'Because it's not at all likely,' Julia retorts. 'You know what, Lottie, you're using that woman as an excuse.'

'For what?' I ask.

'Not accepting that you've broken it off with Chris because you're still in love with Luke.'

'I was never "in love" with Luke,' I object. 'It was eighteen years ago, for heaven's sake!'

'Hopefully I'll still love Jeff eighteen years from now,' she says.

'You're seeing him every day. That's different.'

'I know. But don't you think you have to give it a shot?'

I shake my head. 'Regardless of everything, he still has a life of his own. And I can't go barging into it.'

'Maybe he thinks the same about you. After all,' she reminds me, 'he thought you were getting married. It's not a great incentive for anyone to ask you out, is it?'

'That's true,' I concede. 'But you're not seriously suggesting that I get in touch with him, are you? You wouldn't do it, if you were me.'

'Yes I would,' she says.

I'm shocked. And then I think that it's very easy to say what you'd do in someone else's place. It's a whole different ball game actually doing it. I murmur that perhaps she's being carried away by a romantic notion and she nods.

'I'm a romantic person,' she says. 'Don't you remember when we were younger? I was forever looking for the boy and then the man who would steal my heart with a grand gesture.'

'I thought you were playing the field,' I say.

'That too,' she agrees. 'But I always loved that first date. So much promise. So much excitement. And the guy would always treat you so well. It was lovely. But it tended to go downhill after that.'

'Not with Jeff, though.'

'There are always bad days,' she says. 'That's why marriage is hard work. But when it's the right person, you're prepared

378

to find solutions. And that's why, even though I complain sometimes, Jeff and I are a solid couple.'

'Maybe I don't want to have to work at it with Luke.' I gaze into the distance. 'Maybe that's the real reason I walked away. Because I'd had the romantic day, you see. A totally perfect day. And anything after that could only be a disappointment.'

Chapter 29

Jeux Interdits (Forbidden Games) – Pepe Romero

I'm used to coming home and finding that Chris has been there in my absence, but when I arrive back at Harold's Cross, the fact that I can see he hasn't been here at all makes me realise that we really have broken up. That it's properly over and I'm on my own again.

I phone in an order to the takeaway for chow mein before lugging my suitcase upstairs and beginning to unpack. When the doorbell rings less than ten minutes later, I think that the Fortune Cookie has really upped its game, but when I go downstairs and open the door I see, to my complete astonishment, that Pen Bennett is standing on the step.

She's dressed completely in black – jeans, boots, short jacket – and for a moment I have a horrible feeling that perhaps Dorothea has died and the family is in mourning. I'm terrified it's something to do with her fall, which was partly my fault anyway, as she was doing unnecessary work for the about-to-be-called-off wedding. And I'm thinking that there isn't much more the Bennetts can throw at me when Pen gives me a brief smile and asks if she can come in for a moment. I'm still not entirely convinced she isn't here to break some terrible news, because in all the time I went out with Chris, Pen has never been to my home. She's never even contacted me by phone or email. I invite her in for the first time.

I'm glad that I tidied the house before I went on holiday. I always do – it's a hangover from the times my gran used to visit us at home and make pronouncements about leaving things as you'd want them to be found. She was the sort of woman who'd tell you to wear your good knickers going out in case you were run over by a bus. Even though that's a bit of a cliché, her words stuck with me, and I have a habit of making sure that I leave things neat and tidy, just in case someone should need to break into my house, or my desk, or even my underwear drawer unexpectedly. Mind you, I wear nice undies not because I'm expecting to be run over, but because I like them!

'I thought you might want these back,' she says.

She hands me a set of keys on a Perspex keyring. The keyring is one that Chris's clinic gives to patients. There's a tiny eye chart on one side and contact information for the clinic on the other. The keys, of course, are the ones I gave him to my house.

'Did Chris ask you to return them?'

I'm disappointed that he didn't feel he could drop them by himself. He wouldn't have had to speak to me if he found that too distasteful; all he'd have to do was shove them through the letter box.

'I offered,' she says. 'They were in the hallway and I was coming this way and I asked if he'd like me to do it.'

I picture them at home in Rathgar. Looking at the keys.

Talking about me. Chris too angry to bring himself to return them.

'Thanks.'

We're both standing awkwardly in the hall. I don't know why she asked to come in if all she wanted was to give me the keys. Actually, I don't know why she even bothered to ring the bell. But now she's here, I feel obliged to ask her if she'd like a cup of tea. Which sort of makes me feel like my own mother, offering tea as a kind of bandage to help things along. I'm half hoping Pen will refuse, but she says she'd love a cup, and I've already put the kettle on before I wonder if I've got milk in the fridge and if so, if it's gone off.

I check the unopened litre carton in the door. The milk was best before yesterday, so it's more or less OK. It's only going in the tea after all. I look in my bread bin and see a packet of digestive biscuits. I slide them on to a plate, make the tea and bring it over to the table where Pen is sitting.

'I was sorry to hear about you and Chris,' she says, after taking a biscuit.

'I thought you'd all have been delighted.' I can't keep the bitterness out of my voice. 'You didn't like me, remember?'

'I never said I didn't like you.' Pen bites into the biscuit and it crumbles. I hope it's not out of date too. 'Just that I thought – we thought – you looked down on us.'

'That's nonsense and you know it.'

'You're very different,' she says. 'You can't blame us.'

I'm about to launch into a counterargument about how they disapproved of me, but I realise it's not important. I don't need to redefine my role in the Bennett family any more. It doesn't matter, either to them or to me.

'How's Chris doing?' I ask the question as casually as I can.

'Busy,' says Pen. 'Is it true?'

'Is what true?'

'That you were cheating on him.'

'I wasn't . . .' I sigh. This is exactly the moral dilemma I wrestled with myself. Whether thinking about Luke Evans constituted cheating on my fiancé. In the end, given that I'd planned to split up with him, I'm thinking that it did.

'There was someone in my past who reappeared,' I say. 'I found it difficult to deal with.'

'And now?'

I shrug. 'Nothing.'

'You've split up with my brother but you're not with this other guy?' Pen sounds incredulous.

'It just made me feel that Chris and I weren't right for each other,' I say.

'But he broke up with you.'

'Yes.'

'Weird.'

What's weird is that she's here in my kitchen, drinking tea. And I still haven't fathomed the reason for her visit.

'To be honest, I just wanted to say sorry to you,' says Pen when I can't help asking her.

'You what?'

'I knew, even before what you said earlier, that you felt we weren't as welcoming to you as you would've liked. After Chris told us about your break-up, I thought we might have in some way been responsible. But then he talked about you having someone else. So I thought probably not. All the same, I felt it might be the right thing to come round anyway. To say that if we didn't help, I regret that.'

383

I'm completely astonished by this.

'I know that our family can be difficult,' Pen explains.

She knows but she didn't make things any easier.

'Have they ever been against one of your boyfriends?' I ask.

Pen gives me a wry smile. 'I don't bring people home.'

I don't blame her.

'Not for the reasons you think,' she says.

I look at her inquisitively.

'Oh, for heaven's sake, Carlotta.' She picks up her bag, opens it and takes out a packet of cigarettes. I'm astonished. I didn't think smoking would be one of her vices. She stands up and asks if it's OK to smoke outside. I nod. We both walk out to the patio, where she lights up and then looks at me, a challenging expression in her eyes.

'Haven't you guessed?' she asks after taking a deep drag from the cigarette. 'I don't do men.'

I stare at her as I process this information. And now that she says it, I realise that I should have known all along. It isn't in her looks or her clothes or anything tangible. Not that gay people have to look a certain way. But there's always been something about Pen. And now I know what it is I'm kicking myself for not seeing it before.

'I guess my gaydar wasn't working properly,' I tell her. 'I didn't know.'

'Yeah, well, I wouldn't necessarily expect you to be totally up to speed,' she says. 'I'm not big into the gay scene. I'm not massively butch, nor am I a lipstick lesbian. I'm just a normal person.'

'Normal for a Bennett.'

Suddenly she laughs, a wickedly throaty rasp. 'Maybe you're right about us. Maybe we're a totally weird family.'

'All families have their own level of weirdness,' I say.

'Does yours?'

'I guess so. My mum and dad dress alike and potter around the world together. She wants to be supportive of my career but would prefer me to be married and have kids like my sister.'

'That's not so weird, I'm sure my mum would like at least one of us to be married with kids too.'

'Sorry if I messed that up,' I say.

'Confession time.' Pen takes another deep drag from her cigarette and fans the smoke away from me. 'I was probably a bit down on you because I envied you.'

Another person who envied me! Clearly I've been living a perfect life. It's a pity I didn't realise it.

'You always seemed to be so together,' she elaborates. 'You personally, I mean, not you and Chris. And even though I thought you looked down on us and thought we were sort of hopeless, I liked that you were able to do it. You could deal with Mum. I bloody well can't. That's why she doesn't know about me being gay. It would be hellish.'

I can imagine.

'Anyway,' she says. 'I don't fancy all of my brother's girlfriends. But when you came on the scene . . .'

I don't believe it. She's attracted to me! OK, that's definitely weird.

'I knew right away you weren't gay,' she assures me. 'It's just you stood up for yourself with Mum. I admired that.'

'It didn't help my cause with her,' I say.

'It was good for her to come up against someone like you. And good for me too. For the first time I realised that I could be a different person. Stronger.'

'Stronger as in being able to tell her?'

'Like I said, it would be hellish,' says Pen. 'But I've met someone and I want to be with her and I think . . . Well, you wouldn't keep it quiet, would you?'

'No.'

'So I'm planning to do the great coming-out,' she says. 'And I wanted to thank you for giving me that strength.'

OK. So I thought she'd come here tonight to list my failings and tell me why Chris is better off without me and generally be all Bennett-ish, but actually she's here to say thank you.

The doorbell rings and I remember I've ordered Chinese food.

'Would you like to stay and share?' I ask after I've taken it in.

She shakes her head and grinds the remains of her cigarette beneath her foot.

'No thanks. But thanks for listening. It's the first time I've told someone inside the family circle about being gay. It felt good.'

'I'm not exactly in your family circle any more,' I point out. 'If I ever was. But I'm glad you think I helped.'

'I didn't want you to feel that everyone in the Bennett family hates you because of breaking up with Chris,' she says. 'It was important to me.'

'It's a relief not to be hated by at least one of you.'

'I never hated you,' she says. 'I was just jealous.'

'I'm not sure I'm worth it,' I say. 'I know it must be hard for you, but couldn't you have told Chris and Lisa?'

She shakes her head. 'We're not close enough to talk about things like that.'

'It must be very hard to feel that way,' I say. 'I'm sure they'd have understood. Chris would, certainly. We have gay friends, for heaven's sake.'

'Thing is, people can be OK with it when it's someone else. But when it's closer to home . . .'

'They're your family. They love you. And they might have guessed anyway.'

'You think?'

I nod. 'But even if they haven't, I know they'll still love you. I admit your mum might be tricky at first. But Chris will be absolutely fine.'

She looks at me curiously. 'You still care about him?'

'I . . . I never stopped loving him,' I say. 'But I mixed up what I wanted from love.'

'Would you get back with him, if he asked?'

I think of Julia's exhortations to give it a shot with Luke, to embrace the romance of it all and be good to myself. And I think of solid, dependable Chris, who I hurt because I wanted to have my cake and eat it.

'I'm not the right person for him,' I tell her. 'I thought I was. I wanted to be, but I'm not.'

'I'm sorry it didn't work out,' she says.

'So am I.' I smile at her. 'But life goes on, hey?'

'I guess.' She smiles too. 'Anyway, I'd better go.' She nods towards my food. 'Nothing worse than cold takeaway.'

'Let me know how you get on,' I say.

'Will do.'

Then she leaves.

And I'm left wondering if she was ever here at all.

Chapter 30

Vikingman – Rodrigo y Gabriela

Despite what I'm chalking up as a success with Pen Bennett, I've decided that my strength is business, not personal relationships, and that it's time for me to focus solely on my career. I'm better at dealing with other people's problems than my own. So that's what I'm going to do from now on.

But even as I busy myself with reports and new clients, my mind can't help drifting back to my broken engagement every so often, and I wonder if I've blown my chance at happiness. I also think about my madcap nephews and I ask myself if I've blown my chance at motherhood too. I know women have babies into their forties now, but it's not a precise art, is it? I still have time, but perhaps not as much time as I might have thought. Besides, it also takes time to find someone, to nurture the relationship, to realise that you might have a future together and then, perhaps, consider children. And what happens to my career then? Do I walk away to become someone's wife and someone's mother, like Julia? Do I do exactly what Dorothea wanted and end up being nothing more than a support to my husband? Do I give up everything for an uncertain future?

I tell myself that I'm getting caught up in choices that I might not have to make. Because I might never find someone like Chris again. I would have had to make those choices with him. Now they've been taken away from me. Or, more accurately, I've taken them away from myself.

Joost van Aken taps on the glass door and walks into my office. I'm getting on well with him, although we don't have the same easy relationship as Dirk and I did. Dirk hasn't yet completed his move to South Africa, but he's already handed over the reins to Joost.

'Carlotta,' he says as he pulls up a chair and sits down. 'How was your vacation?'

'Pretty good,' I tell him.

'You're looking well.'

I'm wearing a navy jacket over a jade dress. It's a look that works for me. I thank him for the compliment.

'We have a problem,' he says.

My heart begins to pound. Problems mean politics. And I'm not good at politics because politics are all about other people. It's a vicious circle.

'But I'm hoping you can solve it.'

I am too. Depends on what it is, though.

'A new client,' says Joost.

Dirk would never, ever have called a new client a problem. To him, every new client was an opportunity.

'This client needs someone with experience to help them out of the mess they're in.'

'Who is it?' I ask.

'Kilgarry Foods,' says Joost.

I raise an eyebrow. Kilgarry Foods was once a major player in the health food industry. They concentrate on cereals, snacks and seeds. But last year a dead body was found in one of their processing machines. It turned out that there had been some kind of scam going on within the company with regard to the organic quality of their products that was about to be blown wide open. Apparently the organic cereal, well, wasn't. The body was of the potential whistleblower, and his supervisor is currently awaiting trial for murder.

The story was massive and ran on the news for weeks. The management of Kilgarry blamed rogue suppliers for the problem and said that company policy was to only use ethical sources. The body of the whistleblower, a production manager who had been transferred in from another plant, had been found in a mixing machine. As a murder mystery, it had everything. As something to happen to a health food company, it was a total disaster. Whatever people might feel about non-organic produce being incorrectly labelled and marketed, nobody wants to think that their cereal contains body parts. Apparently the production manager was formally identified through dental records. It makes me want to puke just thinking about it.

'I thought they'd closed down,' I say now.

Joost tells me that they're still in business, although obviously their brands have taken a major hit. They want us to advise them on a way to rebuild. It's a challenge, and I say this.

'I know,' says Joost. 'That's why I'm asking you and Ian McKenzie to go see the chief executive and talk through the options with him.'

Bloody hell. There's no way Ian is going to want to work with me. I might not be great at office politics but I know that he's a dab hand at it. He's well known for taking other people's ideas and turning them into his own. I'm going to have to be really careful with this one.

'I've already spoken to Ian,' says Joost as he stands up. 'Get together and talk it over.'

Right, I think, after he walks out of my office. I need to stop faffing around thinking of the lives I'm never going to lead and get my brain in order. To be honest, it's nice to have something else to worry about instead.

The HQ of Kilgarry Foods is about fifty kilometres outside Dublin. It's an industrial building set in green parkland, and I recognise it from the news stories of previous years as well as from some of their marketing material. Ian and I arrive ten minutes ahead of schedule and he pulls in to the half-empty car park. We came in his car because he drives a BMW and it trumps my Mini for corporate gravitas. But we're both channelling the corporate look: he's wearing a sharp charcoal suit with white shirt and silk tie, and I've gone for my unforgiving navy, white blouse and high heels. As I was checking myself out in the wardrobe mirror before leaving, I imagined how I'd look in a red flamenco dress, but then I realised that my hair was too short and spiky for the coiled sensuality that the dancer in Seville possessed. I'm getting over it. Slowly but surely.

The CEO of Kilgarry, Con Barron, is a snappily dressed man in his mid fifties who brings us on a tour of the plant, during which he complains about the media coverage given to the murder. I understand his frustration, but a dead body among the cereals is a massive story and he can't really blame the papers for running with it for weeks.

Afterwards, he brings us to the staff café, where he offers

us nut clusters and coffee. Even though I've seen how sterile the production line is, I'm not tempted by the nut clusters. I sigh. It can take years to build up a brand and seconds to destroy it. I'm not entirely sure that Kilgarry Foods can ever be the presence it was before. But I don't say this as we continue to discuss Con's ideas about the future. It's an hour or so later before we finish up.

'I'll be in touch,' says Ian as he shakes Con's hand.

'Thank you for an interesting day,' I add.

Con insists on giving us goody bags of Kilgarry products. On the basis that organic should be healthy, I'd be happy to eat them. Except I keep thinking of the dead body in the mixer. Which I'm pretty sure everyone else does too.

Ian talks most of the way back. He's already got an outline plan for Kilgarry. I tell him that he should look at the financials first. Because I know that there are weaknesses that Con Barron has glossed over.

'This will be a good account,' says Ian as we arrive back at the office.

'Maybe.'

'You don't sound keen.'

'I am,' I say. 'I just haven't decided the best way to go about it yet.'

'I have,' says Ian. 'Look, do you want me to debrief Joost?'

I'm not falling for that.

I tell him we'll talk to the CEO together.

Chapter 31

Danza de la Paloma Enamorada (Dance of the Enraptured Dove) – Jaime Guiscafre

The Kilgarry project is keeping me in the office for twelve hours and more every day. Ian and I are working together, but I know that we're holding out on each other too. I'm keeping some of my best ideas to myself and I bet he has a few stashed away that he's not sharing with me yet.

It's only when I add a note to my diary that I realise I should have been getting married this weekend. And it finally hits me. Everything I've been trying to forget. No fiancé. No wedding. No happy ever after. The plans, the dreams, the ideas – all sacrificed for one kiss. I should be getting worked up about floral arrangements and hairstyles. Instead I'm immersed in financial statements and job descriptions. I completely lost my way and I didn't have the sense to see it. I swivel my chair and stare out of the window towards the building where Chris is, even now, helping someone to have perfect sight.

Quite suddenly, I want to cry. I swallow hard and remind myself that crying isn't my thing. Besides, it wouldn't do to be found sobbing at my desk. People might get the wrong idea about me.

But I still feel shaky and unaccountably vulnerable, so I get up from my chair, gather my things and walk out of my office. I tell Verity that I'll be back in fifteen minutes and take the lift to the ground floor. Then I step outside the building. It's a bright day in Dublin – at the end of summer the weather has eventually turned balmy – and the warmth of the sun makes me feel marginally less bereft. There are lots of other people walking along the quays in the mid-morning sunshine. Some of them are suits like me. Others are parents with children. More are tourists who are having their photos taken alongside the street art, or queuing up to visit the *Jeanie Johnston*, the tall ship moored alongside Custom House Quay. Chris and I took a tour of the ship during our lunch hour once. It seemed like a romantic, silly thing to do.

A couple of teenagers, boy and girl, are doing the whole photograph thing, and I wonder what it is that will split them up. Because, like Luke and me, they're too young to be together forever, no matter that he's smiling at her and she's laughing at him and they only have eyes for each other. Well, not quite, because suddenly he asks if I'd mind taking their photo and of course I say yes. They pose, arms around each other, in front of the tall ship and then they check the digital photo to be sure it's OK. It's clearly good enough, because they thank me and then they start to walk along the quays together, their arms still around each other.

That's the thing about teenage love, I think. It's all so bloody intense. That's what Luke and I never got to experience properly. That's why he lunged at me and kissed me in Seville and why I responded so willingly. It was all about repressed passion. A few photos together, a few weeks walking around town wrapped up in each other, and we'd have got it out of our systems.

Well, he obviously already has. And I will.

Eventually.

Even though I've got myself under control again and I know I'm not going to burst into tears, I'm not ready to go back to the office yet. I join the other strollers along the quays and allow the sun to warm my back and warm my heart too. I continue walking until I reach the small café where Chris and I used to meet. I almost go in for a coffee, but I stop suddenly because I can see the couple sitting at the window table, deep in conversation.

It's Chris. And Sive.

If Sive were to look away from him she'd see me, but she's the one who's talking and she's leaning towards him, gesturing with her hands as she speaks. And then Chris grasps one of her wrists and holds it to keep it still. They sit opposite each other, looking silently at each other. I wonder how Sive will react to him imprisoning her wrist. Not well, I think. I can't really see her expression from here. With her other hand she reaches towards him and for a moment I actually think she's going to slap him. But instead she touches his jacket and removes something – a hair, dust, I don't know – from his shoulder. In that instant I'm rooted to the spot. Because her action is unexpectedly proprietorial. I continue to watch them. Chris slides his hand from her wrist to her palm. And then they link their fingers. They are holding hands. Chris and Sive. My ex-fiancé and my ex-best friend. And I can see that they're not talking about me at all.

That's when Sive looks out of the window. Our eyes meet. I know my expression is one of shock, because I'm trying to interpret what I'm seeing. I'm trying not to get it wrong. Sive's expression is different. She's horrified. She says something and Chris looks at me too. His expression is entirely different. It's defiant. But it's also regretful.

The thing is, I'm not sure exactly what he's regretting.

I whirl away from them and begin to walk very quickly in the opposite direction. I'm half expecting to hear either Sive or Chris call out to me, but they don't. I turn around when I get back to the Samuel Beckett Bridge again, but there's no sign of either of them.

I think what hurts more than anything is that they didn't think I was worthy of speaking to at all.

I'd planned to be a human dynamo this afternoon and write up my proposals for Kilgarry Foods, but I'm back at my desk staring into space again. I keep seeing Sive and Chris in the café and I'm trying to figure out what's going on between them. I'm telling myself that it doesn't matter if anything is – in fact, I reason, if Sive and Chris are . . . well . . . seeing each other, that means she's left Kieran, which is a good thing. But there's no denying I feel betrayed. Which is a joke. I've no right to feel anything other than incredibly stupid.

It's almost five thirty and I haven't done a stroke of work when my mobile rings.

'Hello, Sive,' I say when I see who's calling.

'Lottie. How are things?'

'Since we last spoke a few weeks ago?' I say. 'Oh, they're going well. I've been to Canada, seen Julia and the boys.

They're in great form. And I'm working hard on a new proposal for the firm. Still not getting married this weekend but too busy anyway. You know how it is.'

She doesn't speak. Neither do I. I guess we're in uncharted territory here. But eventually she says that Natasha has been asking for me.

'Really?' I say. 'She's not just pissed off at me for not giving her a day out in a pretty dress?' I still have the trinkets I bought for her in Vancouver. And the bracelet I got for Sive too. I haven't been able to bring myself to call her.

'Of course not,' says Sive. 'She's disappointed for you, not for her.'

'I'm sure she's got over that by now.'

'Carlotta . . .'

I wait. It's not that I'm trying to make it hard for her or anything; it's just that I don't know what to say. I don't want to appear to be accusing her of anything when it just as easily might be my imagination running wild. Even though I'm supposed to be the one without imagination.

'Can we meet?' she asks.

'Sure,' I say. 'How about the café on the quays?'

She hesitates for a moment. 'Of course, if you like. But maybe a glass of wine at the Clarion?'

I suppose that whatever conversation we're going to have needs alcohol, not caffeine. I agree.

'In an hour?'

'Fine,' I say, and hang up.

It's funny, but after talking to Sive my head seems to have cleared itself. I pull my laptop closer and open a new document. Then I start to type. Forty minutes later I've finished.

I save the document as Kilgarry Proposals 2, close the laptop, pick up my jacket and walk out of my office.

Ian McKenzie is at the water cooler. He raises an eyebrow as he sees me head towards the lifts.

'Half-day?' he asks.

'I usually stop when I've finished everything I have to do,' I tell him sweetly.

'I didn't think the work here ever ended,' he returns.

'There are times when you know that you can't improve on what you've put together,' I say. 'That's the time to walk away and allow yourself to concentrate on other important projects.'

'Concentrate on what? Where?' he asks.

'My next big assignment,' I reply. 'And sometimes it helps to be in a different place when you're doing it.'

The doors of the lift open and I step inside.

'See you tomorrow,' I say.

He's still frowning as they close again.

Sive is already in the hotel bar with a glass of wine in front of her when I arrive. She stands up and looks awkwardly at me. We usually hug when we meet, but this time it's more of an air-kiss moment. A waitress arrives as we sit down again and I ask for whatever Sive ordered.

We don't speak until my wine has arrived. I tip the glass towards her.

'Cheers.'

'Cheers.' She takes a gulp of wine.

Suddenly I'm tired of playing games. Sive has been my best friend for years. We've shared highs and lows and have always been there for each other. I know I told her stuff about her boyfriend that upset her, and I understand why she was mad with me. If she and the man I treated badly have hooked up, why should I blame her? After all, I wanted her to break up with Kieran, didn't I? Shouldn't I be pleased she's with a man I thoroughly approve of? And I certainly can't blame Chris. He deserves someone in his life. He always liked Sive. But it's still a bit freaky.

'So tell me,' I say in my brisk, businesslike voice. 'Have you and Kieran split up? And are you and Chris an item?'

I can see she's taken aback by my bluntness. But the thing is, Sive and I are good at being blunt. That's why we're good at our jobs.

'Yes,' she says. 'And . . . sorry, Lottie, but it's sort of yes again to your second question too.'

'Right.'

'I'm sorry,' she says again.

I'm not entirely sure what she's sorry for. Being angry with me about Kieran, or taking my abandoned boyfriend. I ask her and she looks embarrassed.

'Both,' she says.

'No need,' I tell her. 'I'm glad that you've dumped Kieran and I don't mind about Chris.'

'You don't?'

'Why should I? We're not together any more. I wish him nothing but happiness. I hope he finds it with you.'

'Carlotta, I know you want to be strong about stuff, but . . .'

'I made a mess of Chris and me. I'm delighted that he's apparently found someone more suitable.'

'Please, Lottie.'

I shrug. 'Really. There was no way back for us. Why

shouldn't you two be happy? Besides,' I add, 'I'm just glad you're not seeing Kieran.'

At least that's the complete truth.

Sive looks uncomfortable. 'I'm sorry about that. I was so angry at you because I was having such fun with him and I couldn't see in him the kind of person you were describing. Then I wondered if I was missing something. If, in my desire to have a man in my life, I was brushing aspects of his character under the carpet.'

'So you decided you were and then decided that as he was free, Chris was fair game?'

She winces.

'I called him for advice. Chris is astute about people and I suppose I felt that we were both in a similar position, having come off the worse from knowing you.'

That hurts. But only for a moment. I ask her what Chris told her.

'Urrgh.' She sighs. 'He said Kieran was a total tosser and that you and he had trashed him on the way home after the dinner party at my house. He didn't say anything about your personal experience with him.'

'Because I didn't tell him. I was afraid he'd clock him if I did.'

'I kind of guessed that. I didn't say anything either. Anyway, I suppose when Chris was so adamant that Kieran was a dick, I believed him.'

'I'm glad you believed one of us,' I say. 'How did Kieran take the news?'

She makes a face. 'Not particularly well. He wanted to know if it was something you'd said. And straight away that confirmed it for me. I'm so, so sorry, Carlotta. I shouldn't have doubted you and I shouldn't have said the things I said.'

I tell her that I don't blame her.

'You should.' She takes a sip of wine. 'I accused you of making it up even though I know you'd never lie to me. And I said that you should've made the tea. That was unforgivable!'

I smile a little. It's true. Telling me I should've made the tea was a betrayal of all Sive's principles.

'I understand why you did it all the same,' I say. 'I wouldn't have wanted to hear stuff like that about my boyfriend either. And you did seem to care for him quite a bit.'

She looks at me ruefully. 'I wanted to care for him. I wanted to love him. I wanted to have what I thought you had.'

I'm so tempted to say 'and now you do', but I don't. Because I know that's not really what she means and it's more important to repair our friendship than score points off each other.

'After you and Chris talked about Kieran, did you talk about me?'

'Yes.'

I watch her as she gathers her thoughts.

'At first he wanted to know what had happened when we went to Spain, and I told him that you hadn't seen Luke – he said you had.'

'I only spotted him in the street,' I protested. 'I didn't talk to him.'

'He didn't believe you,' she says. 'And he thought you'd put me in a terrible position by asking me to come with you. I tried to explain, but . . . well, we ended up sharing stories about you.'

'Which I'm guessing weren't good.'

She looks shamefaced. 'We had a right old bitch, to be honest.'

'Maybe I had it coming.'

'Ah, no.' She takes a bigger sip of wine. 'No you didn't, Lottie. How you felt wasn't your fault. After running out of nasty things to say, I admitted to Chris that you'd agonised over the whole situation. And I'm sure you agonised over telling me about Kieran too.'

I think of how much I wanted to do the right thing, and suddenly my eyes sting with tears. I blink a couple of times then fish a tissue out of my bag and blow my nose. I'm not going to break down in front of Sive. I take a deep breath and put the tissue back in my bag.

'In the end we just agreed that you had your flaws but so does everyone.'

'Thanks.' I try not to sound bitter. I'm *not* bitter. I just wish I'd handled it better.

'Then he asked if I'd like to meet up with him again. I wasn't thinking of it as anything other than two friends.'

'But?'

'But we got on so well, Lottie. He's so easy to talk to. He's—' She breaks off. 'Well, you know.'

I do know. I loved him. My use of the past tense, even to myself, surprises me. Every day since our break-up I've wondered if I did the right thing. If secretly I still love him. Now, sitting here with Sive, I realise I don't. That I was right all along to think that maybe I didn't love him enough. Because the fact that they have become an unexpected couple doesn't hurt me nearly as much as it did when I first saw them together. But perhaps that was the shock of it as much as anything else.

'Carlotta?' Sive is looking anxiously at me.

'What can I say?' I raise my glass. 'I wish you well.'

She raises hers too but I know she's not convinced.

'What about us?' she asks.

I don't say anything.

'We're friends,' says Sive. 'At least, we're supposed to be. I don't want to lose our friendship, but I understand if you feel you can't stand the sight of me. And I'm sorry for not being in touch with you, but I just didn't know what to say. I would have called eventually, you know. I really would.'

I believe her. I know what it's like.

'I want you to be happy,' I say. 'I want Chris to be happy too. If you end up being happy together, then that's a good thing.'

'I might just be his rebound girl.'

'You might. But you might be his forever girl.'

'Jeez, Lottie, you're being very magnanimous.'

I know I am. But that's because I feel as though I've walked out of the fog that's surrounded me for the past few months. I can see clearly again. I thought I loved Chris enough to marry him, but obviously I didn't. And the fact that Luke Evans came along and made me see that was a blessing. It would have been so much worse if we'd gone through with it and lived the wrong life together.

I say this to Sive and she nods slowly.

'But what about you?' she says. 'And what about Luke?'

'You were right about him,' I tell her. 'He was my fantasy. But he didn't try to come after me and he has his own life. That's OK.'

'You sure about that?' she asks.

'Absolutely,' I reply.

*   *   *

We spend three hours together, which means we drink far too much wine and have to leave our cars at the office. By the time the cab drops me home, I'm suddenly exhausted. I go to my bedroom, take off my make-up and fall into bed. I'm asleep in less than five minutes.

Chapter 32

Agua Fuego Tierra Aire (Water Fire Earth Air) – José de Córdoba

I wake up early, totally refreshed and entirely without a hangover, despite the wine. I'm energised in a way I haven't been for absolutely ages and I decide to walk into work rather than get a cab. The sun is beginning to rise in a clear sky, and because the Indian summer is still with us, the air is warm. My walking route follows the Grand Canal from Harold's Cross to Leeson Street Bridge, so I've brought some stale bread for the swans that congregate around Portobello. It's just about bright enough for them to be awake, and as I throw it into the water and watch them hurry across to get it, I can't help feeling lucky. I might have messed up, but it could have been worse. As it is, I'm young (ish), free and single and I'm in complete control of my own destiny. Which, this week, will mean finalising my report for Kilgarry Foods, sharing the information with Ian – while perhaps keeping one or two nuggets to myself for later – and showing Joost van Aken that I'm a valuable member of the Cadogan team who is worthy of promotion.

I hurl the last scrap of bread into the centre of the water so that the swans who haven't quite made it to the previous pieces get something too. Then I continue on my way to the office with a spring in my step. (The springiness is partly due to the fact that I'm wearing trainers. My high-heeled office shoes are in my tote bag. They're not designed for a five-kilometre walk.)

I'm at my desk with my takeaway coffee by eight. Most of the consultants are already in, including Ian, who waves to me as I walk across the office floor. A couple of minutes later he pokes his head around my door and asks how it's coming along. I tell him that I'll have my suggestions ready to go by the end of the day.

'Good,' he says. 'I was talking to Joost last night. Kilgarry are looking to have a meeting on Friday afternoon.'

'No problem.' I nod. 'I'll be ready.'

I'm perfectly aware that the salient point in Ian's comment is that he was talking to Joost last night. Without me. I was mending bridges with my friend instead of concentrating on my career path. It was the right thing to do but it kept me out of the loop. It doesn't matter, though. I don't need to be in their loop. I'm totally on top of this project.

Nevertheless, the knowledge that Ian has been having cosy chats with Joost spurs me on to an increased frenzy of activity on the Kilgarry Foods account. I'm perfectly aware that it might not have been a cosy chat at all, that Joost might simply have spoken to Ian in passing, but I have to assume there's been some ass-licking going on by my colleague. I have to be sure that my work outdoes his smarminess. Even as I think this, I sigh inwardly. Business should be about doing your best for the company, or your clients, or your shareholders. But really it's about doing the best for yourself.

My phone rings.

'Hello,' I say.

'Carlotta. How are you?'

I recognise Mateo's voice immediately.

'I'm great, Mateo. And you?'

'Busy, busy,' he says. 'I'm calling because I've been talking to Antonio Reyes.'

'Yes?'

'Ecologistics have received an offer for a major stake in the business.'

'Oh?'

'It looks like a decent offer,' he says. 'But he wants us to check it out for him. Also, he wonders how it will affect the recovery plan.'

'Depends on the stake the bidder wants to take,' I say. 'What is it?'

'I don't know,' says Mateo. 'Antonio is emailing the information to me. And he wants a meeting with the board tomorrow.'

'I'll look over it,' I tell him.

'He'd like you to be there too,' says Mateo.

I frown. There isn't really any need for me to be there. Despite the fact that Antonio clearly liked the work I did for his company, Mateo is the account manager. I'm just the velvet assassin. I say this to my colleague, who laughs.

'Antonio trusts you,' he says. 'He says you speak the truth without putting on the sugar coat.'

That's true. That's what my job entails.

'I'm very busy here,' I say.

'This is important,' Mateo tells me. 'If Antonio and the board accept the offer, there will be more business for us. And if they don't because we have a better plan, there will still be more business.'

The holy grail for Cadogan is increased business. But if I go to Spain, even for a day, Ian McKenzie will have yet more time to cosy up to Joost. Nevertheless, I like Antonio and I have a sense of ownership of Ecologistics and its future development.

'Meeting in Madrid?' I ask.

'Well we could do that, but I'd prefer us to go to Seville,' says Mateo. 'That way we can talk to everyone.'

I don't exactly shudder, but the disastrous travel arrangements of the last trip are still close to the surface. And although I've dreamed about being in Seville, I'm not sure I ever want to go there again. But this is business, and business is what matters to me now.

'OK,' I say. 'Will I meet you at the office or the train station?'

'At Ecologistics in Seville,' says Mateo. 'I'm going to go there this evening and chat informally to Antonio first, maybe over dinner.'

'OK,' I say again. 'I'll see you tomorrow.'

I end the call and stare into space for a few minutes. I can deal with both Ecologistics and Kilgarry. One is speed-reading and memorising, which I've no problem with. And the other is having my stuff prepared. Which I'll have done in the next half-hour. I call Verity and ask her to organise my flight. Then I click on the computer screen in front of me and start working.

*　　*　　*

I'm on the high-speed train again. The Spanish countryside is whizzing by while I read the offer from the company that wants a piece of Ecologistics. There are lots of business people on this train and all of us are working. At least, most of us are – I did notice that one of the men across the aisle was actually playing Angry Birds on his iPad as we pulled out of Atocha station.

I'm not thinking of the last time I travelled on this train and how things turned out afterwards. I'm totally focused on the document in front of me. Mateo had to resend it to me because the first time he actually sent the Spanish version. When I emailed him back and told him that he'd have to get it translated, he sent back an apologetic response saying that it would take a while. So I didn't get to read it as planned last night. It was waiting for me in my inbox when I landed at Barajas airport this morning.

There's enough material here to keep me busy for the entire two-and-a-half-hour journey, although I allow myself a bit of time to have a coffee and glance at the TV screen at the front of the carriage, which is showing an action movie. Sylvester Stallone is doing his thing with a massive gun. It's a more recent Stallone movie and I can't help wondering how many men in their mid to late sixties could actually run around like Sly. I wonder if Sly himself can actually run around like movie Sly.

Chris likes Sly. And Arnie. He likes action movies. I think most men do. The only times we went to the cinema together were if the movie starred Arnie or Sly or Jason Statham or Bruce Willis. I was fine with that. I like Jason and Bruce, although I find it hard to suspend my disbelief when they get into fights and emerge with nothing more than a few scratches. Chris and I used to argue about it, although in a friendly way. I wonder if he's now going to action movies with Sive. No matter what I said to her, it's incredibly weird and unsettling to think of my ex-fiancé and my best friend together. Does he compare me to her? In bed? On the phone? I shudder at the thought. Do they talk about me? Complain about me? Tell each other that I'm a total flake? I know I've repaired my relationship with Sive, but it's still fragile, and she wouldn't be normal if she and Chris didn't comment about me in some form or another.

I gaze out at the countryside as it flashes by and tell myself that it doesn't matter what Chris and Sive say or do. I've made my choices and I have to live with them. I wish it had been different. That I hadn't overslept, that I hadn't missed the train, that I hadn't met Luke Evans. But who knows what else might have happened anyway? Life is random. You have to get on with it. There's no point wishing you could undo things. You have to concentrate on the future, not the past. And right now, all I have to worry about is doing a good job.

Joost wasn't best pleased when I told him that I was coming to Spain. He's totally keyed up about Kilgarry Foods and Friday's meeting. I explained that even though I wouldn't be able to sit down with Ian and go through my recommendations this afternoon, I would email them to both him and Joost so that they'd be able to go through them before I returned. I would, of course, I assured him, be back in time for the meeting itself.

'You'd better be,' he said, in a way I found disturbingly ominous. There's a distinct lack of warmth about Joost. I know I have a residual loyalty towards Dirk, and I valued the working relationship we had, but that's in the past and it's Joost who matters. Nonetheless, I can't see myself ever wandering into his office simply to shoot the breeze as I used to with Dirk. Lots of people say that business is about being the best and doing your best and that it isn't personal, but that's bullshit. Everything is personal.

I finish reading the report for the third time half an hour before the train arrives in Seville. When I close my eyes I can see all of it, page by page. I can see the good points and the bad points and the hidden points too. It's perfectly clear to me that the offer is a good short-term deal for some of the senior management of the firm – especially Antonio – but that as a long-term proposition it will pretty much wipe out Ecologistics as it's currently run. And within the pages I've seen the clauses about rationalisation, which, as usual, means getting rid of people. My recommendation will depend entirely on what Antonio and his board want from the company. It comes down to a choice between getting some money for themselves now, or sticking with Ecologistics for the long haul and turning it into a profitable business that will reap greater rewards in the future.

I like Antonio, but I'm not optimistic about him or his colleagues wanting to wait for future rewards. Business used to be like that, but it's not any more. It's all about what people can get right now. However, it's not up to me to make moral judgements. Morality is for other people, certainly not consultants. As Dorothea pointed out to me on more than one occasion.

I'm assailed by the heat as I step from the air-conditioned train on to the platform. It's way hotter in Seville now

411

than it was in April. I feel my body begin to perspire as I walk towards the exit and I envy the women who are already using their hand-held decorative fans to cool down. I always thought that fans in Spain were a tourist thing, but I realise now that they're part of daily life. I wish I had one myself.

I get into a cab (no Jeremy Clarkson lookalike today) and am whisked to the Ecologistics offices. I cool down almost as soon as I open the door to the building, because it's air-conditioned to the extent of positive chilliness. Which makes me glad, after all, that I'm wearing one of my suits – a muted purple pencil skirt and fitted jacket, which, along with my black heels, makes me look almost tall.

The security guard tells me to go to the fourth floor, where Antonio and the rest of the board are waiting. I check my reflection in the mirrors of the lift, tug the skirt a little, rearrange my sparkly clip and take a deep breath. Antonio himself is waiting to welcome me and lead me to the boardroom. They've set it up with coffee and pastries. I like the fact that Ecologistics doesn't stint on the pastries, but I stick to my personal rule of no flaky food, and simply accept a cup of coffee.

Mateo is the one who gets the meeting going, talking about the proposed deal in rapid-fire Spanish that completely goes over my head. But then he turns to me and asks me to give my views. I begin by apologising for the fact that my Spanish isn't up to the task and remarking that their own English is probably good enough to understand anything I might say. But I add that Mateo will translate so that there are no misunderstandings on either side.

As I talk about the future of the company and stress the

need to look after the employees, I can see Antonio looking speculatively at me, and I wonder if he's thinking that I'm too soft-hearted to be a velvet assassin after all. But all I'm doing is laying it out in front of them. It's their choice to make, and it doesn't matter to me what they do. Regardless of whether they stick with the plan or not, Cadogan will get the fees due to us. And they're paying more for me to be here today.

'Thank you, Carlotta,' says Antonio when I've finished. 'You've put it all together very concisely.'

Of course I have. That's my strength.

'I think there are a number of issues my colleagues and I would like to discuss. Perhaps we can do this now and you can come back and talk to us again in, say, one hour?'

I tell him that I'll come back whenever he likes and get up from my seat. Mateo joins me and we leave the offices and go to a nearby café bar.

'They're going to accept,' I say after I order a sparkling water. It's too hot for coffee.

'Do you really think so?' asks Mateo. 'I've spoken a lot to Antonio. He loves that company.'

'Nobody turns down money in the hand,' I remark. 'I'd like to think that Antonio is different, but I doubt it.'

'You're very cynical,' says Mateo.

'Experienced is the word I'd use,' I tell him.

He acknowledges the difference. We stop talking about Ecologistics and chat instead about the changes at Cadogan. I tell Mateo about the power battle going on between me and Ian McKenzie and the change in the atmosphere ever since Joost van Aken arrived. He talks about recent changes in Madrid too. He also says that he's thinking of a move to a different company.

'If Antonio sticks with it, I'm sure he'll be sorry not to be working with you into the future,' I say.

'In the end, nobody cares,' Mateo says. 'Life goes on. Business goes on.'

'We're both being cynical today.' I sip my water. 'Which is a pity, because it's too nice a day not to have faith in human nature.'

We sit and watch the world go by while we wait for Antonio to summon us back to the office. After nearly two hours he does. There are more people in the boardroom now, and I'm pretty sure that they're the Ecologistics legal team, which reinforces my view that, despite the picture I painted for them of a potentially rosy future, they're going to accept the offer.

But then Antonio surprises me by saying that they've decided to go it alone. I'm hardly ever shocked by the outcome of any of my business meetings, but I am by this.

'I cannot let somebody else take over,' he explains. 'The board cannot. We have invested too much of ourselves in this company.'

You don't often hear that.

'I'm really glad,' I say to him after the meeting breaks up. 'And you can be sure that Cadogan will work with you to make sure that Ecologistics is as successful as it can be.'

'I know.' He nods. 'It is because the plan has been so successful up to now that we want to continue. It's probably why someone else wants to buy us out. I have to thank you for that, Carlotta. And I want to ask if you have thought any more about coming to work for us yourself.'

'I haven't had time.' I avoid giving him a direct answer.

'When you do have time, let me know,' he says.

I might like it here, I think. With the blue skies and the hot sun and working with people who have a passion for what they do. Even if what they do is something as dry and boring as logistics!

'And we look forward to you visiting us any time,' he adds before giving me the obligatory kiss goodbye.

Mateo and I leave the building. I look at my watch. I'd decided against trying to get back to Dublin tonight, even though I reckoned I'd probably make the evening train. The memories of it not working out in the past are still too raw. Yet once again I've elected to stay in Seville rather than Madrid. This time, however, I'm spending the night in the type of hotel I wanted to before. It's small and classy and it's near the cathedral.

'Nice,' says Mateo when I tell him.

'I know. I picked it myself.'

'Have a good time in Seville,' he says. 'I hope we get the opportunity to work together again soon.'

'Me too,' I say. I mean it. I like Mateo. I don't want him to leave Cadogan. He's one of the good guys.

He gives me a hug and hops into a cab. I hail one myself. I'm still wearing the high heels and it's easier than walking. Cooler, too.

The hotel I've chosen for my night in Seville is perfect. It's in an old but beautifully restored building, and from my window I can see the cathedral in all its magnificence. The room is cool and inviting and both traditional and modern at the same time. The marble floor is dark, and the walls are papered in black with red roses. There are plenty of mirrors and lights that can be adjusted to suit the mood I want, and the bathroom is a treasure trove of high-pressure shower, enormous bath and exquisite toiletries.

I feel calm and relaxed as I slide my iPhone on to the dock and select the Concierto de Aranjuez. I can listen to it again now that I'm no longer with Chris. And hearing it now, in Seville, doesn't make me feel sad and mournful and aching for something else as it did in Dublin. The music suits the room and it's mysterious and joyful and it sweeps me along in its rich cadences. I'm no longer the velvet assassin, or the consultant who's seen a client reject an amazing offer, or the businesswoman who needs to get ahead of her rival. I stand in the middle of the room, raise my arms over my head and move to the music. Even though Aranjuez is more Arabic than flamenco, I'm the dancer in the red dress, stamping my feet, clicking my castanets and draping my shawl around me in a way that's designed to show me at my most alluring.

When the music finally fades, I flop on to the bed and pick up my iPad. I have five emails from Ian, asking for further input ahead of the meeting with Kilgarry. I reply that I'll be sending an email shortly to him and to Joost and that I'll see him, as scheduled, on Friday afternoon.

Then I ring Sive.

'Where are you?' she asks.

'Seville.' I tell her about the meeting with Antonio and the fact that Ecologistics didn't sell out as I expected them to.

'Company in not-getting-rich-quick shocker.' She's equally surprised. 'Are you planning to go anywhere else in Spain?'

'No.'

'Not to Marbella?'

'Sive, it's about three hours away.'

'So?'

'I don't have time to go to Marbella. I hardly had time to come to Seville. I'm really busy right now.'

'Seems an awful waste to be in the same country and do nothing about it.'

'You told me I was crazy before,' I remind her. 'It'd be doubly crazy now.'

'I told you it was crazy when you were engaged to Chris,' she points out. 'You're not engaged any more.'

No, I acknowledge. But I'm not Luke's girl any more either. I'm a different person. I've moved on.

I tell Sive that it's not possible to get to Marbella from Seville and back to Madrid in time for my flight tomorrow. And that Luke could be in Timbuktu for all I know. And that I might have made a fool of myself over him once but I'm absolutely not going to do that again. I also tell her that I've got an important piece of work to get on with and I fill her in about Kilgarry Foods.

As I suspected, her attention is diverted by the work issue.

'Their financials are crap,' she tells me. 'I'm not speaking out of turn because it's common knowledge they're in deep trouble.'

'That's why they've called us in,' I tell her. 'I've seen the financials. I have some thoughts about that myself.'

'You should check out the terms of some of their contracts too,' she says. 'Just to be on the safe side.'

'Do you know something?' I ask.

'Nothing specific,' she says. 'Nothing you can't find out yourself. But some suppliers haven't renewed and the substitutes aren't all certified.'

'That's what got them into trouble in the first place!' I exclaim. 'Con Barron is such an idiot.'

'Just desperate, I think,' says Sive.

'I understand, but he needs to be upfront with us on everything.'

'Make sure he is.'

I like being back on good terms with my friend. I've missed talking to her.

'How's Natasha?' I've had enough of business talk. 'Has she got over not being my bridesmaid yet?'

'You'll have to visit us when you're back,' says Sive. 'She was philosophical about the wedding. She said it would have been worse if you'd said no at the altar.'

'It's hard when even children are more sensible than I am.' I sigh.

Sive laughs.

'Does she know about you and Chris?' I ask her.

'No,' says Sive. 'I'm trying not to have her think she's living on a trailer-trash reality show where people play pass the parcel with each other.'

'She likes Chris,' I say. 'She'll probably be happy when she gets over the awkwardness.'

'She'll be worried about you,' admits Sive. 'And to be honest, I'm not keen on being regarded as the woman who split you up.'

'You didn't.'

'She probably won't see it like that.'

'How is Chris?' I ask. 'And Dorothea? And Pen?'

I haven't said anything to Sive about Pen. I'm hoping that Dorothea's daughter will have the strength to come out sooner rather than later.

'I still have to meet them,' she says. 'But at least I know what to expect. And as for Chris . . .' I can hear her voice soften. 'We're good. We really are.'

'I should have seen it from the start,' I say. 'You and him. Perfect for each other.'

'It *is* slightly weird,' agrees Sive. 'I'm hoping we can all eventually get over it.'

'I'm not sure Chris ever will,' I say. 'He was so angry with me and I can't blame him.'

'I'll put in a good word for you.'

'You're all heart,' I tell her. 'By the way – Pen will be on your side.'

'She will?'

'Yes. She's actually one of the good guys. As for Dorothea . . .' I speak thoughtfully. 'Well, I guess she'll be so glad you're not me, she'll be on your side too.'

'I'm another career girl.'

'She'll like the fact that you have a daughter. It'll make you seem more human.'

'Or more like a trollop,' says Sive cheerfully. 'I can't see Dorothea as a woman who takes kindly to single mums.'

'If she's giving you the evil eye, just keep in mind that she's got those erotic novels on her bookshelf.'

'Carlotta!'

'Whenever she went on a rant to me, I'd imagine her chained to the bed by furry handcuffs,' I confess. 'Helped a lot.'

The two of us laugh. Then I hear a ping in the background and Sive says that she has to go. Dinner's ready.

I could do with something to eat myself now. I think I'll go out and see what Seville has to offer the hungry woman on her own.

It has a lot to offer, actually, but because it's only eight o'clock in the evening, most of the people out and about in the streets are tourists. Nevertheless, the bars and cafés are busy, and each time I walk past one of them I get a refreshing spritz from the cool mist they're pumping on to passers-by. I stop at one of them and order pizza, which is probably a crime against the local culinary culture but which does the job as far as my hunger is concerned. Afterwards, without Luke to guide me, I wander aimlessly around the town's twisting, narrow streets. I can't remember where the flamenco club was, nor the bar where he and I shared tapas together. But as I emerge from a particularly tight alleyway, I realise that I'm in front of the place where we drank mojitos.

I walk inside and, as we did months earlier, I go to the rooftop. Even though it's relatively early, it's very busy. There are people sitting around the pool, dangling their legs in the water; there are people clustered around the high tables; and there are even more people standing at the rail that encloses the entire terraced area. There's more than a few languages being spoken and the buzz of conversation and laughter nearly, but not quite, drowns out the music track, which is a generic sound with a definite bass rhythm.

I changed from my suit and heels to a pale cream summer shift dress and ballet pumps before I came out. It's the only change of clothing I brought because this is such a short visit.

One of the beautiful waitresses asks if I'd like a drink. I order a mojito and sip it leaning against the rail, looking out over the city. Despite the volume of the music and conversation, I feel calm and peaceful. Nobody knows me. Nobody is taking any notice of me. I'm an anonymous person in a strange city. And I like it this way.

Is a part of me expecting Luke to turn up? I know that's

not remotely realistic. And yet I know that I'm conscious of every single person who walks on to the crowded rooftop while not even expecting any of them to be him. It's a peculiar state of mind to be in, wanting something, knowing it's not going to happen, yet preparing myself on the off chance that it does.

But of course Luke doesn't walk into the bar. Luke is miles away. And he'll never know how much I've thought about him since our night in Seville together. It's probably better that way.

Chapter 33

Fuente de la Alhambra (The Alhambra Fountain) – José de Córdoba

I've no idea what time it is when I wake up, because I closed the shutters on the window before going to bed. So when I open my eyes, the room is in pitch darkness. I fumble around for a moment until I find my phone and discover it's a couple of minutes to eight. I push back the covers, get out of bed and open the shutters again. The sun hasn't risen yet but the sky is beginning to lighten in the east. I have a shower, get dressed and go downstairs.

I'm the only person in the breakfast room and I select from a tempting array of fruits, cheese and meat. I add a couple of mini chocolate croissants to the mix and ask the waitress for a cup of coffee. By the time I've got to the coffee and croissants, a few more people have arrived and sunlight is beginning to stream through the windows.

My flight is in eleven hours. I deliberately didn't book a return seat on the train because, even though I'm not a super-stitious person, it was too much like having the same thing happen again. My plan is to rock up to the station with plenty of time and catch the first available train. I know, because I can remember the schedule in detail, that they start at around six in the morning.

I go back to my room and put my bits and pieces into the overnight bag I brought with me. And then I sit on the windowsill and look out at the street below, which is full of people chattering away and pointing their cameras at the cathedral and at the facade of the hotel. I'm watching without seeing, aware of what's going on without really registering it, because I'm thinking about everything in my life that has brought me here. I'm thinking that, at fifteen, I never imagined that one day I would make a business trip to Seville. Or anywhere, to be truthful. At fifteen I didn't have a clear idea of what I wanted. But I knuckled down and worked hard and got my exams and my job and my promotions, and here I am, a successful businesswoman. I'm thinking, too, about my personal life, about Sive and how I nearly lost her friendship. About Julia, who I've always envied without any good reason. And about Chris, who I loved and lost. I think about how I've never been truly satisfied with what I have, always thinking that the grass is greener somewhere else, always chasing some elusive rainbow that's just out of reach.

I need to put an end to this. I need to follow Julia's advice and allow myself to be happy. And I will, because I have a good life and my happiness is in my own hands.

I get up from the windowsill, take my bag and go to reception to check out. The receptionist phones for a cab, and while I'm waiting, I look at my emails. Joost has responded to my recommendations by saying that there are some interesting points and we'll talk in the morning before the clients arrive for our meeting. There's nothing from

Ian McKenzie. I flick through the rest of the emails, trashing most of them before replying to the more urgent ones. I finish with the last as the taxi turns up.

I recognise the driver immediately but I doubt he recognises me. Which might be a good thing, as I don't want Jeremy Clarkson getting on my case about his missed fare nearly six months ago. He nods at me as I get into the back seat and sets off for the station, once again driving through the twisting roads of the old city. This time, however, we look like arriving at our destination in one piece. I can actually see the train station when I lean forward and ask him if he could drive me to Fuente del Rio instead.

I've no idea what makes me do that. I haven't been thinking of Fuente del Rio, let alone going there. And yet something is triggered inside me the moment I see the station.

Jeremy, of course, is completely taken aback by my sudden change of destination. He pulls the car to the side of the road and turns around, unleashing a torrent of Spanish, not a word of which I understand. When he's finished, I repeat that I'd like to go to Fuente del Rio, not the train station. It's embarrassing to be speaking in pidgin English and I think to myself that I really need to learn other languages, especially if I get promoted at Cadogan Consulting and do more overseas work.

Eventually, after a few minutes toing and froing with lots of gestures between me and Jeremy, he gives a massive shrug, puts the car into gear and starts off again.

I know that this is absolutely crackers of me, but I can't help it. I need to see the little town again, to sit at the café and eat bread smothered with Nutella, and to walk the path beside the river. I tell myself that this is a way of getting closure on everything, but I'm not entirely sure I believe my own words. And yet I do feel that returning to the town where I came with Luke will somehow release me from the shadows that still keep forming in my mind, will help me on the road to letting myself be happy.

The cab driver has his radio tuned to a talk show, interspersed with snatches of music. I find myself thinking that if it plays the Concierto de Aranjuez, it's a sign. I'm not entirely sure what it could be a sign of, but that's what I'm thinking. I realise that I'm actually willing the music to change, but, perhaps fortunately, the radio station sticks with generic pop and I don't have to interpret any signs, made up or not.

When we arrive at the town, he pulls in to a parking space near the river and tells me how much I owe. I give him the fare, plus a generous tip. He thanks me with a surprised smile and then pulls away. I take a pair of sunglasses from my bag, put them on, turn from the river and head up to the town square.

It's even hotter here than it was in Seville, and I take off the jacket of my suit and carry it over my arm as I walk along the steep street that leads to the square. Colourful flowers topple over the sides of huge planters and I can hear the hum of bees and the constant shrill of birds over the ripple of the fountain. The bars are open and the tables outside are all shaded by enormous parasols. It's pretty and Mediterranean and as tranquil as I remember, although most of the tables are occupied by people drinking cups of coffee. Or, in some cases, glasses of beer or wine. I glance at my watch. It's nearly midday.

I sit down in the shade of one of the parasols and order

coffee. Then I add that I'd like some bread and Nutella too. The waiter nods and disappears into the café. I stretch out my bare legs so that they're catching the sun. It's hot, even beneath the parasol, so I undo a couple of buttons on my white blouse. I really should've worn the summer dress and pumps again today.

As I wait for the coffee and bread, I feel myself drift. I'm dislocated from everything around me, in a bubble of my own. It's as though I'm observing myself and everything going on around me from a distance. I see two men wearing sharp suits talking animatedly to each other. A woman sipping a glass of water while she keeps an eye on two dark-haired, dark-eyed children playing a game nearby. Two more elderly women wearing black, their hair backcombed and lacquered, sitting on a stone bench beneath an olive tree. A skinny cat lying just out of the sun. It's a different world and I'm not a part of it. But I'm dipping into it, just for a while.

I shake myself out of my reverie and take out my phone. It's a bit ominous that there aren't any more messages, but I'm finding it hard to care. Nevertheless, I fire off an email to Ian, asking if he has any comments on my proposals for the Kilgarry Foods meeting tomorrow. I cc Joost on that too. Then I sit back and wait for my coffee.

By the time it arrives, I'm wishing I'd ordered water, because I'm positively wilting in the heat. I pleat one of the paper napkins that came with the coffee and bread into an improvised fan, which I wave, fairly uselessly, in front of my face. I'm not sure that hot coffee is a good idea at all now, but the bread and Nutella look very inviting; notwithstanding my lovely breakfast earlier, I'm hungry again.

I spread Nutella on the soft, warm bread and take a bite.

Then I take a sip of coffee. Despite the heat, it's absolute heaven. I feel relaxed for the first time in months. Suddenly all my previous feelings of guilt and misery and uncertainty have evaporated. Forced on me or not, I'm content to live with the choices I've made. Because in the end, it's the small pleasures that bring the most happiness. And I'm embracing those small pleasures now.

I smile as one of the dark-eyed children kneels down and pets the sleeping cat.

This is a good place to find happiness.

I think about Luke Evans, but not in a maudlin way. I think of how much he meant to me when we were younger, and I think about how handsome he is now. I picture him with me here before, and then I remember him and the beautiful girl in Marbella.

I think about Marbella.

I see the building he walked out of and the brass plaques on the wall. There were company names – Villanova, Equitos, Caralito, Poco a Poco. There were professional people – Paco Ramirez-Casillas, Abogado. Paloma Suarez-Verdasco-Echaverría, Dentista. Carlos Jimenez, Psicologo. I take out my iPad and begin to type.

Villanova, Marbella, is a property development company. Equitos is a financial services company. I can find nothing for Caralito or Poco a Poco, although I do discover that Poco a Poco means little by little. I don't need to look up the professional people, although for my own satisfaction I discover that an *abogado* is a lawyer. I close my eyes and recall the telephone numbers on the Caralito and Poco a Poco plaques. I remember them perfectly.

I'm not sure why I do it, but I begin to dial.

I try Caralito first. The name sounds like it could be a sort of charity, although I'm not basing that on anything other than a feeling. After a moment, there's a click and then an answering machine whirs into action. Obviously I've no idea what's being said, although I assume there's something in there about leaving a message after the beep. Which I don't.

I ring the Poco a Poco number next. In this case, there's a brief ringtone, then further clicks and then another ringtone. And then the phone is answered. Obviously I don't have a clue what the man is saying, because he's speaking Spanish. I'm ashamed of not having learned any usable languages at school. It's embarrassing to have to ask if he speaks English.

'Yes,' he says. 'I speak English.'

It sounds like Luke. It really does. And the connection is so clear that it sounds like he's right beside me.

'Is that Poco a Poco?' I ask.

'Yes,' he replies. 'How can I help you?'

'Luke?' I say.

'Yes. Who's speaking?'

I recognise him but he doesn't recognise me. I tell myself I'm being very stupid. But I take a deep breath and speak again.

'It's me. Carlotta.'

'Carlotta?' This time it's as though he's behind me, and I can't stop myself from whirling around in my seat. As I do, a man at a nearby table, half hidden by one of the multiple planters full of flowers and the dancing plume of water from the fountain, stands up and looks around him. It's Luke Evans and he's holding a mobile phone to his ear.

I'm stunned into silence.

'Carlotta?' he says again.

He isn't alone at the table. The beautiful girl is with him. I don't know what to say.

'Carlotta, where are you? Where are you calling from? For a moment I thought—'

And then he sees me.

I'm still holding my own phone as though I'm about to speak to him. But I don't.

'Carlotta.' He strides towards me, ending the call as he walks. 'I don't believe it. What are you doing here? How did you find me?'

My mouth opens but no words come out. He disconnects the call and puts his phone on the table beside me. Even though I know he's in front of me, I'm gripping my mobile so tightly I could possibly crush it. He takes it from me and puts it beside his own.

'Carlotta,' he says once more.

I find my voice. I say hello. It's as much as I can manage.

He pulls up a chair and sits opposite me. He's wearing his jeans and T-shirt combo and looks fit and tanned, his blond hair cut a little shorter than when I saw him in Marbella.

'I hope I'm not imagining you,' he says. 'I can hardly believe it.' Then he asks me again what I'm doing here.

'Having coffee,' I say. 'I didn't expect to see you. Or . . .' I glance across at the girl. She's even more beautiful than I remember. Her skin is gently golden, her complexion dewy. She's wearing a white T-shirt over a short blue skirt. Her luxurious mane of hair has been pinned up in an elegantly disordered way. Up close it seems to be all her own. No extensions. She looks at me curiously from chocolate-brown eyes. I realise that my appraisal of her has been equally curious.

Luke waves at her and she walks over to us. They speak briefly in Spanish and then she walks away.

'What was that about?' I ask. 'Is she coming back? Have I upset her?'

'No.' He sits down again. 'She's fine. She's leaving us alone for a while.'

'She's very pretty.' I try not to sound like a sulky teenager.

He grins. 'That's Anita,' he says.

I ask him if she's the Anita who got married when I was here before, and he says that she is. He reminds me that her family have an old house here. I remember him telling me that, of course. I remember everything about the last time we were here. And I wonder what the connection is between Luke and Anita and Richard Evans.

'You went out with her, didn't you?'

'For a while. Now she's married to someone else.' He makes a face. 'Happens to me a lot.'

I don't know why. He's so damn attractive I'd have thought he could keep any girl he wanted.

'Why are you here?' he asks again. 'How did you get my phone number?'

'I saw the phone number on a building in Marbella,' I said. 'I rang it.'

He frowns. 'But when were you in Marbella?' he asks. 'How did you . . . Carlotta, I'm totally confused.'

I take a deep breath and explain that Sive and I visited Marbella a few weeks ago. And that I saw Anita there. And that I saw Luke too.

'You saw me!' he exclaims. 'You saw me and you didn't

say hello? Why on earth not? Carlotta, don't you know how much I wanted to see you?'

I keep my voice ultra-light. 'Ah now, I don't think so, Luke,' I say. 'You were with Anita at the time.'

He tilts his head to one side as he always used to when he was thinking.

'With Anita . . .' And suddenly his face clears. 'Oh yes, I remember.'

'So you wouldn't have wanted me butting in.'

'Carlotta, are you being particularly silly or something?' he asks. 'Why wouldn't I have wanted you to butt in?'

'I thought . . . well, you put your arm around her and I—'

'Carlotta O'Keeffe! D'you think I was having some kind of fling with Anita? She's only just got married!'He sounds truly shocked.

'I didn't know who she was when I saw the two of you together,' I point out. 'I assumed she was a girlfriend.' I take a deep, deep breath. 'And I'd seen her before too. In your father's nightclub. She was with him.'

'Hold on.' Luke raises his hand and calls the waiter over. 'I need something to get me through this. Ideally alcohol, but as I'm driving later, I guess an espresso will have to do. How about you?'

I ask for an espresso too.

'*Dos solos*,' Luke says to the waiter. '*Fuertes.*'

The waiter disappears. Luke says nothing until he returns with two small cups of thick, aromatic coffee. I realise that Luke has asked for doubles. Suits me. I knock mine back and relish the caffeine hit.

'OK,' says Luke as he drains his own cup. 'Let's get this

straight. Any chance you could start at the beginning and put this all into context for me?'

So I tell him about going to Marbella with Sive for a girlie break. I tell him that I remembered his dad's nightclub was there and we decided to check it out. I tell him that I saw Anita and Richard together. And then I tell him that I spoke to his father.

'You talked to Dad!' He's gobsmacked.

'Yes.'

'In the name of God, why?'

'Because,' I say carefully, 'I was looking for you.'

My statement falls between us. Luke is staring at me. I'm looking back at him. I'm trying to keep my gaze steady, but eventually I'm the one who breaks eye contact.

'Why were you looking for me?' asks Luke.

I'd tell him, I really would. But I can't speak again.

'Carly?' His voice is gentle. 'Why were you looking for me?'

I swallow a couple of times as I try to compose myself. Then I give him a tight smile.

'I . . . wanted to . . .'

And then I finally lose it.

I start to cry.

His arm is around me in an instant and he's hugging me close to him. I can feel the warmth of his body, the rhythmic beat of his heart. I can smell his musky aftershave. I let myself be cradled in his arms.

'Oh Carly,' he whispers. 'Don't cry.'

I can't believe I'm really crying. It's so not my thing. And crying for no apparent reason – well, that's definitely not my thing. Yet allowing the tears to flow down my cheeks is alarmingly cathartic. I can understand why people do. I feel a momentary twinge of guilt for every time I told a crying person to pull themselves together. Sometimes it's good to crumble.

After a few moments I sniff a couple of times and sit up. Luke's arms drop and he looks anxiously at me.

'I'm fine,' I say as steadily as I can. 'I'm sorry about that. It was just . . . well, I was overwhelmed for a moment. But I'm fine now, honestly.'

'Good,' says Luke. 'Are you going to tell me what on earth is going on?'

He reaches out, takes my hand and squeezes it. Just like he used to, back in the day.

'Give me a minute,' I say.

'OK.'

It takes a couple before I'm ready to talk. Luke hasn't said anything during that time, but he's kept holding my hand. And he keeps watching me.

'I guess I never really got over the kiss,' I say eventually.

'The kiss?'

'At the train station.'

'Ah.'

'I know it was silly.' I'm talking quickly now because I'm managing to sound almost businesslike. As though I'm explaining a particularly daft proposal to a client. I tell Luke that the kiss knocked me for six and that when I got back to Dublin I behaved a bit like the silly teenager I was when he last knew me.

'You were never silly,' he interjects.

I continue, not acknowledging the comment. I tell him

everything. That I felt guilty about how much I liked it, that I felt the need to see him again. Another moment of silliness, I say. That I tried to find him in Marbella. I tell him about going to Chanzes, talking to his dad and seeing Anita. And about seeing her with him the next day. I tell him that I realised then how incredibly daft the whole thing was.

'But . . .' He looks at me, his blue eyes filled with puzzlement. 'In that case, why are you here?'

I explain about Antonio Reyes and the Ecologistics deal.

'But here?' he asks again. 'In Fuente del Rio?'

'It was so lovely before,' I say. 'I wanted to experience it again. I was thinking about that day. And then . . . I remembered the phone number from the building in Marbella. I dialled it.'

He nods slowly. 'When there is no answer in the office, the calls are diverted to me. But Carly . . . why did you ring? Did you want to see me after all? How could you know I'd be here, in Fuente?'

'I didn't,' I say. 'I was thinking about the phone numbers and I just . . . rang. I was very shocked when you answered. I was even more shocked when I realised you were actually here. I never for a second imagined . . .'

'What were you going to say to me?' he asks.

'I don't know,' I admit. 'Seeing you has made me forget everything.'

'Including your fiancé?' he asks.

'Um.' He'd interrupted me before I'd managed to tell him about Chris and me splitting up. I tell him now.

'So you broke up because of me? Because I kissed you?'

I'm glad that he doesn't sound self-satisfied at this.

Because it's a big thing, isn't it? It could make a person feel really smug. Luke, though, isn't smug. If anything, he's anxious.

'That was just a catalyst.' I keep my voice as unconcerned as is humanly possible. 'It made me realise that what I had with Chris wasn't what I thought I had.'

'You told me he was the one,' says Luke. 'You said you loved him.'

'I thought he was,' I say. 'I really and truly did. I thought we were good together. And we were. We understood each other, at least most of the time. I loved him because he was calm and rational and easy to get on with. The fact that I was prepared to get on with his witch of a mother only made me surer than ever about him.'

'And yet?'

'And yet I came to see that it wasn't enough.'

'Because I kissed you? How did that make you change your mind?'

'I loved Chris but I . . .' I shrug. 'It doesn't matter. The important thing is that you actually stopped me from making a mistake. Don't look so panicked,' I add. 'I'm not trying to substitute you for him. Or stalk you or anything.'

'I still can't believe you're here.' He's looking at me in sheer wonderment.

And then my phone beeps.

I turn away from Luke and pick it up. It's a message from Verity to say that the meeting tomorrow has been brought forward. Con Barron and his team will be coming in for breakfast at seven thirty. I swear softly to myself. A bloody breakfast meeting! I wonder who decided on that. My eyes narrow as I think that it's something Ian might do to put me on the back foot. To give me less time to prepare because he knows I'm away today. I realise that I'm grinding my teeth.

I text back an acknowledgement to Verity and tell her I'll be there. I tell myself that I'll be ready for whatever Ian is going to try.

It's hard to imagine, sitting in the heat of a Spanish village, that tomorrow could be one of the most important days of my professional career. With a sudden jolt I also remember that tomorrow was supposed to have been the most important of my entire life. Tomorrow I should have been getting married to Chris in my beautiful dress, with Sive and Natasha as my bridesmaids. Friday the thirteenth. There's no omen in that. None at all.

Luke is sitting opposite me, watching me as I type on my phone.

'I didn't think I'd ever see you again,' he says when I put it away.

'You and me both.' Although I'd dreamed of it. And now that it's happened, it's not what I expected. Mind you, I don't really know what I expected. For us to run along a beach into each other's arms like in the movies? For Luke to declare undying love for me? For him to kiss me again?

'I tried to find you,' he says.

I stare at him.

'Not at first,' he tells me. 'At first I thought it was right to let you go. You were engaged, after all.'

'Why did you change your mind?'

'The kiss,' he says.

I frown.

'You said it changed things for you. It changed things for me too,' says Luke. He picks up the little spoon on his saucer and turns it over and over in his fingers. He's not looking at me; he's staring at the spoon.

'I couldn't believe it when I met you in Seville,' he says. 'It was like the last eighteen years had suddenly been wiped out. There you were, and you made me feel . . .' He takes a deep breath and releases it slowly. 'The way you always made me feel.'

'I didn't always make you feel anything,' I remind him. 'You had loads of girlfriends when you knew me.'

'I know. I think it was to prove to myself that even though my dad and my brothers thought I was a wimp, I was . . . well . . . manly.'

'Manly!' Luke wasn't at all manly in his teens. Like Mum used to say, he was beautiful.

'They were all so damn macho,' he says. 'All into body-building. All with the "do a deal" mentality drummed into them by Dad. And I thought that if I wasn't like that, at least I could be the kind of cool guy that girls hung out with.'

'Right. You did that. I hung out with you,' I say.

'I didn't consider you to be a girl.'

'Oh? What was I? An alien?'

He laughs. So do I. It's getting easier between us again. Easy like it used to be.

'You were my friend,' he says. 'You weren't there to make me feel good about myself in front of my family. But you did. And when I was with you, I felt . . . I felt good about everything. Not just about me. Everything.'

'So did I.'

'And when we went out together to that movie . . .'

I wonder if he'll remember which one it was.

'. . . *Independence Day*, I had the best time ever. We both liked the film.'

'God knows why,' I say. 'Looking back, it was pretty dire.'

'But fun then,' he reminds me. 'It was a fun night. An easy night. Everything was perfect.'

'Except my dad opening the door.'

He grins. 'Good old Mr O'Keeffe. Protecting his daughter.'

'You think?'

'I'm certain of it. Anyway,' continues Luke, 'I couldn't wait to see you again. But, of course, we left. I kept thinking about what would've happened if I'd kissed you. I kept thinking that it would have changed everything.'

He was thinking the same things I was thinking.

'Maybe it wouldn't have,' he says. 'I was being hauled off to Spain no matter what. And with all the stuff about my dad – well, there was nothing I could do. I couldn't say all this to you in Seville. You kept texting and phoning your fiancé. I was certain that you were happy with him and that you'd got on with your life without me. Well, of course you had.'

'So had you!' I exclaim. 'And a pretty good life it was too. I'm not surprised you never came back to Dublin.'

'I didn't see the point,' he says. 'Raking over the past isn't always a good idea.'

'I agree.' After all, coming face to face with my teenage crush has completely messed up the life I'd planned. 'You know, if we'd just had the damn kiss back then, we'd have got over it in the space of a few months.'

438

'Or maybe not,' says Luke. 'Maybe we'd still be together.'

It's my turn to use a prop. I pick up one of the sachets of sugar and shake it a few times.

'That's not very likely,' I say.

'But you came looking for me. And I tried to look for you.'

'Yes.' I put the sachet down. 'You never got round to telling me how.'

'I rang your house,' he says simply. 'But no one ever answered.'

'You rang my house?'

'Your parents' house,' he amends. 'Lots of times. I assumed they must have moved away.'

'You rang Blackwater Terrace?'

'Of course,' he says. 'How could I forget the number? I rang it often enough in the past.'

It comes back to me suddenly. Walking into the house with the milk and bread for them after their trip to Vancouver. Hearing the phone ringing. Hearing it stop. Not being concerned. Not thinking, for a second, that it might have been Luke.

'And then I realised I was being stupid,' he says. 'Why was I looking? You were getting married, after all. You hadn't turned around at the train station. You hadn't said anything to me other than goodbye.'

I don't know what to say.

Then Anita walks back into the square.

She really is exceptionally beautiful. Every single person in the café looks at her as she walks over to our table in wedge sandals that make her long legs look even longer. She gives Luke a dazzling smile, pulls out a chair and sits down.

'Everything OK?' she asks in English.

'Sure,' says Luke. 'Anita, this is Carlotta. Carlotta, Anita.' We shake hands.

'You are the girl who stayed in Seville.' She gives me an appraising glance, but it's hard to tell what she's thinking.

'Yes. Thank you for your hospitality. Even if it was forced upon you,' I tell her.

'You are welcome.' Her voice is warm and her previously unreadable expression is too. 'Any friend of Luke's is also my friend. And you are an old friend, yes?'

'Very.'

'It's good for Luke to have friends,' says Anita. 'He works too hard.'

'Do you?' I look at him.

'For the charity he is working all the time,' says Anita. 'Making everyone find more and more sources of money. Spending it wisely. We all love Luke.'

She sounds like she really means it.

'You're involved in the charity too?'

'Anita is head of fund-raising,' says Luke. 'She was at the nightclub in Marbella to talk to my father about giving money to one of our projects.'

I try not to look judgemental. I think Richard Evans should be paying back his ex-neighbours, not making himself feel good by making donations to charity.

'I didn't want her to do it,' Luke adds. 'But there is an association of business people in the area who do charitable work, and my father is involved. So she met him.'

'And he is making a donation,' adds Anita.

'He told me that you and he hadn't spoken in years. You

440

said that too.' I know I sound brittle as I say this. 'I'm surprised you'd even think of accepting money from him.'

'It wasn't an easy decision,' he admits.

'I know that Luke's father has a – a difficult past,' Anita says. 'But he can redeem himself by helping less fortunate people now. I tell Luke always that he should speak to his father. We only have one family. We might not approve of everything they do, but they are our family all the same.'

'We don't see eye to eye on that particular issue,' Luke tells me.

'So . . .' Anita looks at me with interest. 'You are here to see Luke?'

Luke and I exchange glances.

'Not originally,' I reply.

'But you have seen him.'

'Yes.'

'And it is OK? You are OK? He is OK?'

'Everyone's OK,' I say.

The ringing of my phone yet again stops us all talking about being OK. It's Verity. She's telling me that she's emailing me more information for the meeting. That Ian and Joost are both in agreement about the strategy for Kilgarry Foods. They've come up with a game plan between them, adapting the notes I've already sent. In fact, says Verity confidingly, she has a feeling that Ian won't mind if I don't make it back.

'Of course I'll be back,' I tell her. 'I'm going to send some additional notes to Joost now. I'll cc you too, Verity. Let me know when you receive it.'

I select a file from my iPad and attach it to an email, giving an apologetic glance to both Anita and Luke as I work. When the email has finally gone, I look at my watch and realise that it's getting late and that I should make my way back to the station. I say this to Luke and Anita, and both of them look at me in surprise.

'To Seville?' says Luke. 'Now? How exactly were you planning to do that?'

'By taxi,' I tell him.

They exchange looks.

'Now? From here?'

'It's not that far,' I say.

'But you have to book in advance,' Anita tells me. 'There is not a regular taxi.'

'What?' I'm astonished. Fuente is a small village, but surely they need to get to the city from time to time.

'There's a bus in two hours,' says Anita.

I look at my watch again. This is beginning to feel eerily familiar. My stomach sinks. I have to get back to Ireland tonight. I have to be in the office for the meeting tomorrow. Missing Dorothea's party sent my personal life into meltdown. Missing the meeting would turn my professional life into toast.

'Don't worry.' Luke grins at my panicked expression. 'I'll take you.'

'Are you sure?'

I know I should protest, tell him to stay here and do whatever he came here to do. But I don't. Because I have to get to Seville and I have to catch that train.

'Sure I'm sure.' He grins again. 'Better get a move on.'

We stand up and Anita holds out her hand.

'Nice to meet you,' she says.

'You too. And thank you again for the night in Seville. Your apartment is lovely.'

'I'm glad you think so.' She smiles and then turns to Luke. 'I will see you later?'

'Yes.'

As she walks away from us, I accept that there was no weird love triangle going on between Luke and Anita and Richard Evans. That she's married, his dad is still a slightly dodgy businessman and Luke is a free agent. But, I remind myself, just because Luke and I met up unexpectedly and cleared the air a little, it doesn't mean that there's something between us. Not any more. I remember Sive asking me what I wanted from him, and the truth is that I don't really know.

We walk through the square together. The gentle perfume of the flower-filled tubs follows us as we make our way towards the river, and I can feel the heat of the sun through my white blouse. I look for the Aston Martin, but Luke leads me instead to a dark green Mini.

'You actually drive a Mini?' I can't help smiling.

'I know it's not a patch on the Aston—' he begins, but I interrupt him and tell him I like Minis, that I drive one myself.

'You do?'

'Yes.' I get into the passenger seat. 'It's red.'

Luke nods approvingly as he opens the driver's door. 'It's exactly the right car for you. I can see you in it.'

He drives the Mini the same way he drove the Aston. Confidently and competently along the roads that snake through the countryside. When we reach the train station, he parks in the car park and gets out.

I look at my watch. 'The next train is in eighteen minutes.'

'Eighteen?' For a moment he's taken aback by my accuracy.

'Of course, you know the timetable off by heart, don't you?'

'I spent a lot of time looking at it when I was trying to get back to Madrid the last time.'

'So we have eighteen minutes to talk about the future.'

I stand outside the station, my travel case beside me.

'What future?' I ask.

'Carlotta! You've broken off your engagement. You came here looking for me. You called me.'

'You think I've been running after you?' I never wanted to be that girl. Never wanted him to think that I needed to follow him around. Even though I did.

'I called you too,' he reminds me. 'Well, I tried. The only thing that stopped me trying harder was the fact that you were getting married.'

'But what now?' I ask. 'You're here. I'm in Dublin. We have different lives.'

'Why did you look for me?' he asks.

'I honestly don't know.'

'If we hadn't met in Seville, would you have given me a moment's thought?'

Tricky, that. Because I regularly thought of Luke, if only to wonder how he was. But I wouldn't have called off my wedding, or at least got into a situation where my fiancé dumped me!

'It's complicated,' I say.

'I suppose it is.' He gives me a half-smile. 'I suppose it always has been.'

But it wasn't, back then. It was simple. Best friends. Forever.

My phone beeps again, and I check it. Verity is confirming that she's got the email and that she's printed off copies. I send a thank you to her and put the phone back in my bag.

'Everything all right?' asks Luke, and I give him a potted history of Kilgarry Foods.

'Wow,' he says. 'Murder on the Organic Express.'

I laugh.

'And you have to bring body-part-free nut clusters to the public again?'

'The company employs two hundred people,' I say. 'I want to save their jobs. That's what the email was about. A new strategy.'

'Saving the world was always on your list of things to do.' Luke isn't teasing me. When I was fifteen, I was big into saving things. The whales. Pandas. Water. Energy.

'Some things can't be saved,' I say. 'I'm not sure if I can succeed with this.'

'Do you think your plan is a million times better than your colleague's?' he asks.

'Not a million,' I admit. 'Just – better.'

'So you're too important and too necessary to your company to chill out and spend another night in Seville?'

For a moment, the desire to do just that is so strong that I stop walking. Which means I have to hurry to catch up with him.

'I can't,' I say. 'This is an important account and I need to be there.'

'This is who you are now?' he asks. 'A corporate suit?'

'Don't you start.' I actually snap at him as we enter the relative coolness of the station. 'I got it in the neck all the time from Chris's mum. I'm sure she's still rubbing her hands in glee at the narrow escape he's had.' Although now that he's with Sive, I suppose she'll think it's a case of out of the frying pan and into the fire.

'I'm sorry,' says Luke. 'It's just that . . . we lost each other. We looked for each other. We found each other. And you're going home?'

Of course I'm going home. I'm not the Carlotta I was in April. I'm not even the Carlotta I was last month. I'm not a flamenco dancer in a red dress either, ready to be carried away by the click of a castanet and the heat of the sun and the rapid beating of my heart. I'm Carlotta with an important career move ahead of her, and I'm not going to be distracted by nebulous ideas of romance. I'm never going to move to Spain to be with Luke. He's not going to abandon his work here to be with me. And if either of us did, and it all went wrong, we'd simply end up blaming each other. I don't want to have to blame Luke any more. Meeting him again was wonderful, his kiss was magical, but I've got to be realistic. This time it really is closure.

'I can't miss this train,' I say as I join the queue.

'So I'm saying goodbye to you in the train station again.'

'Déjà vu,' I murmur.

'Don't go,' says Luke. 'Stay with me.'

Part of me wants to, it really does. But I can't stay. I have a life now, a different life. And I have to finally face up to that.

'You were the one I dreamed of,' I tell him. 'For months after you left. I never stopped thinking that you'd come back.' I smile slightly. 'Well of course eventually I did stop thinking that, I had to. You became a memory. When I met you here before, it made all those memories come alive. But Luke, that's all they are. Memories of when I was young and naive and I thought love was simple.'

'It seems perfectly simple to me,' says Luke.

'I built up a life and I ruined it because I thought there was something more,' I tell him. 'Because I was dissatisfied with what I had. I hurt a man I cared about. I need to be on my own. I need to cop myself on.'

His face is impassive, but I see his jaw tighten the way it used to when he was upset about something. I don't want to upset Luke, but I need to be firm. With him and with me.

'I should have come home,' he tells me. 'I should have trusted you.'

'Luke, we were kids!' I remind him. 'It's not about trust. We would've gone our separate ways sooner or later. We both know that.'

Although doubting that, not knowing for sure, is what messed up my head for the last six months. It's odd that only now, with Luke beside me again, am I accepting it.

The queue of people filing through the barrier has thinned out. The train will be leaving in five minutes.

'Goodbye, Luke,' I say.

'Goodbye, Carlotta.'

I wonder if he'll kiss me.

I wonder if that will change how I feel.

He does. But only on the cheek. The lightest of touches.

I turn away and walk through the barrier.

I know I've done the right thing.

Chapter 34

Concierto de Aranjuez: Allegro – Narciso Yepes

Once again I'm speeding away from Seville at 245 kph. I have my iPad open. I'm looking at my report for Kilgarry Foods, even though I don't need to, because I remember every word of it. Tomorrow morning I'll get up and deliver it without hesitation. I'll show Joost van Aken just what a treasure he has in me. And I'll carve out a place for myself as a real player in Cadogan. Plus, I think, I'll save three quarters of the jobs at Kilgarry. I'm the velvet assassin, but I'm also a guardian angel. I'm doing the right thing for everyone.

From tomorrow, my career will take precedence over everything else in my life. I'll have put Luke Evans back into the locked box in the deepest recesses of my mind. He'll become, once again, my childhood sweetheart. My erstwhile best friend.

Sive is my best friend now. She's the one I confide in. And despite everything that's happened, we will be that way again. We've been there for all of each other's ups and downs. Even if she stays with Chris, I'll be her friend and she'll be mine.

Luke has his own circle of friends. His Anitas and his Begoñas and goodness knows who else in the golden life he leads. He's not the person he was before. Nor am I. I don't need to remember him as being my one true love. Hell, I didn't think of him like that when I met Chris. I didn't think of him at all. I thought Chris was my one true love then. I'm absolutely hopeless when it comes to men. But not any more. It's going to be different from now on.

My phone vibrates.

'Ian,' I say.

'Those are some very interesting last-minute insights you've put together,' my colleague tells me. 'Joost is all excited about them.'

'Good.'

'I thought we were going to share everything.'

'We did.'

'You didn't send me the information about that overseas contract before.'

'Not separately,' I say. 'But it was in the files.'

'Hidden,' he says.

'Slightly tangled,' I agree.

'So you think you'll get a big pat on the back for your efforts?'

'I hope not,' I say. 'I hope I get a lot more than that.'

I end the call and sit back in the seat.

Luke was right. I'm a corporate suit.

And I'm a good one.

The rhythmic motion of the train is lulling me into a state of torpor. The AVE doesn't make the same clackety-clack sound of a traditional train. Something to do with the high-speed rail. The tracks are different. I read that somewhere. I close my eyes to remember. The article was about a gas welding technique that was being proposed for the development of rail track. I think I read about it in a magazine when I was waiting in Chris's eye clinic one day. I don't need to remember any of this. But I do.

I remember the day now, too. I was waiting for him to finish with his last patient, a woman who was having the same laser eye surgery as me. He was apologetic for having taken so long, telling me that she needed lots of reassurance. I remember telling him to put her in touch with Sive, who'd been delighted with the results of her own surgery. We went straight to dinner from the clinic. And afterwards back to my house, where we made love. He left just after midnight. Pen was away and he didn't want to leave Dorothea alone.

He deserves someone better than me in his life. I wonder, in Sive, is that what he's getting? It's still unsettling to think of the two of them together. But they always enjoyed each other's company. Perhaps they were made for each other after all. Perhaps I've done them a favour.

As for me . . . I lean my head against the window, eyes still closed. I wonder if I'll ever find the right person. I wonder if I need to. After all, if I've found happiness, isn't that enough? Besides, we come into the world alone. We leave alone. Where's the big tragedy in that? Isn't it better to be happy on your own than to try to make something work with the wrong person? Isn't it better to do the things you want, rather than shoehorn yourself into someone else's life?

I can't do that. I can't make myself fit into the wrong place. I'm too independent. Too damn stubborn. I didn't want to fit when I was younger and I don't want to fit now. Except, perhaps, at Cadogan. I do the right thing there because you have to fit to get along. And if I'm not going to have someone to kiss me at night, the least I can do is make sure that I'm a good fit in the office.

I moisten my lips. I wonder why Luke didn't kiss me goodbye. I wonder why I thought he would.

I open my eyes again. The countryside, drier and more parched than it was in April, flashes past. I'm leaving Luke further and further behind. Leaving the part of me that allows passionate kisses, flamenco and orange blossom to ruin her life. Well, not ruin. Change. Forever. And no harm in that.

Dammit, I think suddenly. Why didn't you kiss me?

Why didn't I kiss you?

Was it because I was afraid it wouldn't be as good as the last time?

That I'd have discovered I'd given up everything for nothing?

It's hot and busy at Madrid's Atocha station. Much busier than Seville. There are people milling around everywhere, in groups, separately, travelling for business, for pleasure. For necessity. It's noisy and confusing and I stop to orientate myself.

A woman bangs into me as she hurries past. Older than me, so she should know better than to barge into her fellow travellers. And then I see her rush into the outstretched arms of the man who has been waiting for her. He's tall and distinguished, grey hair, glasses, wearing a suit. He folds her into his arms, hugging her tightly. Then he kisses her on the lips before hugging her again.

I feel the tears pricking at the back of my eyes again. Tears of envy, I realise. Envy that she cares about someone so fiercely. Tears that she can show it. I blink them away. I've done my crying. I'm over it.

All the way from Seville I've told myself that I'm happy with my choices. And the truth is that there wasn't another choice for me to make. All the same, I wanted something more from Luke. I wanted him to sweep me into his arms and kiss me like that man did the woman on the train. I wanted some of the fire and the passion I decided I couldn't have with Chris. I wanted romance.

Me. Carlotta O'Keeffe. The velvet assassin. Wants romance. I'd laugh if I wasn't so disappointed in myself. I take a deep breath. I need to pull myself together. I need to be OK with things again. And yet I'm standing here and I can't move. It's as though I'm weighed down once more with everything that's happened over the last few months. As though my stupidity is a burden that's too heavy for me to carry. I literally cannot move.

My phone rings yet again.

What, I wonder, does Ian want now?

I answer it.

'Carlotta.'

It's not Ian McKenzie. It's Luke Evans. My heart somersaults.

'Are you all right?' he asks.

The question surprises me.

'Yes,' I say. 'I caught the train. I'm on time for my flight. I'm fine.'

'Are you sure?' he asks.

What does he want from me? I've already made a fool of myself by chasing him around Spain. I'm not going to make things worse by having fruitless conversations with him now.

There's hardly anyone left on the platform. Soon I'll be alone. A woman in high heels with a sparkly clip in her hair, clutching her mobile phone and trying not to cry.

'It's just that you seem uncertain,' says Luke.

'I'm not uncertain,' I say. 'I'm a bit confused, that's all.'

'Confused about what?'

'Oh Luke.' And suddenly I don't care any more. 'I'm confused about me. About you. About us.'

'Us?' he asks. 'There's an us? After all this time?'

'I think I've always had a dream of us,' I admit. 'Which is probably nothing to do with reality. Because the reality is that you're in Seville and I'm on my way to Dublin and we're like . . . well, we're two trains on separate tracks.'

'But we can still end up in the same station,' he says, and I can hear the warmth in his voice.

I love Luke. I always have. I always will. Which is why I never really had decent relationships with other men. Which is why I fell at the final hurdle with Chris. Which is why, I think, I'll always fall at the final hurdle.

'Carlotta?'

'Mmm.' I'm thinking that emotional stuff is messy. That it's not clear and logical, which is the person I've let myself become. I'm thinking that no matter how much I know that tomorrow morning I'll be at a breakfast meeting talking about balance sheets and corporate plans, I'd much prefer to spend it wrapped in Luke Evans's arms. No matter how fleeting or temporary that time with him might be.

I'm alone on the platform now. Everyone else has left, moved into their own lives, getting on with it. And I'm the one left standing here. I glance the length of the gleaming white train. And I see the person standing at the door of the carriage halfway down the platform. He's holding a phone to his ear. And when he sees me looking at him, he waves.

It's Luke.

He ends the call. My own phone goes silent. I stare at him as he starts to walk up the platform towards me. And then I run. I run to his outstretched arms and I thud into his body and I feel him pull me close to him. And then he kisses me.

It's the best kiss of my life.

It's the kiss from the man I'll always love.

I wake up early the next morning, in plenty of time for the meeting with Kilgarry Foods. All the information I need floods into my mind. All the information that I ran through with Ian McKenzie last night. The financial issues. The staffing issues. The PR issues. They're all there, neatly formulated in my head, just as I memorised them. I hope that Con Barron realises that, working with Cadogan, his company and his brand can be rebuilt. I hope Ian can persuade him.

I turn over in the bed.

Luke is awake too. He's looking at me.

'Sleep well?' he asks.

'Like a log,' I reply.

'I know.' He grins. 'You snore.'

'I do not!'

'Do so.'

'Did I keep you awake?' There's mock-contrition in my voice.

'Not a bit of it,' he says. 'I was exhausted.'

'Not surprised,' I say.

We spent a lot of yesterday just being together. Neither of us could let the other one go. I knew, from the moment I kissed him at the train station, that I wouldn't be returning to Dublin that night. And that the meeting would be going ahead without me this morning. And I didn't care. I still don't. I phoned Ian late last night and told him I'd be missing the meeting, and I went through everything with him. He was astonished at the level of detail I was giving him, and I know he thought that somewhere along the line I had a trump card to play, something to hold over him, but I assured him that everything was fine, it was just that I was taking some personal time. When he said that I was driving a nail into the coffin of my career, I said I'd worry about that later. But I won't worry. I'll think about it. Deal with it. But I won't worry about it, because with Luke beside me, nothing has the power to worry me any more.

He pulls me close and bumps his head against mine, the way we used to do.

'I love you,' he says. 'I always have, I always will.'

'I love you too,' I tell him. 'I'm glad I found you.'

There are lots of things we have to talk about. Lots of decisions that have to be made. But not now. Now is for not being at a breakfast meeting at seven thirty in the morning. Now is for happiness. Now is for us.

Meet Sheila O'Flanagan

Read on to hear from Sheila on her life as a writer, getting married and her favourite travel destinations . . .

What made you want to become a writer?

As a reader I loved getting involved with characters and their stories. I also love spinning stories myself. So it was almost inevitable that I'd start to write them down. It wasn't a conscious decision, it just happened. But I do want to bring the same joy I get from reading to anyone who reads my books.

What's your routine as a writer? Do you always write in the same place, and try to write the same number of words every day?

I have an office in my house where I write and I try to get there every day. I don't set myself a word count for the day. I write in scenes so I stop when I'm happy with the scene I've done. Sometimes that's five hundred words and sometimes it's a few thousand.

What do you like most about writing?

The characters! I love how they evolve and take on their own personalities. They're all like family to me and I'm always interested to find out how they're getting on. I also enjoy not working nine to five, although I do a lot of writing at the weekends . . .

What do you not like about writing?!

Nobody else can do it for you! If you've had a bad week it can be difficult to get yourself into the right mental place to deal with fictional people's problems. And physically typing 120,000+ words is demanding.

You chat regularly to your readers on Facebook (/sheilabooks) and Twitter (@sheilaoflanagan). How do you make sure you don't spend too much time online rather than writing?

I spend far too much time on Twitter and Facebook. I wonder if social media had been developed back in the day would Hemingway have limited his work to tweets and status updates! The thing is, it's really nice to connect with readers through social media but when I'm engrossed in writing I can ignore it.

You've written many bestselling novels. How do you celebrate when your latest novel hits the bestseller list?

I'm always relieved when I see that people other than my mum and my family have bought my books. I ring mum and then usually go out to dinner with Colm, my husband.

Of all the books you've written, is there one that's a favourite? Why?

It's hard to pick a favourite because the characters are so close to me that it would be like picking your favourite child or something. But ISOBEL'S WEDDING is an old favourite, mainly because Isobel's so different to me in almost every respect. THINGS WE NEVER SAY is another one because it's a complex story with lots of very different characters which made it an interesting challenge to write.

Your novels often focus on dilemmas in women's lives. How do you come up with the ideas? Do you sometimes use dilemmas that your friends and family members have experienced?

I don't consciously use dilemmas of people I know but I'm sure over time I must have done. I generally write about things that interest me – women trying to juggle expectations of them; the difficulties in relationships; family problems – we all go through them!

IF YOU WERE ME is partly about choosing the right person to marry. You lived with your partner Colm for many years before deciding to get married while you were writing IF YOU WERE ME. How did you know Colm was the right man for you?

That's a good question! I think it was because although we're very different in lots of respects, we both tend to like the same things and have similar interests. Having said that, he likes shopping more than I do, and I watch more football than he does . . .

And was there a romantic proposal? Do you think couples can still have romance in their relationships after years together?

He asked me to marry him in Spain which made it a bit of a slam dunk as I'm always in a good mood when I'm there. We were staying in a Parador and they brought us a bottle of champagne to celebrate. I think the most important thing in a relationship is not taking each other for granted – that way there's always room for romance. Somewhat weirdly, I was writing about a couple who've been together for a long time when Colm and I got married. Their family doesn't see them as romantic at all but . . .That's now my next book, MY MOTHER'S SECRET.

Some of IF YOU WERE ME is set in steamy Seville, and there are often exotic overseas settings for your novels. Have you travelled a lot, and which are your favourite destinations?

I like travelling because it makes you look at the world in a different way, and being in another place sparks lots of creative ideas. I also have a home in Spain where I edit a lot of my books. My favourite chill-out destination is Antigua, in the Caribbean, where I set my short story collection, CONNECTIONS. Probably the most interesting place I've ever visited is Pompeii which I finally got to last year. Seeing the preserved town reaffirmed my view that people are generally the same, wherever and whenever they've lived.

Can you tell us a little more about your next novel, MY MOTHER'S SECRET?

This is a big family novel, that centres around a surprise anniversary party for Pascal and Jenny who've been married for forty years. But everyone who comes to the party has something going on in their lives, and the couple themselves have a past that they'd rather people didn't know about. When a flood traps them all in the house the secrets come tumbling out.

And if you're already looking forward to
Sheila O'Flanagan's next book,
here's a sneak peek at the first chapter of . . .

My Mother's Secret

Chapter 1

A tiny bead of perspiration rolled along Steffie's eyebrow, gathering momentum as it slid down her cheek before landing with a plop on the enormous cardboard box she was carrying. She used the top of her shoulder to wipe her face as she walked gingerly towards her ancient blue Citroën C3, and sighed with relief as she finally placed the box on the passenger seat. As far as she was concerned, the thirty-second journey from the bakery to her car couldn't have been more nerve-racking if she'd been carrying a box of gelignite. And the consequences of dropping it would have been equally explosive.

She pushed a damp wisp of cinnamon-gold hair from her forehead, and shuddered as she imagined Roisin's reaction to the loss of their parents' anniversary cake. A missing cake would have been a major disruption to the Master Plan, and Roisin didn't allow her plans to be disrupted by anyone or anything. Secure in the knowledge that for once she hadn't fallen short of her older sister's high expectations, Steffie eased into the driver's seat and rolled down the car windows. Then she turned the fan up as high as possible in an effort to combat the unexpected end-of-summer heatwave. During the last fortnight the media had happily replaced gloomy reports on the wettest

August on record with daily guides to staying cool, as fore-casters pointed out that Dublin, Ireland was currently as warm as Dublin, Ohio, and hotter than Madrid, Paris or Rome. Which would be wonderful, Steffie thought, as a weak stream of tepid air finally began to flow from the vents in front of her, if Irish houses had air conditioning and outdoor swimming pools instead of central heating and double-glazing.

A swimming pool in the garden of Aranbeg, her parents' home in Wexford, would have been something to look forward to this afternoon. But even if they could have afforded it, Pascal and Jenny weren't the sort of people who'd install something that would be used approximately one summer in five. Steffie, and the rest of the day's guests, would simply have to cool off with lots of chilled drinks at the fortieth wedding anniversary party instead.

She exhaled slowly as she thought of the surprise they were about to spring on their parents, who were in blissful igno-rance of the fact that they'd be arriving home to a party later. She still wasn't entirely convinced that surprising them was a good idea, but Roisin had been adamant and Steffie knew from long experience that when her sister's mind was made up, changing it was pretty much a lost cause. All the same, she muttered darkly to herself, the next time she rings me with one of her covert plans in which she gives all the instruc-tions and I'm left with the donkey work, I'll do what I keep promising myself and say that I'm too busy to get involved. I'll remind her that I keep proper working hours even if my office is Davey's old bedroom. I'll take a stand and be strong, firm and businesslike and I won't allow her to railroad me into anything because she's twelve years older than me and she thinks that entitles her to boss me around.

She luxuriated for a few minutes in the fantasy of telling Roisin to sod off and then allowed herself a wry smile. It was never going to happen because Steffie knew that in the face of the force of nature that was Roisin in full organisational mode, there was nothing she could say to stop her. Besides, it isn't only me she bosses around, she acknowledged. She's the same with everyone and we all accept it because Roisin is a born leader, methodical and organised, and the rest of us, maybe with the exception of Dad, are too lazy to bother. Which makes it all the more surprising, she muttered to herself as the Citroën surprised her by getting up enough speed to pass a plodding Fiesta, that I'm the one with my own business and Roisin is a full-time mother. Even as the thought crossed her mind, she conceded that the reality of their situations was quite different from appearances. Roisin had been a high-flyer in the insurance company where she worked, only deciding that she needed to devote more time to her family after the birth of Dougie, her third child. And describing herself, as she did, as a full-time mother was disingenuous. Roisin still did occasional contract work for various insurers, while being an active member of the parents' council at the local school, and currently running a summer sports camp for under-tens. Every second of her day was managed and accounted for and she frequently remarked that she was busier now than she'd ever been. Steffie, on the other hand, had set up Butterfly Creative in her brother's old bedroom because she hadn't been able to find a job as a graphic artist anywhere else, and justified the time she frittered away on social media sites as important networking opportunities to get her brand noticed.

She liked to think that working for herself suited her free-spirited nature, but she was uncomfortably aware that her current status as the owner of a company where she was the sole employee had more to do with her lack of corporate solidarity than her entrepreneurial skills. Her previous job, with a design studio on the far side of the city, had come to an abrupt end after she'd refused to work on a campaign where they wanted to use images of semi-naked women to promote a line of jewellery.

Both her parents had been totally supportive of her stance (although she'd had to apologise profusely to her dad, who'd lent her the money to buy the Citroën and whom she couldn't immediately repay), but Roisin hadn't been able to hide her exasperation with her younger sister when she heard the news.

'Are you out of your mind?' she asked, before launching into a diatribe about there not being room for principles when you needed a job. 'You've got to roll with the punches, Steffie.'

'You can't possibly mean that,' retorted Steffie when Roisin finally paused for breath. 'Not when those punches are blatantly sexist. If you can't have principles about your work, then what's the point?'

Roisin said it was all about being pragmatic and realising what was important.

'My principles are very important to me,' said Steffie.

'Oh, grow up. You're in the real world now,' said Roisin. 'You're like all those girls who scream harassment every time a co-worker passes a remark about how they look. You're letting yourself be offended.'

'It depends on the remark, don't you think?' said Steffie. 'But in any event, nobody has ever passed one about how I look.'

465

'Seriously?' Roisin was so astonished she forgot to keep haranguing her.

Her astonishment was due to the fact that Steffie was the sort of person people tended to notice. She was tall and willowy, her open face framed by a tumble of burnished curls. Roisin made no secret of the fact that she felt the looks genes had been unfairly distributed between them, because she herself had inherited their father's darker colouring and stockier frame, which meant she was locked in a constant battle to keep her figure in the kind of shape that Steffie didn't even have to think about. That battle was the only one she'd never quite succeeded in winning, despite her enthusiastic embracing of various diets and workouts, and it infuriated her. Steffie would tell her that willowy implied you could sort of glide into rooms looking cool and sophisticated whereas she was all arms and legs and falling over herself. On the other hand, when Roisin walked into a room everyone knew she was there thanks to the force of her personality, not because she'd tripped over her own two feet.

'But I'd like to tower,' said Roisin. 'It'd give me a greater presence.'

'You wouldn't really,' Steffie told her. 'It's not always comfortable. Besides, you don't need a greater presence. Everyone does what you tell them anyway.'

'That's because I'm always right,' said Roisin. 'And I'm right about this work thing too. You need to grow up, Steffie. Get out there, work hard and prove yourself.'

Which by setting up her own company she thought she had, even if the decision had been forced on her by a continuing failure to find a full-time job following the jewellery debacle. She wondered if she'd been blacklisted from the graphic artist community – if there was such a thing – because she'd never gone through such a job drought before. In the end she'd got her break by designing some flyers for a friend who owned a café on the nearby industrial estate. The flyers were noticed by a marketing manager at one of the estate's manufacturing companies and they'd asked her to be involved in a packaging design for them.

When she got the business she was elated, even though she knew in all likelihood it was because she'd quoted such a ridiculously low price for the job that they couldn't turn it down. Her parents were happy to see her busy, and even happier when she got more work from other companies in the area. They suggested that instead of having the laptop in a corner of the living room, she use Davey's bedroom as a work zone. After he'd moved out a number of years earlier they'd kept it as a guest room, but as they hardly ever had guests it didn't matter if she took it over. So she bought some office furniture from IKEA (which Pascal assembled for her), registered her business and hoped she hadn't made a terrible mistake.

It hadn't been a mistake, but it continued to be a rocky road. She'd built up a small number of regular clients and she occasionally landed more complicated and interesting projects. Nevertheless, her income was erratic and she wouldn't have been able to keep going if it wasn't for the fact that she was living practically rent-free in the house.

Shortly after Command Central, as Roisin called it, was moved to Davey's bedroom, their father took an early retire-ment package from his job at the Revenue Commissioners, and he and Jenny moved to Aranbeg, the Wexford house where they'd spent every summer for the past thirty-five years, leaving Steffie to live in the Dublin house alone.

'It's your corporate headquarters now,' her father had joked the day they loaded up the car. 'We're only in the way.'

'I hope you don't think I'm forcing you out.' She looked at them anxiously.

'Oh, for heaven's sake, Steffie, it's a joke.' Pascal, a good two inches shorter than her, had to reach up to squeeze her shoulders. 'I hope you'll be very successful.'

'So successful that you'll be moving into bigger and better premises in no time,' added Jenny.

That had been a year ago. So far there was no danger of her needing to look for anywhere bigger. But she lived in hope. Not because she didn't like the fact that her daily commute was a matter of walking from one room to another, or because she could work in her PJs if she felt so inclined, though she tended not to, feeling more creative when she was properly dressed, but because she wanted to believe that she could support herself and not have to rely on the generosity and good nature of her parents to keep her going.

She fiddled with the Citroën's air vents again. Thinking about her work always made her hot and bothered, as if the whole party thing hadn't got her hot and bothered already. When Roisin had phoned to say that they should surprise Jenny and Pascal with a celebration of their forty years of marriage and invite all their family and friends to Aranbeg, Steffie hadn't voiced her own opinion, which was that she hated surprise parties and she wasn't sure they'd be their mum and dad's cup of tea either, because Roisin was already well into her stride and telling her what had to be done. Nor did Steffie say that she was too busy to do all the things that Roisin had already designated as her responsibility. Roisin wouldn't have believed her, because Roisin didn't really think that

Butterfly Creative was a proper job at all. And even though she really was occupied with a proposal that could turn out to be her most profitable contract yet, Steffie was simply unable to resist the unstoppable force that was her sister in full flow.

'We'll do it the Saturday before their actual anniversary to properly surprise them. Aranbeg is the ideal place too. So many of us used to gather there when we were younger. It must be years since it was full of people, and Mum loved it so much like that,' Roisin informed her.

That was true. During their childhood years, aunts, uncles and cousins from both sides of the family regularly descended on Aranbeg, turning it into a buzzing hub of social activity. These days Steffie only saw her cousins at family gatherings, where she always felt as though she'd let Jenny and Pascal down by not being as successful as everyone else.

'Obviously there are logistical issues to think about given that Mum and Dad are actually living there now,' continued Roisin. 'However, I have a plan to get them out while you sort things. They'll stay overnight with me and you can nip down and get it all organised. I'm too busy with the summer camp to do it. But you can take time out whenever you like. One of the big perks of working from home.'

Which was true, Steffie agreed, but what Roisin didn't seem to grasp was that if she took time out during the day to do everything her sister wanted, she'd have to make it up later. Whenever she allowed herself to get distracted from her work by looking at cute kittens on YouTube, or playing games on Facebook, she reminded herself that it was her own time she was wasting. It didn't stop her but it did mean that she often ended up working in the middle of the night. It would be the same with party planing. Roisin simply didn't get it. She never would. And she wasn't taking any excuses from Steffie this time either. Steffie had listened as Roisin listed her instructions, which included buying balloons and other decorations for the house, designing the invitations and keeping on top of the guest list. The invitations should be child's play to her, Roisin pointed out, they wouldn't take any time at all. And as far as the guest list was concerned, it was easy for Steffie to co-ordinate that if she was sending off the invitations. As for the decorations – well, she was the creative one, wasn't she, so Roisin would leave it all up to her, but she'd send her a link to a wonderful website that did the most amazing stuff. It was a US site, she pointed out, and Steffie probably wouldn't be able to order in time for the party, but it would give her ideas. Not that you need them, of course, Roisin added. You're the designer, you probably know loads of great sites. And you can probably get a discount too. Steffie's head was reeling when Roisin finally stopped giving orders, and instead of telling her sister that she'd certainly design the invitations but she didn't have time to do everything else, she meekly asked if Roisin had thought about plates and cutlery.

'Of course I have,' Roisin replied. 'I got the most fabulous disposable plates with the cutest little hearts on them from a shop in Blanchardstown. Totally appropriate. Mum will love them. And I've got disposable cutlery too, decent stuff, not horrible bendy plastic.'

'Sounds good,' was all Steffie said. So now, as she hurtled towards Aranbeg with the precious cargo of the cake (chocolate sponge with a ruby-red frosting, for which Roisin herself had taken total responsibility), she had to admit that it was entirely her own fault that she'd been landed with the role of invitation designer, guest-list co-ordinator and home decorator. All she hoped was that it would all have been worthwhile. Despite her personal misgivings about the surprise element of the party, she had to accept that everyone who'd been invited thought it was a brilliant idea and they were all looking forward to it immensely. Roisin had told her to count on a twenty per cent refusal rate, but hardly anyone had turned down the invitation, which meant that they'd be dealing with close to seventy people turning up at Aranbeg to surprise her mother and father.

She supposed the phenomenal acceptance rate had a lot to do with Jenny and Pascal's popularity, and because Aranbeg was actually a fantastic venue for a summer party. Set in a secluded location close to the small village of Castlemoran, it was far enough from Dublin city to be rural and yet near enough to Wexford town not to feel completely isolated. Most of the non-local guests had managed to book rooms in nearby bed and breakfast accommodation and some had opted to stay an extra day to make a weekend trip of it. Fortunately they'd booked before the heatwave had broken out and everyone in the capital had decided to try to take a break near the sea, because there wasn't a room to be had anywhere near the coast now. The traffic was heavy on the main road and Steffie knew that it would take her longer than usual to reach Aranbeg. She hoped that all the guests would take the traffic situation into account. It would be a total nightmare if Jenny and Pascal arrived before the people who were going to surprise them. Roisin would have a fit. And that was something that would make everyone very hot and bothered indeed.

If you can't wait to find out what happens next, pre-order MY MOTHER'S SECRET now at www.headline.co.uk and be one of the first to read it in July 2015